NIGHT TERROR

As I stepped out on the ramparts, a sudden powerful gust of wind whipped at my hair, causing it to stream wildly over my shoulders. A brief rain beat against my face, and a lowering cloud temporarily blotted out the newly risen moon. Drawing my heavy cloak more closely about me to keep out the dank chill of the summer evening, I peered down the long line of the parapet.

What am I doing here? I thought in sudden panic. There was danger here. I couldn't see it, I couldn't hear it, but I could feel it in every pore of my being. Then, over the deafening roar of the wind, I heard a man's voice calling, and there, at the far end of the battlements, I saw a dim figure running toward me, his arm raised in a gesture so heavy with menace that I screamed in terror, holding my arms in front of me in a futile attempt to ward off the threat bearing down on me . . .

DISCOVER THE MAGIC
OF ZEBRA'S REGENCY ROMANCES!

THE DUCHESS AND THE DEVIL   (2264, $2.95)
by Sydney Ann Clary
Though forced to wed Deveril St. John, the notorious "Devil
Duke," lovely Byrony Balmaine swore never to be mastered by the
irrepressible libertine. But she was soon to discover that the human
heart — and Satan — move in very mysterious ways!

AN OFFICER'S ALLIANCE   (2239, $3.95)
by Violet Hamilton
Virginal Ariel Frazier's only comfort in marrying Captain Ian
Montague was that it put her in a superb position to spy for the
British. But the rakish officer was a proven master at melting a
woman's reserve and breaking down her every defense!

BLUESTOCKING BRIDE   (2215, $2.95)
by Elizabeth Thornton
In the Marquis of Rutherson's narrow view, a woman's only place
was in a man's bed. Well, beautiful Catherine Harland may have
been just a sheltered country girl, but the astonished Marquis was
about to discover that she was the equal of any man — and could
give as good as she got!

BELOVED AVENGER   (2192, $3.95)
by Mary Brendan
Sir Clifford Moore could never forget what Emily's family had
done to him. How ironic that the family that had stolen his inheritance now offered him the perfect means to exact his vengeance —
by stealing the heart of their beloved daughter!

A NOBLE MISTRESS   (2169, $3.95)
by Janis Laden
When her father lost the family estate in a game of piquet, practical Moriah Lanson did not hesitate to pay a visit to the winner, the
notorious Viscount Roane. Struck by her beauty, Roane suggested
a scandalous way for Moriah to pay off her father's debt — by becoming the Viscount's mistress!

*Available wherever paperbacks are sold, or order direct from the
Publisher. Send cover price plus 50¢ per copy for mailing and handling to Zebra Books, Dept. 2767, 475 Park Avenue South, New
York, N.Y. 10016. Residents of New York, New Jersey and Penn-
sylvania must include sales tax. DO NOT SEND CASH.*

DARK RENDEZVOUS AT DUNGARIFF
LOIS STEWART

ZEBRA BOOKS
KENSINGTON PUBLISHING CORP.

For Tony

ZEBRA BOOKS

are published by

Kensington Publishing Corp.
475 Park Avenue South
New York, NY 10016

First printing: September, 1989

Printed in the United States of America

Chapter 1

I shivered, feeling a sudden bitter chill, although the sun was still shining brightly and it was unusually warm for a springtime afternoon in the Scottish Highlands. A soft breeze ruffled the grass on the gentle mounds marking the graves of the clansmen, but I could sense a clammy coldness rising from the earth. For a fleeting, frightening moment, I thought I could hear the anguished cries of the men who had fought and died for Bonnie Prince Charlie over a hundred and fifty years ago on this bloodstained field of Culloden.

I shivered again, and then, catching a flicker of movement out of the corner of my eye, I looked up in surprise to see a tall man standing not far from me. He was wearing Highland dress, and from beneath his wide bonnet his eyes were fixed upon me in a silent, unblinking stare.

I took an involuntary step backward. How had he managed to appear so suddenly, so unexpectedly, giving no warning of his approach? As he continued to stare at me without speaking, my uneasiness grew. Smiling to hide my nervousness, I said, "Do you live around here? Perhaps you could tell me—is it true that heather has never grown in the grass above the clansmen's graves?"

Before he could reply a voice behind me called, "Glenna! Glenna MacDougall! Are you going to stand out there all day? It's time to start back for Inverness."

I swung around to wave to my aunt, who was sitting in a smart brougham drawn up on the narrow roadway bisecting the moor. "I'll be with you in a moment, Aunt Aillie." Turning back to the Highlander, I gaped in astonishment. He had disappeared as suddenly as he had come.

How odd, I thought. Then, shrugging, I walked over to the brougham. The coachman solicitously helped me up the steps, and as the carriage moved off I remarked, "I wonder why that man wouldn't answer my question? He's the first rude Scotsman I've met on this trip. No, that's not fair. Maybe he couldn't understand English. So many people in this part of Scotland speak only Gaelic. It's odd, though, how he seemed to materialize out of thin air—"

"What man?" Allison Murray interrupted.

"Why, that man I was talking to. The Highlander in the kilt and bonnet—" I paused, drawing a sharp breath. The man hadn't been dressed in the rough jacket and short skirtlike kilt and jaunty Glengarry bonnet I'd been seeing during our travels in Scotland. No, the man had been draped in the voluminous folds of the "belted plaid," which I knew from my reading was an archaic form of the Highland dress, and his broad, flat bonnet resembled the headgear I'd seen in pictures of Bonnie Prince Charlie's doomed Highland followers.

"You must be imagining things, Glenna," said my aunt. "There was no man out there with you."

I felt my stomach muscles contract into a painful knot. The man *had* been real, I was sure of it. Aunt Aillie had simply failed to observe his brief appearance, that must be it. However, her face wore the troubled expression that had become so familiar to me during the past three months, since that day in late February when the letter arrived that would change our lives so completely. Even without the letter, it would have been a memorable day, I reflected, thinking of William Simpson and my first proposal of marriage . . .

William reined in his buckboard in front of the gate in the white picket fence. He helped me down from the vehicle and stood looking at me with a rather strained smile. "Good-bye. I'm sure we'll see each other again soon."

"William . . ." I couldn't think of anything to say. He was such a fine person, kind and considerate and yes, handsome in his quiet, diffident way. He was also the president of the Atwater, Massachusetts Commercial Bank and the greatest "catch" in town. This afternoon when he arrived at the library to take me to a very special dinner at his mother's house, he had presented me with an expensive bouquet of my favorite white roses, saying, "I want you to remember this evening all your life."

The meal had indeed been a special one, and Mrs. Simpson had made the most transparent of excuses to leave us alone together in the parlor after supper. Until the very moment that William asked me to marry him, I'd intended to accept the ring that he was holding out to me. But I didn't. I couldn't. Without any conscious thought, the words came tumbling out: "I'm so sorry, but I can't marry you. I'm very fond of you, but I don't—I don't love you."

William's face seemed to collapse. "But I was sure— Glenna, you can't mean that. You don't need to give me your answer right now. Take a little time to decide. I'll ask you again later."

"No, William. I won't change my mind." And I knew I wouldn't, though the shrewder, more practical side of my nature was urging me to reconsider. I was already twenty years old, and I was realistic enough to know that I would never meet anyone else even remotely as eligible as William. Time would pass, and in three more years the twentieth century would begin, and there I'd be, still working as a librarian, still living with my widowed aunt in this dull little New England village.

"Will you come into the house, William? I think Aunt Aillie has made that spice cake you're so fond of." I made the offer out of cowardice, to postpone facing Aunt Aillie with news that was sure to disappoint her.

William was far too upset to come in and sip tea and behave as though nothing had happened. "No, thank you," he said. "Another time, perhaps. Say hello to your aunt for me."

Latching the gate behind me, I walked slowly up the path to the house, pausing in the tiny foyer with a sudden qualm as I heard the rattle of teacups and observed that the lamps were lit in the parlor rather than in the kitchen where we took our everyday meals.

Aunt Aillie's smile faded as I entered the parlor. "Why—where's William? He didn't propose, then?"

"Yes, William proposed. I meant to accept him, but—suddenly I realized that I didn't love him enough to spend the rest of my life with him."

Her eyes kindling, my aunt opened her mouth to protest. Then she reverted to her usual composed self, pressing her lips firmly together against an unguarded remark. After a moment she said quietly, "Well, it's your affair. I hope you won't live to regret it. I think you'll find, though, that romance is a poor substitute for financial security."

I looked at her affectionately as she busied herself with pouring the tea. Allison Murray was my father's sister, a tall, slender woman, still quietly handsome, though her once flaming red hair had faded to light brown. When my parents had died of typhoid fever ten years previously in a small town near Boston, Aillie had brought me to Atwater to live with her and her husband Malcolm. She was an undemonstrative woman of decided views and strict convictions, but I had never doubted her deep affection for me. Malcolm had died five years ago, and, although Aillie had a small income from the sale of her husband's haberdashery business, she had had to scrimp to make ends meet until I finished normal school in Fitchburg and obtained the position of town librarian in Atwater.

"This is your best spice cake ever, Aunt Aillie," I said with my mouth half full. "How was your day?"

"Oh, nothing special. I tidied up a bit in the attic. I was thinking of starting the spring cleaning this week, but the weather's not quite warm enough to put the rugs out. Oh." She paused, her forehead furrowed in a deep frown. "I almost forgot. A letter came for you. I'll just fetch it from the kitchen." When she returned, she handed over the letter so slowly, so reluctantly, that I knew immediately that she hadn't forgotten the letter's arrival. I stared at her curiously for a moment before turning my attention to the envelope.

We seldom received mail. We had no relatives to write to us, and our infrequent letters came either from the lawyer who handled Uncle Malcolm's affairs or from one of my former classmates. Certainly I could never remember having received a letter with a foreign stamp.

"It's from England. No, Scotland." I turned the envelope between my fingers. "I wonder who could be writing to me from Scotland?"

"You can find out easily enough by opening the envelope," said Aillie tartly.

"So I can," I laughed. "Will you hand me the letter knife, please?" I opened the letter, which consisted of several pages. "It's from a man named Duncan Livingstone in Oban, Argyllshire. He's a solicitor. Isn't that what the English call a lawyer? He says . . ." My voice trailed away as I read on with a growing sense of shock:

2 March, 1897

"My dear Miss MacDougall: I write to inform you with great regret of the recent death of your uncle, Niall Alexander MacDougall, on 20 February last in Oban, County of Argyll, Scotland.

"I enclose a copy of Mr. MacDougall's last will and testament, which I am sure you will wish to study at your leisure. The main provisions of the will are as follows: you are named as Mr. MacDougall's sole legatee, subject, however, to a certain condition: in short, before you can receive the bulk of your inheritance, you must agree to live for one year in Argyllshire, in a place and residence of your own choosing. In the event that you die without issue, Mr. MacDougall's estate will pass to the residuary legatee, Mr. Lorne MacDougall, or, if he predeceases you, to whoever then occupies the position of Laird of Dungariff.

"Upon receipt of your consent in writing to the provisions of the will, I will forward to you such sums as you may require to pay for your journey to Scotland and to live in a manner commensurate with your inheritance, which will be in the neighborhood of 500,000 pounds sterling.

"I remain, Madam, your humble and obedient servant, etc."

I lifted my eyes from the letter and looked blankly at my aunt. "This man, this Mr. Livingstone, tells me I've inherited half a million pounds—what's that, about two and a half million dollars in American money?—from an uncle I never knew I had."

Aillie extended her hand. "May I see the letter?" she asked in a tightly controlled voice. She read both the letter and the will, her face devoid of expression, and then, with a frighteningly cold voice, she remarked, "I saved my brother Niall's life once when he was very small. I pounded his back until he coughed up the bit of mutton gristle that was choking him. It would have been better for all of us if I had just let him die."

"Aunt Aillie!" I exclaimed in horror. I sat down, forcing myself to be calm. "Why didn't you ever tell me that you and Daddy had a brother? A brother who, it now turns out, was alive until a short time ago."

"Niall was a thief and a liar and an adulterer. Your father and I put him out of our lives many years ago. We hoped he was dead."

"Is Uncle Niall the reason why you've never wanted to talk about your family? I remember asking you more than once about your childhood in the old country, but all you ever told me was that you and Daddy grew up on a farm in Scotland, that you were very poor, and that when your father died the two of you decided to come to America."

"Your father and I were miserably unhappy in Scotland. That's why I never talked about our lives there. Why rake up hurtful old memories?"

I motioned to the lawyer's letter. "I'm afraid you must, now."

"Yes, I suppose so." Aillie sighed heavily. "We—my brothers Ian and Niall and I—grew up feeling proud that the MacDougalls were once the most important family in Argyll," she began. "We were related to the Laird of Dungariff, who lived down the road from us in a great frowning castle. Indeed, Father never ceased reminding us that our branch of the family had once owned Dungariff. But for all his great ancestry, Father was just another poor farmer, trying to scrounge a living from a few rocky acres and a flock of scrawny sheep. Many's the day we didn't have enough to eat, or warm clothes on our backs." Aillie's voice throbbed with an old bitterness. "Worst of all, we were expected to bow and scrape and smile gratefully when the Laird's wife sent us a bundle of outgrown clothing or a bit of meat during the holidays."

Aillie sighed again. "Even so, by the time I was eighteen, things were looking up a bit for us. We'd had good crop weather for several years running, and the price of wool had held up. Niall even found a position as a clerk in an Oban bank. Then he fell in love with that actress. She was a member of an acting troupe that came to Oban for a season of repertory. Niall bought himself some fancy clothes and gave the actress presents he couldn't afford, and when the repertory group left town Niall simply helped himself to the bank's cash and went with them. The disgrace killed my father. He persuaded the bank not to prosecute, provided the stolen money was replaced. To do that, Father sold off everything he owned. He'd scarcely had a sick day in his entire life, but he was dead in six months."

I reached out to put a sympathetic hand on her shoulder. "And that was the last you heard or saw of Uncle Niall?"

"Oh, no." Aillie's lip curled. "About a year after Father died, Niall wrote to your father and me from America. He'd heard about Father's death and he was beside himself with remorse. He enclosed money for steerage tickets and urged us to join him in Boston." Aillie shrugged. "Ian and I decided to go. We were eking out a hand-to-mouth existence in Oban, at best, and it wasn't pleasant, either, being stared at on the street. Oh, Father had done his best to hush up the story, but almost everybody in town knew that Niall had embezzled money from the bank. But when Ian and I arrived in Boston, Niall wasn't there; his landlady told us he had been fired from his job and had gone off to seek his fortune in South America. I guess I was more relieved than sorry. Now I wouldn't have to pretend that I had forgiven Niall for Father's death. I tried never to think about him. After a time I forgot that I'd ever had a younger brother.''

I shook my head at Aillie's story. Apparently my newly discovered uncle had had a checkered past. How had this man, so seemingly at odds both with the law and his own wild impulses, been able to accumulate the vast fortune I had now inherited? Would I ever learn any of the details, I wondered.

Aillie, too, was deep in thought. After a long silence, she murmured, "This is probably some monstrous joke that Niall is playing on us from beyond the grave."

"Aunt Aillie! What a grisly thing to say!" I picked up the lawyer's letter and reread it. "I've always heard that the Scots are very practical, serious, hardheaded people. Somehow, I can't believe that Mr. Livingstone would allow himself to be part of a two-and-a-half-million-dollar joke!"

"What are you going to do?"

"Do?" I must have looked as puzzled as I felt. "Why, what else? I'm going to Scotland to claim my inheritance. Surely you don't think I should refuse Uncle Niall's money? I realize he didn't lead a very proper life, but there's no reason to think his money is tainted!"

My aunt didn't reply immediately. "No, of course you shouldn't refuse the money," she said at last. "I'll feel so much easier in my mind, knowing that you'll never have to worry about your future. But it shouldn't be necessary for you to go to Scotland. Write to this Mr. Livingstone and tell him that he'll have to find some way to release you from this silly requirement to live in Argyll."

"Nonsense, Aunt Aillie. I want to go to Scotland. I'd

like to know something about my roots. And you're going with me. You may have left Argyll in steerage, but you'll be returning in style!"

"Of course there was a man, Aunt Aillie! I told you, he seemed to appear and disappear like the genie in the bottle, but he was there all right."

Shifting her gaze, as if she didn't want to meet my eyes, Aillie looked out the window of the brougham with an interest scarcely justified by the bleak moorland landscape with its occasional plantation of fir trees. "I think we should go home," she said after a long pause. "We don't need Niall's money. We still have the house in Atwater—it's probably not rented out yet—and I'm sure you'd have no difficulty getting back your job at the library. And William—"

"Aunt Aillie, look at me. What's put this bee in your bonnet?"

"All this gallivanting about Europe isn't good for you—for us," Aillie burst out. "Too much has happened, too fast. Look what it's doing to your nerves! Take that man you claimed you saw today. There wasn't any man, Glenna. And those nightmares you've been having. They remind me of—" Aillie broke off, clamping her lips tightly shut.

"They remind you of what?" I asked with a composure I didn't feel. I had to tamp down a sharp twinge of apprehension. I didn't like to think about those terrifying nightmares that had haunted my dreams intermittently since the evening I'd learned about my Scottish inheritance.

"They remind me of my mother," Aillie said in a low voice. "She was a Lowlander—born in Dalbeattie, she was—and she never ceased to be homesick for Galloway.

14

She used to have nightmares that her old home was burning, or her father was dying, or one of her brothers had drowned. She died young, and that was probably a mercy. She . . . we all thought she would have been quite mad, if she'd lived much longer."

"What are you suggesting? That since I have nightmares, and I've left my home in Atwater, I'm a candidate for madness, too?" I could hear my voice rising, becoming shrill.

Aillie's eyes widened in shock. "Of course I didn't mean that. How could you think such a thing?"

I was sure that she had merely spoken without thinking about her mother's mental illness. Nevertheless, the remark was one more indication of Aillie's continuing reluctance to leave the safe haven of the New England town where she had lived for so long. Nursing a vague sense of injury, I lapsed into a rather stiff silence that lasted until we entered the outskirts of Inverness, a pretty town on the River Ness at the northern end of scenic Glen More. The hired brougham deposited us at our hotel, a small, comfortable establishment near the Town Hall at the foot of Castle Hill.

"I'd like a nap before dinner," Aillie said in a rather subdued tone as we parted at the doors of our respective bedchambers. "Give me a call about seven, will you?"

I'd never been one to take naps, and I wasn't sleepy now. I took off the jacket of my tailor-made, removed my hat with its upturned halo brim, and stood at the window for several minutes, watching the children playing around the Town Cross in front of the hotel. Embedded in the cross, so I'd been told, was a lozenge-shaped stone, the Stone of the Tubs, so called because it was here that the women of the town had from time immemorial rested their water pitchers on the way to the river.

Laughing at the altercation that had broken out

15

between two pugnacious little boys at the foot of the cross, I sat down in a comfortable chair and reached for what had become my favorite reading in recent months, *A History of the Clans*. It had been exhilarating to learn that the MacDougalls could once lay claim to fully a third of Scotland and were actually related to the British royal family through a common descent from the legendary Fergus of Dalriada. Unfortunately, the clan over the centuries had been remarkably prone to choose the wrong side in any dispute, thereby forfeiting their lands and possessions. My own distant ancestor had marched off to follow Bonnie Prince Charlie in 1745, forfeiting Dungariff Castle to a distant cousin after the defeat at Culloden, and was hanged for high treason. As Aunt Aillie had once remarked, "Being descended from kings never helped Father put food in our mouths!"

I yawned, placing my book on the table next to my chair. Time to dress for dinner. I glanced around the large, pleasant room, more than adequate in size for two people. But I don't have to settle for the adequate any more, I reflected. Aunt Aillie and I can occupy separate rooms as a matter of course. Money had never been the most important thing in my life, but it was certainly better to have too much of it rather than too little! I smiled reminiscently, remembering the heady shopping trips to the smart stores along Washington and Summer streets in Boston, when Aunt Aillie and I had ordered everything that struck our fancy, without inquiring about the price tags. We'd crossed the Atlantic in the elegant new *Carpathia*, feeling awed initially, but soon taking for granted first-class staterooms and seats at the captain's table for dinner. Even our tour of Scotland, on our way to our final destination in Argyll, had been as luxurious as the local amenities would allow.

If only Aunt Aillie would try to enjoy the trip more, I

thought. The closer we came to Argyll, the more she seemed to dwell on the grievances that had haunted her youth. Well, only time could change that, I supposed. I walked over to the wardrobe, where I selected a white shirtwaist lavishly trimmed in lace and a black satin yoke skirt finished with a flared flounce.

The ensemble looked very well, I reflected, glancing approvingly at my image in the mirror after I had dressed. Just the proper amount of formality to dine in a country hotel. My hair looked well, too, the heavy dark masses brushed away from my forehead and coiled in a heavy knot at the back of my head in the newly fashionable Greek mode. I lingered in front of the mirror, not dissatisfied with what I saw. My hair and my eyes—large and deeply blue—were my best features. My mouth was a trifle wide for classical perfection, but I had a good complexion and an engaging smile, and my figure was trim and well proportioned.

A little later, as my aunt and I crossed the lobby on our way to the dining room, Aillie's lacy shawl slipped from her shoulders and trailed on the floor. A tall man, who had just entered the front door of the hotel, hurried over to pick up the shawl.

I recognized him instantly. "Why, you're the man I met at Culloden this afternoon," I blurted.

The man, who was wearing not a kilt but a sober tweed lounge suit, removed his Homburg hat when I spoke to him. He hesitated for an instant, looking at me intently. Then, with a curt "I'm afraid you've confused me with someone else, ma'am," he bowed slightly and moved on to the registration desk.

My face was burning with embarrassment at the near-snub. I muttered to Aillie as we walked into the dining room, "I can't believe he isn't the same man. He looks enough like that Highlander to be his identical twin." But

I wasn't quite so sure anymore. If the two men were identical, what reason would the man in the lobby have for denying it?

Aillie shot a quick, concerned glance at me but didn't comment on the incident during dinner. Instead she chatted gaily about our forthcoming steamer trip on the Caledonian Canal. Later, after drinking our coffee in the lounge, we were standing in the lobby, debating the merits of an evening stroll, when she said with a trace of uneasiness, "That man is coming toward us. What could he want, I wonder?"

"Miss MacDougall? Miss Glenna MacDougall?"

I looked coldly at the man who had stopped in front of us. I was half-tempted to pay him back in his own coin by snubbing him royally. Instead, I raised a haughty eyebrow, saying, "Yes, I'm Glenna MacDougall."

"Forgive the intrusion, but I've been inquiring at the desk, and I think we may be related. I'm the MacDougall of Dungariff."

I studied the thin face, as austerely handsome as the carved likeness on an antique coin. His thick waving hair was as intensely black as my own. I exclaimed in surprise, "You're the Laird of Dungariff?"

"Yes, I'm Lorne MacDougall, and unless I'm mistaken both of you ladies are my cousins." His closed-in, aloof features relaxed in a sudden smile that lighted up the still, blue-black depths of his eyes.

I caught my breath as my heart began to pound and an unfamiliar, enticing, sensation of warmth flooded my body. So this, I thought incredulously, is what it means to be powerfully, sensually attracted to a man. No wonder it had cost me only a passing qualm to refuse William Simpson's proposal. Never once in his presence had I felt such overwhelming physical magnetism.

Swallowing hard, I forced down this strange new

clamor in my blood, grateful that Lorne MacDougall's attention was momentarily distracted away from me when he greeted Aillie. "It's Mrs. Murray, isn't it? You must be Niall MacDougall's sister Allison." Turning back to me, he said, shaking his head, "When you spoke to me earlier, you seemed strangely familiar, although I was positive we had never met before. Finally, feeling like Paul Pry, I asked the desk clerk about you. You have the look of the MacDougalls, you know. I should have recognized you at once. There's a strong resemblance to your Uncle Niall." Glancing around the lobby, he added, "Can't we go somewhere and talk? Perhaps we could have coffee in the lounge."

Aillie, normally so gracious, said brusquely, "We've already had our coffee."

"Oh, but I'd like a second cup," I said hastily, and promptly wished I hadn't. I suspected I sounded like an overeager schoolgirl.

"Very good. Will you change your mind, Mrs. Murray?"

"No, thank you. I'm going up to my room now. Glenna, I'll see you later." Aillie marched toward the stairs, her back held more rigidly erect than usual.

I shrugged at the question in Lorne's eyes. "You're not seeing Aunt Aillie at her best, I'm afraid. Shall we go to the lounge?"

After the attentive waiter had left, Lorne poured a cup of coffee for me and sat down beside me on the sofa with his own cup. He said stiffly, "If you'll tell me how I've offended Mrs. Murray, I'll be happy to apologize."

"You didn't do anything," I assured him. "It was your grandmother. Aunt Aillie has always resented being treated as a poor relation when she and her brothers were young."

"I see." Lorne lapsed into silence.

I studied his face covertly. I still thought he was the

image of the man at Culloden. Perhaps they were doubles. Hadn't I once read that everyone has an identical double somewhere in the world? I wondered idly why Aunt Aillie hadn't mentioned how much I resembled Uncle Niall. Apparently the resemblance was strong enough to cause Lorne MacDougall to think for a moment that he recognized me when we met in the lobby earlier.

He said thoughtfully, "I'm afraid my grandmother was a Tartar and a snob. To me she was an indulgent granny, but I can see now that she definitely enjoyed playing the lady of the manor. I think I can understand your aunt's resentment." He poured himself a second cup of coffee and, apparently glad to change the subject, said, "It's such a coincidence, meeting you and your aunt here. Only yesterday, as I was leaving on a business trip to Inverness, my mother remarked that she was going to write to your lawyer, Mr. Livingstone, to find out when you would arrive in Oban."

"Oh. I'm not sure . . . As you probably know, the terms of my uncle's will require that I live in Argyll for a year, and Aunt Aillie's been talking of finding a house in Inverary. It's a beautiful place, she says."

"You're not coming to Oban?" Lorne asked incredulously.

"If it were up to me—but Aunt Aillie has so many unhappy memories of the place. For one thing, she seems to think that people would point their fingers at us because of Uncle Niall's criminal past."

"He didn't have a criminal past. The money he embezzled was paid back and he was never prosecuted. As a matter of fact, he died a most respected citizen of the town."

I began to laugh. "Which did the townsfolk admire more, Uncle Niall's good character or his money?"

Lorne looked startled. It was obvious that he was a man

little given to levity. "A little of both, I think," he replied in a tone of discovery. "He may have been something of a rascal, but he was a charming man. He and my mother became great friends during the last years of his life when he returned to Oban. He often spoke of you, you know. I think you'd have enjoyed knowing him."

"I wish I knew more about him."

"Then come to Oban. Come to Dungariff. My mother's been hoping that you'll pay us a long visit at the castle."

"Well . . ." The invitation seemed genuine enough. I thought I could detect a definite warmth there, beneath that facade of cool formality. "Thank you," I said. "I'll speak to Aunt Aillie." Suddenly I knew I wanted to go to Dungariff. I wanted to see more of this handsome, intense man whose brooding eyes both attracted and repelled me.

As it turned out, it didn't do any good to speak to Aunt Aillie, at least initially. After I said good-bye to Lorne in the lounge I went up to my aunt's room.

"Stay at Dungariff?" she exclaimed in tones of horror. She might have been referring to a place quarantined by the Black Death. "Why should we visit people who wouldn't notice we were alive if you hadn't suddenly inherited a vast fortune?"

"We're not talking about the same people," I protested. "Lorne wasn't even born when his grandmother treated you and Daddy and Uncle Niall so badly." I set my jaw. "I want to go to Dungariff, Aunt Aillie. If you're so set against it, I could go there by myself for a short visit. You could wait for me here in Inverness."

Aunt Aillie stared at me. She must have realized she couldn't change my mind. "All right, then. Don't say I didn't warn you. No good will come of such a visit."

I went to my own room with a sense of quiet triumph and the hope that, even though my aunt's assent had been so grudging, the visit would eventually enable her to come to grips with the painful memories of her childhood.

As I prepared for bed, my thoughts lingered on Lorne MacDougall. How strange to reflect that, until tonight, he'd been only a title, an abstraction in Uncle Niall's will. Now it seemed likely that I'd be seeing him frequently during my coming year of exile in Argyll. Somehow, it didn't seem so much like exile any more.

I fell asleep with a pleased little smile on my lips, still thinking of the dark stranger I'd met tonight, and of the visit I'd soon be paying to his ancient ancestral home . . .

. . . As I stepped out on the ramparts, a sudden powerful gust of wind whipped at my hair, causing it to stream wildly over my shoulders. A brief rain squall beat against my face, and a lowering cloud temporarily blotted out the newly risen moon. Drawing my heavy cloak more closely about me to keep out the dank chill of the summer evening, I peered down the long line of the parapet. What am I doing here? *I thought in sudden panic. There was danger here. I couldn't see it, I couldn't hear it, but I could feel it in every pore of my being. Then, over the deafening roar of the wind, I heard a man's voice calling, and there, at the far end of the battlements, I saw a dim figure running toward me, his arm raised in a gesture so heavy with menace that I screamed in terror, holding my arms in front of me in a futile attempt to ward off the threat bearing down on me . . .*

I jerked myself upright in bed, my heart pounding, my body drenched in cold perspiration. I uttered a stifled scream of fear. For an instant, I couldn't separate nightmare from reality. Then, my eyes clearing, I realized that the now familiar nightmare had returned. Throwing off my blanket, I leaped out of bed, thrusting my arms into my red velvet dressing gown. I stood by the window, staring down into the deserted square in front of the hotel. Once again I'd dreamed that I was standing on those dark ramparts. Once again I'd seen that menacing figure racing toward me. I stirred uneasily. This time the figure had come closer, so much closer that I could distinguish that the man was wearing what appeared to be a jacket and a short kilt made of some kind of red and black checked material.

Why did the ghastly dream keep recurring? Mercifully, not every night. Actually, there'd been no recurrence on our transatlantic crossing, and none since our arrival in Scotland, but the memory of it was often enough to make me reluctant to fall asleep. And why had I never experienced the nightmare before the night that I learned of my Scottish inheritance? I tried to shift my thoughts to another subject, but my mind kept returning to the terror-filled dream interval on the ramparts, every detail as vivid, as clear, as if I had experienced it in reality, although normally when I awaken from a dream I can remember only fleeting fragments and indistinct impressions.

Chapter 2

I stood at the railing of the ship, drinking in the wild and desolate beauty of the Argyll landscape. I was looking forward to exploring this land of wooded glens and barren passes, tall gaunt mountains and lonely woods and lochs. After several days of sightseeing around Inverness, Aillie and I had gone by boat down the Caledonian Canal, transferring to a coastal steamer for the voyage to Oban along the shores of Loch Linne.

My aunt joined me at the railing. "Lismore," she murmured, motioning to the elongated island we were passing. "Soon we'll be entering the Firth of Lorn."

A large island loomed to our right, a place of deeply indented shores and mist-shrouded mountains. Aillie stood motionless at the railing, her body rigid with tension as she gazed ahead, obviously searching out familiar landmarks. At the same time, I could feel my heart beginning to thud. This landscape, I acknowledged with foreboding, was as familiar to me as it was to my aunt. As Aillie exclaimed excitedly, "There's Duart Castle," and "I see Kerrara," I could feel my lips soundlessly forming the same words. When the steamer edged into a pier on the northern side of a broad harbor backed by wooded hills, I didn't need to be told that this was Oban. I clenched my fists so tightly that my nails bit into my palms. I knew with a sudden chilling burst of intuition that I could step off the ship and wander confidently through the town without once losing my way.

"Well, we're here at last," Aillie said resignedly. "I think I'll pop down to our cabin to make sure that they've taken our luggage up." She left, apparently without noticing my agitation.

During the brief interval that she was below deck, I tried hard to recover my composure. I told myself that I must have acquired my startling familiarity with the town from my reading. But as soon as the thought occurred to me, I rejected it. The books I'd read before beginning this Scottish tour were generalized histories and geographical works: Oban had been mentioned only casually as the principal port of the Western Highlands.

However, starting down the gangplank after my aunt's return, I felt my spirits rise as I spotted a very tame and friendly seal in the water. "Look, Aunt Aillie," I exclaimed in delight, "have you ever seen a speckled seal before?"

"That's a harbor seal, and he's hoping for a free meal from a gullible tourist," called a laughing voice.

The owner of the voice was a tall, broad-shouldered young man with fair, curly hair, pleasant handsome features and twinkling gray eyes. As I stepped off the gangplank he came up to me, extending his hand. "Hello there, would you be Miss Glenna MacDougall?"

"Why, yes. Who . . ."

"I'm Colin MacDougall, your cousin. Well, your very distant cousin! My Aunt Ellen asked me to meet your boat."

"Your Aunt Ellen? Oh, you mean Mrs. MacDougall from Dungariff. How kind of her. I wrote her that I was coming to Oban, but I certainly never expected to be met. This is my aunt, Mrs. Murray."

Aillie gave the young man a long, fixed stare. Then she said with a slow smile, "Would you be Andrew's son, then? Colin's grandson?"

"Yes. I'm Lorne's first cousin. I was raised at Dungariff after my parents died."

"Aye, you have the look of Andrew. He was one of the fair MacDougalls."

Colin's eyes crinkled. He said in broad Scots, "Ach, Mrs. Murray, ye may ha' gaed away fra' us these many years, but ye still sound like a Scotswoman."

My own ears had begun to be attuned to the Scottish accent with its soft gutturals and charmingly rolled r's, but I hadn't noticed until now that the overlay of Aillie's New England twang had been fading fast since our arrival in Scotland.

"If you'll follow me, ladies, I have Aunt Ellen's landau waiting at the end of the pier. She sent along two of the lads with a farm cart for your luggage, so it will be coming on after you. Lorne sends his regrets," Colin continued over his shoulder as he led the way. "He had an appointment in Fort William today, so I'll be escorting you to Dungariff in his place. Here we are. Mrs. Murray, Miss MacDougall, may I introduce Lorne's fiancée, Flora Cameron?"

I felt a curious jolt in the pit of my stomach, as if someone had caromed into me with a large, heavy object. Why hadn't it occurred to me that Lorne might be engaged to be married?

The slender, petite girl standing beside the landau had a small, heart-shaped face, large light blue eyes and fine reddish blond hair worn with a curly Alexandra fringe. Though rather primly dressed in a tweed skirt, short form-fitting jacket, and a straw hat trimmed with daisies, she was undeniably pretty. But I unaccountably found myself being put off by the girl, who was staring at me with an open, almost avid curiosity, as if she were mentally cataloging every aspect of my appearance. Her greeting, while cordial enough, was delivered in a flat, rather grating voice.

"Flora will be coming to Dungariff with us," Colin said, handing my aunt into the carriage. "I usually drive her out to the castle every weekend. Though not usually in as grand a fashion as this, eh, Flora? Most times we come out in my gig."

"Yes, it's kind of Colin to take me out to Dungariff every week," Flora said in that oddly flat voice of hers. "Otherwise Father would have to send someone out with me."

"Actually, it's a bit of tit for tat," Colin said, laughing. "I work for Flora's father—Mr. Cameron's a ship chandler—and in return for acting as Flora's escort, I get to leave work early on Saturdays to go to Dungariff."

As the landau moved away from the pier, along the long curving esplanade, Colin began pointing out the landmarks of Oban. Trying to mask my growing nervousness, I pretended that I was hearing about George Street and the Railway Pier and Pulpit Hill for the first time, although, to my dismay, I found myself anticipating every remark that Colin made. I was relieved when he broke off to say, "You'll think I'm the village idiot, Mrs. Murray. Here I was forgetting that you used to live here."

"It hasn't changed much," Aillie said shortly.

"I expect Oban must look very small and provincial to you, Mrs. Murray, after you've seen great cities like New York and Boston," Flora commented with a tinkling little laugh that did not quite disguise what appeared to be a lurking envy of more well traveled acquaintances.

Catching a glimpse of a large pillared stone structure atop a hill above the town, I exclaimed involuntarily, "But that building wasn't here before—" I paused, feeling both confused and foolish. "What's that big pile of stone up there on the hill, Mr. MacDougall?" I asked, trying to cover my slip. "I don't recall reading about it."

"Oh, that. We call it McCaig's Folly," Colin grinned. "No, you wouldn't have read about it. Construction only started a few months ago. One of our local bankers—a man named McCaig—is building it to provide work for our local unemployed. Looks a bit like the Roman Coliseum, doesn't it? We all wish he'd picked a different design."

I listened to Colin with only half an ear. McCaig's Folly was a new building, and it was also the first Oban landmark that had seemed unfamiliar to me. Was my haunting sense of recognition selective, limited to a period now past? Giving myself a mental shake, I pushed this disturbing new idea to the back of my mind and tried to pay closer attention to the conversation.

"See here," Colin was saying, "must we be so formal? I wish you'd both call me Colin. We *are* cousins, after all."

"I'd like that," I replied, smiling at him. I glanced inquiringly at Flora, who promptly chimed in, "Oh, yes, I'd be so pleased if you would call me Flora. I'll be your cousin, too, one day soon," she added archly.

Colin turned his attention to Aillie. "How about you, Mrs. Murray? Couldn't I call you Cousin—no, Aunt—Allison? That's it, you'll be my Aunt Aillie."

In the face of Colin's beguiling smile, Aillie's instinctive stiffness relaxed. She even managed a rather wintry smile herself as she replied, "Well, now, Colin, I don't see how it could do me any harm to acquire an instant nephew."

As the carriage reached the end of the long incline leading up from the town and turned south, Colin remarked, "We've not far to go. It's about ten miles to Dungariff. Oh, sorry, Aunt Aillie, you know exactly how far it is." He motioned to the folded-down top of the landau. "I'm glad we have such a lovely day for your arrival. It might so easily have been raining buckets."

"Yes," Flora agreed. "It can be very wet in Argyll."

It was, indeed, a lovely day, and lovely, too, was the countryside, as the road began gently climbing into an area of low green foothills. The fields were scattered with wide expanses of brilliant yellow gorse and broom, and the hedgerows were starred with the white blossoms of hawthorn and the red flowers of fuchsia. I gasped with pure delight at the sight of high hedges of riotously blooming rhododendrons lining both sides of the road. "Aunt Aillie, you never told me!" I exclaimed.

Aillie eyed the heavy masses of purple and pink and deep red blossoms and said softly, "I'd forgotten."

Soon afterwards, the carriage crested a high ridge and began descending again toward the bright azure water of what appeared to be a long and narrow lake. Suddenly my chest felt constricted, and my breath began coming faster. I knew, without knowing how I knew, that this body of water wasn't a lake. It was Loch Fingorm, a slender, elongated arm of the sea, and there on a promontory, guarding the entrance to the loch, reared a lofty cliff crowned by the forbidding walls of a great castle.

"Dungariff," Colin said.

I wondered what he would say if he realized that it was superfluous to tell me the identity of that frowning structure. Oddly enough, I ceased to be nervous as the landau wound around the southern shore of the loch and began the final climb to the Gothic gatehouse. Actually, I had entered into an almost trancelike state, in which I accepted with a fatalistic calm the fact that I knew this place, deep in my bones, as intimately as did my new-found cousin Colin.

"There used to be a moat here," Colin remarked as we passed under the deeply recessed portals of the gatehouse, "but it was filled in long ago, and Aunt Ellen has made it into a flower garden. It will be lovely next month when her roses come into bloom."

We drove into a great ward, or courtyard, which sloped slightly upward toward a massive, rectangular building at the far side of the curtain wall. Standing in the courtyard was a tall, generously built woman in early middle age. She had masses of sandy hair, only a little touched by gray, and a pleasant, open face.

"Welcome to Dungariff," she called, coming up to me and Aillie with outstretched hands. "I'm Ellen Mac-Dougall." She studied my face for a moment, catching her breath.

Like Lorne, she's noticed my resemblance to Uncle Niall, I thought.

"I was imagining a bonny lass exactly like you," she exclaimed with a quick, charming smile. She turned to Aillie. "I believe we met years ago, Mrs. Murray, shortly after I was married. I'm looking forward to renewing our acquaintance."

Aillie responded to Mrs. MacDougall's welcome with a rather forced smile and a murmured word of thanks.

"Come along and I'll show you the Great Hall," said Ellen. Chatting as she walked along beside us, Ellen explained that when the castle was remodeled in the thirteenth century the center of defense had shifted to the newly built gatehouse, and the old keep had been pulled down and replaced by a hall house. "It certainly made for much more comfortable living. The family must have been terribly cramped in the gatehouse. I'm told that this type of hall house is rather rare in the British Isles. It's much more common in Europe." She added, "We're entering by the Great Hall, because I thought you'd like to see it, but except on formal occasions we usually use the side entrance over there to your left. It leads directly to the family living quarters."

As we stepped into the great central room of the hall house, the "Great Hall," I noted with a mixture of apprehension and resignation that it appeared exactly as I had already seen it in my imagination. The thick stone walls had been paneled over and were hung with a large collection of archaic weapons. There was a raised platform at one end of the room, and massive screens of ornately carved wood enclosed the other end, with the musicians' gallery above. An enormous triple fireplace occupied most of the facing wall.

"Of course, this room and the rest of the hall house looked very different in the old days," Ellen remarked. "We've added windows, for one thing, removed the old center hearth fireplace, put up partitions, and laid down wooden floors."

She led us out of the huge room into a comfortably furnished drawing room, saying, "This is part of what used to be the solar, or Lord's quarters. Flora, would you please show Mrs. Murray to her bedroom? It's the rose room next to yours, at the far end of the corridor." To me she said, "If you'll follow me, I'll take you to your room. I hope you'll be pleased with it," she added, going from the drawing room through a series of smaller rooms into a dimly lit, circular area, from which a spiral staircase with roughly hewn steps led upward. "This tower was built especially to house the stairs to all floors of the hall house," she said, motioning me to follow her. "Now it's no longer needed, because my husband's grandfather installed wooden stairs to connect all the floors to the Great Hall. But we still use the room at the top of the tower for its original purpose—to accommodate important guests—and we thought you might enjoy staying there."

As we rounded the last curve of the steep, winding staircase, I was puffing, more than slightly, and I was chagrined to observe that my hostess, so many years older than I, wasn't breathing heavily at all. We entered a large circular room, bathed in light from a series of deeply recessed windows in one wall. I noted with one corner of my mind that I felt no disquieting sense of familiarity with this part of the castle. I wondered why, but I had no time to think about it as I continued my appreciative inspection of the room. Muted old tapestries covered most of the rough rock walls, and there was a tall canopy bed hung with heavy worn velvet, a massive Jacobean wardrobe and several comfortable chairs.

It would be easy to feel at home here, I thought, drinking in the view from those deep-set windows. Far below, at the end of a dizzying perpendicular drop, was a rock-strewn beach, and to the right and left I could glimpse the curving beaches and rugged cliffs of the Argyll mainland. Straight ahead, across a narrow sound, was the outline of a large island, rising from the sea in a shimmering violet mist.

"That's Mull. We'll take you over there for an excursion one day," Ellen said, coming to stand beside me. "Now, over there, my dear, in the corner of the room, is a door leading out to the curtain wall. The only other direct access to the battlements is from the Laird's Bedchamber. Otherwise, you must go by way of the gatehouse or one of the flanking towers."

"I love the room, Mrs. MacDougall. I'm looking forward to exploring the rest of this wonderful place."

Ellen smiled. "Somehow, I suspected you might share something of our feelings for Dungariff. It's one of the great MacDougall strongholds, you know, and the only one that's been uninterruptedly in MacDougall hands since the twelfth century. If you're really interested in knowing more about Dungariff, you must get Lorne to tell you about it. He's always loved this place with a passion, and he knows the history of every nook and cranny." A wistful expression clouded her face. "He was never happy away from here. It was a struggle even to get him to go away to school! And yet he voluntarily exiled himself for more than ten years."

I raised a questioning eyebrow.

"He quarreled with his father shortly after his twentieth birthday and left to join the merchant navy," Ellen said with a sigh. "Lachlan—my husband—wanted to lease the estate to a wealthy English industrialist, who intended to use it for sporting holidays—hunting, fishing, the like. Lorne opposed the lease, because it would have meant eviction for most of our crofters, and he refused to sign the agreement releasing the estate from entail. I don't think he and Lachlan ever forgave each other over the affair. Lorne never came back except for brief visits until after his father died last year."

"That must have been an unhappy time for you."

Ellen shrugged. "All things pass." Quickly she changed the subject. "Your Uncle Niall would have been overjoyed to see you here. I think he loved Dungariff as much as Lorne does."

"I'd like to talk to you about my uncle. Lorne told me that you and he became very close in his last months. I know practically nothing about him, you see. He'd lost touch completely with the family."

"There'd been a quarrel," Ellen said, nodding. "Terrible things, these family quarrels."

"I don't even know how he made his fortune."

"It was a diamond mine. He'd wandered all over South America for years, working at ill-paying odd jobs, and then, at the very end of his life, he stumbled on a diamond mine in Brazil. He came back to Oban to retire and enjoy his wealth, only to discover soon afterward that he had a bad heart condition. That's when he decided to look up his family in America. He was so pleased to find he had a niece. I think he put that provision in his will requiring you to live in Argyll for a year because you're the last of his family line, and he hoped that you might put down roots here."

"Thank you, Mrs. MacDougall. I understand Uncle Niall much better now that I've talked to you."

"I'm happy if I've been of any help." Ellen hesitated. "My dear, may I call you Glenna? And I heard that scamp Colin calling Mrs. Murray Aunt Aillie, so perhaps I could be your Cousin Ellen? I really am, you know! I was a MacDougall, too, before my marriage. Lachlan's third cousin once removed."

"I'd love to call you Cousin Ellen."

Reaching out to clasp my hand, she said, "That's all settled, then. Oh, Jane, come in. Glenna, this is our housekeeper, Jane Henderson."

Standing at the door was a very tall, rather rawboned woman in her early forties, with plain unsmiling features and cool gray eyes. She was carrying a tray. "Guid day tae ye, Miss MacDougall. I've brought ye some tea." She spoke in the broadest of Highland dialects, and I knew it would be some time before I could easily understand her.

"Why, thank you, Mrs.—is it Mrs.?—Henderson."

"Nay, ma'am, it's Miss. But Jane will do verra weel. Ye maun let me know if ye need anything."

After the housekeeper had left, Ellen remarked, "You're probably wondering why one of the maids didn't bring up your tea. I suspect that Jane wanted to have a firsthand look at you! She was Colin's nurse. He came to Dungariff as a mite of four when his parents died in an accident, and, since Lorne's nurse was leaving at that time to be married, Jane stayed on to care for both boys. But none of us has ever had the slightest doubt that Colin was her favorite! After the boys grew up she gradually took over the duties of housekeeper. Now I'm afraid that her work is her life. She has no family, no close friends. The other servants tend to keep their distance, because Jane is supposed to have the second sight."

"The second sight? What's that?"

"Oh, Highlanders tend to be a fanciful lot, I fear. They believe that folk with the second sight can predict which of their acquaintances are about to die."

"But that's nothing but pure superstition. Surely you don't believe in it?"

Ellen looked oddly indecisive. "I can't say I disbelieve in it," she said finally. "I've seen too many strange things happen, things that couldn't be explained in any other way, except . . ." She smiled at my shocked look. "In any case, you needn't be the least bit apprehensive about Jane. If anything, she views this gift of hers as distrustfully as the rest of us." Moving to the door, she said, "I'll leave you now to rest and change and enjoy your tea without my constant chatter. Don't hurry. We may have to delay dinner for a bit this evening, if Lorne is late returning from Fort William. Come down to the drawing room any time after eight o'clock."

The memory of Ellen MacDougall's warm welcome lingered after she had gone, but I was glad to be left alone with my thoughts. I sipped a cup of tea and ate some of the thin sandwiches and tiny cakes that the housekeeper had provided, while I tried to sort out my impressions of this disturbing day.

Why did I have so strong a sense of familiarity with this corner of Scotland? After leaving our ship in Glasgow, Aillie and I had traveled leisurely through the Lowlands, up to Edinburgh and north to Inverness, and I'd never felt anything more than a normal sightseer's interest in the landscape. Was there any real reason to feel frightened by this curious sense of recognition? Could it be that I was simply experiencing a puzzling affinity for the area where my aunt and my father had spent their youth?

A knock at the door put an end to my reverie. A pair of sturdy farm servants arrived with my trunk and suitcases, followed soon after by a young maid, whose speech was so larded with marvelously rolling r's, that I had to listen closely to every syllable. The maid's name was Meg, she announced, and she had come to unpack my belongings.

"And wha' will ye be wearing the nicht, Miss?" Meg

inquired with an obvious delight in seeing and handling a fashionable outlander's wardrobe.

I hesitated. My elaborate new evening gowns would be as out of place at Dungariff as they had been at the hotel in Inverness. "The lace blouse and the white satin evening skirt," I decided.

"They need a wee bit o' pressing, Miss. I'll ha' them back tae ye in no time at all."

Glancing at the pendant watch pinned to my bodice, I decided I had time for another cup of tea before I had to dress for dinner. I was stirring the milk and sugar into the cup when Aillie entered the room.

"I think there's enough for another cup if you'd like some, Aunt Aillie."

"No, thank you. I've had my tea." Aillie glanced around the tower room with an air of reluctant curiosity. "I hope you appreciate the fact that you've been given the most important quarters in the castle. At least one of the Stewart kings stayed here," she observed. She added grudgingly, "I must say, Ellen MacDougall is sparing no pains to make us feel at home."

"Yes, she's being very hospitable. Aunt Aillie, I've been wondering: did you or Daddy ever describe Dungariff to me?"

Aillie frowned. "Why do you ask?"

"Oh, it's—I've an odd feeling that I've been here before, that's all. I thought I might be remembering something that you and Daddy told me when I was very small."

"I told you, Ian and I never talked about Argyll. We wanted to forget that we'd ever lived here. You're imagining things again." Abruptly Aillie changed the subject. "It's past seven-thirty. I believe I'll go change for dinner."

Half an hour later, I jabbed the last hairpin into the heavy coil at the crown of my head and checked the hang of my skirt in the mirror before starting down the winding corkscrew stairs of the tower. The lanterns hanging at intervals on the wall had been lit, but I picked my way carefully along the worn steps, grateful for the curved handrail that had been added long after the original construction. Outside the drawing room, I came upon Colin standing in conversation with the housekeeper, Jane Henderson.

"Now, Maister Colin," Jane was saying, "ye're looking a wee bit peely wally. Ha' ye been getting enough sleep the nicht?"

"Stop your blethering, woman," Colin said, grinning. "You're always thinking I look pale, or tired, or out of sorts. I'm feeling perfectly fit, though I daresay you'll outlive me by a couple of centuries."

After Jane had gone off, grumbling that even as a bairn her former nursling would never listen to good advice, Colin remarked, "She'll never believe that I've grown up, even after I've turned forty, or grown a full gray beard."

He was wearing a black velvet jacket decorated with silver buttons and a short, skirtlike garment in red and black plaid; from his waist hung a sort of purse made of fur, and he wore knee-length hose with what appeared to be a dagger tucked into the stocking on the right leg.

I flashed him an admiring look, saying, "Do you often wear the kilt?"

Looking down at himself a shade complacently, as if he were well aware of the dashing figure he presented, Colin replied, "Yes, for special events, like the Highland gatherings. Lorne and I also like to wear the kilt in the evenings, at dinner."

"Is that the MacDougall tartan? And why on earth do you put a knife inside your stocking?"

"Indeed, this is our clan tartan. The knife's a *sgian-dubh*. After the battle of Culloden, the English government outlawed the carrying of weapons by the clans, with the exception of the *sgian-dubh*. I guess the English didn't mind if we carved each other up, as long as we didn't try to mount a rebellion against *them!*"

Colin and I were still laughing together as we entered the drawing room, a large hospitable-looking room with dark paneled walls, faded old Persian carpets, and rather shabby old-fashioned furniture. A brisk fire burned in the fireplace on the wall facing the door. The rest of the household was already present. Aillie and Ellen Mac-Dougall, who appeared to be chatting very comfortably together, were dressed similarly in conservative, high-necked dark gowns. Flora wore a blue silk dress.

I went straight to the fireplace, holding my hands to the flames in an attempt to ward off the decided chill of the room. Ellen said with a laugh, "You'll have to get used to our climate, Glenna. Today is really very warm for May. Colin, please help yourself and Glenna to sherry."

Ellen returned to her conversation with Aillie, and I walked over to sit beside Flora on a sofa upholstered in worn velvet. She stared intently at my off-the-shoulder, lace evening blouse. "Are those small sleeves fashionable this year?" she asked with a dissatisfied glance at her own enormous puffed sleeves.

"So I was told," I replied, stifling an urge to inform her that the vogue for immense gigot sleeves had collapsed like a pricked hot-air balloon at the end of the previous season.

"It's difficult to dress stylishly in an out of the way place like this," Flora remarked discontentedly. "I wish that Lorne and I could live in Edinburgh or Glasgow for at least part of the year after we're married, but . . . Oh, well, at least I'll be going to Edinburgh to buy my trousseau." Her eyes lighted up. "Perhaps you could go to Edinburgh with me and help me shop. My stepmother doesn't know anything about fashion."

"Oh." I felt taken aback. "I'm no expert, but if I could be of any help— Will you be married soon?"

38

"In September." Flora giggled. "Do you know, I can't quite believe that when school starts in the fall, I won't be in the classroom."

"So you're a teacher. I thought I heard Colin refer to one of your pupils on the drive out here."

"Yes, I've taught in the Oban lower school for four years now."

"Flora's an excellent teacher," Colin interjected, coming up with my sherry. "Her pupils won both the regional spelling championship and the county essay contest this year. She also does most of her father's bookkeeping."

"Oh, you, Colin." Flora blushed faintly, but it was obvious that she was pleased by Colin's praise. They appeared to be on the best of terms, and it occurred to me that Flora probably saw more of Colin than she did of Lorne.

"Will you miss teaching?" I asked.

"Not especially," Flora replied candidly. "Oh, I like the children, but I really started teaching because I was a little bored living at home. My father remarried about five years ago, and . . . well, you know how it is. Sometimes it can be a little awkward for two women to share a house."

Probably, I surmised, Flora had become accustomed to managing her father's household to suit herself, and it must have been difficult to relinquish her place to a stepmother. I wondered suddenly if there would be any friction between Flora and Ellen after Flora's marriage to Lorne. It would be another case of two women sharing the same household.

"Glenna, Aunt Ellen was saying that you're interested in the family history," Colin said after a moment. "Come, have a look at this."

Rising, I followed Colin to what appeared to be a tiny door in the wall. "It's an aumbry," said Colin, pulling it open. "A keeping hole. These old castles didn't have cabinets or chests of drawers for their owners' valuables. It's completely useless today, of course, but Lorne won't hear of boarding it over.''

"Here you are at last, Lorne," his mother said. My pulse quickened as I turned to watch the tall lithe figure enter the room. Lorne was also dressed in the kilt, wearing it with a natural swinging grace that made Colin, by contrast, appear to be attired for a costume ball.

Jumping up, Flora rushed to the door to greet her fiancé. "I thought you'd never get here," she scolded playfully, lifting her face to him.

"I left Fort William as soon as I could," Lorne said quietly, bending down to kiss her on the forehead. He looked tired and withdrawn. "I hope I haven't delayed dinner too much," he said, going over to his mother. He greeted Aillie and then crossed the room to me. I rose to take the hand he was extending to me.

"So you've come at last, Miss MacDougall. Welcome to Dungariff. Welcome home."

Once again his brief, radiant smile transformed Lorne's dark somber features, and as our eyes locked together, I was dismayed to feel a powerful sensual awareness throbbing between us. Almost snatching my hand from his grasp, I looked away from him, hoping that he hadn't noticed the effect he was having on me. It was ridiculous, feeling this way about a man who was already engaged to another woman. In a moment, when Flora came up to put a possessive hand on Lorne's arm, the spell was broken. In what I hoped was a casually friendly tone, I said to Lorne, "Please call me Glenna. We're all family here except Flora, and she soon will be!"

Dinner was simple but well prepared, featuring potatoes cooked in four different ways and a meltingly tender leg of lamb that I wolfed down hungrily, even though I had never cared much for lamb. The talk at the table had an easy family friendliness, although Flora tended to monopolize the conversation. I was unsure whether Flora's talkativeness resulted from an excess of nervous energy, or merely reflected a pronounced self-absorption. Lorne, on the other hand, said very little; he sat back, listening to what the others were saying and throwing in an occasional quiet remark.

"I was thinking today, Flora, that term must be nearly over," Ellen observed.

"Yes," Flora nodded, "only five more weeks of school." To me she said, "I'll be spending part of the summer here at Dungariff, getting ready for the wedding. Mother MacDougall and I have all sorts of plans for refurbishing the family living quarters."

I thought I saw a shadow pass across Ellen's face, and I wondered how eagerly the older woman looked forward to Flora's renovations.

At one point Ellen said to Lorne, in a tone that was rather too casual, "And how did it go today at Fort William?"

"It could have been better, Mother," he replied briefly. He immediately changed the subject.

In the drawing room after dinner, as Lorne was handing around the coffee cups, he remarked, "It's still quite early, Glenna, our twilights are very long at this time of year. Would you like to make a brief tour of the castle?"

"Yes, I would. Thank you."

"I'll come too, Lorne. I like an after-dinner stroll," Flora said quickly.

"No, you don't, my girl. Last week you promised me a chance to revenge myself at draughts," Colin exclaimed.

Flora seemed less than pleased, but Colin insisted on having his game, and Lorne and I started off alone after we finished our coffee. Lorne proved to be an adept guide. He not only had an intimate knowledge of every aspect of Dungariff, but the enthusiasm and affection he felt for the place broke through the barrier of his usual reserve to communicate his feelings. His dark face glowed with a warmth and a spontaneity that made him suddenly look years younger.

"There, to your left, is the buttery," he said as we stood in the Great Hall of the hall house. "Nothing to do with butter, of course; it's the room where they issued the ale and wine to the minions." Tapping on a groin in the vaulting of the hall, he said, "Behind here is a small chamber accessible only from a trapdoor in the Laird's Bedchamber, from which he could hear every word spoken by those sitting on the window seat of the hall." He smiled slightly. "The story goes that more than one unfaithful wife was caught out by her eavesdropping lord."

Outside, in the great courtyard, I became more and more silent as we looked briefly into the stables on one side of the curtain wall and paid a visit to the tiny medieval chapel on the other side. My sense of familiarity with this part of the castle was so powerful that I seemed to hear an inner voice forecasting Lorne's comments before he made them. From his puzzled glances, I knew that he had noticed my altered mood, but he said nothing. After we had poked into the guardrooms on either side of the gatehouse and had ventured down into the dungeons below—now used only for storage, Lorne assured me—he proposed a walk along the ramparts.

Entering a door beside the gatehouse, we climbed up winding stone stairs that were even narrower and steeper than the flight leading to my quarters in the tower. I was glad when we emerged onto the ramparts, high above the courtyard. A brisk breeze tugged at my hair and made me wish that I had brought along a shawl. It was still quite light, though the sun was low on the horizon. Far off to our left was the view I had previously seen from my tower window, with the jagged mountains of Mull outlined in a silvery purple glow against the ocean beyond.

"The curtain walls are ten feet wide and forty feet high,"

Lorne explained as we sauntered slowly along the parapet walk. "Dungariff, you see, was one of the castles scattered along the coast in strategic places to guard against attack, first by marauding Irish and later by the Norsemen."

We had now reached the part of the curtain wall directly behind the Great Hall. Looking down at the sheer, nearly perpendicular cliff face below the wall, I could understand why the castle would be impervious to attack from that quarter.

Suddenly the wind freshened, tearing fiercely at my hair. I began to feel chilled to the bone, and then, as I glanced back along the line of battlemented walls leading to the gatehouse, I was seized with a kind of creeping horror as I gazed at the scene of my nightmares. I choked back a scream.

"Glenna, what is it? Are you ill?" Lorne exclaimed, putting his arm around me.

Acting purely on instinct, I pushed at him violently. I leaned back, trembling, against one of the corbels of the battlements, while I fought to calm myself.

"I'm all right now," I said at last. Unwilling to reveal the real reason for my discomfiture, I improvised. "I—I felt a little faint. I'm not very good at heights." I looked down at the rocks directly below, lashed by the pounding turf, and shuddered.

"I wish I'd known," Lorne apologized. "I should never have brought you up here. Give me your arm. Do you think you can manage the stairs?"

Later, in my tower chamber, I prepared for bed more leisurely than usual, postponing the time when I would be obliged to confront my thoughts. But after I had turned out my lamp and slipped into bed, I had to face the most alarming aspect of my experience earlier on the ramparts. It wasn't so much that the parapet walk at Dungariff had turned out to be the scene of my nightmares—that seemed almost natural, almost inevitable at the end of this long, troubling, unnerving day. No, what had really frightened me was the sensation that I was actually reliving a part of the nightmare while I was still in a waking state. For a few fleeting seconds before Lorne's voice had recalled me to reality, I'd had to fight down the paralyzing fear that the menacing figure of my dreams was in some fashion physically present on the ramparts.

I closed my eyes reluctantly, suspecting what would follow when I'd fallen into slumber, but helpless to prevent it.

I couldn't have been asleep very long when I woke up, strangling a scream of terror, my nightdress damp with perspiration. Gazing about the bedroom, dimly lit by the moonlight slanting in through the windows, I felt grateful that the tower was so isolated that no one was likely to have heard my scream. Sitting up, I hugged my knees tightly to my chest with a growing sense of panic. In tonight's episode of my nightmare, the threatening figure had again moved closer to me. Only a few feet more, and I'd surely have been able to identify him.

Chapter 3

The rays of the early morning sun were creeping across my pillow. I stirred, opening first one reluctant eye and then the other, sitting up to stretch luxuriously. After almost a month at Dungariff, it no longer felt strange to awaken in this circular, stone-walled room. Rising, I slipped into a dressing gown and moved to the wide bank of windows, to savor the view that seemed fresh every time I looked at it. There had been a light rain during the night, and the mountains of Mull were slowly emerging from a veil of pearly iridescent mist.

The door opened quietly and the little maid, Meg, came into the room with a tray. "Ach, ye're up, Miss," she beamed. "Miss Flora, I usually ha' tae wake her. She says she works hard a' the week and deserves to sleep in on the Sabbath."

"Good for Miss Cameron. Back in America, where I worked as a librarian, I used to enjoy a late sleep on Sundays, too."

Meg's eyes widened. "Really, Miss? We heard ye were sa hivy—sa rich. A vera great heiress."

Laughing outright, I replied, "I wasn't always an heiress. I used to work almost as hard as you do, Meg."

This interval at Dungariff had certainly been more

tranquil than my old busy life in Massachusetts, I reflected, settling into a chair to drink my tea. One long quiet day had drifted almost imperceptibly into the next. I'd gone for leisurely walks, caught up on my reading, helped Ellen weed her flower garden. Aillie, too, had changed her life-style; now she had time to knit and embroider to her heart's content. Even more important, Aillie seemed to have come to terms with her ancient grudge against the MacDougalls of Dungariff. She and Ellen had grown close, spending long, companionable hours together each day.

And yet, the slow, uneventful days here at Dungariff might have grown somewhat boring, I suspected, if Lorne hadn't taken time from his estate duties to show me the beautiful Argyll countryside. There'd been a long stretch of perfect weather, day after lovely day of smiling sunshine, though Lorne had warned me that the rainy Highland weather would certainly return. On most of our excursions, I'd felt that nagging sense of familiarity—a feeling, though I shied away from the thought, of having visited these places in some previous existence—but as the days passed and nothing alarming happened, I gradually ceased to be disturbed by these fancies.

Except—I turned my head to stare at the inconspicuous door that led to the ramparts. Unwillingly, as if drawn by a giant magnet, I left my chair to walk to the door, where I made sure that the massive bolt was drawn securely. Since my first night at Dungariff, when Lorne had taken me up to the ramparts, I'd been unable to shake off a conviction that something malevolent lurked in waiting for me outside this door, and I'd grown into the habit of checking the bolt frequently. One part of my mind told me that I was being illogical, or plain superstitious. Perhaps Aunt Aillie was right. Perhaps I was developing an overactive imagination. There was nothing, surely, that threatened me on the ramparts. In any case, if there *was* anything out there, it couldn't be a physical presence . . . Could it? So of what use was a metal bolt, however sturdy, to protect me from it?

The clock on the mantel chimed the hour, and I turned away from the door to the ramparts to dress for breakfast. I was arranging my hair when Jane Henderson came in with one of my light summer frocks draped carefully over her arm.

"The rent mended vera weel, Miss Glenna. Ye'd never know the dress had been torn."

"Why, thank you," I said, examining the exquisitely executed darn. "But I never meant to bother you with it, Jane. Meg offered to take the dress away and mend it when she noticed the tear."

"That Meg," the housekeeper scoffed. "She's no' a real needlewoman, though she means weel. Forbye, I was happy to do it."

"Well, it was very kind of you." I reached for my handbag. "I'd like you to have this."

Shaking her head at the coins in my hand, Jane took a quick step backward, an offended look crossing her usually composed features. "I couldna accept anything, but thank ye."

After the housekeeper left, I shook my head ruefully. It seemed I had a great deal to learn about dealing with servants. Jane had taken to coming to the tower room every day to inquire if there was anything she could do for me. Was it really customary for housekeepers to be so attentive to guests? The slight mystery was still on my mind when I met Ellen at the entrance to the dining room, and mentioned Jane's kindness in mending my dress.

Ellen laughed. "Oh, I think you've made a conquest. Jane never goes out of her way to please anyone except Colin!"

In the dining room, I greeted Aillie and Flora. The latter had arrived the night before with Colin for her usual weekend visit. Flora was dressed very attractively in a dress of pale green percale, sprigged with tiny yellow flowers that enhanced her reddish blond hair and pale skin. Looking up as she buttered an oatcake, she remarked, "I hear that Lorne took you to see Serpent Mound the other day, Glenna."

"Yes, I enjoyed it so much. I'm grateful to Lorne for taking so much time from his busy schedule to show me around the countryside."

"This is his busiest time of the year. Sometimes, when I come out for the weekend, I swear that I almost have to make an appointment to see him!" Flora laughed, an angry little titter. It came to me with a mild shock that the girl was actually jealous of the amount of time I was spending with her fiancé. Catching an amused, ironic smile from Aillie, I was relieved to have Flora's attention distracted by Colin's entrance into the room.

"You're looking lovely this morning, Glenna," he remarked with an admiring gleam in his eye. "Our Argyll air must agree with you." As he passed by her chair, he put a light hand on Flora's shoulder, inquiring, "Do you feel more rested today?" He said to the table at large, "Flora's been wearing herself out. She filled in this week for one of her father's clerks who was out sick. And of course she's preparing for the end of the year examinations."

Flora shot him a pleased smile. Now, why, I thought suddenly, didn't Flora fall in love with Colin? They obviously felt familiar and relaxed in each other's company, and Flora seemed to bask in the warmth of Colin's solicitude. There was no accounting, I supposed, for the ways of the heart. For that matter, why hadn't *I* succumbed to the very decided attentions that Colin had been paying to me since my arrival at Dungariff?

"Good morning, dearest," Flora greeted Lorne, who had just entered the dining room, dressed in riding clothes.

As usually happened when I caught my first daily glimpse of Lorne, I felt my heart giving a sharp little thump, and I mentally berated myself. During the past weeks, I'd schooled myself to think of him only as a kind and thoughtful distant cousin, but my wayward heart kept betraying me. Oh, I knew he was out of reach, engaged to Flora. What's more, he wasn't an easy person to know. He was quiet to the point of reticence, serious and reserved and preoccupied by estate matters. I gathered that Lorne's father had been a poor manager. All the same, I'd never been able to block completely my response to the appeal of his dark, smoldering good looks.

"Where've you been, Lorne? The morning's half gone." Flora's tone, meant to be teasing, had a barb to it. She put out her hand as he approached the table.

Dropping a light kiss on her cheek, he glanced over at me, saying, "I've been checking out that horse I told you about. Jim Kennedy at Barnacarry sent the mare over late yesterday, and I rode her this morning. I think you'll find that she's very gentle. A nice-looking horse, too. A dark sorrel color."

"Why, thank you! I'm looking forward to riding her," I replied, pleased. Lorne had been teaching me to ride for the past several weeks, but he had concluded that the estate saddle horses were too spirited for a beginner.

"You've bought a horse especially for Glenna, Lorne? That was kind of you," Flora spoke up. Her lips wore a sugary smile that concealed what I was sure was acute displeasure.

Apparently unaware of any conversational undercurrents, Colin observed to Lorne, "I had a good look at the boat this morning from my window. She seems in fine shape. We haven't had her in the water since—how long has it been? Last August, last September?"

"September, I believe it was. Yes, I think she's ready for our outing this afternoon. She needed considerable caulking, though, and I had to replace the sail."

"I can't wait to climb aboard her. I've been looking forward to our first sail of the season all week," Colin said. "How soon can we start?" He cocked an eyebrow at Ellen. "You aren't going to insist that we go to church first, are you?"

"I don't think your Sunday will be totally ruined if you give an hour or two to the Lord," Ellen said severely, but she gave in when Colin shot her one of his coaxing smiles and raised his clasped hands in mock supplication. "Well, this one time, I suppose it can't hurt."

Colin blew his aunt a kiss. "How about you, Glenna? Are you a sailor?"

"I've gone out in a rowboat a few times."

"I don't think that's what Colin had in mind," Aillie said, laughing.

Entering the dining room to ask Ellen a question about the picnic hamper for the sailing excursion, Jane Henderson beamed at Colin, saying, "I've baked your favorite cream cakes. Mind ye give the Maister and Miss Glenna and Miss Flora a taste." Suddenly Jane gasped and turned deathly pale, standing rigidly immobile for several seconds. Her eyes rolling in her head, she put out her hand blindly to grasp at the table for support. Before anyone could reach her, she fell heavily, dragging the tablecloth and the breakfast dishes after her.

Ellen was the first to react. She jumped up, disregarding shards of broken china and glass, to kneel beside Jane, who soon opened her eyes in a blank stare. Almost immediately, her eyes cleared and she sat up abruptly, her face flaming a mortified crimson. She struggled to her feet and left the room. Slowly Ellen rose from her kneeling position, saying, "Let's spread out the tablecloth and use it to collect the worst of the broken china and glass."

"Cousin Ellen!" I exclaimed. "Aren't you going to call a doctor for Jane? At the very least, shouldn't someone go after her to make sure that she's all right?"

"It's best to leave Jane be," Lorne said shortly.

"But she's obviously ill. And she may have injured her head, falling like that."

Lorne compressed his lips together, clearly reluctant to continue the discussion. At last he said, "Jane's not ill. She probably saw a fetch. Don't worry about it."

"I don't understand. What's a fetch?" I asked, bewildered.

Straightening up from her task of picking up broken china, Ellen put her hand on my arm, saying quietly, "My dear, remember that I told you Jane has the gift of the second sight? She's a taisher, someone who sees events happening at a distance, or who forecasts things that will happen in the future. Sometimes the taisher sees the fetch—a double, or other self—of a person he knows, and usually this means that the individual will die."

"Of course, each case is different," Flora said, her eyes wide with a kind of ghoulish fascination. "If the taisher sees the fetch in a coffin, or wrapped in a shroud, death is imminent. If the fetch is dressed in ordinary clothes, death won't take place for some time. The position of the shroud is important, too. If the shroud isn't seen above the middle of the body, death may not take place for a year or more, but if—"

"Flora," Lorne said sharply. "That's enough."

I stared at the other people in the room. They looked subdued and vaguely uncomfortable. Not one of them would meet my eyes. "All of you believe in this superstitious nonsense, don't you?" I blurted. "You think that one of us is going to die!"

Ellen hugged me impulsively. "Glenna, dear, I hope we haven't alarmed you with our foolish talk. Of course we don't actually *believe* in the second sight. Well, not unconditionally, anyway! It's just— Oh, sometimes we feel a twinge. We're all Celts at bottom, you know. So are you!"

"But if you believe that Jane saw something—"

"Supposing she did. It could have been the fetch of any one of hundreds of people! But I don't want you to think about it anymore, Glenna. Be off with you, now, all of you, to get ready for your boat ride."

Later, climbing the steps to the tower room to change into boating clothes, I found myself wondering uneasily about the staying power of centuries-old superstitions. I knew, despite Ellen's reassurances, that every one of the modern, civilized people living in this castle—including my own aunt—retained some belief in the ability of the taisher to foretell the future. Shaking my head, I tried to put thoughts of fetches and shades out of my mind as I dressed in a jaunty modified bicycling costume, consisting of a short jacket, a full skirt two inches off the ground, and a little visored cap.

"What a practical outfit for sailing," Flora complimented me when she joined our boating party. She was still wearing the dress of delicate sprigged percale she had worn to breakfast.

The boat was moored below the castle on Loch Fingorm, near the spot where the lake suddenly narrowed to flow into the sea between giant facing cliffs. Instead of taking the long walk by road from the gatehouse to the lake, we descended to the shore by a steep path at the rear of the castle, exiting through a long disused postern gate next to the stables. Parts of the path had been improved, but there remained rough spots where I was glad to feel Colin's supporting hand beneath my elbow. Near the end of the descent, I glimpsed Lorne and Flora ahead of us, poised momentarily at a bend in the path as Lorne helped Flora scramble over a large boulder. "They're a handsome couple, aren't they?" Colin remarked.

There was an oddly wistful note in his voice, and I paused on the path to look at him with a question in my eyes. His lips widened in an open, unembarrassed smile. "You're very quick, Glenna. Yes, I used to be a little in love with Flora. It was when I first came to work for her father, and it might have worked out, I suppose, but about two years ago Lorne and Flora fell deeply in love. Lorne had come home briefly, between voyages, when his father was taken sick. It was the beginning of Uncle Lachlan's last illness, though we didn't know it at the time."

"I'm sorry, Colin."

"No need to be. Flora and I have stayed good friends, and I'm happy for her and Lorne." Colin put his hand on my shoulder and squeezed it. "In fact, I'm thinking of following their example, if I can only find the right girl!"

The boat, bobbing gently on the clear, blue-green water of the loch, looked like any other smallish craft to me, but it was, as Colin explained "what you Americans call a catboat," rigged with one mast, a boom, and one sail. It was a day of bright sunshine, with a steady light breeze that sent the boat skimming exuberantly through the waves. Sitting in a corner of the deck, out of harm's way, I became an almost instant convert to sailing as I watched Flora and Colin and Lorne, working together like experienced old hands, guide the boat out of the channel below Dungariff into the waters of the Firth of Lorn.

After several hours on the water, we sailed into a secluded harbor on Kerrera, an uninhabited island forming a natural breakwater for the town of Oban. Near the beach, we spread out a blanket and unloaded the hamper that Jane Henderson had packed with enough food to feed twice our number. Several bottles of white wine had been included, chilled by being trailed along beside the boat on suspended ropes.

It was an informal, cheerful meal, with Colin and Lorne sprawled comfortably on the grass, resting on their elbows, as they consumed vast amounts of food. Colin and Flora did most of the talking, keeping up a light-hearted, teasing banter that largely concealed the fact that Lorne seemed far-away, lost in his private thoughts. At one point, Colin remarked, "I can't remember when we've had so many beautiful days in a row. You must have brought some of your red Indian weather with you, Glenna."

"You mean Indian summer. And you've got the time of year all wrong."

A little later, Flora said accusingly, "Colin! That's your third cream cake. What a pig you are!"

"Dear old Jane. She never forgets our favorite foods." Colin reached for another cream cake.

"You mean *your* favorite foods," Flora retorted. "You'll notice that Jane didn't pack any of those jam tarts that poor Lorne likes so much."

"Well, it's only natural," Colin replied blandly. "She raised me from a baby, don't forget. When she first met Lorne, he was a scruffy, unappealing eight-year-old. Isn't that right, Dungariff?" he added, pelting Lorne with a handful of grass.

"What?" Lorne sat up, rousing himself from his reverie. Colin repeated his joking remarks. "Oh, no doubt about it," Lorne said, a derisive quirk curling the corner of his mouth. "Jane never gave me a moment's notice."

I was intrigued to hear Colin playfully using Lorne's personal title, Dungariff. Seeing Lorne every day in his prosaic role of hardworking estate owner, it had been easy for me to forget that, before the middle of the eighteenth century, the man holding the title, MacDougall of Dungariff, had exercised a very real power as senior member of the cadet branch of the clan and as second in command to the Chief in time of war. In the old days, the simple title, Dungariff, identified its owner as unmistakably as Argyll identified the head of the mighty Campbells. Even today, when the servants referred to Lorne as The Master, I could hear the vivid echo of a colorful past.

Yawning, Colin rolled over on his side. "I ate too much,

I'm ashamed to say. I'm not going to move a muscle until I've digested all those cream cakes."

Flora nudged him with the point of her shoe. "What a lazy lout you are," she giggled. "What you should do is get up and exercise off all that food you've eaten, or you'll end up as fat as my Uncle Archibald."

I rose to stretch my legs. "What's that building up there on the cliff?" I asked idly.

Lorne followed my gaze. "That's Gylen Castle. Another of the ancient MacDougall strongholds. In ruins, like most of the clan possessions." A barely suppressed note of bitterness sounded in his voice.

"Could we go and have a look at it?"

Lorne hesitated, glancing sideways at Flora. "If you like."

I felt a flutter of surprise. During the past month, Lorne had always seemed at his most outgoing when he was proposing a jaunt to one of his beloved Argyll landmarks.

"It's a terrible climb up there," Flora protested, looking down at her dainty frock and elegant kid boots. "The castle's a heap of ruins, anyway. I don't understand why you're so interested, Glenna."

"Because it's there?" I replied lightly. "However, if you think it's too hard a climb, Lorne—"

"Not at all. I'm game if you are. Flora, Colin?"

"You exercise fiends go ahead. I'm for a nap," Colin said, closing his eyes.

"I'll stay with Colin." No doubt about it, Flora was sulking.

Toiling behind Lorne along the steep trail leading to the castle, I soon realized that Flora hadn't exaggerated the difficulties of the ascent. More than once during the climb, I regretted my impulse to visit the ruins, perched on a rocky pillar rearing up from the shore, with sheer cliffs protecting three sides. It was only after Lorne and I had scrambled up a circular turret stair to emerge into a gabled watch chamber that I conceded the effort had been worthwhile. Standing beside Lorne, our shoulders companionably touching, I gazed at the spectacular scenery surrounding us on all four sides, and sighed dreamily, "Argyll must be the most beautiful place in the world. Have you ever thought, that I would never have come here except for an accident of fate? What if Uncle Niall hadn't discovered that diamond mine?"

Lorne didn't reply. He stood looking into the distance, shoulders hunched, his thoughts elsewhere.

I touched his arm. "Have I offended you in some way, Lorne?"

He stared at me blankly. "No. Of course not. Why do you ask?"

"Well . . . you haven't been very talkative today. I wondered if I'd done something . . ."

"It's nothing to do with you," Lorne said quickly. "I'm in one of my moods, that's all. Didn't my mother warn you about us Celts? She'll tell you that we're always brooding about something!" He changed the subject, obviously attempting to make up for his previous inattentiveness. "The famous Brooch of Lorn, which was once owned by King Robert Bruce, used to be kept here at Gylen Castle," he began. "Before it was stolen a few hundred years ago, it was one of the great MacDougall treasures. It turned up again in 1825, and it still has the place of honor at Dunollie House, where the present Chief of the clan lives."

"I'd love to see it. Is it on view to the public?"

"No, but you're not the public. I don't know why it didn't occur to me before, but I'm sure the Chief would be delighted to greet you as the newest member of our family. I'll take you to Dunollie House some time soon." Lorne's black mood seemed to have evaporated. Pulling out his watch, he sounded genuinely regretful as he said, "I'm afraid we should be going. Mother will be expecting us for

Sunday tea at four o'clock."

If the climb up to the castle had seemed steep, the way down seemed even steeper. Lorne went ahead, reaching back frequently to extend a helping hand. As we neared the bottom of the cliff, my luck ran out when I skidded on a patch of slippery pine needles. I lost my footing, crashing into the back of Lorne's legs and knocking him down. Scrambling to his feet, he helped me up. "Are you all right?" he inquired.

I slumped against him, nestling my head against his chest. "Yes. No. I'm a little woozy. I think I hit my head when I fell." His arms tightened around me, and despite a slight sensation of vertigo, I could feel electric sparks shooting through me at his touch. It felt so natural, so fulfilling, to be cradled against his tautly muscled body. I didn't want him to release me. I wanted his arms to hold me ever more closely.

"Well! Is that what you call cousinly affection?"

Startled, Lorne and I pulled away from each other to confront Flora, who was standing at the entrance of the path near its junction with the beach. "Please excuse the interruption," she exclaimed in a voice shrill with angry sarcasm. "I came to tell you it's time to go." Spinning on her heel, she rushed away down the path.

"Flora—" Muttering a curse under his breath, Lorne went after her. When we caught up with her a few moments later, she was standing in Colin's embrace, sobbing into his shoulder. Lorne walked over to her, putting his hand on her arm. He said, very quietly, "Flora, stop that crying. I want to talk to you."

"Better leave her alone for a bit," Colin murmured. But Lorne was insistent, tightening his grip on Flora's arm. Gradually responding to that silent pressure, she turned around, still snuffling forlornly, and allowed Lorne to lead her away to the other end of the beach, where they sat down together on a piece of driftwood.

"What happened to throw Flora into such a state?" Colin demanded.

After I had explained, he said with a sigh, "Poor Flora. She's got a jealous streak, I'm afraid. Not that she doesn't have reason for it, I suppose. Her mother died when she was a baby, and she grew up very close to her father. It was a real shock for her when Mr. Cameron remarried a few years ago. He used to depend on her so much, and now I think she feels out of place at home, unwanted. So naturally, with Lorne—" He cut himself short.

"Go ahead and say it. Flora's transferred all her affections to Lorne, and it was inevitable that she'd be jealous of any attentions he paid to me."

"Well . . ."

"It's all right, Colin. I'm not embarrassed. I'll make sure this kind of thing doesn't happen again, that's all."

After a long, low-voiced conversation with Lorne, Flora surprised me with an apology. Wan but composed, she came over to help pack away the remains of the picnic lunch, and, as we were folding up the blanket, she murmured, "I'm sorry I made a scene. Lorne's explained everything to me."

Nevertheless, the return trip to Dungariff was a subdued affair. Flora kept to herself, taking no part in sailing the boat, and Lorne, after muttering a brief "Sorry" to me, had reverted to his usual reticence. Even Colin's normally high spirits were muted. I settled back in a corner as the boat got under way with Colin at the tiller. Not far from the entrance to Loch Fingorm, I heard a loud cracking noise. Lorne lifted his head to glance up at the sail and called out sharply, "Colin, you idiot! You're sailing by the lee."

Following Lorne's gaze upward, I could see that the top of the sail was fluttering noticeably.

"Sorry," Colin exclaimed. He sounded chagrined. "Stand by to jibe." Seeing my puzzled expression, he explained, "Nothing to worry about. The wind is coming over the same side of the boat that our sail is on, and we could capsize if we didn't jibe, or tack." A moment later he shouted, "Jibe ho."

Picking up the mainsheet, Lorne began trimming the rope hand over hand, telling Flora and me, "Keep your heads down." As the boom came halfway across the middle of the boat, the wind filled the sail again and Lorne began paying out the sheet rapidly. Suddenly a sharp gust of wind caught the sail. Lorne yelled, "Shift weight to the port side."

I hesitated, feeling stupid. Earlier in the afternoon, Colin had taught me some rudimentary nautical expressions, but every one of them had slipped from my mind. With an impatient grunt, Lorne grabbed my shoulder and shoved me to the opposite side of the boat just as the craft heeled sharply.

I plunged overboard, panicking at the shock of the icy water. I'd never learned to swim, and I flailed my arms desperately in an attempt to keep my head above the choppy waves. I was pulled under, my lungs desperately straining against the impulse to inhale, and then I blacked out.

I opened my eyes to find myself lying on the beach below the rear walls of Dungariff with Colin astride my midriff. Protesting the painful pressure on my rib cage, I croaked, "Don't do that—it hurts!"

He got up, grinning. "Better than drowning, love." His smile faded. "Fool me, for not paying attention to that wind shift. I could have capsized us all."

Struggling to sit up, I said, coughing, "You certainly didn't try to drown me on purpose, I know that."

A strong hand beneath my armpit helped me to my feet. Putting his arm around my waist for support, Lorne said, "You gave us the fright of our lives. It didn't occur to me and Flora that you couldn't swim. We've been like fish, all of us, since we were bairns. But thank God for Colin. He went into the water seconds after you did. I followed him, but he was the one who found you. You'd been pulled under the boat and out the other side."

My teeth were chattering, and the heavy sodden masses of my hair felt like ropes of ice against my neck. I swayed back against Lorne's arm.

"She's perishing with cold," came Colin's worried voice. "We should get her into bed right away, before she catches pneumonia."

"She's too weak to climb up to the castle," Lorne said. "Look, Colin, I'll go up by the back path, while you and Flora get Glenna into the boat and sail into the loch. By the time you moor the boat, I'll have a carriage at the landing."

Even though I was encased in a cocoon of blankets during the drive to the castle from the dock, I was still shaking with cold when the carriage entered the court-yard, where Aillie and Ellen were waiting. As Lorne helped me out of the carriage, carefully redraping the blankets around me, I was able to muster a smile for my aunt. "Don't look so worried, Aunt Aillie. It will take more than a cold dunking to kill me."

Instant relief flooded Aillie's face, although she said scoldingly, "Ach, Glenna, I could never take my eyes off you for a minute when you were a child, for fear that you'd get into some kind of mischief, and you're still a handful now that you're grown."

"Lorne *said* you were all right, but I don't think Aillie quite believed him," Ellen exclaimed. "Now, Glenna, it's out of the question for you to climb the tower stairs, and I don't think Lorne or Colin should try to carry you there, either. So I've arranged for you to stay tonight in the green bedroom near your Aunt Aillie."

I didn't resist the change in sleeping quarters. After expending that brief flurry of energy to reassure Aillie, I felt close to complete exhaustion. No doubt, over the centuries, servants must have transported furniture and other heavy objects to the tower room, but I didn't relish the thought of being carried, even in Lorne's careful arms, or Colin's, up those narrow, wickedly curving steps. "Thank you, Cousin Ellen," I said, observing with a kind of muzzy surprise that my voice was coming out in a mere sliver of sound. Ellen reached out to grab me as I went limp and started to slump to the paving stones.

Lorne carried me into the green bedroom on the second floor, where Jane Henderson was waiting for us. She took immediate charge of the situation with her usual competence. "Lay Miss Glenna on the bed, Maister, and leave her to me."

As Lorne set me down, I hugged my arms to my chest, missing the warmth of his body. My teeth were chattering audibly.

"You need some whisky for that chill," he said abruptly. "I'll be right back."

"I dinna hold wi' strong drink at a time like this, Maister," began Jane, but Lorne was already gone. "Ye maun get out o' those wet clothes, Miss Glenna," she grumbled. "Ye'll die o' the cold afore the Maister comes back."

Lorne returned in several minutes with a small glass of smoky-colored liquid. He supported me with his arm around my shoulders and put the glass to my lips. I choked at the taste of the fiery brew and began to cough.

"'Tis enough, Maister. Be off wi' ye," Jane ordered.

In an incredibly short time, she had stripped off my drenched garments, popped me into a tub of hot water before a roaring fire, dried me off with a large towel so briskly that my skin felt scraped, and propped me up against a mound of pillows in a bed piled high with blankets and comforters. Relaxing completely, I was almost asleep when Jane returned a little later with a tray containing a light meal. "I feel almost human already," I said gratefully, as the housekeeper held a cup of hot broth to my lips.

"A good night's sleep will cure anything that's wrong wi' ye," replied the housekeeper stolidly. She put another pillow behind my back and placed the laden tray on a small table close to the bed. "Can ye manage by yersel'?"

Jane sat quietly by the bed while I, with more appetite than I would have thought possible, drank some tea and ate some toast and part of an omelet. At one point, the housekeeper inquired casually, "Did Miss Flora no enjoy the sailing, then? She seemed a wee bit crabbit when I spoke to her juist noo."

"She's probably tired. It was a long day." I had no intention of talking about Flora's tantrum, but it was clear that Jane already had a shrewd idea of what had happened today at Gylen Castle. Possibly she had wormed an account out of Colin. There was little that concerned the family at Dungariff that did not reach Jane's ears eventually.

Thinking back over the day's events, I was struck by a chilling thought. I was horrified to hear my voice asking, "Was it my fetch you saw this morning?"

The housekeeper froze, her lips clamped tightly together. After a moment she said, "Ye mustna talk o' such things."

I persisted. "I almost drowned today. Did you know I was going to have an accident? Mrs. MacDougall—everybody—is convinced you saw *something*."

At last the housekeeper said reluctantly, "It's true, I ha' the sight, but I canna talk o' it. And forbye ye didna die, praise the Almighty . . ." She left the sentence unfinished. I knew it was useless to pursue the matter. Jane left the room after tucking me under a mountain of blankets.

It was only a few hours later—the night outside the windows was still pitch-black—when I awoke with an attack of acute nausea. I stumbled out of bed to the basin on the washstand. Afterward, I stood at the window, gulping in the cold, fresh air.

Could I have internal injuries, I wondered, remembering Lorne's violent shove that had sent me plummeting into the chill waters of the Firth of Lorn. No, that couldn't be it. I felt no pain, except for a slight soreness in my ribs from Colin's well-meant attempt at lifesaving. It was more like . . . I shrugged my shoulders impatiently. What a ridiculous thought! I must still be light-headed from shock. What could have put the idea of poison into my mind?

Chapter 4

I woke up the next morning feeling completely disoriented. Swathed in a cocoon of blankets, I lay staring around the unfamiliar room, wondering muzzily why I couldn't see that glorious sweep of light streaming in through the bank of windows on my turret wall. As the sleep cleared from my brain, I gradually recalled what had happened yesterday, and why I had spent the night in a strange room. I eased myself cautiously into a sitting position. Apparently I'd suffered no permanent ill effects from the boating accident, though I did feel a sudden twinge of soreness in my rib section, where Lorne had shoved me roughly to the opposite side of the craft. But, to my relief, there wasn't a trace of the agonizing stomach cramps that had roused me in the middle of the night.

Noticing a slight movement at the door, I called out, "It's all right. I'm awake."

Jane Henderson's face peered around the door. "I've brought Miss Flora and Maister Colin tae see ye for a wee bit, if ye feel up tae it. They're aboot tae gae back tae Oban."

"Oh, of course, they have to return to work today, don't they? Send them in. I'm quite at leisure," I said cheerfully.

"Noo, mind ye dinna stay tae lang," Jane cautioned, as she ushered Flora and Colin into the room. "I'll juist be bringing up yer tea, Miss Glenna."

"I told Colin it was far too early to disturb you," Flora apologized. She was dressed for town in a prim toque and a three-quarter length coat. There were dark circles under her eyes, as if she hadn't slept well.

"Oh, I knew you wouldn't mind, Glenna. You know we're both working people who have to be up with the tide." Colin grinned, coming with Flora to stand beside my bed. "We didn't like to leave Dungariff without finding out how you are this morning."

"I'm fine."

Looking at me closely, Colin said with a touch of anxiety, "Are you sure? You look a little pale. I could never forgive myself if you became ill as a result of that boating accident. How I could have been so stupid and inattentive—"

"No, really, I'm perfectly well," I interrupted him. I saw no point in adding to poor Colin's guilt by mentioning my bout of stomach cramps. In fact, remembering my nocturnal fears of being poisoned, I was beginning to feel foolish. The cramps had probably been caused by ingesting a large quantity of sea water. "Don't forget," I reassured him, "there was some stupidity on my part, too, Colin. If I'd followed Lorne's orders, I wouldn't have fallen overboard."

"Colin, I think we should be going," Flora said. "You know how Papa hates for you to be late to work."

Glancing at his watch, Colin said, "Good Lord, yes. Mr. Cameron will have my hide. You get lots of rest, now, Glenna, and we'll see you next weekend. We'll try to find something less strenuous than boating!"

Flora touched my hand. "I hope you'll soon be feeling better, Glenna." She smiled, a brief wintry smile that didn't seem to reach her eyes. "Doubtless Lorne will see that you get some fresh air by taking you out on another excursion."

I felt acutely uncomfortable. Flora had apologized for making a scene yesterday, and she was apparently trying to be gracious this morning, but clearly she was still jealous of the amount of time I was spending with Lorne.

Appearing with a tea tray, Jane shooed Colin and Flora out. "The gig is waiting in the courtyard, Maister Colin."

Giving his old nurse a brief hug, Colin said to her with a show of mock severity, "You be sure to take good care of Miss Glenna. I want to see the roses in her cheeks when I come back next week."

As the door closed behind him, I shook my head. "Poor Colin. He feels so responsible for my accident, even though he's the one who saved me from drowning."

Arranging the teapot and cup and a plate of buttered toast on the tray table she had set in front of me, Jane said seriously, "Aye, Maister Colin ha' a tender heart. He's a guid laddie. Always has been, since he was a wee bairn."

I had to smother a smile. I wondered if the possibility that her ex-nursling had a flaw had ever crossed Jane's mind.

Rather to my surprise, I felt hungry. I devoured the strong hot tea and the buttered toast, wishing that Jane had brought me some porridge or a rasher of bacon and eggs as well. When she returned for the tray, I said, "Please ask Meg to bring me something to wear. She can pick out whatever she thinks suitable."

Jane recoiled. "Ye'll never be wanting tae get out o' bed sae soon, Miss Glenna. Ye should juist bide where ye are for the rest of the day."

"I feel fine," I said impatiently. "I've never stayed in bed a day in my life. Back in Massachusetts we don't hold with such laziness!"

The rigidity of Jane's back as she went out the door expressed her strong disapproval, but a short time later the little maid, Meg, appeared with a change of clothing, including a fleecy shawl, which I was glad to have. Even in the spring, a Highland morning can be decidedly chilly.

After I had dressed, I went downstairs to the family living quarters, where I paused to look into Ellen's sitting room. She and Aunt Aillie spent much of their time there, busy with their correspondence and their voluminous knitting and sewing projects, but the room was empty now. They were probably at breakfast. Eyeing the softly glowing fire on the hearth, I sank into a high-backed easy chair facing the fireplace, put up my feet on a hassock, and reached for the book I had started a few days before.

I must have dozed off. The next thing I was aware of was the sound of Ellen's agitated voice, just inside the threshold of the sitting room. I was swinging my legs off the hassock, about to rise and greet her, when I froze in place as I realized that she was speaking to Lorne on a very private matter. Keeping my head down, I sat huddled in miserable silence, desperately hoping that they wouldn't come farther into the room to discover me in my involuntary eavesdropping.

"But Lorne," Ellen was saying, her voice rising on a note of panic, "doesn't this mean we'll be ruined?"

"It's not quite that bad, Mother."

"Isn't it? The bank's informed you they won't renew your notes unless you agree to lease three-quarters of the property to that sporting syndicate. That means most of our crofters will be forced to leave. We'll have the castle and enough land to graze a few sheep. After all your work this past year, after all the sacrifices you've made to pull us out of the financial mess your father left, we'll be no better off than we would have been if you'd given in to Lachlan and agreed to break the entail so he could lease the estate to that hunting baron."

"A little worse off, actually. Father wanted to lease the entire estate for fifty years in return for a very decent income. The MacLeod Bank in Fort William is proposing a ten-year lease only, allowing us to remain living in the castle. But after we make the loan payments, there won't be much left. Father had run the estate pretty much into the ground."

"His gambling and other extravagances didn't help," Ellen said bitterly. "It's not fair, Lorne. Will . . . will there be enough money to maintain the property if we manage carefully?"

I couldn't see him, of course, but apparently Lorne shook his head.

"What will you do, then? How can you get married now? You'll have to postpone the wedding."

"I can't do that. It wouldn't be fair to Flora. Look, Mother, we do have some options. If worse comes to worst, I can always go back to sea. I was making a fair salary as a merchant captain, and you and Flora could make do with it."

"Oh, no, Lorne. You can't leave Dungariff, now that you've finally come home." Ellen paused for a moment. "How did it come to this? I remember so well—it was the day Glenna and Aillie arrived—you came home from seeing Mr. MacLeod at the bank in Fort William, and you told me he had some hope of persuading his father to renew the loan. What happened?"

"Alan MacLeod doesn't have the final say in the bank, Mother. His father does. And his father decided against renewing my notes unless I would agree to the lease. I have exactly six weeks to consider the offer. On the other hand, there is one more possibility, a slim one. You know I've always been interested in developing the silica deposits on the property. Alan MacLeod's promised to try to interest some of his Glasgow banking friends in financing such a project."

"Lorne, would you consider—?" Ellen broke off. She tried again, her voice hesitant, "Have you thought of speaking to Glenna? There's all that money, more than

68

she can ever think of spending, and it's really MacDougall money . . ."

"Under no circumstances would I ask Glenna for a loan," Lorne exclaimed with a harsh finality. "Listen to me, Mother: I don't want Glenna or Aillie to know anything about our money problems. It has nothing to do with them."

"Yes, you're right, I suppose." Ellen sounded doubtful. "Well, let's hope those Glasgow bankers decide to invest in our silica. I think I'll go up to see how Glenna is doing. She's probably awake by now."

"I'll go with you."

As soon as their voices had receded toward the stairs, I seized my shawl and ran down the corridor in the opposite direction. If I pretended I'd been on an early morning walk, neither Lorne nor Ellen could suspect that I'd been in the sitting room, overhearing their conversation.

Leaving the hall house by the side door normally used by the family and servants, I slipped out into the courtyard under the massive portals of the gatehouse to Ellen's rose garden, which occupied the area of the filled-in moat. I paused, glancing at the tightly furled buds. Before long, the garden would be a mass of perfumed blossoms. Poor Ellen, how she would miss her roses if she were forced to leave Dungariff, I thought with a pang. Surely it wouldn't come to that. But no, that was wishful thinking. From what I had overheard, it seemed more than likely that, rather than hang on at Dungariff in straitened circumstances, Lorne would choose to sell the property outright. Barring, of course, that slim chance that the Glasgow people would invest in the silica deposits. The next few weeks might very well see the end of over five centuries of occupancy by the MacDougalls at Dungariff.

I stamped my foot in sudden exasperation. Lorne must know I'd be happy to loan him any amount he needed from the vast fortune that Uncle Niall had left me. As Ellen had said, it was really MacDougall money. But no, in his stubborn, stiff-necked pride, Lorne had made up his mind not to approach me for a loan, and as long as I was supposed to be officially ignorant of his money problems, I couldn't very well bring up the subject myself.

A sharp breeze ruffled my hair, and I pulled my shawl closer around my shoulders. Bright Highland spring day or no, it was far too cold out here without a jacket. Walking quickly, I reentered the hall house by the side door, pausing in some confusion as I rounded a corner of the corridor and nearly ran into Lorne.

"Where've you been, Glenna?" he said accusingly. "Jane told us that you insisted on getting out of bed, and I've been looking all over for you."

"Whatever for? I simply went out to get a breath of fresh air."

Lorne took my arm. "Jane thinks you ought to rest today, and so do I. Now, she may not be able to manage you, but *I* can. I'm marching you right back to that bedroom."

I pulled away, laughing. "You may be the Master of Dungariff, Lorne MacDougall, but I think you're a petty tyrant. Oh, all right, I'll go lie down for a bit, but only in my own room in the tower."

Tucking my arm into his, he retorted, "You won't mind if I make sure of that, will you? I'll take you up."

By the time we reached the landing at the head of the winding tower stairs, my legs felt distinctly rubbery, although I wasn't going to admit that to Lorne. He walked into the bedroom, gazing around him with a thoughtful expression, almost as if he were seeing the room for the first time. "I haven't been up here for a while," he observed. "It does have an atmosphere, doesn't it? Mother says you're enjoying staying in the tower."

"Very much. I feel at home. And I love the view."

70

He went over to the windows, staring out across the sound to the fog-shrouded outline of Mull. "It *is* beautiful," he murmured. A wistful note crept into his voice. "I used to dream about the views from Dungariff when I was at sea. Of all the places I've seen, Argyll's the only place I've ever wanted to be."

Joining him at the windows, I reflected that I had never really seen him with his guard down to this extent. His thin dark face looked strained and vulnerable, and I knew he was thinking of the possibility that he might lose the estate. Impulsively I reached out to grasp his hand. "You're home now, Lorne. You won't have to dream about Dungariff any longer."

It was a mistake, I realized at once. His hand tightened in mine, and a powerful current seemed to be flowing between us. I was trembling, and my breath was erratic, and there was a curious roaring sound in my ears. I had a light-headed sensation that I was being drawn irresistibly closer and closer to Lorne, and yet the eons passed— actually I suppose it was only a second or two—and we were still standing apart, except for our clasped hands, staring at each other in hard-breathing silence. Neither of us had said a word, but I knew, deep in my being, that whatever I was feeling, he was feeling, too.

I don't know what might have happened if Jane Henderson hadn't broken the spell. We heard her voice saying tartly, "Miss Glenna, why aren't you in bed?"

Like two children caught in the cookie jar, Lorne and I broke apart and turned to face Jane, who was standing in the doorway, carrying a tray.

"Will you excuse me, Glenna? I've got work to do," Lorne mumbled, not meeting my eyes. "Get some rest now. I'll see you at dinner, I hope." He walked to the door, passing Jane with a curt nod, and disappeared down the stairs.

"What's that you have for me?" I asked Jane, pointing

71

to the steaming pitcher on the tray.

"Hot milk, Miss Glenna. There's no a better remedy for what ails ye, even if the Maister believes in the strong drink. Here ye are, drink it doon."

As she bustled about with her usual efficiency, helping me out of my blouse and skirt and tucking me under a mound of comforters, I wondered uneasily if her stern Calvinistic soul had been offended by the sight of Lorne and me holding hands in my bedroom. If so, there wasn't a trace of disapproval on her stolid features. She left the room with a brisk injunction, "Mind, dinna ye be wasting yer time wi' one o' them dreich buiks ye're always reading, Miss Glenna. Juist close yer eyes noo and get some sleep."

That was easier to say than do. I closed my eyes obediently, but I couldn't stop thinking about Lorne. Of course I wasn't falling in love with him. He was engaged, happily engaged, to Flora, and he had never given me the slightest indication that he felt anything except cousinly affection for me. And yet—my cheeks burned—and yet there was *something* between us, some overwhelming physical impulse that made each of us achingly aware of the other's body.

Eventually I did fall asleep, wakening several hours later feeling perfectly refreshed. Dressing quickly, I wandered downstairs, finding Ellen and Aunt Aillie in the sitting room, watching one of the young farm servants as he carefully removed a large portrait from a packing case.

"There you are, Glenna," my aunt said giving me a long, scrutinizing look. "You don't seem any the worse for wear, thank the good Lord. But you were always a strong, healthy child." She motioned at the painting. "Look at what arrived this morning. Lorne's official portrait."

It was Lorne to the life. Dressed in a velvet jacket and the short kilt, he was standing against a hazy, indeterminate background, his lean body poised and graceful, but with the faintest suggestion of tension. His dark eyes stared out at me with their familiar aloof, inscrutable expression.

"It's a speaking likeness, isn't it?" Aillie remarked. "Ellen says she practically had to hit Lorne over the head before he'd agree to be painted. But she was determined he wasn't going to be the first Laird not to have his portrait in the family collection."

"Do you really have portraits of all the Lairds of Dungariff?" I asked Ellen, impressed.

"What?" Ellen appeared abstracted. She gave herself a little shake, as if to collect her thoughts. "Oh . . . no. We have an unbroken series of portraits of the Lairds and their consorts from the late fifteenth century on. But the earlier Lairds . . . well, I fear they were an uncivilized, blood-thirsty lot, engaged in constant feuds with their neigh-bors," she added with a smile. "It probably never occurred to them to have their portraits painted!"

She called to the servant, who was about to carry the pieces of the discarded packing case out of the room. "Leave that till later, Donnie. We'll put up the Master's portrait now. Aillie, Glenna, you come along with us to the Great Hall. I want you to see how the portrait looks when it's hanging in its rightful place."

As we walked to the Great Hall behind Ellen and Donnie, who was carrying the painting, Aillie said to me in a low voice, "There's something wrong with Ellen this morning. She's not herself, did you notice? She seems to be a million miles away."

"Maybe she has a headache," I murmured. I knew exactly what was wrong with Ellen, but I had already decided not to tell Aunt Aillie about the conversation I'd overheard. If or when Lorne and his mother wanted us to know about their financial situation, they would tell us.

When we arrived in the Great Hall, I looked around me with a sense of discovery. Ellen had shown us through the huge room on the day we arrived in Dungariff, and I had walked through it a number of times since, but I had never really examined it closely. Though it was the showpiece of the hall house, and during earlier periods had been the very heart of the castle, the Great Hall was used now only for the most ceremonial of occasions. It was so vast that it was dankly chilly even in the height of summer, and I presumed that it was impossible to heat it adequately in the colder months.

A long line of family portraits occupied the wall opposite the enormous medieval fireplace. As young Donnie mounted a ladder to hang Lorne's portrait near the courtyard entrance, I left Ellen and Aillie to supervise the boy's efforts, while I walked to the far end of the hall so that I could examine the pictures in chronological order.

Some of the earliest portraits, of fierce-looking men dressed in antique kilts and of equally fierce-looking women, were quite primitive. They had probably been painted by wandering artisans. Later pictures displayed a higher degree of technical skill. It raised goose pimples on my flesh to reflect that I was gazing at the features of my direct forebears extending back through the centuries. Well, that wasn't quite accurate. My family's direct line had ended with the battle of Culloden, when my ancestor, Angus MacDougall, had forfeited the estate of Dungariff for treason. All the succeeding Lairds were related, not to me, but to Lorne.

I paused before an empty space, about the width of two of the paintings. The metal plaques on the two pictures preceding the empty space read: "Alan MacDougall, 1690-1743; Margery Forbes MacDougall, 1696-1740."

I felt a pang of disappointment. The missing pictures must be those of Angus MacDougall and his wife. I thought I knew Lorne and his mother far too well to suspect them of refusing to hang Angus's portrait because he had died a traitor—half the Highland clans, after all, had followed Bonnie Prince Charlie to defeat at Culloden—or because he wasn't their direct ancestor. Besides, two pictures had obviously been hanging there until recently.

Giving the remaining portraits only a cursory inspection as I walked by them, I returned to the other end of the hall, where Donnie was climbing down from his ladder.

"It looks splendid, Ellen," I said, standing back a little to get the full effect of the newly hung portrait. "I'm sure Lorne will be pleased." Feeling oddly hesitant, I went on, "I noticed an empty space in the middle of the row of paintings, about where pictures of Angus MacDougall and his wife should be. Did they ever have their portraits done?"

Ellen appeared startled. "Oh, yes. Angus and Catriona," she replied hastily. "I had their portraits removed for cleaning. The nearest reliable painting restorer is in Edinburgh, so it takes the longest time to get one's pictures back. I'm sure, though, that they'll be returned well before your visit ends."

"But, Mistress—"

At Donnie's strangled exclamation, Ellen turned to the boy in surprise. "Did you want to say something to me, Donnie?"

Turning a beet red, the boy busied himself with folding up the ladder. "Nay, Mistress," he muttered. "It wasna' anything, ye ken."

As he walked off with the ladder, Ellen remarked, "Glenna, I'm going to the village with Aillie this afternoon to see Pastor Munro about the summer festival. Would you care to come along?"

"I'd love to," I replied absently. I couldn't put my finger on it, but I had a vague feeling that there was something rather strange going on. Take the portraits of Angus and Catriona, for instance. Why were these the only two pictures, out of a long row of paintings, that needed cleaning? And when I'd asked Ellen about the whereabouts of the portraits, I could swear, in hindsight, that she seemed not only startled, but faintly guilty, as if she were extemporizing a story to explain their absence. Then there was Donnie. Listening to Ellen's talk of having the paintings cleaned, he'd started to blurt out something, and then he'd changed his mind.

I was still mulling over the mystery of the paintings—if mystery it was—when I climbed into the landau with Ellen and Aunt Aillie after lunch to drive to the hamlet of Finlay, a mile down the coast from the castle toward Oban.

Ellen seemed more cheerful this afternoon. I presumed that she had decided, with her usual calm good sense, to push her worries to the back of her mind until Lorne's money problems actually reached a crisis point. "You look so pretty today, Glenna," she observed as we drove along, eyeing my simply cut tailor-made costume of pale blue tweed. "You're always so suitably dressed. I wish Flora—" She broke off, biting her lip. "Isn't it a bright, beautiful day?" she added quickly. "I sometimes think you and Aillie are responsible for bringing us this stretch of lovely weather."

I exchanged a glance with Aunt Aillie. I was sure that she, too, knew the reason why Ellen had so abruptly changed the subject. It was to avoid criticizing her future daughter-in-law's rather atrocious taste in clothes. Last Saturday at dinner, for example, I'd noticed Ellen's involuntary look of distaste when she glimpsed Flora in her new gown of bright yellow trimmed with pink and light green, colors that couldn't have been more unbecoming to her pale transparent complexion.

Finlay was a dreary little place, consisting of a pub, a tiny church, the minister's house or manse, a small general store, and a straggling string of dilapidated fishermen's cottages. Its only feature of interest was the crumbling remains of a *broch*, a hollow circular tower of drystone masonry which had once, Ellen told us, served as a refuge from Viking raiders.

As we walked up the path to the minister's door, Ellen murmured, "I hope you're not put off by Pastor Munro. He's a fine man, but he does tend to be a trifle dictatorial. Nothing much happens in Finlay that he doesn't know about."

I had already observed from attending services in the church that the Reverend Aidan Munro was a stern-looking man with a penchant for preaching strong sermons. Up close, as we sat facing him in front of his desk, he appeared to be every bit as austere as his pulpit performances indicated.

"I hear, Miss MacDougall, that ye had a bout with death on the Sabbath last," he said, fixing me with a penetrating eye. "Ha' ye been sitting in the kirk instead of sailing around in a boot, ye'd no ha' been in sich peril."

"That's very true, Pastor," I replied meekly. I didn't dare look at Ellen's face, or Aillie's, for fear of giggling.

Having made his point, the pastor turned his attention to the summer festival, which, I noted mirthfully, he apparently intended to supervise without doing any of the actual work. I had an idea that Ellen would efficiently manage the whole thing. Before the end of the meeting, she had persuaded Aunt Aillie to take charge of the fancywork booth, and I suspected that I would soon be enlisted, too.

As we stood up to leave, Ellen said hesitantly, "There's something else I'd like to discuss, Pastor. It's about Morag Armstrong, who used to work in the kitchen at Dungariff. You've heard, I suppose, that she's had . . . well . . . family problems."

The Reverend Munro drew his eyebrows together in a forbidding frown, making no bones of his opinion. "I ha', that. Her puir husband caught the woman in the act o' adultery." Catching my eye, he pursed his lips, saying,

77

"Ye'll forgie us for discussing sich a subject in front of a young unmarried lady, Miss MacDougall, but I maun concern mysel' wi' the affairs of my congregation." To Ellen he said, "Wha' did ye wish tae discuss, Mrs. MacDougall?"

"Well, I know Morag's conduct was very bad," Ellen said hastily, "but I don't think she was entirely to blame, either. Duncan Armstrong is a hard man, much older than Morag, and I think he left her alone too much. She came to me the other day in tears, telling me she's begged her husband to take her back, but he'll have none of it. So I thought—Pastor, will you speak to Duncan? Morag is truly sorry for what she did, and I'm sure he'd listen to you."

After a long silence, during which his frown grew more pronounced, the Reverend Munro nodded reluctantly. "If the lass ha' repented, Duncan ought tae consider pardoning her fault. Verra weel, I'll ha' a wee talk wi' him."

As we emerged from the gate of the manse, Ellen said with a worried frown, "I do hope I haven't made things worse for poor Morag. Pastor Munro is very rigid in his views about women losing their virtue, in or out of marriage! But if Morag's husband doesn't take her back, I don't know what she'll do. The villagers are even more censorious than the pastor, and they've already made the girl a pariah. Perhaps I should have spoken to Duncan myself."

"You did your best, Ellen," Aunt Aillie assured her.

"I suppose," Ellen sighed. "Can you two occupy yourselves for a few minutes? Old Mrs. MacIntyre has been under the weather and I should look in on her."

While Ellen was playing lady of the manor, my aunt and I wandered down to the shore, empty except for several aged men, mending nets, and a handful of small children. "You know, Aunt Aillie," I said thoughtfully, "I never realized before how intimately Cousin Ellen concerns herself with the folk living on the estate and in the village. She treats them all like family—" I broke off, hugging my arms close to my chest.

"What is it, Glenna? Aren't you feeling well?"

"Yes . . . I don't know. I feel so cold all of a sudden . . ." I stiffened, transfixed with horror at the sight of the young woman who was running down the beach toward us, screaming in terror. Pursuing her was a man whose hate-twisted face was even more frightening than the ugly-looking knife he brandished in his hand.

"I'll kill ye, ye faithless woman," the man was yelling. "I'll drain every bit o' bluid frae yer worthless carcass."

As the woman came nearer, her racing steps began to slow, and I observed with a sick apprehension that she was nearing the end of her strength and her pursuer was rapidly catching up to her.

"Help me, oh help me," she moaned, her voice barely audible above her wheezing gasps. She might have been speaking to the wind; her eyes were vacant from fear, and she seemed hardly aware that Aillie and I were there.

Her heartrending plea roused me out of the sort of inexplicable paralysis into which I had fallen. I launched myself at the man, hurling my body between him and his prey, screaming to the woman, "Run, run! I'll hold him until you can get away."

A pair of strong hands gripped my shoulders, shaking me so violently that my head jerked back and forth like a rag doll's. Struggling to free myself, I cried fiercely, "Let me go, Aunt Aillie. We've got to help that poor woman before her husband kills her."

Aillie gasped, her eyes widening in shock. "What woman, Glenna?"

Drawing a deep, ragged breath, I turned my head to look up and down the beach. I saw no one except the two old fishermen, still engrossed in their net-mending, and the knot of children, who had stopped their play to watch the

79

outlander ladies who were behaving so strangely.

"Aunt Aillie, tell me the truth," I said with a desperate intensity. "You must have seen that young woman fleeing for her life from a man with a knife. I'm sure it was the girl Ellen was telling us about. Morag Armstrong, and her husband Duncan."

Aillie shook her head, her face taut with anxiety. "No, Glenna. There wasn't anyone to see. It's like that time at the battlefield of Culloden, when you thought you saw the Highlander who wasn't there."

"You're lying," I exclaimed angrily. "I saw those two people as plainly as I see you standing in front of me now. I can even tell you exactly what they were wearing—"

The words stuck in my throat. Yes, I could describe the clothes worn by "Duncan" and "Morag." He'd been swathed in the voluminous folds of the belted plaid, and she was wearing a striped wrap known as the *Arasaid*. Garments that hadn't been worn in Scotland since the Highland dress was abolished by the English authorities a hundred and fifty years ago after the '45.

Chapter 5

"Glenna, are you all right?"

I swallowed hard against the lump of panic in my throat. I wanted to respond to the concern in my aunt's voice, but the words wouldn't come.

"Glenna!"

This time I managed to say, somewhat shakily, "I'm fine. Feeling a little silly, maybe."

"You mean . . . you're talking about those people you thought you saw?"

"Oh, don't worry about that, Aunt Aillie," I replied, laughing. It was a poor excuse for a laugh, it didn't sound convincing even to my own ears. "I think I must have had a touch of the sun. It's so bright on the water today." I cast a quick look around the beach. The old net-menders were gone, and the children, no longer curious, had returned to their game. No one else was there, of course. "We'd better be getting back. We don't want to keep Cousin Ellen waiting."

Ellen was already sitting in the landau when we came up from the beach. Immediately she exclaimed, "You're pale, Glenna. Are you ill? You know Jane thought you shouldn't get out of bed today."

"It's only a headache. Probably a touch of the sun,"

Aillie cut in. By some sort of unspoken agreement, she continued to cover for me during the ride back to the castle, chattering like a magpie to Ellen to hide the fact that I was as tense as an over-wound watch spring. I don't think Ellen noticed anything amiss except that I was unusually silent. When we arrived at Dungariff, I used the boating accident as an excuse to get away. "Perhaps I did overdo a bit today, Cousin Ellen. I think I'll go lie down."

I shook off Aunt Aillie's instant offer to accompany me, and, as soon as I was out of sight of both of them, I fled with a sense of desperate urgency up the twisting stairs of the tower to the haven of my room. Only then did I allow myself to face the implication of what had happened today at Finlay.

Those two people on the beach—the terror-stricken woman and the man I took to be her vengeful husband— had been figments of my imagination. The proof? Aillie had been with me during the whole encounter, and she hadn't seen a thing. And if those people weren't real, what about the man I'd met at the Culloden battlefield, the archaically dressed Highlander who so closely resembled Lorne? Aunt Aillie hadn't seen him, either.

I began pacing the floor. Was I seeing things? Did my frightening nightmares, my eerie sense that I had lived here in Argyll in another time, have anything to do with these apparitions, if that was what they were? Into my reluctant mind crept the memory of Aunt Aillie's chilling revelation that there was a streak of mental instability in her mother's family, and I stopped my nervous pacing abruptly. Standing in the middle of the floor, I clenched my fists in anger at the growing wildness of my thoughts. What was I afraid of? Madness? The supernatural? But that was ridiculous. I was a perfectly normal, well-balanced modern woman. There had to be some logical explanation for what had been happening to me, if only I had the wit to discover it.

Suddenly I remembered Sophronia. I hadn't thought of her in years. She had never existed, either. She was one of the companions I'd invented as playmates to populate my lonely childhood. I smiled to myself, remembering the times when I'd also made up narrow escapes from pirates and encounters with hostile Indians. My overly vivid imagination had been a great trial for my practical, down-to-earth aunt while I was growing up.

Limp with relief, I collapsed into a chair. That must be it. My imagination. The bane of poor Aunt Aillie's life. Here in Scotland I'd simply been responding to an atmosphere charged with the turbulence and tragedy of centuries. At Culloden I'd felt a pervasive sadness over the death of the clansmen, and the appearance of the Highlander in battle dress could have been merely a reflection of my own thoughts. Similarly, at Finlay today, having heard so much about the unfortunate young woman caught in adultery, perhaps it was inevitable that the image of poor Morag would materialize in the flesh.

Satisfied that I'd resolved my fears in a rational manner, I went downstairs a little later in a thoroughly relaxed frame of mind. I ate heartily at dinner, challenged Lorne to a game of draughts afterward in the drawing room, and went up to bed still in a mood of near euphoria, a mood, unfortunately, that didn't carry over until the morning. Several hours after falling asleep, I woke to the familiar cold sweat, the pounding heart, the feeling of infinite menace emanating from that shadowy figure racing toward me on the rainswept ramparts.

"Where are you off to, Glenna?" Aunt Aillie called from the sitting room as I walked past the door. I paused, feeling a stab of irritation. It was Saturday morning, and in the five days since our visit to Pastor Munro at Finlay my aunt had been keeping me under what amounted to constant surveillance. Wherever I turned, she seemed to be dogging my steps, and not even the haven of my tower room was totally exempt from her watchful eye.

She stepped out into the corridor, eyeing my straw hat and parasol. "Oh, you're going for a walk," she said. "If you'll wait a moment, I'll fetch my bonnet and a wrap, and I'll go with you. Or perhaps we could take a drive. I'm sure Ellen wouldn't mind if we ordered the landau."

"No, I'd rather walk. I need the exercise. I don't think you'd enjoy going with me, though. I'm going down to the beach by the path at the rear of the castle."

"But that path's much too rough for you to go it alone," Aillie protested. "You might fall, and you could lie there for hours before anyone thought to go looking for you."

"Oh, I'm sure you'd miss me soon enough," I said with a touch of dryness. "Don't you worry about me, Aunt Aillie. I'll be back in an hour or so, safe and sound."

Slipping away from my aunt's clutches before she could think of any further objections, I went into the courtyard, where I found Lorne emerging from the stables with his saddled horse. In his boots and breeches and worn jacket, he looked like any other farmer in the British Isles, I suppose, but he had an ingrained elegance that belied his nondescript clothes, and the jaunty Balmoral bonnet marked him as a Scotsman. As usual, my heart gave the odd little flip I'd come to expect whenever I saw him.

"Hullo, Glenna. Where are you off to?"

"I'm really escaping from Aunt Aillie," I replied, laughing. "She thinks it's too dangerous for me to go down to the beach by the rear path. Sometimes I don't think she realizes I've grown up."

"The path *is* a little rough. Look, I'll take you down."

"Don't be silly. You'd only have to climb up again, and you have work to do."

"Maybe I should play hooky." His lips curved in a slow smile. "I'd like to." He reached out to brush a gentle finger across my cheek.

I could feel the warmth creeping into my face. "You're too old to play hooky," I said hastily, "especially since you've already invited me for a ride this afternoon."

Lorne chuckled. "Very well, I won't argue with a New England Puritan," he said, putting his foot in the stirrup and swinging into the saddle. "Until later, Glenna."

I waved good-bye and turned to tug open the heavy double-leaved iron gate or yett, which in the old days had provided the one exit on the seaward side of the castle. Circling some huge rocks and a few scrawny fir trees that had managed to root themselves precariously in the thin soil outside the gate, I began the steep descent to the beach. More than once in my scrambling progress, slipping and sliding on the loose stones of the path, I regretted not accepting Lorne's offer to play hooky. The touch of his strong, capable hand would have made me feel much more secure.

Reaching the end of the path, I found a comfortable perch on a large boulder near the water, put down my parasol beside me, and, after a moment's thought, removed my straw boater. I sat for several minutes in utter stillness, lifting my face to the gently warming rays of the sun and listening to the muted ripple of the waves. I reveled in the feeling of being solitary, free of Aunt Aillie's presence, at least for a while.

The incident at Finlay had apparently revived all my aunt's latent anxieties about me. I'd been trying to keep in mind that she had nothing but my best interests at heart, but her constant hovering, however well meant, was beginning to be oppressive, especially since, in my own mind, she had nothing to be concerned about.

I stirred, hunching my shoulders as I shook off my resentful thoughts. Aunt Aillie would come around if I gave her a little time. My slight movement affronted an inquisitive sea gull that had wandered too close to my motionless form, and he flew away, squawking indignantly, carrying with him the last remnant of my black mood. Laughing as I watched the gull soar off above the water, I settled myself more comfortably on my rocky perch, thinking ahead with a good deal of pleasure to my ride with Lorne that afternoon. Today was Saturday, so we might have to curtail our outing slightly, in order to get back to the castle in time to greet Flora and Colin as they arrived for their regular weekend visit.

As the sun rose higher it burned more hotly on my hatless head, and I cast a guilty glance at my parasol and straw boater lying on the ground beside me. Aunt Aillie would have a conniption if I returned home with my complexion imperilled by reddened cheeks and a peeling nose. Rising, I shook out my skirts and picked up my belongings. Jamming on my hat, I began the climb back up the path, which turned out to be, as any beginning student of logic could have told me, much more difficult than the descent. A number of times I nearly lost my balance, and it was only by snatching at any handhold, a scrawny bush, a jutting rock, that I saved myself from some nasty falls. As it was, by the time I reached the postern gate, my hands were covered with scratches and my light-textured dimity dress was badly soiled and ripped about the hem.

As I rounded the stables on my way to the hall house, I encountered Ellen and Aunt Aillie emerging from the portals of the gatehouse. They were wearing old clothes and carried trowels, and had, I presumed, been weeding in Ellen's rose garden.

"Back already, Glenna? I hope you didn't get too much sun . . ." Aunt Aillie broke off, staring at me in disapproval. "What on earth have you been doing with yourself? You look as if you'd been rolling in the mud."

"It's only a little honest dirt, Aunt Aillie. It will wash out. Go ahead and say I told you so. You were right. I shouldn't have made that climb alone."

"Honestly, Glenna, it's getting so I can't take my eyes off you for a minute," Aillie grumbled.

For a moment she sounded as she had years ago when I soiled my Sunday-go-to-meeting dress before it was time to leave for the services. I didn't snap back at her—I was much too fond of her for that—but I made up my mind that I wasn't going to spend the rest of the afternoon playing lone chick to her mother hen.

Ellen must have noticed the touch of irritation in my face. She said quickly, "I hope you'll not be too disappointed, Glenna. Lorne won't be able to ride with you this afternoon. One of our crofters has had an unexpected death in the family, and Lorne's gone over to see what he can do to help."

I nodded and went up to my room.

When I came down to lunch I was wearing my riding habit. Still determined to escape my aunt's vigilance, I announced calmly that I saw no reason to forego my ride, even if Lorne weren't available. One of the grooms could accompany me.

However, when I entered the stables, only one groom was present—young Donnie, the lad who had helped to hang Lorne's portrait in the Great Hall a few days before. Busily polishing harness, he glanced up, startled, as I entered. "Miss MacDougall! Ye didna get the Maister's message, then?"

"Oh, yes, I know he's been detained and won't be able to ride today," I replied over my shoulder, as I walked over to Jeannie's stall. She was the gentle mare Lorne had insisted on buying for me. We'd become fond of each other. Greeting me with a soft whinny, she lifted her head to be scratched between the ears. "I thought you might be kind enough to fill in for the Master, Donnie," I continued.

"I'd like tae oblige ye, Miss, it's juist that I'm the only one here, ye ken," he apologized. "Jock, he's the other groom, he's out helping the vet'rinary today, and—"

"And you have more than enough to do to keep two people busy," I finished, smiling. "I understand, Donnie. Just saddle up Jeannie and I'll go off for a short ride by myself."

Donnie looked disapproving. "The Maister wouldna like ye tae do that, Miss. Ye dinna ha' the experience, ye havna been riding verra lang."

"Then we won't tell him about it," I laughed. "I'll be quite all right. I won't go galloping off like a steeplechase rider, and I won't go so far that I might get lost."

As I watched the young groom put the sidesaddle on Jeannie, I asked him on a sudden impulse, "Donnie, you remember those two paintings that Mrs. MacDougall sent away to be cleaned?"

The strong capable hands paused for a second in their task of cinching the girth on Jeannie's saddle, and an expression of discomfort clouded his open, cheerful face. "Oh, aye, Miss, the paintings."

"When did that happen? When were the pictures taken down?"

"I dinna recall exactly."

"Well, about how long ago?" I persisted. "Six months? A month?"

"Aye, ye ha' the richt o' it. 'Twas juist aboot a month," Donnie replied hurriedly. "Jeannie's a' ready, Miss MacDougall. Can I help ye tae mount?"

I was in a thoughtful mood as I rode out of the courtyard. I couldn't imagine what her reason might be, but I was sure now that Ellen didn't want me to see the portraits of Angus and Catriona. Likely as not, the portraits were still in a storeroom somewhere in the castle, where Donnie had taken them shortly before or after I arrived at Dungariff. Even though it was hard to see how it could be a matter of world-shaking importance, my curiosity was intrigued. Perhaps the explanation was simply that the artistic quality of the two portraits was so inferior to the other family pictures, that Ellen was too embarrassed to let me see them.

As I had told Donnie earlier, I had no intention of becoming venturesome during my unescorted ride. I walked Jeannie sedately down the drive leading from the gatehouse and turned south in the direction of the Serpent Mound. This was an easy meandering route that Lorne and I had taken several times before, and one that shouldn't present any surprises even to a neophyte rider like me. I had never been astride a horse before I came to Scotland. I didn't own a riding habit. When Lorne first started teaching me to ride, I'd worn one of Ellen's old habits. The divided skirt and short, tight-fitting jacket of dark blue broadcloth I was wearing today had been delivered from the tailor in Oban only the week before. Leaning forward, I patted Jeannie's thick sorrel mane. Lorne was a wonderful teacher, patient and conscientious, but his task would have been far more difficult if he hadn't bought this gentle intelligent creature for me.

I paused for another look at the Serpent Mound, which was composed of boulders arranged in an elongated letter S and was supposed to be a relic of primitive snake worship. A short distance farther on, I glimpsed a narrow track running off to the left. Vaguely recalling that Lorne had once mentioned an abandoned graveyard with a particularly fine Celtic cross lay down this road, I turned Jeannie into it.

No one had come down the rutted track for a long time. It was overgrown with rank grass, so that Jeannie had to pick her way carefully, and the straggly brush on either side of the road had grown so high that it occasionally met overhead. Now and then as we plunged deeper into the miniature wilderness, I heard a rustling in the under-brush, but I thought little of it. I knew there were no dangerous wild animals in the vicinity. So it came as a heart-stopping surprise when a large shape crashed through the brush and lunged straight into Jeannie before staggering off into the thicket on the other side of the track. I think now it must have been a red deer, but at the time I was too startled to pin down the creature's identity.

My frightened horse reared sharply and uncontrollably, and even as I grabbed at her mane with frantic hands, I could feel the saddle sliding down her back and out from under me. I landed in the middle of a large prickly bush that broke my fall but held me a prisoner for several seconds until I could pull myself away from the razor-sharp thorns. Lurching to my feet, I gazed rather numbly at my tattered gloves and the rents in my new riding habit. My saddle lay incongruously collapsed on the track before me, but Jeannie had disappeared. I could hear faintly the thud of her hooves as she sped back along the track the way we had come.

Uttering an unladylike curse, I bent over to retrieve my new bowler hat, which, though it sported a few twigs and bits of dried grass, looked considerably better than the rest of me. Jamming the hat on my head, I started trudging after Jeannie. I even managed to view my predicament with a certain amount of philosophical detachment. I wasn't hurt, after all, and I wasn't lost, either. All that had really suffered was my dignity.

The tall grass overgrowing the track made walking difficult, and to compound my misfortunes it began to rain. Soon I was a sodden mess, my riding habit clinging damply and uncomfortably to my body. A cold rivulet spilled over the rim of my hat and down the back of my neck, and the long blades of wet grass began to wrap themselves tenaciously around my boots, impeding my progress almost like quicksand. Sliding along in chill misery, I fell more than once. When Lorne cantered around a bend in the track a short time later, he found me sprawled motionless on the ground, momentarily too disgusted even to make the effort of getting up.

Hearing his panic-stricken voice calling my name, I lifted my head abruptly, feeling an overwhelming relief as I saw him racing toward me across the slippery grass. I was halfway to my feet when he came up to me, reaching out to fold me into his arms. "Glenna, oh, Glenna, I thought you were hurt when I saw you lying there," he exclaimed, his arms tightening around me.

"Not hurt at all, just cold and wet, and oh, so glad to see you, Lorne." I smiled up at him, noticing inconsequentially how the raindrops clung to his long dark eyelashes like tiny jewels.

A muscle flicked in his cheek and he pulled me closer to him, muttering, *"You're* glad . . ." With a little moan, he bent his head, crushing my lips against his in a kiss that went on and on, sending waves of unfamiliar fiery longing surging through me, making me conscious as I had never been before of the enticing rightness in the feel of his lean, hard body against my own. I was oblivious to the still-falling rain, I was gasping for breath in that burning embrace, sinking ever deeper into a mindless abyss of passion. Danger flags were flying in some distant corner of my consciousness, but I paid them no heed. All that I cared about, all that existed for me, was the urgent pressure of Lorne's mouth on mine.

He came to his senses before I did, abruptly relaxing his hold, pushing me away from him. "Glenna, I'm so sorry," he blurted. "I never meant to grab you like that. You must think I'm some kind of savage. It was just—I was so worried about you, you see, and then when I saw you there, still as death—"

I moved away from him, feeling my face flame with embarrassment. He'd been carried away by his concern for me. But *I*, what excuse did I have? What must he think of me, responding to his embrace with such wild abandon? "I'm the one who should apologize," I said with an attempt at lightness. "I brought this on myself. Donnie tried to talk me out of riding alone. I should have listened to him."

"Donnie should have tried harder," said Lorne grimly. "You could have been badly injured."

The rain, which had tapered off, began again with a gust of wind and a chilling squall. Suddenly aware once more of my drenched garments, I started to shiver.

"You'll die of pneumonia if we don't get you home," Lorne exclaimed with a worried frown. "Here, I'll put you up in front of me in the saddle."

I relaxed against him as we moved off. I was still chilled and clammy, and he was as wet as I was, but with his arms clasping me close to him, I felt at least a hint of warmth. "How did you know where to find me?" I asked curiously.

"I didn't. It was a stab in the dark. When you didn't come back from your ride, we were convinced that something had happened to you, so we went looking for you. Unfortunately, Donnie had no idea where you'd gone, not even in which direction. I sent him and Jock, the other groom, north, toward Oban. Colin and Flora arrived then, and Colin volunteered to search Glen Fingorm while I rode south. My heart was in my mouth when I spotted Jeannie grazing near the Serpent Mound. Her saddle was gone, you were nowhere in sight. I took a chance on this track. I remembered we'd talked of visiting the abandoned graveyard. What happened, Glenna? How did Jeannie come to lose her saddle?"

"It was the oddest sensation, feeling myself sliding off Jeannie's back," I said as I finished my story. "One of the straps—I know that isn't the right term—one of the straps on the saddle must have come loose, I suppose. Perhaps Donnie was in a bit of a hurry, he was working alone in the stables today."

Lorne stiffened. "That's impossible," he said coldly. "Donnie could never have been that careless. And the saddle was almost new. I bought it for my mother on her last birthday." I could feel him taking a deep breath. "I'm sorry, Glenna. I didn't mean to snap at you. We'll soon get to the bottom of this. I'll send Donnie out to collect the saddle the moment we get back to the castle. Meanwhile, young lady, I have a bone to pick with you," he added with mock sternness. "What did you think you were doing, going out riding alone?"

"You told me I was becoming an accomplished equestrienne," I retorted. "If that's true, I don't need an escort. You can't have it both ways, Lorne."

Even though my back was to him, I could almost see the surprised look on Lorne's face. Then he chuckled. "I can so have it both ways. I'm the Master of Dungariff, remember?"

I smiled to myself. Lorne, usually so somber and withdrawn, was actually developing a sense of the absurd. We rode along in companionable silence in the gathering twilight. Though the rain had stopped, I was no less wet and uncomfortable, but somehow it didn't seem to matter. Nestled against Lorne's shoulder, clasped in his arms, I gradually slipped into a dreamlike state of mindless contentment. I wasn't fully aware of my surroundings until we clattered under the heavy portal of the gatehouse into the courtyard of Dungariff. Colin, who had obviously ridden in with Donnie only moments ahead of us, tossed his reins to the groom and rushed over to us, shouting, "Lorne, by all that's holy, you've found her!" He reached up to help me down from the saddle, giving me a brief, hard hug as my feet touched the ground. "Thank the good Lord, Glenna."

The side door of the hall house burst open and what looked like the entire population of the castle erupted into the courtyard, apparently alerted by Colin's exultant shout. Aunt Aillie pushed Colin aside, gathering me to her with arms that trembled. Behind her, Ellen smiled at me wordlessly, brushing a tear from the corner of her eye.

"Where did you find her, Lorne?" Colin asked. "I went clear to the end of Loch Fingorm, and Donnie must have gotten at least halfway to Oban before he gave up the search."

"I'll tell you about it later," Lorne said shortly. "Right now, I don't want Glenna bothered with questions. She needs to get out of those wet clothes before she perishes with the cold. Mother, give me your shawl, please."

Taking the shawl from Ellen's willing hands, Lorne wrapped it carefully around my shoulders. "There, that should help a bit until we get you up to your room," he said, smiling down at me. For a fleeting second, I had the strangest impression that we were quite alone in the courtyard. "Do you feel up to climbing the tower stairs? I could carry you—"

"Oh, don't be ridiculous, Lorne," Flora interrupted him. She had been standing back on the edge of the little crowd, but now she came forward, putting a possessive hand on his arm. "Of course Glenna doesn't want to be treated like a wee bairn," she added, with the forced little titter I'd come to recognize. "As a matter of fact, Glenna, I expect you're becoming tired of being fussed over all the time as our honored guest. Why, you'd have been embarrassed to see what an uproar this place was in this afternoon when Colin and I arrived from Oban. Mrs. Murray was actually talking about finding your dead body! I tried to tell Lorne there was nothing to worry about. You'd taken the wrong turning, that was all, you'd be home in your good time. But nobody listens to me, naturally—"

"Flora."

Lorne's quiet voice cut like a whip. Flora bit her lip, the angry color flooding her cheeks and receding again, leaving her face pale and pinched. She snatched her hand away from Lorne's arm, as if his very touch was burning her, and stalked off toward the house.

An appalled silence lasted until Aunt Aillie, with her usual calm good sense, said briskly, "You're all in one piece, Glenna, praise Heaven, but Lorne is quite right: we'd best get you out of those clothes before you catch your death. Come along, child."

Chapter 6

"Here, Glenna, if you'll sit at the dressing table, I'll towel your hair dry," Aunt Aillie said after we had climbed up to the tower room and I had removed my sodden garments.

I sat down, relaxed, feeling much more human after a complete change into dry clothes. Watching Aunt Aillie in the mirror as she vigorously wielded a towel on my hair, I was relieved to observe that she didn't look especially upset. Apparently she wasn't going to make a great to-do about my riding accident. Probably she considered it a perfectly normal, run-of-the-mill incident, without any element of the inexplicable—like seeing people who weren't there! It could have happened to anyone.

"Well, what did you make of the little scene with our Flora?" Aunt Aillie inquired after a moment.

I shrugged. "Nothing very much. Flora's always a bit . . . well, prickly, don't you think?"

"Prickly, my hat! The girl's jealous of you and Lorne, that's what. You should have seen her this afternoon when she and Colin arrived at the castle. She tried to talk Lorne out of going out to look for you. Said the most that could have happened was that you'd gotten lost, and the grooms could find you as easily as he could. My Lord, I thought there was going to be a battle royal between the two of them, but Lorne simply ignored her. Which is more than I did."

"Aunt Aillie, I hope you didn't have words with her," I said uneasily.

"Nothing of the sort," she snorted. "I did make it perfectly clear, however, that falling off a horse can cause fatal injuries, and you weren't the world's most expert rider!" She shook her head. "Do you know, try as I might, I've never been able to cotton to that young woman. I don't think Ellen cares much for her, either."

"Aunt Aillie!"

"No, I mean it. Not that Ellen's ever said a word to me against Flora. It's what Ellen doesn't say, I guess. Haven't you noticed how uncomfortable she looks when Flora keeps talking about the improvements she wants to make at Dungariff after she and Lorne are married?"

"Ellen doesn't approve of Flora's plans?"

"Well, she's never actually said so," Aunt Aillie admitted grudgingly, "but I'm sure she doesn't like the thought of major structural alterations to the castle. And let's face it, she can't really be looking forward to having two mistresses at Dungariff." The towel stilled in Aillie's hands. She added casually, "Lately I've been wondering if Ellen wouldn't be much more enthusiastic about that wedding if Lorne were marrying you, instead of Flora."

Twisting my head so abruptly that the towel tore out of Aillie's hand, I stared at her, too dumfounded to speak.

"Well, why not?" she said with a trace of defensiveness. "Lorne likes you, that's obvious. Ellen likes you. She told me once that she knew you'd be good friends the minute she first saw you. And I've always thought you were fond of Lorne."

"Of course I'm fond of Lorne. We're fond of each other," I spluttered when I finally found my voice. "What does that have to say to anything? Aunt Aillie, what's put this bee in your bonnet?"

She didn't answer immediately. Instead, she picked up a brush from the dressing table and began pulling my thick wavy hair off my forehead into a Grecian knot at the back of my head. For a person who cared little about her own appearance—her reddish brown hair had been tortured into a tight bun at the crown of her head for as long as I could remember—her fingers had a rare deftness when it came to arranging my hair becomingly.

"Look, you may not care for Flora," I went on. "Ellen may not care for her. As long as we're speaking frankly, I'll admit that I don't much like her myself. But Lorne loves her, and she's his choice for a bride. And that's all that matters."

"I know," Aillie sighed. "You're right, of course." Putting down the brush, she tucked a tiny jewelled butterfly into my heavy coil of hair.

"No, really, what put a strange idea like that into your head?" I persisted.

She hesitated. "Oh, it was something Ellen let slip the other day, I guess. Now, don't imagine that she's been pouring out her troubles to me, but we do spend a lot of time together, and we've become . . . well, rather fond of each other. And occasionally she drops a remark or two, and I put the bits and pieces together. Glenna, I think she's very worried about money."

"Oh? What bits and pieces?" I asked, hoping that my expression didn't betray that I was already very familiar with the subject.

"Oh, well . . . I've gathered that Lorne's father used to squander huge sums when he took those trips to Edinburgh without Ellen. Glenna, Lachlan was a *gambler!* I believe the family financial cupboard was nearly bare when he died. Do you remember that Lorne wasn't here to greet us the day we arrived at Dungariff? He was in Fort William on business, they told us. I think he'd gone there to try to arrange some kind of emergency loan.''

Aunt Aillie looked at me with a sheepish smile. "The long and short of it is, that I got to thinking about all that money you inherited, and how Flora doesn't have any, and since I'm positive Ellen likes you much better than Flora, well, it occurred to me that perhaps . . .'' She shrugged. "So there. Go ahead and call me a foolish old woman.''

I jumped up to give her a quick hug. "You're no such thing, Aunt Aillie. You *have* been letting your imagination run away with you, though, the way you're always accusing me of doing! Please, *please*, don't say a word about this to Cousin Ellen.''

As Aillie was leaving to change for dinner, the sandy-haired young maid, Meg, came in the door with a tray. "Mistress thought ye'd fancy a cup, Miss, since ye werena here at teatime.''

I had to smile at yet another indication of Ellen's rooted belief that a cup of tea could put almost anything to rights, but I was glad of the excuse to linger for a while in the tower room. While Meg moved quietly about, picking up my wet garments and straightening my dressing table, I sipped my tea and tried to put my thoughts in order.

Aunt Aillie's remarks had hit far too close to the mark. Unbidden, the memory of Lorne's fiery kiss came into my mind and my heartbeat quickened, even as I told myself firmly that the kiss didn't mean anything, couldn't mean anything. It was a temporary physical aberration, that was all. Nothing like that would ever happen again. There was no possibility that we could be in love with each other. Lorne was engaged to be married, happily engaged, despite Flora's occasional bouts of jealousy. For the first time, though, I began to think about leaving Dungariff. Perhaps my presence here was too much of an irritant to Flora, who would soon be living at the castle full-time until her wedding. But as soon as the thought of leaving occurred to me, a seductive image flashed into my mind.

Suddenly I saw myself living here with Lorne, presiding over the castle as the Mistress of Dungariff, a place refurbished and modernized with Uncle Niall's money, a place of joy and passion and . . .

"Idiot!" I exclaimed aloud.

"Is there something wrong, Miss?" Meg inquired, sounding startled.

"No, not at all," I replied hastily, feeling even more like an idiot. I'd been so deep in thought that I'd completely forgotten Meg was in the room.

"Is there anything I could do fer ye afore I gae downstairs, Miss? Would ye care fer a shawl?"

"Oh, thank you, Meg. Would you bring me the white silk shawl with the fringe?"

Meg walked over to the huge old wooden wardrobe in the far corner of the room. A moment later I heard a high-pitched scream of terror, and I leaped out of my chair to rush to her. She was standing beside the open door of the wardrobe, trailing my shawl in one hand, literally paralyzed with fright as she stared at an object on the floor beside her foot.

"What on earth is that thing?" I said, bending down to retrieve the object.

"Don't touch it, Miss! It's *evil!*" Poor Meg's face was chalk-white beneath the sprinkling of freckles.

"Nonsense." I picked up the doll—though it was stretching the meaning of the word to call it a doll—and turned it over in my hands. It was fashioned out of wax, with a blob for a head and four sticklike appendages representing arms and legs. A few strands of black yarn were glued on its head, apparently meant to suggest a woman's flowing hair, and the figure was wrapped in a bit of familiar-looking cotton material sprigged with tiny blue flowers. Several large pins were jabbed into the torso of the doll.

"Good Heavens, what an ugly thing," I exclaimed.

"And isn't that a piece of my dress? The one I tore this morning on the beach?" I looked into the bottom of the wardrobe, where I had tossed the ruined dress before I went down to lunch. It was still there, but now there was a large square piece missing near the hem.

Finally Meg stirred out of her fear-ridden trance. "It's the *Droch Shuil*, Miss. The Evil Eye," she said in a shaking voice. "A witch ha' put a spell on ye."

I looked incredulously at the figurine. "You mean this . . . this thing is supposed to be *me?*"

"Aye, Miss. That image is a *Corp creadha*. Wherever those pins are stuck in't, ye'll begin tae feel a dreadful pain in that part o' yer body. I thank God there's no pin near the heart. That would mean yer *death.*"

In spite of the absurdity of what she was saying, the absolute conviction in Meg's voice sent a shiver down my spine. I expostulated, "Oh, Meg, you know there's no such thing as witches."

"There are, there are!"

"Well, have you ever seen one with your own eyes?"

"Nay, but I dinna need to. I've seen wha' happened tae my own uncle's cow. A witch put the Evil Eye tae it, and the puir beastie wasna giving any milk, naething at a', 'til the charmer—that's a white witch—told Uncle tae tie a string o' three colors around the beastie's tail."

"And that made the cow give milk again?"

"Aye, she did, as much as ever she did." Even in her distress, Meg recognized the skepticism in my tone. "Miss, ye must believe me, there are witches a' around ye. They can turn themsel' intae beasties. Most often hares, but frogs and cats and ravens, too. Aye, verra often ravens. I heard o' a crofter over Benderloch way, he was attacked by a huge cat, and he knew it were really a witch, so he put a silver coin in his musket and juist pointed the gun at the creature, and the cat turned intae the woman who lived down the glen. And eggshells, Miss. Witches use the shells fer boats, sae ye maun always be sure tae pierce a hole in the bottom o' the shell . . ."

There was a peremptory knock at the door and Jane Henderson entered the room, her forehead creased in a frown. "There ye are, Meggie, lass, ye havna turned down the beds yet." She choked on her words as she spotted the wax image in my hand. Darting across the room, she snatched the figure from me and swiftly, methodically, tore the pins out of it. "Get tae yer work, lass," she ordered Meg, "and dinna make the gossip aboot this." After Meg had scuttled out of the room, Jane said to me, "I'll get rid o' the figure, Miss. Dinna fash yersel', it canna hurt ye noo I ha' the pins out."

I put my hand out to her as she turned to go. "Jane, you can't really believe that something terrible would have happened to me if you hadn't removed those pins."

She stared back at me with the same intractably stubborn expression she had assumed when I questioned her about her own powers as a taisher. At last she replied, slowly and reluctantly, "I dinna ken for sure, Miss. There's black magic a' around. Aye, it's there, for a' ye willna admit it," she added when I instinctively shook my head. "But I canna imagine wha' enemies ye could ha' made, and so . . ." Her voice trailed away.

"Perhaps it was one of the servants' children, making a little mischief?" I suggested, grasping at a straw. Even as I said it, I didn't believe it for a moment. Jane kept far too sharp an eye on her domain for any of the servants' children to have the opportunity to roam at will through the family quarters.

However, she seized on my remark with evident relief. "Oh, aye, that could be it," she replied. "I'll juist be looking into it. Goodnight, Miss." When she reached the door, she paused, her expression troubled, to say, "I wouldna wish the Mistress tae be distressed, so mayhap if ye didna mention this tae Mrs. MacDougall . . ."

"Oh, I quite agree," I said hastily. I had no desire to upset Ellen. Then there was Aunt Aillie. What would she make of this, I wondered? I told Jane, "It will be much better if you take care of this by yourself."

After Jane left, I stood quietly for a moment, slowly arranging and rearranging the folds of the white silk shawl around my shoulders, while I thought about the incident of the doll. It was clear that Jane Henderson shared Meg's conviction that a black witch had tried to put a spell on me. Naturally, I dismissed their belief as pure superstition, but it made me feel uneasy, all the same, to reflect that someone had actually put the revolting object in my bedchamber. It could have been meant as a practical joke, I supposed, although such a cruel sense of humor didn't seem to belong to any of the people I had met at Dungariff. Or could I have offended someone without knowing it, one of the servants who worked in the castle or on the estate, perhaps?

I shrugged, refusing to speculate on the matter any longer, and went down the tower stairs to the drawing room, where the other members of the household were already assembled. A glass of sherry in either hand, Colin came up to me as I entered. "Allow Dr. MacDougall to prescribe for you," he said with a cheerful grin. "Strong drink is what we both need after that perishing rain, actually. Or would you prefer a whisky?"

"No, thanks," I shuddered. "The sherry's fine." One dollop of that pungent, powerful national drink of the Scots had been enough for me.

Colin touched my shoulder gently. "We were terribly worried about you, Glenna," he said, his blue eyes sober. "Don't put us through anything like that again, please."

"I won't," I promised, sipping my wine. My eyes were glued on Lorne as he crossed the room to us. Standing side by side, the two tall cousins were distinguished-looking in their velvet jackets and kilts, the one man broodingly dark, the other blond and laughing.

Lorne appeared ill at ease, speaking only a few brusque words to me. "You seem fully recovered, Glenna, I'm happy to see. I had visions of you succumbing to pneumonia." With a brief, curt little nod, he swung away, returning to Flora, who was sitting on a sofa near the fireplace. I watched as he sat beside her, bending his head to her in an intimate conversation that enclosed them snugly in their own little corner of the room. She was visibly blossoming under his attention. Once she leaned toward him, brushing her cheek against his shoulder in a fleeting gesture that revealed wordlessly her feelings for him.

Colin's eyes followed my gaze. "He's been mending fences with her, thank the good Lord," he murmured.

Light dawned. I understood why Lorne had spoken to me so briefly, with that curious air of constraint. Flora was watching him, and he was trying to avoid any suggestion of closeness between us that might spark her jealousy.

"After you left the courtyard to go up and change your clothes, Lorne spoke to Flora rather sharply, and she was devastated," Colin added in a low voice. His open handsome face looked troubled. "She's so sensitive, always has been. She overreacts to things that make her unhappy, and then she often says and does something she doesn't really mean."

There was a faint note of apology in his voice, and I knew he was being protective of Flora again, tacitly asking me to understand and overlook her temperamental faux pas. "I wouldn't want you to think I was criticizing Lorne," Colin went on, "but sometimes, you know, he can be a bit rigid. He's always so completely in control of himself, I think he finds it hard to understand when other people are more . . . more emotional."

I made a sudden, abrupt movement. Colin was wrong.

104

Lorne wasn't always in complete control of himself.

Whatever he was saying to Flora, it seemed to bring her completely out of her sulky mood. At the dinner table she was talkative, almost vivacious, especially on the subject of the annual ball that would take place in two weeks' time. This was *the* single grand social occasion of the year at Dungariff, when friends and relatives from all over Argyll and the rest of the Highlands were invited to the castle to share the MacDougall hospitality. The servants had been cleaning and polishing and refurbishing in every spare moment, and Ellen's little sitting room was a snarl of lists of supplies to be ordered and tasks to be done.

Personally, I hadn't been able to summon up much enthusiasm for the ball. I felt uncomfortable at the thought of meeting so many strange people all at the same time. What's more, I knew that inevitably, as the visiting American heiress, I would be the object of much intense curiosity.

"I was so excited to hear that the Chief will be coming," Flora observed, her eyes sparkling. "It's been a number of years, hasn't it, Mother MacDougall, since the Chief of the clan was a guest here at the annual ball?"

"Yes," Ellen nodded. "He's often away in Edinburgh or London at the time of the ball, and last year he was ill." She smiled at me. "It always seems so much more exciting, Glenna, when the Chief of the MacDougalls comes to our ball. Perhaps it's because, for a few brief hours, we can imagine that the old clan society of the Highlands is still intact."

"It rotted away years ago," Lorne muttered in a tone of quiet ferocity. "Sorry, Mother," he added immediately. He'd been in a distant mood all during dinner, taking little part in the conversation. It didn't surprise me that he was abstracted, with all the worries he had on his mind. There was Flora and her insecurities, and the looming

105

possibility that he would lose Dungariff.

"You're right about the impact of the Chief's presence, Aunt Ellen," came Colin's quick, smiling response, which covered the slight awkwardness of Lorne's comment. "At any moment you expect him to order a raid on the MacLeans over in Mull, with the war cry *Buaidh no bas* thundering to the rafters and Lorne standing by as our war chief, brandishing his claymore as he prepares to lead the clan into battle!"

"Oh, Colin, you're so silly," Flora said with an indulgent smile and the air of a schoolmistress tempering the remarks of an overly enthusiastic pupil. For myself, however, I could easily visualize Lorne at the head of a Highland charge, his dark face alive with the fever of battle.

"You're going to do the Sword Dance for us this year, aren't you, Lorne?" Flora inquired.

"What?" When Flora repeated her question, he shook his head, saying, "Oh, the Sword Dance. I think I'll let someone else do the honors this year. The dance is really for younger men, anyway. Colin, for instance."

"Thanks—I think. You're all of four years older than I am, Lorne," Colin retorted. "Glenna, now that we're discussing dancing, what about you? Are you up on your Scottish dancing? At some time during the evening on the night of the ball, Aunt Ellen orders in the pipers, and then we all go mildly berserk doing the schottische and the reel and the strathspey. Even our decrepit and ancient Master of Dungariff!" he added with a wicked glance at Lorne.

"I don't know how to do any of those dances," I replied in alarm. "I never even heard of them. I can manage a waltz or a two-step, but that's my limit."

"Allison Murray, how is it that you didn't teach Glenna the important things of life while you were living in that place with the unpronounceable name?" Colin demanded of Aunt Aillie with a mock severity. "Oh, well, we'll have to remedy the oversight. Aunt Ellen, you'll play for us after dinner, won't you? So we can teach Glenna something of her Scottish heritage?"

"I'll be happy to," Ellen laughed. "I wish you'd given me warning, though. The piano hasn't been tuned for ages."

In the drawing room, after Lorne and Colin had rolled up the faded old carpets, Ellen sat down at the piano. "I think, Lorne, as long as Glenna doesn't know any of the Scottish dances, we might start with 'The Far Northland,'" she said. "It's simple, and it's fun to do. Well, then, ladies and gentlemen, choose your partners!"

As Ellen was speaking, I turned, smiling, to Lorne, who was standing closest to me. With an instinctive gesture, he reached out for my hand, then froze in mid-movement. He dropped his arm, not looking at me, and muttered, "I don't think I'm a very good teacher, Glenna. Flora and I will do the dance first, so you can see how it goes, and then you can try it with Colin."

Looking pleased but rather self-conscious—did I imagine her quick little glance of triumph?—Flora took her place beside Lorne, their left hands clasped, his right arm across her upper back as he grasped her other hand at the shoulder. They were an attractive, graceful couple, and I was fascinated with the dance, which was full of turns and running steps and hops, but it didn't look in the least simple to me. However, when it was my turn to dance with Colin, I did my best to follow his patient instructions. "Place your left heel diagonally forward, like this, then step left foot behind right, then right foot sideward . . ." By the time he got to "turn on the ball of the left foot and raise your right knee high," I was hopelessly confused.

"It's no use," I exclaimed in despair. "I think I was born with two left feet."

"Nonsense," Ellen called from the piano. "It's just that this is all so new to you, Glenna. Let's start over. Lorne, you be Glenna's partner this time."

Slowly, with an almost visible reluctance, Lorne clasped my left hand and put his right arm over my shoulder. His right hand grasped mine in a sudden spasmodic grip, and I didn't have to wonder if he were feeling the breathtaking jolt of electricity that seemed to be pouring through my body at his touch. Curiously, though my mind was in a hopeless jumble and afterwards I couldn't remember a word that he said to me about the steps, I sailed through "The Far Northland" as if I'd been dancing it all my life. I seemed to know instinctively how to respond to the slightest pressure of his hand and the rock-steady support of his arm around me.

"I feel about two inches high," Colin complained when the music stopped. "Would you believe it, Glenna, I'm usually considered an excellent dance teacher? You'll have to give me another chance. Aunt Ellen, can we have a reel next?"

It developed into a magical evening. With first Colin as my guide, and later Lorne, I whirled through the gliding, springing steps of the reel, the more energetic if majestic movements of the strathspey, and the exhilarating hops of the schottische. By the end of the night I actually believed that I could take my place on a real dance floor without disgracing myself. We all seemed to drop any inhibitions that might have been part of our mental baggage earlier. By the time the session had ended, Lorne's eyes were sparkling with enjoyment, and Flora wasn't showing any sign of jealousy when I chanced to be her fiancé's partner. Even Aunt Aillie was coaxed into taking part in a reel.

"What would the Reverend Macomber have to say to this, Aunt Aillie?" I teased her when she came off the floor, breathless and laughing. Our pastor in Atwater had been a straitlaced man who equated social dancing with the devil's work. He was the reason I hadn't learned to waltz until I went away to normal school.

Aunt Aillie shot me a sheepish glance. "Maybe it's never too late to learn new tricks," she replied, shrugging.

As we were putting the drawing room to rights, Colin suggested a stroll. "I haven't had a minute's quiet talk with you on this visit, Glenna, what with runaway horses and dancing lessons and other distractions," he grinned. "I'm sure you're panting to hear about how much cordage and canvas I sold this week."

I agreed to go with him and went up to the tower room to fetch a warmer wrap, pausing for a long moment in front of the wardrobe before I opened the door. There were no unpleasant surprises waiting for me when I reached inside, however, no sign of a crude image with black strands of yarn plastered on its gruesome skull. Replacing my white silk shawl with a wool waist-length cape, I wrapped a scarf around my hair and returned downstairs. On my way to the drawing room I noticed a light in the small room that Lorne used as an estate office, and glanced in to find that he was seated at his desk before a mass of papers.

"You keep long hours," I chided him. "Longer hours than any of the people who work for you, I don't doubt."

He put down his pen, quickly drawing a ledger over the papers he was working on, but not before I caught a glimpse of rows and rows of figures. He leaned back in his chair, absently smoothing the tired crease between his eyes. "Long hours are part of my privileges as Master of Dungariff," he replied with a crooked smile.

"Why don't you put all those papers away and come for a stroll with me and Colin?" I said on an impulse.

"That's kind of you, but Colin wouldn't thank me for making an unwanted third. Being here only on weekends, he doesn't get much of a chance to see you."

I wanted to cry out that Colin and I weren't courting, that I would like nothing better than to have Lorne accompany us, but of course I didn't. Lorne's unstated message was quite clear; he wasn't going to risk upsetting Flora by any repetition of the emotional interval we'd shared that afternoon. He'd been raising the height of the defensive wall between us for most of the evening. And he seemed quite frankly relieved to be interrupted when Donnie appeared in the doorway.

"Could I ha' a word wi' ye, Maister?" Donnie's young face was unusually solemn.

"Yes, what is it?"

Donnie looked from Lorne to me and back again, shuffling his feet and pulling his cap between his hands. It was obvious he wanted to speak to Lorne privately, and I was about to excuse myself when Lorne said impatiently, "Speak up, man. Did you find Miss MacDougall's mare and the saddle?"

Donnie's discomfort increased. "Aye, I did, and Jeannie's fine. She hadna wandered verra far frae where ye spied her near the Serpent Mound. But the saddle . . . Maister, I ken ye've been thinking I was careless wi' Jeannie's harness—"

"I never thought that, Donnie," I interrupted him.

He flashed me a grateful glance, but his expression was still troubled as he said to Lorne, "I maun tell ye, Maister, there *was* a guid reason why the young lady fell off Jeannie. Somebody ha' cut the cinch nearly through. From the under side, it was, so I didna notice the cut when I put Jeannie to the saddle. The cinch held as lang as Miss MacDougall kept the mare tae an easy pace, but didna ye tell me that Jeannie reared and bolted when a deer or some such beastie frightened her? That was when the cinch parted altaegether."

Lorne's brows drew together in a straight black line.

"Don't be a blether-skate, lad. Are you saying that somebody deliberately caused Miss MacDougall to have an accident?"

"Weel, the cinch *looked* as if it were cut wi' a knife. I suppose it could ha' worn thin, though it wasna an auld saddle . . ."

"It had to be a defective cinch. The alternative doesn't bear thinking about," Lorne said grimly.

"Aye, Maister," Donnie said slowly. "Naebody at Dungariff would wish tae harm the young lady, surely?"

Chapter 7

Jane Henderson must have a magic needle, I thought, looking down at the exquisite darns in my riding habit. I had considered it ruined beyond all saving after I fell off Jeannie's back into the briar bush. This habit would do very well until the industrious tailor in Oban finished making me a new one.

I went over to the wardrobe to get my hat, pausing to admire the ball gown hanging on the door, Meg had brought it up shortly before, newly pressed. The dress was made of deep blue silk surah, with short double-puffed sleeves and deep lace falls surrounding the décolletage and the ends of the sleeves. It was my favorite of all the new clothes I had bought in Boston, and I would be wearing it tonight for the first time. It was too elaborate a gown for anything except the most formal of occasions. It would be perfect for the Dungariff annual ball.

Standing in front of the cheval glass to check that my hat was on straight, I found my eyes straying to the door in the corner of the room, the door opening onto the parapet walk. I hadn't been able to rid myself of my unreasoning conviction that danger awaited me on the ramparts. Most nights before going to bed, I checked to make sure the bolts on the door were secure. And I hadn't ventured out there since Lorne had taken me up to the battlements on the night of my arrival at Dungariff. But it was a case of out of sight, out of mind, I suppose. I simply hadn't thought much about that vague menace on the ramparts in recent weeks.

Until last night. Or, rather, early this morning. I'd awakened before dawn, very briefly, turning over in bed and burrowing deeper into my coverlets with a luxurious feeling of gratitude that I needn't rise for hours yet. Then I heard a sharp, thumping sound, as if an object had struck a hard surface like wood. Perhaps it was the repetition of an earlier sound that had awakened me. I sat up, listening intently. At first I heard nothing, but gradually I became convinced, against my will, that there was someone—something—on the other side of the door leading to the ramparts. A few seconds later I heard a faint scraping noise. The sound of a shoe against the rough stones of the parapet? It was so faint, I couldn't be sure I had actually heard it.

I hadn't gone to investigate. Instead, I'd swathed the comforter more securely around me. I'd even succeeded in going back to sleep. It was the wind, if it was anything, I told myself. While I was dressing for breakfast, I'd kept my eyes averted from the door, and I hadn't allowed my thoughts to dwell on the nocturnal noises.

Turning away from the cheval glass, I picked up my riding crop and headed for the door opening on the landing. I stopped in mid-stride. Was I going to give in once more to the superstitious fears that had so nearly engulfed me after the episode on the beach at Finlay? There was nothing out there on the ramparts, nothing except a wraith of my overactive imagination. I marched to the parapet door, boldly shoving back the heavy bolts, and lifted my foot to step out on the walk. And brushed against a large black bird lying in front of my boot. It was a raven. A very dead raven. Meg's voice flashed into my consciousness: "Witches can turn theirsel' intae beasties, hares and frogs and cats and ravens. Aye, verra often ravens." With a smothered scream, I slammed the door and shot home the bolt.

My panic lasted only for an instant. I was immediately ashamed of myself. Birds and animals died of natural causes more often than not. A sick or dying raven had plummeted to his death against my door in the early morning hours. It was as simple as that. I ignored the niggling question that popped into my mind: it was pre-dawn when I heard the object striking against my door, and ravens didn't fly in the dark, did they?

A little later, as I was passing the door of Ellen's sitting room, Aunt Aillie hailed me. She came out into the corridor, embroidery hoop dangling from her hand. "Ellen asked me to remind you to come back a little early from your ride. She says it will probably take you longer than usual to dress for dinner, and then, too, some of the guests who are coming from a distance will probably arrive a little early." She added pensively, "You know, Glenna, I'm so glad you insisted I buy that gray silk gown from Madame Lucille's shop in Summer Street. None of my other dresses would be half grand enough for tonight."

I felt a quiver of inner amusement. Aunt Aillie was really looking forward to the ball tonight. Listening to her talk about it, you would never suspect that she had fought tooth and nail against coming to Dungariff in the first place. Luckily for me, in fact, she'd become so engrossed in helping Ellen prepare for the festivities, that she'd had no time to cluck about after me, for which I was heartily grateful.

A quizzical smile curled her lips. "I imagine you and Lorne won't be going riding together as often after today."

"Perhaps not," I replied calmly. "Flora's school term ended yesterday, so she'll be in residence here until the wedding. Of course, she doesn't ride."

"And wouldn't like to see you and Lorne going off without her," Aillie retorted. "I know, I know, I should bite my tongue before saying things like that." She laughed, waving me off. "Enjoy yourself, then, it may be your last ride for a while."

As I left the hall house by the side entrance and crossed the courtyard, I reflected that it was uncanny how often Aunt Aillie made remarks that echoed my own secret thoughts. I, too, had been wondering if this afternoon's jaunt would be my last ride with Lorne. Flora had been all sweetness and light when she visited last weekend, and I suspected Lorne would go to considerable lengths to keep her that way, including a hiatus in his solitary rides with me.

When I entered the stables, Donnie was already saddling Jeannie. The beautiful sorrel-colored mare neighed gently when she saw me. I had been told more than once that horses have brains the size of a pea, but I was firm in my belief that Jeannie not only knew me, but liked me. I even suspected that she'd tried in her dumb way to apologize for throwing me on that afternoon two weeks ago. Certainly in the time that had elapsed since the accident, I hadn't experienced the slightest fear in climbing on her back again.

"Guid day tae ye, Miss," Donnie said. "I'll ha' the bonnie mare ready for ye in juist a moment. I maun check the cinch again."

"Oh, Donnie, that's not necessary," I exclaimed. "I've told you before, nobody thinks you were careless with Jeannie's harness. The cinch gave way, that's all, for whatever the reason."

"Aye, Miss." Donnie looked grateful for my comment, but he meticulously tested the cinch strap nonetheless. He peered out through the open stable doors. "It's anither braw day for riding. Do ye ken where the Maister plans tae gae this afternoon?"

"I haven't a notion," I laughed. "It's just as well. I like to be surprised. Mr. MacDougall never tells me where we're going until the very last minute."

"That's because I don't know myself until the last minute." Lorne came hurriedly into the stables, dressed in his usual worn jodhpurs and ancient hacking jacket. "Sorry to keep you waiting. I had to speak to the bailiff."

"Well?" I asked in amusement a few moments later after we were in the saddle and making our way beneath the portals of the gatehouse. "Have you brought yourself to a decision about where you're taking me today?"

"Let's ride all the way into Glen Fingorm. There's not much of a road—it's little more than a very rough farm track—but you're making such strides with your riding that you shouldn't have any difficulty. I'd like you to see the prettiest spot on the estate."

There was an odd note in his voice that I couldn't identify. Finality, perhaps, tempered with a hint of regret. Were his thoughts running parallel to mine and Aunt Aillie's? Did he think, too, that this might be our last ride together? I looked quickly at his face, but his thin, aloof features were inscrutable. Since my riding accident two weeks ago, he'd retreated even farther behind his usual wall of reserve. He was acting very much like the withdrawn stranger I had met that first evening in the hotel in Inverness, or the polite, formal host of my earliest days at Dungariff. The degree of closeness we had achieved—or that I thought we'd achieved—might never have been.

Lorne and I had previously made several short excursions into the glen, riding from the head of Loch Fingorm along the banks of the spirited little river as it splashed through a long lonely valley backed by steep, craggy hillsides, bare save for an occasional small cottage, a scattering of scrub trees, and flocks of grazing sheep. However, we had never penetrated into the wild and difficult country at the end of the glen, where the River Fingorm, erupting exuberantly from the hills, plunged through a rocky ravine and emerged in a series of foaming cascades and rapids.

"It's lovely, Lorne," I murmured, as we stood beside the stream, watching for the sudden leap of a trout in the roiling waters. "Thank you for bringing me here." I didn't mention, naturally, that I could have described the austere beauty of this spot without ever seeing it. Once again, as I had so often and in so many places in Argyll, I was experiencing a bone-deep conviction that I had been here before. The feeling no longer startled me. I'd merely come to accept it.

"I knew you'd like this spot," Lorne said. "Colin and I practically lived on the banks of the Fingorm when we were lads, fishing for trout. In the spring and summer, Colin still spends most of his spare time here with his rod and reel." He added offhandedly, "This year Colin seems to have lost some of his zest for fishing."

"Yes, I wasn't aware that he was such an enthusiastic angler," I replied innocently. I wasn't going to comment on the obvious, that Colin spent most of his time with me on his weekend visits to Dungariff.

His hands shoved deep into the pockets of his jacket, Lorne stood staring into the rushing water in silence. At length he murmured, half to himself, "I love to come here. I can leave all my problems behind me for a while. When I'd come home from sea before my father died—" He broke off. "Look, Glenna, I think that's the grandfather trout that Colin's been after for such a long time."

My eyes followed his pointing finger, but I didn't see the trout. I didn't think Lorne had seen it, either. It was an excuse to get away from a personal topic. He'd thrown up his wall again.

Before I could stop myself, I blurted, "It must have been difficult for you, when you quarreled with your father."

He tossed me a startled look. For several moments he kept his lips clamped mulishly shut. Then he burst out, "It was hell. Father was asking me to give away Dungariff, to break the entail so he could lease our home to strangers. *We* became like strangers, avoiding each other's company, never speaking if we could help it. Eventually I couldn't bear it anymore. I went to sea, vowing never to come back, but of course I couldn't do that. I had to return periodically to see my mother. The visits were so unpleasant, I'd storm out of the castle at least once a day and come to this place to nurse my wounds. I'd find a kind of peace here, until I could gather up enough patience to face Father again without putting my fist into his face." He paused, then said with an air of surprise, "You're the first person I've ever talked to about that time. Even my mother . . ." He shook his head.

I said quietly, "Sometimes it helps to talk."

"Yes, perhaps." But he didn't volunteer any further confidences. I suppose he already regretted letting down his barriers. Rather hurriedly he said, "I believe Mother wants us back a little early. Shall we go?"

Another excuse. It wouldn't be necessary to return to Dungariff for almost an hour.

As we started back down the glen, I commented on how beautifully the handful of lonely crofters' cottages blended into the gaunt hillsides.

"If you were to see them up close, you'd notice that most of them badly need repairs," Lorne replied bleakly. "My father . . . oh, well, I won't go into that. You probably know he neglected the estate badly in his last years. Of course, during the eighteenth century, the glen contained many more cottages and many more people. The crofters were driven out when my great-great-great-grandfather cleared the land and brought in the sheep. That was the time of the famous, really infamous, 'Clearances.' The hills looked much different then, too, covered thickly with birch. The trees were all cut down during the Napoleonic Wars to provide for the iron smelters over on Loch Ettive."

I nodded. "It's hard to believe that the Highlands were once heavily forested, when you look at these lovely bare hills."

"If I had the capital, I'd start an extensive program of reforestation on the estate," Lorne said forcefully. "It would create jobs for our people, more than anything I could do to improve the agriculture here. The soil in Agryll is poor, and we're really too far north for successful grain crops. Even sheep farming isn't as profitable as we once thought it would be. There is something, though, that could provide more jobs on the estate: the silica sand deposits on my land at Dunard Point, across from Dungariff. I have a geologist friend who tells me that silica of this quality is rare in Europe. It could be used for making first-class lenses and optical glass."

His eyes kindling with enthusiasm, Lorne seemed a changed person as he talked of his hopes for the estate that obviously meant so much to him. After a moment, however, his eyes lost their sparkle. He added drily, "Well, so much for daydreams. Don't you Americans have an expression for that? Pie in the sky? Something like that. It would take enormous amounts of capital to reforest the land and mine the silica. I don't have it, nor am I likely to."

No, and you won't ask me for it, either, I thought with asperity. There *must* be some way to persuade this cantankerously proud man to accept a loan, if I could only think of it. I guided the conversation back to the improvements Lorne envisioned making on the estate, and I marveled again at how completely he seemed to come out of his shell when he talked of something so close to his heart.

We were about halfway along the steeply rising drive to the castle, still deep in a discussion of the most economical methods of mining the sandstone beds, when Lorne said, "Look, if we dismount here and walk a few yards to the edge of the cliff, I can show you the place where my geologist friend spotted the silica deposit."

Dunard Point, opposite Dungariff on the far side of the mouth of the loch, wasn't as towering and craglike as the promontory on which the castle stood, but it appeared wild and difficult of access. Peering across, I could make out, scattered over the cliff face, gleaming patches of silvery white. "Won't large-scale mining operations destroy much of the beauty of the site?" I asked.

Lorne shrugged. "That's the other side of the coin, I'm afraid. I think what I'd regret most is the destruction of the Paleolithic cave at the foot of the cliff. Inside it there are some marvelous cup and ring markings. A friend, an archeologist from the University of Glasgow who was working in the area some years ago, told me that the cave was in use well over six thousand years ago. I've always wondered if the earliest ancestors of the MacDougalls landed at Dunard Point in coracles from Ireland during the Stone Age."

"Lorne, I'd love to see the cave." I looked at the tiny watch pinned to my habit. "It's still quite early. Why don't we go over there now?"

"I don't know . . . the path is quite rough," Lorne said doubtfully.

"Rougher than the path from the castle to the beach?"

"Well, no. Not much rougher, anyway. Mind, I haven't been down it for years, not since Colin and I were in school." A look of reminiscent pleasure crossed his face. "All right, why not?"

We circled the head of the loch, dismounting shortly after we passed over the wooden bridge spanning the river. The path looked difficult but passable, winding steeply down around outcroppings of rock overgrown with lichens and an occasional scrawny fir tree. "Those Stone

Age sailors must have used this path after they landed at the mouth of the loch," Lorne commented as he went before me, occasionally reaching back to give me a hand over a difficult stretch. "The archeologist told us that the path had been worn down by so many feet over the millennia that it would probably always be visible."

Near the mid-point of the descent, as he rounded a large boulder, Lorne suddenly dug in his heels, calling sharply, "Wait, Glenna." At the same time, stumbling over a projecting stone, I lost my balance and lurched forward, missing the hand he frantically extended toward me and plunging headlong toward the sheer precipice that had been created when a rock slide had obliterated the lower reaches of the path. I plummeted head over heels into nothingness, dimly aware that only the jagged rocks on the shore would break my fall. Then, miraculously, I struck a small projecting ledge and my clawing fingers grasped the branches of a tiny tree growing from a cranny in the cliff face.

From above me came Lorne's anguished voice. "Glenna, my God! I can't reach you from here. Can you hold on while I circle around to the side of this break in the path?"

"I'll try," I gasped, and even as I spoke my flailing feet found another slight projection and I could relieve the intolerable strain on my arms. After a few moments, listening anxiously to the sound of Lorne's scrambling progress above me, I spotted a number of other trees and wiry shrubs off to my right. Now, if the narrow foothold supporting my weight extended also to my right . . . Cautious exploration proved that it did. Slowly, agonizingly, I moved away from the ledge that had broken my fall, alternating clutching grabs for a scrubby branch with a desperate pawing motion of my feet to find a toehold when the narrow rock projection supporting my weight petered out.

I continued my crablike progress until I arrived at a point on the cliffside undisturbed by the rock slide. Then I collapsed in a relieved heap. Lorne clambered down to my side almost simultaneously. "Glenna, you made it," he panted. "I watched you inching along down here with my heart in my mouth. I didn't dare utter a sound for fear I'd startle you into falling!" He put his hands under my arms to help me up. "Come on. Let's get out of here before anything else happens."

After a laborious climb to the top, enlivened more than once by an ominous loosening of scree beneath our feet, I gazed down at the shore far below and shuddered in reaction. "I'm beginning to think I need a keeper . . . or a guard dog," I said in a feeble attempt at a joke. "Before I came to Scotland I'd never so much as taken a bad fall. Now it's not safe to let me out! I fall out of boats, I tumble off horses, I miss my footing on a cliff path!"

Lorne didn't answer my smile. His face looked pale and strained. "Glenna, I'll never forgive myself. I should have caught you before you went over the edge. I should have made sure the path was safe before I let you set foot on it."

"Nonsense," I scoffed. "Don't blame yourself for my clumsiness. I'm getting accident-prone." I looked at my watch, rather surprised to find it was still pinned to my lapel after my scrabbling fall. "We'd better make tracks, as we say back home. We don't want Cousin Ellen annoyed with us."

By the time we reached the castle, I'd managed to divert Lorne from his feelings of guilt about my near brush with disaster by asking another question about the silica deposits. We were still talking about the feasibility of tunneling beneath the sandstone at Dunard Point when we dismounted in the courtyard. As we entered the vestibule of the hall house, Lorne paused, looking down at me with a glint in his dark eyes. He took one of my hands in both of his. "You know, Glenna, in spite of the fact that

I nearly killed you, I really enjoyed this afternoon."

Jane Henderson walked briskly into the vestibule and interrupted Lorne with considerable asperity. "Maister, do ye ken the hour? Yer guests will be at the door at any moment noo. Miss Flora and Maister Colin arrived hours ago." She stared disapprovingly at my stained and torn riding habit and at my tattered gloves, but said merely, "Gae along wi' ye, Miss Glenna. Ye maun hurry wi' yer dressing. I'll send some tea up shortly. The Mistress and Mrs. Murray and Miss Flora and Maister Colin finished theirs long ago."

As she stalked off, I raised an eyebrow at Lorne. "We have our marching orders," I said, laughing.

"Yes, I'm sure Jane believes Dungariff would fall to wrack and ruin if she weren't in charge of the house-keeping. Perhaps it would."

The little maid, Meg, had just arrived in the tower room with my tea when Aunt Aillie joined me.

"Ach, Mrs. Murray, dinna ye look grand?" Meg exclaimed with an admiring gaze at my aunt's gray silk gown. It was true. I had never seen Aillie look so distinguished.

"Isna that the Murray tartan?" Meg went on, eyeing the red and black plaid sash draped across Aillie's bosom.

"Yes, my husband's tartan," Aillie replied with a faintly self-conscious expression. "As you can see, Glenna, it's very like the MacDougall plaid. Ellen thought I should wear it tonight. I think Malcolm would be pleased."

"Uncle Malcolm would be delighted," I said warmly.

Meg lingered to stare at my ball gown, draped over the door of the wardrobe. "Ye'll look simply beautiful the nicht, Miss Glenna," she sighed. "Shall I come back tae help ye dress?"

"No, thank you, Meg, I can manage. You'll have quite enough to do tonight with the castle full of guests without waiting on me."

After Meg had gone, Aunt Aillie said, "I was beginning to worry about you. I thought you might have fallen off that dratted horse again, and now I see you did exactly that. Honestly, Glenna!"

"No such thing, Aunt Aillie. I won't have you maligning poor Jeannie! Actually, Lorne and I decided to explore a prehistoric cave at Dunard Point and I took a tumble. It's made us a little late, I'm afraid."

"It certainly has. Flora's been fidgeting and worrying about Lorne's whereabouts since three o'clock. What a tiresome girl she is! Not but what I can sympathize a bit with her feelings. It must be galling to know that her fiancé is constantly in the company of another woman. Someone who's much more beautiful and interesting than she is, what's more."

"Go on with you. You're prejudiced," I said lightly. I sat down and poured my tea. "Would you like a cup?" I offered, in an attempt to change the subject.

She didn't hear me. She was staring off into the distance, lost in thought. "You know something, Glenna?" she said suddenly. "I think I know why my brother Niall wanted you to live in Argyll for a year. I think he hoped that you and Lorne would get married, so that our line of the MacDougalls would live at Dungariff again, and with enough money to put the estate in order."

Biting my lip, I stirred the milk into my tea so vigorously that some of the hot liquid spilled over into the saucer. "That's nonsense, and you know it, Aunt Aillie," I snapped.

"Well, I don't know that. But it's beside the point, I agree, since Flora's already in the picture." Aunt Aillie reached into her reticule for a small, worn satin-covered box. "I almost forgot what I came for. Here. I was going to give you these on your twenty-first birthday, or your wedding day, whichever came first! But I think you should wear them tonight."

Opening the box, I lifted out the string of small but perfectly matched pearls. "They're lovely, Aunt Aillie. What . . ."

"They belonged to my mother. The only thing of value she ever owned. How she would have enjoyed seeing you wear them to a gala evening at Dungariff!" Aillie sniffed to hide her brief show of emotion. She shook out her silvery gray skirts and gazed at her image in the mirror with a faintly embarrassed air of approval. "Do you need any help dressing? No? Then I'll be going along."

After she had gone, I took off my grubby riding habit and began dressing for the ball. While I was brushing out the heavy strands of my hair, my mind kept reverting to my aunt's conjectures about Uncle Niall's will. Remembering snatches of conversations I'd had with both Ellen and Colin, I began to be convinced that Aunt Aillie was right. Uncle Niall *had* hoped to maneuver me into a marriage with Lorne. The facts all fit together. Niall had returned to Argyll well before Lorne and Flora became engaged. Then, at about the same time that Niall became an invalid, Lorne's father, Lachlan MacDougall, had suffered the first of his heart attacks. Returning to Dungariff to visit his sick father, Lorne had renewed an old acquaintance with Flora and had fallen in love with her. Later, after Lachlan's death, Lorne came home for good and officially announced his engagement to Flora. By that time, however, Uncle Niall himself was dying. He hadn't changed his will—though, doubtless, I would have remained his heiress in any case—and so the clause requiring me to reside in Argyll had remained in effect.

All of which was unprofitable speculation, I thought in annoyance, jabbing the hairpins into the chignon at the back of my head. Whatever Uncle Niall had wished or intended, events had caught up to his plans in the form of Flora Cameron.

I had just slipped into my blue evening frock when a

light tap sounded at the door and Ellen entered the room.

"I'm so glad to see you," I exclaimed in relief. "I refused both Meg and Aunt Aillie when they offered to help me dress, but now I find that I can't reach the last few buttons at the back of my gown."

"I thought you might need a hand," she smiled. As her capable fingers fastened the tiny buttons at my nape, I suddenly began to feel embarrassed, thinking of Aunt Aillie's other comment that Ellen would have preferred me as a daughter-in-law rather than Flora. I had always thought that Ellen liked me for myself, but certainly her cordiality had always exceeded the bounds of affection or even of hospitality. My self-consciousness grew as she stepped back and picked up an object that she had placed on a table as she entered the room.

"Aillie's pearls are beautiful, but Lorne and I wanted you to have these, too," she said as she deftly fastened a sash of black and red silk tartan to my left shoulder with a silver brooch. She brought one end of the sash across my back and the other diagonally across my breast, knotting both ends on the right at my waistline. She herself was wearing a duplicate of the sash over her green taffeta dress.

"The MacDougall plaid," I exclaimed in delight, walking over to inspect myself in the cheval glass. "And the brooch is so lovely." I moved closer to the mirror to examine the exquisitely detailed workmanship of the pin.

"It's the crest of the Chief of the MacDougalls," Ellen explained. She put out her forefinger, outlining the details of the brooch. "See that armored hand holding the cross? Well, actually, in heraldic language, it's a dexter arm in armor embowed! Beneath the arm there is our clan motto: *Buaidh no bas*—To conquer or die. And around the edge of the brooch is a coiled metal strap. In the old days, the Chief would give his followers a metal plate replica of his crest to wear as a badge, which was fastened to the clansmen's clothing by a strap and a buckle."

She paused with an apologetic smile. "I'm probably overwhelming you with all these details."

"No, not at all. I want to know everything about the brooch."

"Well, then, when the clan badge wasn't in use, the strap and buckle were left coiled around its edges. Some badges are still made that way, but most of them take this form, a metal representation of the crest with a metal strap and buckle circling it. Incidentally, only the Chief and his heir can wear the badge without the strap and buckle."

Reaching out, I grasped both her hands tightly. My eyes were filming with tears as I said softly, "Thank you for your gift, and even more for your thoughtfulness. Every time I wear it, it will bring back memories of Dungariff and the Highlands." I laughed shakily. "After this, I almost feel like a full-fledged member of the clan."

"But you *are* a member of the clan, my dear," Ellen replied with a look of surprise. "You've been away for a while, that's all. Now you've come home. Are you ready to go down to the drawing room? Our dinner guests will be arriving soon."

Lingering for a last look in the mirror, a final adjustment to my new tartan sash, I followed Ellen down the turret stairs. A nervous knot was beginning to form in my stomach. The ball would be my first real introduction to local society. Large numbers of people from the countryside and from Oban had been invited, even a smattering of old friends and relatives from Glasgow and Edinburgh. Most of them, I was sure, would be intensely curious to see the fabulously wealthy American heiress who had suddenly appeared out of nowhere.

At the door of the drawing room, I encountered Colin, who was looking especially elegant in the much ruffled shirt he was wearing with his kilt and jacket. His eyes lit up with admiration when he saw me. "You're a braw lass tonight, Glenna. I'd best claim my dances immediately, for there'll be no getting near you, once our male guests get a good look at the belle of the ball.''

"Hold on, laddie, ye're talking a wheen o' blethers," I laughed, attempting a broad Scots accent, but Colin's obviously sincere compliment helped to ease my nervousness.

The members of the family and a number of guests who had been invited to the gala dinner that would take place before the ball were already gathered in the drawing room as I entered with Colin. Flora, very pretty in soft lavender organza, came over to bring me to meet her father and stepmother.

Both Flora and Mrs. Cameron were wearing sashes of the Cameron tartan. Mr. Cameron was a stolid, humorless-looking man who seemed to be faintly ill at ease in such a festive gathering. He was a prosperous Oban merchant in his own right, but perhaps he felt somewhat out of place in a group composed primarily of representatives of the local Highland gentry. Listening to his dry, unresponsive remarks, I found it easy to believe Colin's frequent hints that Mr. Cameron had never given Flora much outward indication of his affection, especially since his remarriage. Much younger than her husband, Mrs. Cameron was a pretty woman, but her personality was bland, even mousy. After a few minutes conversation with her, I found myself thinking uncharitably that, although she and Flora weren't actually related by blood, they were so much alike that they might as well have been mother and daughter.

"What a pretty dress, Glenna. Did you buy it in Paris? And you're wearing the MacDougall tartan, how nice," Flora said graciously. She looked at the brooch more closely. "That's lovely. Is it new?"

"Yes, very new. Cousin Ellen gave it to me tonight. I told her it made me feel like a real member of the clan!"

My little foray into humor fell quite flat. A cloud passed

over Flora's face, and her stepmother speared her husband with a meaningful glance. I wondered if Flora had complained to her parents about my protracted presence at Dungariff. Aunt Aillie came up to us, breaking an uncomfortable silence with her remarks, but unintentionally making the situation even worse.

"Ellen was so happy you liked the brooch, Glenna," she beamed. "Of course, I knew you'd adore it, when Ellen and Lorne first told me they wanted to give you a very special gift tonight, something that would always remind you of Dungariff."

Flora did her best to cover up, but her jealousy and chagrin were so obvious that I almost regretted receiving the brooch. While I was trying to think of something mollifying to say to her, Ellen walked over to me. "Glenna, the Chief says he won't wait another minute to be introduced to you. Come along, my dear. We mustn't keep the MacDougall of MacDougalls waiting!"

Alastair, Chief of Clan MacDougall, was an awesomely dignified man, tall and stately in his Highland dress, but he and his equally stately wife made me feel comfortable immediately.

"Well, now, Miss Glenna MacDougall, we've been hearing a great deal about you," the Chief said, his eyes twinkling. "Haven't we, my dear?" he said to his wife.

"We have, indeed," she laughed. "It's refreshing, to find a clanswoman returning to Scotland, rather than the other way around. We've lost so many of our Argyll people when they emigrated to America. But now you, at least, are back where you ought to be!"

"That's what I was telling Glenna," Ellen interjected. "I told her she had come home."

I touched her hand affectionately. "It was dear of you to say that, Cousin Ellen, but Aunt Aillie and I are American citizens, you know. We only planned to come to Scotland for a visit. You've beguiled us into a long stay here at the castle, but eventually we'll be returning to our home in Massachusetts."

"We must put our heads together and hatch a little plot to make you and Mrs. Murray change your minds," the Chief said, smiling. "Now, then, Lorne tells me you're interested in seeing our clan treasure, King Robert's Brooch. My wife and I would be delighted to welcome you to Dunollie at any time. Come for tea one day soon."

As Ellen took my arm and led me around the room, introducing me to the other dinner guests, I felt the last of the butterflies disappearing from my stomach. No one could have been more gracious than the Chief and his wife, and the other guests were unaffectedly friendly. At no time did I have the impression that I was a specimen under a microscope.

Pastor Munro was there, to my surprise. He looked decidedly out of place in his severe black suit and white bands.

"Ye seem surprised tae see me, Miss MacDougall," he said with his tight smile.

"Well . . . our minister in Massachusetts didn't approve of dancing."

"I dinna dance mysel', naturally, but I see naething amiss wi' decent folk dancing i' the company of the MacDougall of MacDougall."

I suppressed a smile, wondering how many social vices were made antiseptic by the presence of the Chief of the clan.

One of the people to whom Ellen introduced me was a tall, gangling young man whose nearsighted eyes peered out at his surroundings through thick glasses.

"Here's still another relative, Glenna," Ellen announced gaily. "My cousin, Dr. Thomas MacColl. You have something in common. He's recently returned to Argyll, also, to start a brand-new medical practice." She bustled off, saying over her shoulder, "I'll leave you two together to get better acquainted."

"Actually, you and I aren't related at all, Miss MacDougall," Dr. MacColl said with the painstaking air of one making sure that his facts are precisely right. On further acquaintance with him, I was to discover that he always spoke in this careful, exact manner, the result, probably, of a scientific training superimposed on a naturally reflective personality. "I'm distant kin to Cousin Ellen through her mother, not through the MacDougalls," he went on. "It's very kind of her to invite me to such a grand affair. Not at all what I've been used to as a poor medical student!"

"Where have you been studying, Dr. MacColl?"

"I received my degree from the University of Edinburgh. I also spent a year in Paris, studying mental diseases."

I looked at him alertly. "Mental disease? Do you plan to specialize in such cases?"

A shadow crossed his long, bony face. "No, I'll be practicing general medicine. My father died recently, you understand, and it's necessary for me to make some kind of living for my mother, who's become an invalid. If I could choose . . ." He shrugged.

"If you could choose, you'd prefer to pursue your studies in mental disease."

"Yes, I would," he replied, his eyes kindling. "It's such a fascinating field, Miss MacDougall. Until only a few years ago, it was thought that mental symptoms were caused by strong emotions like guilt, and they could be cured by inducing the patient to lead a moral life. Today we know there is such a thing as the unconscious part of the mind, in which the real guilt that underlies a patient's symptoms is often unknown to him."

Now Dr. MacColl's eyes were positively glowing. He rushed on, "For example, there's a young doctor in Vienna—well, perhaps I should say youngish, Dr. Freud is about forty—who has been doing amazing work with nerve cases. He's virtually abandoned electrotherapy, which he considers useless, and is treating patients who have hysteric symptoms by putting them under hypnosis, during which the doctor discovers the pyschic reasons underlying their illnesses. Dr. Freud wrote a book about a year ago outlining his theories. I heartily recommend it to you, Miss MacDougall." Pausing, the doctor added in a doubtful tone, "Of course, the book was written in German, so perhaps you might find it somewhat difficult."

I burst out laughing. "Even if it were written in English, Doctor, I doubt that I could understand it. So, if you had the opportunity, you'd like to study with this Dr. Freud."

"I'd give five years of my life to do that," he said simply. "I understand he's now working on the relationship between dreams and mental disease—" He broke off as I drew a quick involuntary breath. "You're interested in dreams, Miss MacDougall?"

"Oh, a librarian is interested in practically everything, without knowing a great deal about anything," I replied lightly.

"So you're a learned lady," he said with delight, and plunged into an enthusiastic discussion about books, from which I was rescued moments later by the announcement that dinner was served.

Tucking my hand under his arm, Colin bore me off to the dining room. "Lorne's taking in Mrs. MacDougall, and the Chief's doing the honors with Aunt Ellen, so that means you have to put up with me, Glenna," he said cheerfully. He added under his breath, "Look whom Aunt Aillie's bagged as a partner: one of the MacLeans from Mull, just the right age, and a bachelor to boot!"

"Don't let Aunt Aillie hear you talking nonsense like that," I scolded, but one glance at my aunt convinced me that she was hugely enjoying the attentions of the tall, attractive, middle-aged cavalier from Mull. She was more animated than I had ever seen her.

Extra leaves had been inserted into the massive old oaken dining table so that the twenty guests were easily accommodated, together with all the members of the family. The table groaned with racks of lamb and game and salmon, with Loch Fyne herring and Aberdeen Angus beef, and a number of dishes that were new to me, such as Cullen Skink, a fish soup, and Partan Bree, which turned out to be crab with rice and cream. Midway through the second course, I murmured to Colin, who was sitting beside me, "What's wrong with Flora, do you know? She's hardly saying a word, and she's even paler than usual. Is she ill?"

Colin squirmed uncomfortably, keeping his eyes fixed on his plate. At last he muttered reluctantly, "It's the same old thing. Before dinner Lorne told her he was going to ask you to open the ball with him as his partner."

"This is the first I've heard of it," I said, biting my lip. "Surely the correct protocol would be for Lorne to open the ball with the Chief's wife? She's the highest ranking female guest."

"Well, of course you're right." Colin cast a cautious look around him, but everyone at our section of the table was busily talking. He continued in a low voice, "Lorne thinks, though, that you and Aunt Aillie should be offered some mark of distinction as our honored guests from America. So he talked with both Aunt Ellen and the Chief's wife, and they concurred. Lorne will open the ball with you and the Chief will lead out Aunt Aillie."

"Oh, the devil," I exclaimed under my breath. The last thing we needed was Flora in a sulk on the night of the grand ball. "Colin, do something."

"Such as?"

"You and Lorne will be staying in the dining room after dinner to have port with the other gentlemen, won't you? Tell Lorne he'll have to change his plans."

Colin tossed me a look of pure scorn. "My dear girl, it's easy to see that you've never tried to talk my cousin Lorne out of *anything* he'd decided to do! It wold take more eloquence than I'm capable of to change his mind."

Giving up on Colin, I made another try at remedying the situation after dinner in the drawing room where the ladies were having coffee. I succeeded in getting Ellen off by herself and begged her to speak to Lorne.

"My dear, I wouldn't dream of interfering," she said quietly. "Actually, I agree with Lorne. As the Laird of Dungariff, he's duty-bound to pay you and Aillie some special attention as Niall MacDougall's niece and sister and as the last of your branch of the clan."

"But Flora—"

"Flora isn't a MacDougall, although I hope that some day she'll learn to act like one." Ellen's face flooded with color as she spoke, and I knew she would have taken back the comment if she could. It was the only time I had ever heard her directly criticize Flora.

I walked into the Great Hall a little later, feeling a distinct sense of foreboding about the outcome of the evening, a state of mind that was only exacerbated when I discovered that Aunt Aillie and I were to stand beside Lorne and Ellen in the receiving line. Soon, however, as the Great Hall began to fill with guests, I forgot my apprehensions. I gazed about the enormous room with an awed feeling of unreality, seeing with a fresh insight the armor-covered walls, the long row of family portraits, the roaring fire in the great fireplace, the orchestra softly playing in the musicians' gallery, the crowd of men in multipatterned kilts, and their ladies in elaborate ball gowns with tartan sashes across their bosoms. The blazing torches of old had been replaced by chandeliers and sconces filled with candles, but otherwise the scene must closely resemble the gatherings that had taken place in this vast space in the days when Dungariff was one of the formidable fortresses protecting the West Highland coast from Viking raids.

I described my feeling to Lorne, who was standing beside me, adding, "I feel like rubbing my eyes to make sure I'm not seeing things. I could easily convince myself that I'd regressed five hundred years and this ball was taking place in 1397."

Rather to my surprise, Lorne responded to my pleasantry with a slight frown. "Some people think that we Highlanders have too much of a tendency to live in the past," he said shortly. He looked down at his kilt and the froth of lace at his throat, fastened with a jeweled pin. "Even the Highland dress is an anachronism, you know."

Perhaps so, but I thought he looked magnificent in the finery of another era. A completely irrelevant bit of information he had once given me crossed my mind: the MacDougall surname was derived from the Gaelic word *dughall*, the black stranger. No term could have fitted him more exactly. "The Highland dress may be an anachronism, Lorne," I said softly, "but I think it fills some deeply instinctive need of the heart."

He smiled then, that slow, radiant smile that so transformed his somber features. "How is it that you know these things, Glenna, when you've been amongst us for such a little while?" He put out a gentle finger to the brooch on my shoulder. "Mother says you like our gift. I kept wondering all afternoon during our ride if the brooch would strike your fancy. Your aunt assured me that it would, but . . ." He paused, looking embarrassed. Speaking on a deeply personal level didn't come easily to him. Quickly changing the subject, he added, "We practically had to tie Aunt Aillie down to keep her from telling you about the brooch beforehand. Mother and I wanted it to be a real surprise for you tonight."

"I've never had a gift that pleased me more, Lorne. I'll treasure it for a lifetime." As I was speaking, the orchestra struck up a fanfare, and I could see Alastair MacDougall advancing toward Aunt Aillie. "Lorne," I pleaded, "won't you reconsider, please, and dance the first dance of the evening with the Chief's wife?"

"No," he said curtly. "You and I are opening the ball." Bowing deeply, he extended his arm to me. Giving in to the inevitable, I placed my hand on his arm and walked with him out on the dance floor to the opening strains of a lilting waltz. We were followed by the Chief with Aunt Aillie, and the four of us danced briefly alone. Then other dancers gradually joined us in the waltz, but I scarcely noticed their presence. I was aware only of Lorne and his overwhelming male magnetism that seemed to be drawing our bodies closer and closer together until we were floating across the floor as one. I forgot all about Flora and her possible jealousy, as I revelled in the sinewy strength of the arm that cradled me and the intimate pressure of our two hands locked together. I breathed deeply of the clean, spicy, intensely masculine scent that was so uniquely Lorne's own.

When the music ended, I wasn't aware of that, either. I'd been dancing with my eyes closed, lost in a dream world of sensuous delight, from which I emerged, slightly dazed, to hear Lorne's voice saying with a ripple of amusement, "The waltz is over, Glenna."

I opened my eyes to look up at him as his arm slid lingeringly, reluctantly, from around my waist, but not before I realized that his breathing was erratic and there was a flickering flame behind his dark eyes.

"Well, Glenna, you've been hiding your light under a bushel."

Flora's flat voice, spiced with the familiar undercurrent of anger, broke the spell that had enveloped me, giving the illusion that Lorne and I were alone in the vast expanse of the Great Hall.

"You told us that you'd never had the opportunity to dance very much," Flora went on, an artificial smile pasted on her thin lips, "but here you and Lorne have given us practically a professional waltzing exhibition. I heard the Chief saying he'd rarely seen a more graceful couple."

"That was kind of him," I said quickly, "but remember, Flora, the Chief hasn't seen you and Lorne dancing together yet."

"Yes, I hope you've saved all the rest of your waltzes for me, Flora. You're the best waltzer I know," Lorne chimed in. He'd withdrawn into his normal reserve, and his quiet voice exerted its usual calming effect on Flora's nerves. She smiled, taking his arm possessively as the next waltz began.

Unobtrusively, without calling attention in the slightest to what he was doing, Lorne avoided my company from then on. He danced his duty dances with the Chief's wife and his mother and Aunt Aillie, but most of the time he didn't leave Flora's side. For myself, I never lacked a partner, from the Chief to Doctor MacColl, who proved to be surprisingly light on his feet, to Colin, but the savor of the evening was gone for me.

I was standing beside Colin when the orchestra filed out of the musician's gallery and the rear doors of the Great Hall were thrown open to the wild keening wail of the bagpipes. This wasn't the first time I had heard the pipes, of course. You couldn't be in Scotland very long without being exposed to them. But as the kilted and bonneted bagpipers filed into the room, skirling a plaintive, electrifying tune, I was seized with a powerful surge of atavistic emotion. I knew I hadn't heard that rousing tune before, but in some deep recess of my soul it was

137

entirely familiar.

"They're playing the clan pipe music," Colin murmured. "The *'Caisteal Dhunolla'*—'Dunollie Castle.' No matter how often I hear it, it does something to my heartbeat. Soon, though, they'll swing into some proper reels and strathspeys and hornpipes. Are you ready to display your skills to all your new acquaintances here?"

"Colin," I exclaimed in sudden panic. "I can't do it. Oh, I know how much we practiced over the last two weekends, but I'm afraid I'll fall flat on my face, or catch my heel in my gown, or *something!*"

"Nonsense. You're our star pupil," Colin assured me.

The clan anthem died away in a series of the disjointed squeals that seem to be an integral part of playing the pipes, and before the pipers started up again, I saw Lorne walking across the room toward me.

My skin began to feel clammily cold, and my heart thudded harshly against the wall of my chest as he came closer to me, and I realized that his appearance had changed completely. Now his hair was powdered and queued under a Highland plumed bonnet, and, instead of his formal velvet jacket and short kilt, he seemed to be wearing a coat and skirt in the MacDougall plaid, with a great length of the tartan fastened to his shoulder and trailing behind his back. A great broadsword was attached to a wide leather crossbelt. It was, some small coherent corner of my brain was telling me, the Highland dress of a much earlier day, the great plaid, or *filleadh mor.*

Beside Lorne there suddenly materialized a tall graceful young man, his handsome features imperious beneath his powdered hair. He was dressed in a velvet coat and brocaded waistcoat, with a blue satin ribbon across his chest and jeweled orders sparkling on his lapel and the shoulder of his sword belt. The great plaid in a tartan of red and black and blue trailed from his shoulder.

I knew that plaid. It was the royal Stewart tartan. I knew

138

that face, too. I had seen it only recently in the National Gallery in Edinburgh. It belonged to a man who had been dead for over a hundred years.

As the strangely altered Lorne and his companion came up to me, the insidious coldness that had been invading my body overwhelmed me. I gave a great gasp and slipped boneless to the floor of the Great Hall.

Chapter 8

There was a roaring sound in my ears, and I could also hear a babbling voice penetrating the depths of the black tunnel from which I was slowly emerging.

It was my own voice. It was repeating over and over the same few words: "I saw him . . . it was the Prince . . . Bonnie Prince Charlie."

"Glenna. Wake up," came Aunt Aillie's voice out of the void, and I could feel her fingers gripping my shoulder, shaking me when I didn't respond.

Slowly I opened my eyes, gazing about me uncomprehendingly. Gradually I became aware that I was lying on a sofa in the drawing room. Aunt Aillie was crouched beside me and Lorne was standing behind her, his face drawn with concern.

"How . . . ? What am I doing here?"

Lorne said quickly, reassuringly, "I carried you here, Glenna. You fainted in the Great Hall."

Suddenly my memory returned, and I was reliving that last terrifying scene in the ballroom. Panicking, I tried to sit up, struggling with such strength against Aunt Aillie's arms that she called out to Lorne for help.

My tense muscles began to relax the moment I felt the touch of his strong capable hands, and heard his quiet voice saying, "It's all right, Glenna. There's nothing to be afraid of."

"But there is," I whispered, looking up at him apprehensively. "I saw him—Bonnie Prince Charlie. I couldn't have, though, could I? He's long dead . . ."

"Lorne. She's still not herself," Aunt Aillie said harshly. "Let's get her to bed. One of the family bedrooms would be most convenient. Those dreadful twisting stairs to the tower—"

"No!" I exclaimed with a childish, unthinking forcefulness. "I want to go to my own room."

"I'll carry you up, Glenna," Lorne said, bending over me. "Don't worry. I won't let you fall." Over his shoulder, he snapped to someone—one of the maids, I presume; probably it was Meg—"Tell my mother to ask Dr. MacColl to come to the tower room."

"Oh, I don't think Glenna needs a doctor," Aunt Aillie objected. "Not for a faint."

"She may have hit her head. She may have a concussion. Of course she needs a doctor," Lorne said curtly.

Aunt Aillie choked off a reply and I closed my eyes and rested my head trustfully against Lorne's broad shoulder as he carried me effortlessly up the corkscrewing turret stairs. Never for an instant did I feel the slightest fear that he would stumble and drop me.

By the time we reached the tower room my mind had begun to clear. When he deposited me carefully and tenderly on my bed I turned my head away from him, saying, "Thank you, Lorne. I'm fine now. You needn't stay. You should go back to your guests."

"Glenna's quite right, Lorne," Aunt Aillie said instantly. "This is the most important night of the year at Dungariff. You have an obligation to your guests."

"Hang my guests. Glenna, I don't understand. What was that you were saying about seeing Bonnie Prince Charlie?"

Still keeping my face turned away from him, I mumbled, "Oh, it was nothing. I didn't know what I was saying. I must have been talking gibberish. Perhaps I did hit my head."

"Lorne, I wish you wouldn't keep bothering Glenna. What she needs is rest," Aunt Aillie snapped.

"Lord, I don't use the brains I was born with," Lorne burst out. "Goodnight, Glenna. I'm sorry I went on as I did, pestering you about a trifle. I'm sorry, too, that you'll be missing the rest of the ball."

As soon as the door closed behind him, Aunt Aillie silently helped me to my feet and began removing my ballroom finery. It was only after she had slipped a nightdress over my head and tucked the covers around me that she broached the subject foremost on her mind. "Glenna, you've been imagining things again. You know that, don't you?"

I remained stubbornly silent, averting my face.

"Glenna! You've got to face this . . . this thing. I heard you say, plain as plain, 'I saw the Prince—Bonnie Prince Charlie.' He wasn't there, my dear. I don't know what you saw, or thought you saw, but it wasn't Bonnie Prince Charlie. Nor his ghost, either, if there are such things as ghosts."

Neither of us had heard the light knock at the door. Dr. Thomas MacColl startled both of us when he appeared at my bedside carrying his black medical satchel.

"Thank you for making Miss MacDougall comfortable, Mrs. Murray," he said, bending down to place a hand on my wrist. "You return to the ball, now. I'll take care of the patient."

"Oh, I'd rather stay, Doctor."

"That won't be necessary, Mrs. Murray."

For all of Thomas MacColl's appearance of gangling awkwardness, his voice carried an air of quiet authority. Aunt Aillie left.

Drawing up a chair, Dr. MacColl sat down beside me, taking my pulse rate with his eyes fixed on his old-fashioned turnip seed watch. Afterward he leaned over to place a cool hand on my damp brow. "How are you feeling now, Miss MacDougall?"

"Very foolish." I grimaced. "I've never done a thing like that before in my life. Faint in front of all those people!"

"And what do you suppose caused you to do that? Had you been feeling ill? Overly tired? Not eating properly or regularly?"

"No, no, it wasn't any of those things. I was just . . . it was so hot, and I'd been dancing every dance, and then the pipers started playing . . ."

The doctor nodded. "Aye, it was uncomfortably hot. All those candles. I would hate to pay Mrs. MacDougall's candle bill for the evening! Doubtless, too, you were a wee bit excited about meeting all these folk who were strangers to you. Heat, excitement, overexertion. The pipes, too. They can come as a dreadful shock if one's ears aren't accustomed to them! Yes, all or any of those things might cause a person to faint." He paused, then said with a sudden sharpening of his voice, "There is one thing that's not quite clear to me: something about seeing the ghost of Bonnie Prince Charlie?"

I stared at him, making my features as blank as possible. "Bonnie Prince Charlie? I think you must have misunderstood, Doctor."

He returned my stare. Behind those thick, distorting lenses there was a pair of shrewd eyes boring into me. "Aye," he said after a moment. "Doubtless I did misunderstand." He rose, closing his case. "I'll give one of the servants a sedative for you. I certainly wouldn't advise you to return to the ball, but I don't think there's anything wrong with you that a little sleep won't cure." At the door he turned, his hand on the knob. "If at any time you would like to see me, Miss MacDougall, my surgery is in Oban, off the north end of the Esplanade. Anyone can direct you to me."

I held myself rigid beneath the covers until the door closed behind him. Then I sat up, burying my face in my hands and rocking from side to side in an ineffectual effort to drive out of my mind what I'd seen—what I thought I'd seen—in the ballroom. It had happened at last, the thing that Aunt Aillie had so feared. I'd hallucinated in front of a roomful of people. More than that, there had occurred a merging of nightmare and reality, a repetition, in a sense, of what had happened on the castle ramparts on my first evening at Dungariff, a moment in which, while I was wide-awake, I had glimpsed for a fleeting instant a presence from another plane.

By great good fortune, only Lorne had realized that something out of the ordinary had happened, and Aunt Aillie's quickness of wit had prevented him from delving into the meaning of the incident. Dr. MacColl . . . well, he might have his suspicions, but he was bound by professional ethics from probing further into the matter.

Aunt Aillie would continue to shield me, I knew. She would continue to be watchful. She would probably keep up the pretense that I was imagining things, that common sense and proper rest would solve the problem. But I could no longer ignore, even to myself, the possibility that something was wrong with my mind.

After the most perfunctory of knocks, Jane Henderson entered the tower room, carrying a tray, followed by Lorne's mother.

Jane deposited her tray on the bedside table, saying scornfully, "There now, Miss Glenna, a cup o' my herbal tea will do ye a great deal mair guid than that wee pill Dr. MacColl left fer ye."

"Well, be sure Miss Glenna takes the pill with your tea," Ellen reminded the housekeeper. "How are you feeling?" Ellen asked me anxiously.

"I'm fine. I only hope you'll forgive me for spoiling your ball."

Ellen pressed my hand. "My dear, there's nothing to apologize for. What's important is your health. Thomas MacColl assured me you'd only fainted, but—"

"No, really, I'm perfectly well. I wanted so much to go back and dance. What a shame that I couldn't take part in the Scottish dancing, after all that practice with Colin and Flora and Lorne! But the doctor wouldn't let me. So please, stop worrying about me, and go back to your guests."

After Ellen, appearing somewhat reassured, had left the room, Jane poured my tea and popped the pill into my mouth. While I sipped the tea, she bustled about, rearranging my pillows, pulling the coverlets more snugly around me, placing my ball dress into the wardrobe. As she picked up the tray, preparing to leave, she hesitated, shifting her weight from one foot to the other. At length she said, in an elaborately casual tone, "I hear that ye fainted verra suddenly. One moment ye were perfectly composed, smiling and talking to Maister Colin and waiting for the pipers tae play the opening reel, and then ye stiffened up, a-staring straight ahead o' ye, as if ye were looking at something scary, something the other folk couldna see."

For a moment, I stared at Jane haughtily, hoping that my silence would induce her to go away without asking any further questions. But I was immediately aware that she wasn't merely indulging her curiosity. Her face was troubled, try as hard as she might to preserve her usual impassive expression. I thought, suddenly, of her reputed gift of the second sight and the anguished concern it occasionally caused her, and then, almost without conscious volition, I heard myself blurting, "Jane, I must talk to someone, and I think—I'm sure—that of all the people at Dungariff, you would be the one to understand."

Instantly I felt an enormous surge of relief, as if I had already transferred a part of my crushing load of anxiety to her bony shoulders.

Putting down her tray, Jane drew up a chair beside the bed and sat down, her hooded eyes fixed on my face, her strong capable hands clasped primly together in her lap. "I'm verra willing tae listen, Miss Glenna."

After the first few difficult seconds, I found my words pouring out in an effortless torrent. I told Jane everything that had been troubling me since that day, months ago, when I had learned that I was the heiress to Uncle Niall's enormous fortune. It was odd, it was really inexplicable, I told myself, but until this talk with Jane, I had never consciously dated the beginning of my fears for my mental state to the day I read Uncle Niall's will. Now, of course, it was quite clear. That night I had experienced the first of those threatening nightmares that had been occurring intermittently ever since. I went on to describe to Jane my pervasive sense of familiarity with the Argyll countryside, and my illogical fear of the parapet walk at Dungariff. Last of all, I told her about my visions, apparitions, whatever they were, in which I saw people who weren't visible to my companions, ending with my unnerving sensation at the ball tonight that I had skirted the dimensions of another world, that I had, in fact, slipped momentarily into the past.

"The Prince was so real to me, Jane. He might have stepped right out of his picture at the National Gallery. And Lorne . . ." I shivered. "Lorne frightened me. He was both himself and another person, from another time, and this other person . . ." I shivered again. "This other person was evil. I knew he meant harm to me." I looked straight into the housekeeper's eyes. "Can you think of any sane explanation for what's been happening to me, Jane? That's what I'm afraid of, you see. That there's nothing sane about this. I'm afraid of losing my mind."

Jane seemed stunned by what I was telling her. Her eyes shifted away from me, and my heart sank. I realized I had been counting on her—what would you call it?—on her sense of otherworldliness, perhaps, for reassurance.

At last she said regretfully, "I dinna think I can help ye, Miss Glenna. Had ye thought of talking tae Pastor Munro? I could ask him tae come up."

I stared at her blankly. "Why would I do that? Are you suggesting some kind of demoniacal interference? Possession, I think Roman Catholics call it."

"The Evil One is all around us," she muttered, still refusing to meet my eyes. She sat in silence for a moment, her shoulders hunched as she kept her gaze fixed on her clenched hands. Then a startled expression crossed her face and she looked up. "What ye saw the nicht sounds juist like—" She broke off, biting her lip.

"Like what? Jane, if you've thought of something that might help me, something that might explain . . ."

Her forehead furrowed in a deep frown, she interrupted me. "I've told ye afore this, there are some things we maun best leave alone."

Slumping back against the pillows, I turned my face away from her. "Very well, then. I can't force you to talk to me against your will. Goodnight."

The moments slowly passed and Jane remained in her chair. At last she said heavily, "It's juist that I dinna ken if it would really help ye, Miss Glenna, and forbye we'd be meddling with matters we shouldna concern oursel' aboot. Mayhap, though, ye should judge fer yersel'."

I could hear the sound of her chair creaking as she got up, and I turned my head to see her walking purposefully toward the door.

"Jane—"

"Bide awee, Miss Glenna. I'll be back."

So thoroughly mystified that I temporarily forgot about my problems, I waited impatiently for Jane to return. In five minutes she was back, puffing heavily from her rapid climb up the turret stairs and the apparent weight of the large unwieldy flat object she was carrying. The object or package was wrapped in what looked like several thicknesses of old blankets.

"No one saw me," she reported with satisfaction. "All the sairvants are still busy in the kitchens or they're peeking intae the Great Hall, where the Laird and Maister Colin are performing the Sword Dance." She carefully removed the wrappings from what proved to be a pair of paintings, each at least four feet high. She propped them, side by side, against the wall next to the fireplace.

After one quick unbelieving glance at the pictured faces, I slid out of bed and walked over to the paintings for a closer look. No, I hadn't been mistaken. The metal tags on their frames identified the paintings as the missing portraits of my ancestors, Angus and Catriona Mac-Dougall, the portraits that Ellen had had removed from the wall of the Great Hall before I had a chance to see them.

Arrogantly handsome, tall and slender of figure, straight-browed and lean of face, Angus MacDougall was Lorne's twin. With his longish hair powdered and clubbed back in a queue, his figure swathed in the voluminous folds of the Great Plaid, Angus was also the man I had seen in the ballroom with Bonnie Prince Charlie.

In the matching painting of Angus's wife, Catriona's hair was powdered and dressed closely to her head in the style of the mid-1700s, and her elaborate brocade gown, stiffly boned and low-bodiced, was profusely decorated with lace at the neck and sleeves. The face looking out at me from her portrait, however, was my own. To anyone who knew Lorne and me, these portraits could easily have been our likenesses as we might have looked dressed for a costume ball.

The faintest glimmer of understanding began to penetrate my fog of bewilderment, and I turned to Jane for corroboration. She was gone. Lost in my examination of the portraits, I hadn't noticed her leave. Before I could become too impatient, however, she returned to the room, handing me a large leather-bound book.

I turned the book over in my hands. It had a deeply embossed cover, thick, gilt-edged pages and an ornate metal clasp.

"'Tis the history of Clan MacDougall," Jane explained in answer to my inquiring look. "'Twas written round about fifty year ago by an elderly clergyman, a distant relation of the Maister's grandfather, I believe. The old gentleman was verra interested in the history of Argyll, and he wanted tae trace the MacDougalls back tae the ancient times. The Mistress tells me that the buik was privately printed; this is the only copy that still exists, sae far as anybody knows. Mrs. MacDougall considers it one of the family's great treasures."

Feeling somewhat bemused, I opened the book and riffled through its pages, wondering as I did so why Ellen, with her great family pride, hadn't shown me the book herself. "Yes, I can understand why the book would be a prized possession, but I don't quite see why you've brought it to me . . ." I paused, looking at the two tipped-in facing pictures in the middle of the book. Grainy and a little indistinct, they were obviously copies of the portraits of Angus and Catriona. They were why Ellen hadn't shown me the book.

"Ye'll understand all aboot it when ye read the buik, Miss Glenna," Jane said quietly. "Ye may keep it fer as lang as ye like. It sits on a shelf in the library day in and day out, and never a pairson picks it up. Best tae hide it frae prying eyes, it may be. But I darena leave the portraits here fer verra lang. There isna any place tae hide them where the maidsairvents wouldna see them."

She didn't add, "where the Mistress wouldn't see them, either," but I knew what she meant. I knew it would be useless, too, to ask her to confirm what I already suspected, that Ellen's motive in removing the portraits of Angus and Catriona, and in not showing the family history to me, had simply been to spare the other inhabitants of the castle the spectacle of Flora's jealousy when it was called to her attention how closely Lorne and I resembled an earlier Laird of Dungariff and his lady. And called to Flora's attention it surely would have been, had the portraits remained on the wall after I arrived at the castle. It was a kindly if rather misguided thought on Ellen's part. I had made far too great a mystery out of it.

"Of course you'll want to put the paintings back into safekeeping as soon as possible, before they're missed," I told Jane, taking one last long look at the portraits. "Here, let me help you wrap them up again."

After we had encased the portraits in their snug wrappings, Jane picked up the massive parcel, supporting its heavy weight with surprising ease against her tall, raw-boned frame. She paused in the doorway, her face deeply troubled. "I hope I havna done the wrong thing, fetching yon buik tae ye. I couldna forgie mysel' if harm were tae come o' it."

"Books can't hurt people," I scoffed. "Especially not a librarian. Goodnight, Jane. Thank you for letting me see the book and the paintings."

After the door closed behind her, I put the old book on my writing desk. I sat down, gazing at the book without touching it, as if it were a kind of Pandora's box better left unopened. Mired in my gnawing apprehensions about my mental state, I'd asked Jane for help, and she'd responded with family portraits and a family history. The more I thought about it, the more her behavior reminded me of the Oracle at Delphi, whose ambiguous answers could be interpreted to mean anything the petitioner preferred. On the one hand, Jane seemed to be saying that this old book could answer my nagging questions; on the other, she seemed to be warning me against the danger lurking inside its pages.

Slowly, gingerly, reluctantly, I opened the book.

The Reverend Mr. Archibald MacDougall wrote like a clergyman, or at least as I supposed a clergyman would write. His style was dry, prim, and proper, and he had a strong tendency to sermonize. An image of Pastor Munro shot into my mind. Yes, the pastor at Finlay, modernized a bit, probably strongly resembled the author of this book. The Reverend Archibald also appeared to have an enormous pride of family. Anybody reading his book would have had to conclude that the MacDougalls were the noblest beings on the face of the earth.

Well, not quite all the MacDougalls. When I leafed through the book to the section on my direct ancestors, I soon learned that the reverend gentleman profoundly disapproved of Angus and Catriona. At first it was difficult to understand the meaning of what the Reverend Archibald was trying to say, because he began his account in a tone of fiery moral indignation, speaking turgidly, but in the main incoherently, of "dark, primal impulses" and the "uncontrollable yearnings of the flesh." These were the very qualities, I discovered, as my eyes raced over the closely printed pages, that most frequently characterized the lives of Angus MacDougall and his wife.

Before I inherited Uncle Niall's money and came to Scotland, I had never heard of Angus and Catriona, or of Dungariff, for that matter. Aunt Aillie's reticence about her early life and my father's had left me only with the vague knowledge that I was of Scottish descent. After my arrival in Argyll, I was very little the wiser about my ancestors. From scattered comments by Lorne and Ellen, I had gleaned the bare-bones information that Angus had been the Laird of Dungariff in 1745, when he had joined other rebellious clansmen in a rising to restore the Stuart pretender to the throne of the United Kingdom. After the disastrous defeat of the pretender's son, Bonnie Prince Charlie, on the field of Culloden, Angus had lost both his estate and his life.

I read on eagerly, no longer put off by my clerical chronicler's dry, tortuous prose. Even my personal problems receded temporarily from my mind as I lost myself in the fascinating details of my ancestry.

In many ways, Angus MacDougall should have felt on top of his world in the period immediately preceding the '45. He was young, handsome and Master of Dungariff, and he had a beautiful, well-dowered wife. However, according to the Reverend Archibald, Angus's wife was apparently the thorn in his well-being. As a very young man, before he became Laird, he had fallen desperately in love with a girl of inferior station, to whom marriage was out of the question because of his father's disapproval. Instead, Angus was forced to marry Catriona MacLean in order to cement his family's alliance with the powerful MacLeans of Duart on the island of Mull. Refusing to break with his first love after his marriage, Angus installed his lover as his mistress in Oban. He grew to loathe Catriona, even though, in the very beginning, he had succumbed to the powerful sexual attraction she exerted for him, and a son had been born to them in the first year of their marriage. It was the birth of an heir that turned Angus's hate for his wife into an obsession; his mistress became pregnant at the same time, and Angus agonized over the fact that he would never be able to legitimize this second child.

Shortly after the birth of Angus's son, the old Laird died. Now Angus was Master of Dungariff, and there was nothing to prevent him from channeling his hatred and resentment into a more sinister outlet. Much later, court records and local testimony disclosed that he had fashioned a number of schemes to have Catriona killed, even resorting to black witchcraft. The attempts at murder failed, leaving Angus in a desperate quandary. He could neither divorce Catriona outright, nor could he appear to be in any way personally implicated in her death, because he feared retaliation by her powerful family. He was at a standstill at the time of Bonnie Prince Charlie's landing in Scotland.

Putting his personal affairs aside, Angus declared for the Prince, helping to raise the clans. On the eve of their departure for the campaign, Angus hosted a grand ball in the Prince's honor in the Great Hall of the castle. Immediately before the ball, he had learned that Catriona, unhappy and neglected, had been unfaithful to him with a rival chieftain. As he led her out on the dance floor as his partner in the reel, he muttered to her that if he returned home alive from the war he would kill her with his bare hands.

After the bloody field of Culloden, Catriona received word that Angus had been among the clansmen who were killed in the battle. The report was untrue. Not long afterwards, Angus arrived at Dungariff, a fugitive from the vengeful detachments of the British army who were tracking down the traitors of the rebellion throughout the Highlands.

In a wild mood of rage and despair, Angus pursued Catriona from room to room in the castle, finally catching up with her on the ramparts, from which he hurled her to her death on the rocks below. He was immediately captured by the British, who, after a summary trial, hanged him as a traitor and a murderer. Angus's lands and fortune were made over to one of his cousins who had remained loyal to the Crown. This cousin, of course, was the direct ancestor of Lorne and Colin. The child born to Angus and Catriona lived to found my own branch of the family.

I closed the book with a dry mouth and shaking fingers. My mind was racing, chaotic. No sooner did one appalling thought fly into my brain than a second image succeeded it, more ominous, more horrifying than the first, followed by still another, and another after that, until my head felt as if it were being savagely bombarded by a series of giant sledgehammers. Gradually one grotesque, terrifying idea crowded out all the others: I had crossed into another plane, or, rather, Catriona MacDougall had crossed into mine. She had become reincarnated in my body. Since my arrival in Scotland I had been reliving her brief, miserably unhappy life, and soon now I would meet the same tragic end.

No! I screamed, jumping up from my chair and clutching my hands to my temples in an agonized effort to break the chain of my thoughts. The scream was silent, all in my head. Panting, swallowing hard, I tried to force myself to be calm. I couldn't give way to these imaginings, so much more fevered and fanciful than anything Aunt Aillie had ever accused me of entertaining.

I began pacing the floor, avoiding obstacles such as a chair or my bed instinctively. I scarcely saw them in my intense concentration on dispelling the bizarre notion that Catriona and I were one.

True, ever since my arrival in Argyll, I had felt a haunting, disturbing familiarity with the castle and with so many other places in this part of the Western Highlands. The very places where Catriona had lived and loved a hundred and fifty years before.

True, there were rough parallels between some of my own recent experiences and events in Catriona's life. The Reverend Archibald had described the different methods by which Angus had tried to murder his wife. He had had one of his retainers push her into the sea on a storm-tossed voyage to Oban from Loch Fingorm; she was rescued by another retainer who wasn't in his master's confidence. I, too, had very nearly drowned in a boating accident. Lorne, trying to shove me out of the way of the boom—or so I thought—had instead pushed me into the water and Colin had rescued me.

Another time Angus had poisoned Catriona's wine; the dose wasn't strong enough to kill her, only make her very ill. When Lorne had carried me to my bed after the boating accident, he'd insisted that I drink a glass of whisky to alleviate the chills that were wracking my body. Later that night I experienced nausea and stomach pains that I had attributed as a matter of course to food poisoning.

Another time Catriona had been induced to ride an outlaw horse that bolted and threw her in what might have been a fatal fall. Instead she had suffered only a broken wrist. Jeannie was no outlaw horse, but she had certainly given me a toss, and young Donnie had been firmly convinced that someone had tampered with the cinch.

According to the chronicle, Angus had also employed the black arts of witchcraft to injure his wife. It took little effort on my part to call up the image of that disgusting doll Meg had found in my wardrobe, or the raven that had plunged to its death against my door.

And finally, it was true that Angus had at last succeeded in killing Catriona by throwing her off the ramparts of Dungariff. Those same ramparts were the scene of my recurrent nightmares, in which I was being menaced by a tartan-clad figure who was racing toward me along the parapet walk.

I stopped dead in my tracks as one last horrifying parallel forced itself into my mind. While Catriona lived, Angus couldn't possess the woman he loved, and so he'd tried to get rid of his wife. Was it possible that Lorne, loving one woman—Flora—and seeing his plans for a happy marriage going down the drain because of his money problems, had attempted to dispose of another woman who was in his way—myself—in order to obtain my fortune, which, under the terms of Uncle Niall's will, Lorne would inherit if I died childless? If I were reincarnated as Catriona, wouldn't Lorne, of necessity, be reincarnated as Angus?

"No, I won't believe it, it couldn't be," I screamed. This time the scream wasn't silent.

"Glenna? What's the matter?" Lorne called from the other side of the door leading to the stairway.

"Nothing. Go away." As I spoke, I instinctively moved to the door and turned the key in the lock. It was the first time I had ever used the key in all my weeks at Dungariff.

Now I could hear several voices behind the door.

"Glenna, it's Aunt Aillie. Are you all right?"

"I'm fine. What are you doing up here at this time of night, Aunt Aillie?"

There was a blank pause on the other side of the door. Then my aunt said tentatively, "It's not really so late, do you think?"

I looked at the clock on the mantel. It seemed an eternity since I'd begun reading the Reverend Archibald's book, but only a little more than an hour had elapsed.

"The ball just ended, so Lorne and I decided to come up and see how you were," Aunt Aillie went on. "We tapped lightly, and when you didn't answer we thought you might be asleep. So we were about to go, and then we heard . . . Glenna, could I come in for a moment?"

"I'd rather you wouldn't. I'm tired. I'd like to get some sleep."

There was another pause, and then Lorne said forcefully, brusquely, "We heard you scream, Glenna. And you've locked your door. If something's wrong, please let us help."

"Nothing's wrong. All I need is *sleep!*" I fought back the hysteria in my voice and added more calmly, "Thank you for checking on me, but I'd really rather you'd

156

go. Goodnight."

"Glenna's right, Lorne. We're keeping her from her rest," Aunt Aillie said quickly. She was protecting me again and I blessed her for it.

I waited until I heard their retreating footsteps before I turned the key to the unlock position and moved away from the door. I couldn't bear to see or talk to anyone, especially not to Lorne, until I had put some order into the maelstrom of ideas and emotions that were tearing me apart. Throwing myself into an armchair, I tried to arrange my thoughts calmly and logically.

My entire being revolted against the concept of reincarnation. To me it was a medieval superstition that had no part in an enlightened world that was reaching toward the twentieth century. But how then to account for my visions, for my series of accidents that seemed to parallel the attempts on Catriona's life?

I drew a deep, shivering breath. I felt as if I were in a maze, baffled at every turn, unable to find my way out. I thought suddenly of a favorite childhood story, "The Lady or the Tiger." Like the man in the story, I could choose to open one of two doors, but behind both of them I would find only destruction.

If I didn't accept reincarnation, if I refused to believe that Lorne and I were reliving the same tragic course we'd pursued in another lifetime, then I had to consider my only alternative. I would have to admit into my consciousness that ravening fear that had been lurking in the dark recesses of my mind since my strange vision of a changed Lorne earlier in the evening, perhaps since the moment when I had first begun to suspect that I had visited Dungariff in another existence. I would have to question whether I was losing my sanity.

I huddled wakefully in my chair throughout the night, drawing a blanket around me when the coals in the fireplace burned into darkened slag, while I searched for a way—a third door—out of the macabre dilemma that was enmeshing me.

Toward morning, I became acutely aware of my cramped and stiffened limbs when I jerked upright involuntarily at the loud, quavering mournful call of some kind of sea bird. For a single moment it sounded like a human voice, crying out in extreme misery.

Chapter 9

When I walked into the dining room next morning for the usual late, ample Sunday breakfast—late by conservative Highland standards; it was a little past nine o'clock—I was greeted by a momentary blank silence as the people gathered around the table turned their heads to look at me with mild surprise written on their faces.

Aunt Aillie was the first to speak. "I was planning to trot up right after breakfast to see how you were feeling, Glenna. I thought you'd probably want to stay in bed today," she added as a careless afterthought, but she didn't deceive me for an instant. I knew what she was really saying. If there was the faintest possibility that I was still suffering from the aftereffects of my latest vision, she wanted me to remain in the seclusion of my tower room where I wouldn't run the risk of blurting out any of the details of my experience.

"Why should I stay in bed, Aunt Aillie? I'm not sick," I replied coolly, settling into my usual place at the table. Unfolding my napkin, I waved away the huge bowl of steaming porridge that Meg was about to place in front of me. "Just some coffee and a scone, please."

"I'm so glad you're feeling better, Glenna, but you do look tired," Ellen said. "Did you get much sleep? When

Lorne and Aillie went up to the tower room last night after the ball, they said you were still awake."

Out of the corner of my eye I saw the quick lift of Flora's head. Was she unaware that Lorne had come up to check on me? I glanced at him, catching a momentary tightening of his lips, but he didn't say anything, keeping his eyes fixed on his plate. I said quickly, "Well, yes, I am a little tired. Dr. MacColl's potion made me sleep," I lied, "but I don't think it was a very natural sleep. If you wouldn't mind, Ellen, I'd like to beg off from attending services this morning."

"Oh, of course, my dear. Pastor Munro's sermons are sometimes a trifle long."

"Sometimes they go on forever, Aunt Ellen, and well you know it," Colin interrupted her genially. "I tell you what, Glenna, that was a very sensible notion of yours, not to attend the Free Kirk today. I'll stay home to keep you company."

"You'll do nothing of the sort," I retorted, breaking off a tiny corner of my scone and throwing it at him. "Cousin Ellen's accused you of being a heathen more than once, and I'm certainly not going to contribute to your delinquency!"

Colin continued to argue during the remainder of breakfast, but he eventually trooped off to the village church with the rest of the family, to my vast relief. I needed to be by myself awhile longer.

I wandered into Ellen's sitting room, where Jane Henderson tracked me down shortly after I had curled up in a corner of the sofa facing the fireplace. She planted a tray on the low table in front of the sofa. "Ye didna eat mair than a wee bit o' scone at breakfast, sae Meggie tells me," she said disapprovingly. "I've brought ye some coddled eggs and a pot o' tea."

She lingered while I drank the tea and dutifully ate a mouthful or two of the eggs. "Did ye read the buik, Miss

Glenna?" she asked after a moment.

"Yes, I did."

"And was it helpful?"

"I'm not sure," I said slowly. I looked directly into her eyes. "Jane, did you realize from the very first that I look like Catriona MacDougall?"

"Nay, I didna. Ye had the look o' someone, but juist who it might be, I didna ken."

"The portraits in the Great Hall—"

She shook her head. "Those old things, I hadna looked at them in years. Nay, Miss Glenna, it wasna until the nicht, when ye fainted awa', that I remembered the story of the great ball that Angus MacDougall gave for the Prince afore Culloden. Then I recognized yer face. That was why I brought ye the paintings."

Perhaps Jane hadn't glanced at the family portraits in years, I thought, as I watched the housekeeper put the tray to rights, pick it up, and leave the room, but I was sure that Lorne, with his love for everything connected with Dungariff, had looked at them often, and that he'd recognized immediately my resemblance to Catriona's portrait that first night when we met in the hotel lobby at Inverness. He'd given me such an odd, intent stare when I blurted, "You're the man I saw at Culloden," that I was initially convinced he was lying when he denied meeting me earlier that day. Now I was equally convinced that he'd told Ellen, when he arrived home at Dungariff, about my resemblance to the portrait, and the two of them had decided to remove the paintings from the Great Hall as a safeguard against a possible jealous outburst from Flora.

I shifted my position on the sofa. I wasn't comfortable thinking about Lorne, even though, in the early hours of the morning, I'd been able to achieve an uneasy balance between my nighttime terrors and daylight common sense. Unlike the man in "The Lady or the Tiger," I'd found my third door and bounded thankfully through it.

I'd decided it was absurd to think that Lorne was trying to kill me. The parallels between my life and Catriona's were vague and inexact. None of the incidents of a threatening nature that had happened to me were identical to any of the attempts on Catriona. The Reverend Archibald, for example, had mentioned in the family history that Angus had employed witchcraft in an attempt to destroy his wife. In Catriona's case, however, the witchcraft had taken the form of a framing spell, involving the use of intricately knotted colored threads. Angus hadn't made use of a gruesome effigy pierced with pins like the one that Meg had found in my wardrobe.

There was, of course, an even more significant difference between me and Catriona: Lorne wasn't my reluctant husband. Yes, he badly needed money to save the estate that he appeared to love more than anything else in life. Still, I couldn't bring myself to admit I was such a poor judge of character that I had failed to see that Lorne's attentions and many kindnesses to me were merely a screen behind which he was plotting to take my life. He was nothing like the mad doctor in Mr. Stevenson's terrifying tale of a dual personality.

Nor was I losing my mind. I saw things occasionally that weren't real, but I told myself I was simply more receptive to outside stimulation than most people. My hallucinations resembled the made-up stories of an imaginative child. Save for my rare visions, I was as sane and functioning a personality as any of the people around me.

By the time the others returned from attending services in the kirk, I was essentially back to my normal self. Lunch was a relaxed affair. No one dwelled on my fainting spell at the ball the night before. Flora did bring up the incident with a facile display of sympathy, but I suspected her main purpose in mentioning it was to inform me about the compliments the Chief had lavished on her dancing after I left the ball. Even Aunt Aillie, after a sharp glance at my calm, smiling face, seemed to relax her vigilance.

"Pastor Munro outdid himself today, Glenna," Colin observed, as Meg was clearing the table for dessert. "He spoke for an hour and fifteen minutes on the subject of suppressing the temptations of the flesh. What's more, he seemed to be singling me out for most of his attention. Every time I looked up, I found his eyes boring into me."

Flora giggled. "He wanted to make sure you weren't falling asleep on him, Colin."

"Oh, you." Colin shook his spoon at Flora. "Actually, Glenna, I'll have you know I ended up poorer in worldly goods by performing my Sabbath duty. I made a small wager with Aunt Aillie that Pastor Munro's sermon would last no more than an hour." He dug into his pocket and solemnly handed Aunt Aillie a shilling. She accepted it with a good-natured grace. Colin and his fooleries had made a conquest of Aunt Aillie from their very first meeting.

"I hope you know how much Pastor Munro would disapprove of betting on his sermon, Colin," Ellen said, repressing a smile. Her face clouding, she turned to me. "We heard some very bad news after the services. Do you remember that young woman I spoke to the pastor about, the day we went to see him about the festival?"

"Why, yes. Morag, wasn't that her name? Her husband abandoned her, I believe." I answered readily, but a cold chill of apprehension was beginning to creep over me.

"That's the one. Morag Armstrong. Her husband agreed to take her back into his house after the pastor had a talk with him, and I thought everything was all right. But late last night, or early this morning, Morag and Duncan apparently had a quarrel. A neighbor found her dead in the street outside her cottage. Duncan has disappeared."

I put my hands to my face, fighting back a sudden rush of tears. I was deeply sorry for the unfortunate Morag, but there was another element in my distress. I remembered my hallucination on the beach at Finlay, in which I'd imagined seeing Morag fleeing for her life from her husband, and now my vision had come true. How many of my other visions, dreams, nightmares, would also come true?

I felt Lorne's strong sure hands on my shoulders. "What is it, Glenna?" he asked, his voice throbbing with concern.

How odd, came the fleeting thought, that Lorne should be the first to comfort me. "It's nothing. I'm being foolish," I insisted. "Aunt Aillie, do you have a hand-kerchief?" I wiped the moisture from the corners of my eyes. "I was thinking how terrible it must have been for that poor girl to be struggling for her life at the very hour when we were celebrating so grandly here at Dungariff, totally oblivious to her plight. Why didn't we feel something, some kind of a bond between us, communicating her pain?"

"It's a lovely thought, Glenna, but life isn't like that, you know," Ellen said gently.

"Yes, I know." Giving my eyes a last wipe, I pasted a smile on my face and changed the subject. "We didn't have much of a chance to talk last night amid all the festivities," I said to Flora. "I wanted to ask you if it was something of a wrench, saying good-bye to your pupils for the last time."

"Oh, it was," she sighed. I liked her better for the obvious sincerity in her voice as she said, "I'll miss the children. I really did love teaching. Not the long hours and all those papers to correct, but being with the children was a joy." She brightened. "I haven't cut all my ties with them. I'll continue to teach in the Sunday School. And then, of course," she added with that tinkling laugh that always irritated me, "I'll be far too busy from now until August to miss my pupils overly much. I never realized before how many things were involved in planning a wedding."

"Or planning a honeymoon, either, I'll warrant," Colin teased. "Or is Lorne taking full charge of those arrangements?"

Blushing prettily, Flora reached across the table to put her hand on Lorne's. "That's a great secret, isn't it, darling?"

"Indeed, and none of Colin's business," Lorne replied, smiling faintly. He was never demonstrative, I thought; right now he wasn't returning Flora's handclasp, but you could sense his quiet affection for her.

On Sunday afternoons since Aunt Aillie and I had been visiting at Dungariff, Ellen usually arranged for some kind of outing if the weather was fine. Today it was sunny with a slight breeze—"Glenna's fine weather," as Colin persisted in calling it—and we went for a short drive to nearby Loch Nell, ladies in the landau, Lorne and Colin on horseback.

I stole frequent glances at Lorne, riding slightly ahead of the carriage. He was a superb horseman, graceful and controlled, man and animal moving as one. He was very quiet during the drive, not atypical behavior on his part, of course, allowing the rest of us to do all the talking.

Flora was far more chatty than usual, although she had only a narrow range of subjects, herself and her wedding and her future housekeeping arrangements. "I haven't had a chance to tell you that Papa said last night at the ball that he wants me to have my mother's drawing room furniture," she remarked to Ellen. "It's been stored in the attic all these years, because my stepmother wanted to refurnish the drawing room to suit her own taste." Flora's tone was matter-of-fact, but I thought I could detect a faint note of the resentment that Colin had told me she felt at being superseded in her father's household by his second wife.

"Why, that's splendid, Flora. I'm sure your mother's furniture is beautiful. I wonder, though . . ." Ellen hesitated. "Have you considered where you'd like to put it? We have so much furniture in the castle . . ."

"Well, Mother MacDougall, I've been thinking. Why couldn't we create a little private suite for Lorne and me by cutting a connecting door between the Laird's bed-chamber and the small room next to it? That way we could have our own sitting room, and my mother's furniture would fit in there quite nicely."

"I see. It's certainly something to think about, isn't it?"

Flora smiled with satisfaction, and I suppose she considered the matter a *fait accompli*. I recognized Ellen's slight air of strain, however, and I felt for her. I didn't suspect her of being unwilling to hand over the domestic management of the castle to her son's wife when he married. She was a very sensible woman. I was sure she'd already accepted her inevitable change of status. No, it was more than that. Ellen loved Dungariff almost as passion-ately as Lorne did, and I knew from her confidences to Aunt Aillie that she was firmly opposed to any structural alterations in the castle, and that included cutting new doors and throwing rooms together.

When we arrived at Loch Nell, a pretty freshwater lake surrounded by low mountains, Flora rounded up Lorne and dragged him off for a private walk along the lake shore.

"Well, I guess I can tell when I'm not wanted," Colin complained in pretended high dudgeon. "Come on, Glenna, we'll take a stroll in the opposite direction. You ladies coming with us?"

"No, thank you, Colin. Aillie and I will wait comfort-ably in the landau and watch the waves."

Arm in arm, Colin and I walked along the pebbly strand, tossing an occasional stone into the water, making conversation when the spirit moved us. I felt relaxed and comfortable as I always did with Lorne's cousin. He was a good companion.

"Did you notice how quickly Flora moved to get Lorne off by herself?" Colin asked. "She's been complaining all year that she doesn't see enough of him on the weekends, especially since you—" He cleared his throat.

"Especially since Aunt Aillie and I have been staying at the castle," I finished. "It's all right, Colin. We *have* been in Flora's way. Now that she's here for the summer, however, she'll be able to be with Lorne as much as she likes."

His eyes dancing, Colin exclaimed, "You and I can be very helpful to Flora by staying out of her way. Tomorrow, for instance, we could take the boat out, just the two of us. Oh, I know you haven't seemed enthusiastic about sailing, after what happened to you the last time we went out in the boat, but I promise I'll stick close to shore and we won't go out at all if there's the least sign of bad weather."

"Oh, I don't know . . ." Suddenly I felt again that sense of utter helplessness as I plummeted into the chill dark depths of the Firth of Lorn. I seized at an excuse. "How could we possibly go sailing tomorrow? You'll be leaving at the crack of dawn to go to work in Oban."

"Well! That proves how important I am around here," Colin huffed in jest. "You've forgotten I start my annual holiday tomorrow."

"Colin, I only forgot temporarily! Honestly, I've been looking forward to having you around for a spell."

"That's better," he grinned. "I must say, I'm anticipating my holiday more than usual this year. You're going to give me a good deal of your time, aren't you? We'll go sailing and riding, and we'll take those long walks you dote on." He glanced over his shoulder. "For now, though, we'd better turn back. Lorne and Flora have returned to the carriage, and we mustn't keep Aunt Aillie waiting. I've noticed she's a bear if she doesn't get her tea on time!"

As we approached the landau, I gazed around at the trim farms ringing the lake and asked idly, "Are we still in MacDougall territory?"

"If you mean, does Lorne own these farms, definitely not. There's some kind of an amusing story, though . . . Lorne," he called out, "Come tell Glenna how the MacDougalls lost Loch Nell. I know it didn't happen yesterday."

"Far from it," Lorne said as he came up to us. "It wasn't our branch of the clan, mind, but back around 1500, the MacDougall of Torr-an-Tuirc, having no heirs, decided to bequeath his lands on Loch Nell to the MacDougalls of Dunollie. When he arrived at Dunollie Castle with the title deeds, some pranksters played a practical joke on him—I think they poured water in his scabbard—and he became so angry he mounted his horse and rode straight to Inverary, where he deeded his lands to the Campbells." I saw the familiar somber, hooded look descend on his face. He seemed to forget that I was standing beside him. "One way or another," he muttered, "we MacDougalls manage to find a way to ruin ourselves." He stood staring at the water, lost in some bleak private despair.

"Lorne . . ." My heart ached for him, but there wasn't anything I could say. I knew he was thinking of the financial abyss into which he was sinking. Until he asked me for help, though, I had to pretend I was ignorant of his problems.

All during the drive back to the castle, and later, while I was dressing for dinner, I racked my brain for some feasible way to entice the bullheaded Master of Dungariff to accept some of Uncle Niall's money, but I didn't come up with a ready answer.

Giving my hair a final smoothing and clasping Aunt Aillie's pearls around my neck, I revolved slowly in front of the cheval glass, quite frankly liking what I saw. I was wearing a clinging yellow silk tea gown I'd bought at

Madame Celeste's shop on Summer Street in Boston at a perfectly exorbitant price. I fell in love with the gown at first sight, without having any idea of where I might wear it. The dress was in the Empire style, short-waisted and low-necked, with a pleated overdress of transparent yellow chiffon. It was a wildly impractical creation for any function in Atwater, Massachusetts, or, indeed, anywhere, except possibly some stately ancestral mansion in England or one of the millionaires' "cottages" in Newport. However, I'd taken to wearing it occasionally here at Dungariff after it became apparent that my conservative Scottish hosts were not shocked by a gown that I'd initially considered quite daring.

"You should always wear yellow, Glenna," Colin said admiringly when we met later in the drawing room.

"Last week you said I should always wear blue," I reminded him, laughing.

"Yellow *is* lovely on you, Glenna," Flora agreed, overhearing our remarks as she came up to us. "It's considered *the* color this year." She opened the fashion magazine she had in her hand. "Look at this sketch in *Cassal's*. Do you think it would be becoming to me?"

The dress in the sketch was made of yellow silk draped with scarlet chiffon and it had red velvet puff sleeves. With her reddish blonde coloring, Flora would look like an illustration on a candy box in it. I said cautiously, "Perhaps it's a little elaborate for Argyll? Where would you wear it?"

"Oh, that's no problem," Flora replied airily. "Lorne and I will be doing a lot of entertaining."

Elaborate evening dresses. Extensive alterations to the castle. Ambitious plans to entertain. Had Flora given any thought to the expense of the projects she was planning? Had Lorne even hinted to her that he was short of money?

After dinner Colin persuaded Ellen to play the piano for dancing. I doubt that anyone else noticed, but Lorne carefully avoided dancing with me. He waltzed and one-stepped with Flora, and he partnered Aunt Aillie through the intricacies of a reel. He even planted me at the piano, where I fumbled inexpertly through the "Blue Danube" while he danced with Ellen. Finally, toward the end of the evening, he came over to me, arms extended. "This is our dance, I believe, Miss MacDougall."

I could tell from the expression on his face, a mixture of apprehension and anticipation, that he knew as well as I did how dangerous it was for us to be in each other's arms. It's some kind of chemistry, something neither of us can resist, I thought, as his arm closed around mé and I became the captive of that magical enticing thrall of the senses that Lorne seemed able to evoke with his lightest touch. His arm tightened around my waist and he bent his head, murmuring, "Colin was right, you should always wear yellow. You're stunning tonight, Glenna. I've never seen you look so beautiful."

Colin's voice jerked us back to reality. "Here, you two," he said merrily, "I'm cutting in. Aunt Ellen's digging in her heels and refusing to play any more, and I want the last waltz of the evening with Glenna."

"And I with Flora," Lorne said instantly. He'd recovered his composure. There wasn't a trace in his dark face of the caressing warmth I'd heard in his voice moments before.

I glanced over at Flora, sitting talking to Aunt Aillie. Had she observed anything in my dance with Lorne to arouse her jealousy?

Certainly Colin didn't seem to have noticed anything out of the ordinary. As he swept me off to the last strains of the waltz before Ellen rose determinedly from the piano bench, he said with one of his infectious grins, "Let's take a little stroll before we go to bed. I'd like to see how Aunt Ellen's roses are coming along."

"About the same as they were this afternoon when we

drove out of the gatehouse," I retorted.

"A few more may have opened."

"So they might." I chuckled at Colin's light-hearted nonsense. "Let's go, then."

As we walked down the corridor toward the side door opening into the courtyard, Jane Henderson loomed before us. "And where be ye thinking of taking Miss Glenna, Maister Colin?"

"Good God, Jane, you must have eyes in the back of your head. If you must know, Miss Glenna and I are going for a walk."

"Haud yer wheesht," Jane said severely. "Ye mustna make light o' the Almighty. Miss Glenna, I'll juist pop intae the mistress's sitting room tae fetch ye ane o' her shawls against the chill."

As Colin and I strolled across the courtyard, he remarked, "If ever I seem to you to be acting childish, Glenna, you can lay it to Jane's door. That woman doesn't want me to grow up."

"She's very fond of you, Colin."

"I know. She's taken a fancy to you, too."

The long northern twilight was drawing to a close, but on this summer evening, approaching the longest day of the year, there was still enough light to enjoy the enchanting bower that Ellen had lovingly created from what once had been the castle moat. She had artfully mingled the large, intensely fragrant blossoms of the old-fashioned cabbage roses with the glowing hues and lustrous foliage of the damask rose and the newer hybrid teas.

"Look, Colin," I said, plucking a rich pink blossom from one of the damask rose bushes. "Cousin Ellen tells me that this is called the Marie Louise Rose. It was found growing in the Empress Josephine's gardens at Malmaison in 1813. Over here, though—" I crossed over to the small white roses growing at the rear of the garden against the wall. "These are my real favorites. They have such a simple, dignified grace."

"You and Aunt Ellen. Jacobites, both of you," Colin chuckled. "You know, don't you, that this is the wild Scottish rose? It really has no place in a formal garden, but Aunt Ellen is a sentimentalist. When Bonnie Prince Charlie landed in the '45, this wild rose became his symbol."

"I didn't know that. What a lovely idea," I said, delighted. Then, almost immediately, a dark thought took over. If I believed in reincarnation, I might well wonder if my lifelong love for white roses was a carryover from a previous existence. Shaking off the impression, I picked one of the little roses and placed it in Colin's buttonhole. "There, now we're Jacobites together," I laughed.

He grasped both my hands, holding them tightly, his amused smile fading. "Oh, Glenna, I love you so much. I want us to be together always. I want you to marry me." Bending his head, he put his lips to mine in a kiss that sent a pleasurable tingling all through my body. For a moment, I responded with an ardor that surprised me. Poor William Simpson back in Atwater. His chaste kisses were simply not in the same class with Colin's.

"Well?" Colin murmured, pressing his face against my hair. "Will you marry me, Glenna?"

I pulled away abruptly. "Colin, dear, I like you so much, but . . . You know as well as I do that liking isn't enough for marriage."

He caught my hand. "I don't want to shock you, Glenna, but there was more than just liking in your kiss. Admit it, you wanted me to go on kissing you, longer and harder."

As I snatched my hand away, my face flaming crimson, Colin blurted, "I shouldn't have said that. Please, will you forgive me?"

"Don't worry about it, Colin. I'm not angry."

And I wasn't, except at myself. I *had* responded physically to Colin, and yet I knew that I wasn't remotely in love with him and never would be. Was I becoming crude, common, like those girls that Aunt Aillie had warned me about in my early teens, couching her remarks in such elliptical, obscure terms that I was left totally mystified about her meaning?

Colin hugged me briefly. "I give you fair warning, I'm not giving up. I'm going to ask you to marry me again. I'll keep after you until I wear you down at last."

I shook my head, laughing a little, as I took his arm for the walk back to the castle. Even though I would have to be careful not to encourage him, it was comforting, it was infinitely flattering, to be courted by such an attractive, lovable man.

I was about to turn out my bedside lamp when Jane came to the tower room later that evening. She was carrying a piece of knitting, a partially completed sweater. "Here's that pattern I was telling ye aboot, Miss Glenna. Ye'll not find this exact stitch anywhere except juist in these parts. I'll be happy tae show ye how tae do it." She added with elaborate casualness, "Maister Colin's been a-telling me that he's proposed marriage tae ye."

Of course. Showing me the knitting had only been a transparent excuse for Jane's late-night visit. Her feelings for Colin were the only soft spot in her austere nature.

"Maister Colin, he says ye didna accept him. I maun tell you, Miss Glenna, as one who's known the laddie frae his cradle, ye'll never find a better man fer yersel'."

"I know Colin's a wonderful man," I said hastily. "The thing is, I'm not sure I love him well enough to marry him. You'd want me to be sure, for both our sakes, wouldn't you?"

"Aye. Indeed." The softer look vanished from Jane's

face, and she was back in character, dour and reserved, the real chatelaine of Dungariff.

I sat for awhile after Jane left, pondering the oddities of life. Who could have imagined, less than a year ago, that before long I would receive proposals from two handsome, eligible suitors? Or that I would refuse both offers? Or, most incredible of all, that I, staid proper New England librarian Glenna MacDougall, would, in a span of a few short months, be kissed by three different men?

Chapter 10

Life at Dungariff, I discovered in the next few days, was decidedly different with Flora in residence. I hadn't realized previously, during her short weekend visits before the school year ended, how much she disliked being alone. Apparently she had few inner resources, few interests except planning her wedding and her trousseau. Throughout the day, when Lorne was out on the estate, she would attach herself to one or another of the persons in the household. When Lorne was present, of course, she monopolized his attention, clinging to him like a limpet. In his absence she often sought me out. I did wonder at her motive once or twice. I was positive she didn't like me very much. Perhaps, by staying close to me, she could be sure I wasn't off somewhere with Lorne!

I scolded myself for the uncharitable thought. Actually, I supposed, Flora simply felt more comfortable associating with a girl of her own age. Ellen and Aunt Aillie had become such a closely knit duo, deeply absorbed in their mutual interests, that Flora might well have felt left out if I hadn't been there to provide her company.

Colin's presence on holiday was a ray of sunshine in the changed atmosphere of the castle. He and Flora had known each other for such a long time and they were fond of each other. Whenever I started to feel that I couldn't bear such a prolonged exposure to Flora, Colin came to my rescue and took her off my hands for a walk, a drive, a game of draughts.

Not that Flora had all of Colin's attention by any means. He lived up to his promise to monopolize my time that next week. We rode, we sailed—close to shore, I insisted on that—and we visited the local spots of interest. Colin didn't have Lorne's comprehensive knowledge of the area, or his all-consuming affection for every nook and corner of Argryll, but I enjoyed our outings. I'd be sorry to see him return to Oban and his job in Mr. Cameron's store.

One afternoon toward the end of his first week of holiday, we went riding into Glen Fingorm. I thought wistfully of the afternoon Lorne and I had spent there on the day of the annual Dungariff ball. In all probability he and I would never ride alone into the glen again.

As Colin and I stood watching the swiftly cascading waters of the little River Fingorm, he told me about the prize trout he'd once caught.

"Now, Colin, don't fib. Lorne tells me you've been after that grandfather trout for ages and the creature's still out there," I said wickedly.

"That Lorne," Colin scoffed. "He's jealous of me. I've outfished him ever since we were bairns." He reached out to clasp my hand. "This is the best holiday I've ever had, Glenna. It's meant so much to me, these hours we've spent together." He was silent for a moment, gazing out over the glen. "I've been doing a lot of thinking of late," he said at last. "For most of my life, I've thought of Dungariff as my home. Now that Lorne and Flora are about to be married . . . well, it's occurred to me that perhaps the newlyweds won't want a cousin on their doorstep every weekend and every holiday."

"But Dungariff's your home, Colin," I exclaimed, aghast. "You've lived here since you were a baby. You've been a second son to Cousin Ellen, and as for Jane! Can you imagine the commotion she'd raise if she didn't see you every weekend?''

Colin's open face looked unwontedly serious. "Dungariff's not really my home, you know. I've lived there on the kindness of my relatives. Not that I've ever felt the slightest unwillingness to have me." With a quick change of mood, he said cheerfully, "Anyway, a married man should have his own home. Which reminds me, I've found the perfect place for *our* home, once you've made up your mind to marry me. There's a steep, wooded hillside below Pulpit Hill in Oban, with a precipitous drop to the sea. We could build a beautiful home there for ourselves.''

"Doubtless we could, but I'm far from agreeing to marry you, Colin."

"But you will think about it?''

"Oh, yes, I'll think about it, but don't count on my saying yes. Perhaps I'm one of those women who can't fall in love," I joked. "Perhaps I'll be a permanent spinster."

Colin shook his head. "No. Not with your eyes and your lips, Glenna. I could tell, soon after I met you, that you were ripe to love someone. I only hope it's me."

I thought about what Colin had said as I walked several days later along the winding road that led around the promontory to the beach below Dungariff. The beach had become my refuge when I wanted to be alone to sort out my thoughts. Here I could escape from Flora, and even from Colin, who seemed to have only one topic on his mind these days, persuading me to marry him. Even a proposal, I'd found, could pall when it was repeated too often!

I perched on my favorite rock, gazing out over the view that never grew stale: the hills sweeping down to the beach on Dunard Point opposite the castle, creating the narrow inlet that made Loch Fingorm almost an inland lake, with glimpses to the north of the green hills of Kerrera, and to the west the mountains of Mull.

I certainly had enough to think about this morning. For starters, I'd been wondering if Aunt Aillie and I should leave Dungariff earlier than we'd planned. Ellen had indicated she expected us to stay through the summer until the wedding, but I wasn't certain that Flora and I could stand such prolonged exposure to each other! She seemed friendly and forbearing enough *now*. Lorne had scrupulously refrained from suggesting any riding excursion that she couldn't share, and I really never saw him now except in her company. But it was asking rather a lot of an engaged girl to have another woman in constant attendance. Perhaps Aunt Aillie and I could go off on an exploring trip to other parts of Argyll until the wedding.

And what was I to do about Colin? Remembering his remark that I was ripe for love, I could feel the hot color surging into my face. He sensed, of course, the strain of elemental passion in my personality that I had fought against acknowledging even to myself. I was sure he also knew *he* didn't arouse that kind of feeling in me.

The sun was becoming hotter, glaring into my eyes. I pushed my straw boater lower on my forehead. What if I did marry Colin? I wasn't overwhelmingly, romantically in love with him, but I did feel an enormously strong affection for him. Perhaps that would be enough? If we married, I needn't leave Argyll. Somehow, during the past weeks, my old life in Massachusetts had receded into the mists of an unreal past. I didn't want to go back there. I wanted to stay in Scotland. Then what about Aunt Aillie? She'd made her peace with the ghosts of her Argyll girlhood, and she had few remaining ties in America. A few old neighbors in Atwater, that was all. I thought it likely she would want to stay here, too. She could live with us in Oban, or in a little house of her own. We'd be close enough to Dungariff to visit Ellen often. Lorne and Flora, too.

A loud crashing noise from above and behind me jarred

me out of my reverie. I turned my head, gasping at the sight of the enormous boulder that was hurtling down the cliff face, gathering a horrifying momentum as it plunged toward me. Recovering from a split second of frozen shock, I dove frantically to my right, knowing with whatever part of my brain that was still functioning, that I couldn't avoid the monster's path.

Moments later, lying with my face pressed uncomfortably into the rough gravelly sand of the beach, I lifted my head to gaze disbelievingly at the giant boulder, now resting innocuously on the shore at the water's edge, near the small jetty where the family sailboat was moored. I scrambled to my feet on rubbery legs that at first refused to support me, staring down at the flattened remnants of my parasol on the sand beside my rocky perch. The boulder had missed crushing me by inches.

A handful of small stones skittered down from somewhere above me, and I glanced up in alarm. Perhaps the entire area beneath the castle walls was becoming unstable. Far above me I caught the merest glimpse of movement near the clump of scrawny fir trees masking the postern gate into the castle.

I kept my eyes glued to the area around the gate, but, as the seconds ticked by and there was no further sign of movement, the tense knot in my stomach began to relax. Apparently I needn't fear another huge boulder roaring down upon me. Perhaps what I'd seen had been a small animal, one of the stable cats, for instance, dislodging a fall of pebbles as it prowled around the gate.

Suddenly the sunny, solitary beach seemed hostile and forbidding. Still feeling shaky, I brushed off some of the sand and slimy seaweed from my skirt, picked up my mangled parasol and started trudging back along the narrow road that wound tortuously around the promontory on which the castle stood.

As I passed under the portals of the gatehouse into the

courtyard, I saw Lorne emerging from the stables. "Hello, Glenna. Enjoy your walk?" he called. He waited, smiling, until I came up to him. Then his smile faded. He stared at my badly scratched hands and the wreck of my parasol and the large rent in my skirt. "What happened to you? Did you fall? Are you hurt?"

"No, I'm not hurt. I fell flat on my face trying to get out of the way of a falling rock. I'm either very agile or very lucky. The thing just missed me."

"A rock? Where were you, on the beach?"

"Yes, right below the postern gate. Actually, the rock was more of a boulder. About the size of a small house, I'd say." Lorne didn't smile at my feeble attempt at humor. "I suppose I could have been badly injured."

"You could have been killed," he said angrily. "It's that loose scree at the rear of the castle. Pieces of rock are always falling, though nothing as big as you're describing. I've been afraid for years that someone might get hurt while we were taking the boat out. My father would never do anything about it. He said I was borrowing trouble. He simply didn't want to spend the money for repairs. This settles it. I'll put the men to work immediately, fixing up some kind of wire netting to contain the rock falls. Please don't go down to the beach again until the netting is in place."

He took my arm as we walked toward the hall house. "If anything had happened to you as a result of my negligence, Glenna, I'd have wanted to put a bullet through my head," he muttered.

I recoiled at the naked emotion in his voice. What was this primitive elemental bonding between us that wouldn't stay hidden in the depths where it belonged? "Lorne, don't say things like that," I protested. "There's no harm done. Let's forget it."

Though I didn't realize it at the time, the incident of the rock fall marked the beginning of the end of the precarious peace of mind I'd been enjoying since I'd rationalized away my fears during my dark hours of torment on the night of the Dungariff ball.

That afternoon Flora dragged me into the family living quarters to inspect the Laird's Bedchamber on the third floor, which I had seen briefly when Ellen gave Aunt Aillie and me a tour of the hall house after our arrival at Dungariff. It was a large, rather gloomy room, furnished with massive old furniture and with one large window looking north to Dunard Point. I knew from Ellen that it was the only one of the family bedrooms, besides my bedchamber in the tower, that had direct access to the ramparts, and I could recall Lorne's telling me, on my first night at the castle, that from this room the lairds of a more primitive time could eavesdrop on the conversations of their unfaithful wives in the Great Hall below.

I could see all around me the traces of Lorne's occupancy of the bedchamber, his shaving gear on the washstand, a glimpse of his familiar clothing in the wardrobe, a volume of his favorite Robert Burns open on the night table. And I felt faintly uncomfortable, like an intruder in this room that Lorne would soon be sharing with Flora.

"Have you ever seen anything quite as hideous as these furnishings?" Flora demanded.

I was no expert on antique furniture, but I knew that these heavy oak pieces, ornately carved and ornamented with grotesques and scrolls and heraldic devices, especially the enormous bed with its paneled wooden canopy, must be three or four hundred years old. "I rather like the furniture," I told Flora. "It fits the scale and age of the room."

"That's the right word, age," Flora said discontentedly. "I don't doubt this furniture has been here since the castle was built."

"Oh, I don't think so. Dungariff was in use as a fortress

before the thirteenth century. None of these pieces looks any earlier than Elizabethan."

"That's old enough," Flora said emphatically. As we left the room and walked down the stairs to the first floor, she added, "I was hoping you'd agree with me about the furniture."

"Why?" I looked at her curiously.

"Oh, so I'd have a little extra ammunition, I suppose." Flora giggled. "Lorne and Mother MacDougall seem to think this place is perfect the way it is, but really, I don't see any reason why the castle couldn't be modernized a bit, do you?"

I hesitated. "There's a lot of tradition and family pride involved, Flora."

"Yes, and there's such a thing as being hidebound, too," she retorted. "We'll see. I'll talk to Lorne about it."

Flora didn't have a chance to speak to Lorne until the dinner hour. He was still out on the estate in late afternoon and missed taking tea with us, arriving in the dining room slightly out of breath after an obviously hasty change of clothes.

"You work too hard, Lorne," Flora pouted. "Surely it isn't necessary for the Master of Dungariff to work longer hours than his own bailiff, or his crofters, for that matter. We scarcely see you."

"Sorry to be late, Flora." Lorne tasted his soup, saying in an aside to Meg, "Tell Cook this is excellent," before turning his attention back to his fiancée. "I stopped off to see Jock MacCabe, and we had a long talk about entering Sandy in the field trials at the Highland Gathering in Fort William in July. Jock says the dog is ready. In fact, Jock is so confident that he actually made me a wager that Sandy will win the competition."

"I can't believe it," Ellen said, laughing. "Jock's a very warm man with a shilling." To me and Aillie she said, "Jock's our head shepherd. If he could win a sheepdog trial just once, I think he'd die happy."

"I'd love to see your dog compete, Lorne," I said eagerly. "Perhaps we could all go to the Gathering at Fort William."

"Mother and I are ahead of you there, Glenna. We'd already planned to ask you and Aunt Aillie to attend."

I could tell from the slight tightening of her lips that Flora didn't appreciate Lorne's solicitude in planning entertainment for Aunt Aillie and me. She never liked his attention to be diverted away from herself for too long, either. Reaching over to put her hand on his sleeve, she said, "Glenna and I were up in the Laird's bedchamber today. She says the furniture is Elizabethan."

Lorne smiled at me. "You were nearly right. It's very early Tudor, mid-fifteenth century. What did you think of it?"

"It's so massive and heavy it would look out of place in most homes. It's perfect for Dungariff."

"Yes, I've always thought that. You have a feeling for this old place, Glenna."

"The furniture's terribly old-fashioned, Lorne," Flora put in. "I suppose it must be very valuable, though. To people who like old things, I mean."

"I suppose it is valuable," Lorne said, raising an eyebrow. "I never gave it any consideration. The furniture's simply always been there."

"Well, but that's the thing, Lorne. I'd like something a little different, something lighter, more modern. Now, I'm sure we could get a good price if we sold the older pieces, a large enough sum, probably, to completely furnish the bedchamber."

"Replace family heirlooms with cheap factory-made pieces? Not on your life. I like the room the way it is."

"But Lorne—"

"I don't think we should talk about this at the dinner table, Flora." Lorne looked at Ellen. "Was there anything in the post, Mother?"

"Only the one letter." Ellen's voice sounded curiously reluctant. "I put it in your study. It's from Alan MacLeod in Fort William."

As his mother was speaking, Lorne made a jerky movement reaching for his wineglass, and some of the liquid spilled on the tablecloth. Recalling the conversation I'd overheard between him and Ellen about the estate's desperate financial straits, I recognized Alan MacLeod's name immediately. He was the young banker who'd promised to contact his banker friends in Glasgow about raising funds to mine Lorne's silica deposits. Very possibly the contents of Mr. MacLeod's letter would decide the immediate future of Dungariff. If Lorne couldn't secure financing to mine his silica, he would have to sign away the property on a long lease.

I wasn't surprised when he refused dessert and left the table, telling Ellen he would have his coffee later. Jumping up from her chair, Flora followed him out of the dining room, saying hurriedly over her shoulder, "Excuse me, Mother MacDougall, I want to talk to Lorne."

"Flora—" Ellen shrugged resignedly. To me and Aunt Aillie she said, "Let's go have our coffee in the drawing room."

A little later Flora joined us, looking chagrined. "Lorne read his letter and then said he was going riding," she grumbled. "Now, why would he do a thing like that, after being in the saddle from dawn to dark? Mother Mac-Dougall, do you know what was in that letter? Could it have been bad news?"

"I don't know, Flora. I don't read Lorne's mail, naturally," Ellen replied briefly. She knew right enough, I thought. If Alan MacLeod's letter had reported favorably on the financing for the silica deposits, Lorne would never have rushed off on a solitary ride at this time of the evening. It would be pitch dark before long.

With his usual tact where Flora was concerned, Colin distracted her from her speculation about Lorne by asking her about the preparations for her birthday ball. Flora would turn twenty-one on the following Saturday, and Ellen was giving a small dance for her. Nothing on the order of the annual Dungariff ball. This would be a cozier affair, attended by immediate neighbors and a number of Flora's friends and relatives from Oban.

After we had our coffee, Colin challenged Flora to a game of her favorite draughts, and I made an excuse to the others that I wanted to finish the book I'd been reading. I made my escape to Ellen's sitting room, where I dutifully sat down with my book. However, after I caught myself reading the same page repeatedly, I slammed the book shut. Sir Nigel Loring and his men of *The White Company* would have to wait for another try at my attention.

Leaning forward, my elbows braced on my knees and my chin cupped in my hands, I concentrated on Lorne and his predicament. Was there any way I could persuade him to accept the money he needed to settle his debts and put Dungariff on a sound footing again? Even with the disastrous news I was positive he had received tonight, I was convinced he would simply refuse my offer of money out of hand. What if I approached him from the standpoint of Ellen's welfare, and Flora's? In the end I concluded my most likely course was to stress the point that I was a MacDougall, too, and to suggest that I had the right to use MacDougall money to keep the estate from going under. I was prepared to make it a loan, not an outright gift, if that would salve his pride.

I decided to put the question to Lorne immediately, before my courage evaporated, but I didn't feel at all confident about my chances for success as I walked down the corridor to his study. I had never met a man who went his own way with more dogged stubbornness than the

Master of Dungariff.

There was no answer to my knock, no light coming from under the door. He wasn't back yet from his ride. Well, then, I'd wait for him. Opening the door, I groped my way into the room, which was in almost total darkness despite the one oil lamp burning dimly at the end of the corridor. I knew there was a lamp on Lorne's desk, but before I could strike a match to light the wick, I heard footsteps outside the door and then the sound of Flora's voice, and I dropped my hand to my side with the unlighted match still in it.

Flora and Lorne had paused in the doorway. I could make out their figures indistinctly against the faint light coming from the corridor lamp, but they couldn't see me. She was saying, "Let's go in your office and discuss it a little more. I don't think I've made myself clear—"

"Flora, I don't want to talk any more tonight. We're both tired—" Lorne broke off, and the two indistinct figures merged into one in an embrace that went on and on in a rough-breathing silence broken only when Flora wrenched her lips from Lorne's with a low moan.

"Lorne, darling, I adore you. Let's not quarrel about the stupid furniture. Just hold me, tighter, tighter . . . Oh, Lorne, you make me feel . . ."

I shivered. Could that husky voice, throbbing with passion, belong to prim, ladylike Flora?

"My God, Flora, I don't want to quarrel, either," Lorne burst out. "I only want to make you happy. I'd do anything, I'd ransom my soul to make you happy. Once I thought I could do it, but now . . ." His voice broke off, smothered in the unmistakable sound of a kiss.

"Darling, don't talk like that. Of course you'll make me happy, you're my whole world, you know that," Flora said shakily. "You were right, let's not talk any more now. We'll go say goodnight to your mother. I know she was worried about you, riding off into the night like that."

I waited until I could no longer hear their footsteps in the corridor, and then I scurried up the winding stairs to the tower room. I felt an aching sense of loss, which I tried angrily to deny. Tonight I'd had my answer to that nagging question, what does Lorne see in Flora? He loved her, that was all. There didn't have to be a reason. He loved her and he was half out of his mind with despair and rage, now that the silica deposit financing had fallen through and he couldn't provide the financial security that would enable Flora to live happily ever after as the mistress of Dungariff. Well, I could fix that. Tomorrow I would force Lorne to accept the money, even if it meant destroying our friendship. A friendship that was bound to end, anyway, with his marriage to Flora. I crept into bed, trying to keep my mind blank so I could fall asleep. I managed to slip into a light, brief slumber that ended when I heard a keening, sobbing cry emanating from the battlements, a weird disembodied sound that echoed quaveringly through the tower room for several seconds. The sea bird again. Why did it sound so much like a woman wailing in agony?

Chapter 11

I rose early the next morning. Sometimes Lorne ate an early breakfast and went out on his estate rounds before the rest of the household awakened. Perhaps I could catch him alone and get the uncomfortable business of offering him a loan out of the way so it wouldn't hang over me for the rest of the day.

Dressing quickly, I pulled my hair into a careless bun at the top of my head, threw a shawl over my shoulders, and opened the door to the staircase. I paused on the landing. Lamps were kept burning on the staircase night and day, since the only light reaching the tower came through a few slitlike apertures spaced at wide intervals. This morning, however, the lamp outside my door was out. No matter. I'd have no trouble navigating the first sweeping curve in the semidarkness. I could see a faint light below indicating that the lamp on the next corkscrew turn was lit.

Keeping a hand on the iron railing, but moving as quickly as usual because I was so familiar with the stairs, I started down. Halfway along the bend I stumbled, saving myself from a sickening fall by my convulsive grip on the railing. I sank down on the steps, mopping the cold perspiration that had broken out on my forehead. My other hand brushed against a length of something that felt like coarse string. My fingers followed the string to its end, where it was secured to a small screw in the wall. Slowly I moved my hand up and down on the facing wall, where I found another screw. The string that had tripped me had obviously been torn loose from this second screw by the impact of my fall. With a quick hard yank I pulled the string, and the screw to which it was attached, away from the wall and walked slowly up the stairs.

I examined the string in the bright natural light of the tower room. It was really a very thin rope, although exceptionally strong, and it had been stained black with a substance that might have been bootblacking. With the landing light extinguished, the rope hadn't been visible against the darkness of the stairs. I could easily have been killed, at the very least seriously injured.

With a deep, shuddering gasp, I threw myself into a chair, covering my eyes with my hands. The rope was real. I hadn't imagined it. Nor had I imagined Lorne's desperate cry to Flora last night that he would do *anything* to make her happy. The anything had included an attempt to make me fall to my death on the tower stairs, so that he could inherit Uncle Niall's money as my residuary legatee. He'd had to choose between killing me and losing control of Dungariff to the leasing combine. Was it much of a struggle? I wondered bitterly.

I'd been deluding myself these past few days, refusing to believe that Lorne had been responsible for my accidents. They weren't accidents, they were deliberate attempts to kill me. Only a few days ago, on the day of the ball, pretending to put out his hand to catch me, he'd allowed me to fall into the rock slide at Dunard Point; I'd extricated myself, no thanks to him. Looking back over my weeks at Dungariff, I could trace Lorne's trail to every dangerous incident that had happened to me—our sailing excursion; the drink of whisky and my becoming deathly ill; Jeannie's broken cinch strap. Why, he could have been the "castle cat" I'd observed moving around near the postern gate yesterday after the boulder had crashed down on me at the beach. Certainly I'd run into him shortly afterward at the stables, only a few steps away from the postern gate.

My thoughts slowed, began circling around. Yes, Lorne could have been responsible for the ugly doll, pierced with pins, that Meg had found in my wardrobe and the dead raven against my door. His was the only room in the family quarters that had access to the ramparts. But the doll and the dead bird hadn't placed me in any danger, they'd merely been an attempt to convince me I was being threatened by witchcraft, so why . . . ?

Now my blood ran cold. I remembered the Reverend Archibald's statement in the family history that Angus MacDougall had attempted to kill Catriona by the powers of witchcraft. I remembered, too, that Angus, despite his hatred for Catriona, hadn't been able to resist her sexual charms. So much for my secret, shameful belief—hope— that the physical attraction I had always felt between Lorne and me might eventually prove stronger than his attachment to Flora.

I had the terrifying sensation that my entire being was disintegrating. I couldn't force myself to think coherently. I was either losing my sanity or I had assumed Catriona's identity and I was proceeding inexorably to the same fate that had overtaken her. There was no other choice, no other explanation. And either way I would be destroyed.

I don't know how long I sat there, drifting deeper into despair. It must have been hours, because when Jane Henderson entered the room she was carrying a tray containing a teapot and a plate of scones. "Yer lamp is out, Miss Glenna. I'll see tae it at once," she said briskly. "Since ye didna come down tae breakfast, I ha' brought ye a bite—" She interrupted herself, staring at me in concern. "Are ye ill, Miss Glenna? Ye look bad."

Moved by a stubborn, obscure impulse to conceal the dark morass into which I had fallen, I shook my head. "I'm a little tired, that's all. I didn't sleep very well." As she continued to stare at me, clearly unconvinced by my denial, I added, snatching at the first thought that came to mind, "I heard the strangest sound last night. It made me shiver. It was some kind of bird, I suppose, but it sounded like a woman crying, as if her heart were broken. It seemed to come from the ramparts, right outside my door."

A startled look crossed Jane's face and disappeared.

"Did you hear it too, Jane?"

"Nay, Miss Glenna, not last nicht." She clamped her lips shut with the familiar expression that meant, yes, I know what you're talking about, but I don't want to discuss it.

"But you *have* heard it," I insisted, feeling vaguely comforted that at least this time I wasn't hallucinating. The disturbing cry hadn't existed solely in my imagination.

"Aye," she admitted after a long pause. "Juist the once, a lang time ago, it were." Her deep-set eyes seemed to bore into me. "I think ye maun be a sensitive. Ye be the first guest at Dungariff who ever has heard Catriona Mac-Dougall's cry of mourning."

My eyes widened in shock.

"Aye," she nodded. "The story goes that Catriona still walks the ramparts, unable tae find rest, a-crying for the bairn she never lived tae see grow up."

"That's silly," I said automatically. "There are no ghosts. I heard a sea bird."

But I didn't convince Jane, any more than I convinced myself. After she left, still looking troubled, I continued to wallow in my chaotic thoughts for a brief spell. Then, suddenly, Dr. Thomas MacColl's long solemn face flashed into my mind. If I were indeed going mad, only a doctor could confirm my fears. He might even be able to help me.

Reaching for a lingering remnant of the sturdy New England gumption on which I'd always prided myself, I vowed not to go down without a fight. I'd go to Oban to see Dr. MacColl.

Changing into one of my tailor-mades, I arranged my hair carefully in a low coil at the base of my neck and put on my hat. I crept down the turret stairs, willing myself not to think of the blackened rope that had caught my legs and caused me to fall. As I neared Ellen's sitting room I heard the murmur of voices. I didn't want to see or talk to anyone, but I knew I'd upset Ellen and Aunt Aillie if I went off without a word. I stepped into the room, where Ellen and Aunt Aillie and Flora were sitting together, busy with needlework.

"Come join us, Glenna," Ellen smiled. "We're embroidering antimacassars for the church festival."

"Later, maybe. I'm off to Oban to do some shopping."

Aunt Aillie said instantly, "Now, Glenna, I hope you're not going off by yourself on that horse again."

"No, I'll ask Donnie or Jock to take me in the gig. Is that all right, Cousin Ellen?"

"Of course, my dear. If you'd like one of us to go with you . . ."

"I'd be happy to come with you, Glenna," Flora interrupted. "I could tell you the best shops, not that we have anything to compare with the stores in Edinburgh or Glasgow. What did you have in mind to buy?"

But I was prepared for Flora. "Thank you, I think it would be better if I went alone. There's a certain birthday coming up . . ." I allowed my voice to trail away on a teasing note.

Flora simpered and blushed. "Oh. I see. Well, then, do enjoy yourself, Glenna."

Aunt Aillie sounded puzzled. "But Glenna, I thought—"

I headed her off, too. She knew I'd planned to give Flora

a silver bracelet I'd purchased in Edinburgh during our stay there. "I've changed my mind, Aunt Aillie. I have a much better idea," I said mysteriously.

Donnie was working alone in the stables when I entered. "I'd be happy tae drive ye to Oban, Miss Glenna," he said with a delighted grin on his young face at the thought of escaping from his duties for several hours. "It willna take me a minute tae hitch up the beastie."

Donnie was about to help me into the gig when Lorne cantered into the courtyard with Colin. As they dismounted they both looked at me in mild surprise.

"You planning to drive that gig, Glenna?" Colin inquired with a grin, as he and Lorne strolled over to me. "I had no idea Lorne had taught you how to drive, too. What a talented young lady."

"I'm not. Donnie's driving me. I'm going into Oban to buy Flora's birthday present."

"Oh." Lorne appeared startled. "Well, you shouldn't go alone. I'll drive you. That will be all, Donnie, thank you."

As he reached for my hand to help me mount, I involuntarily took a step backward. On the surface he was the same man I'd come to know so well, quiet, detached, undemonstrative, but with that glimmer of warmth behind his eyes whenever he looked at me. Now I knew that warmth had been an illusion. I was gazing into the face of a murderer, and I couldn't bear to have him near me.

I said coolly, "I wouldn't want to interfere with your work, Lorne. Donnie will take care of me very well."

Lorne tensed, his eyes narrowing at the sound of ice dripping from my voice. "Glenna, have I done—?" Breaking off, he said woodenly, "You're quite right. You don't need me. Donnie's an excellent driver. I hope you have a pleasant shopping trip." He turned away to lead his horse into the stables.

Colin's eyes followed Lorne's retreating back. He raised

an eyebrow. "Something wrong?"

"No, of course not."

"Look, Glenna, I'd be happy to go with you."

"You're on holiday. Oban's the last place you want to be. You'll be back at work there all too soon. Besides, I like to shop by myself."

"Well, if you're sure . . . Do you have something in mind to buy for Flora?"

"No, I thought I'd browse in the shops until I found something suitable."

Colin's eyes sparkled. "If you wouldn't mind a suggestion, I can tell you what Flora would really like. I mentioned it to Lorne not long ago, but he said it was too expens—" His face turning a deep red, Colin stammered, "Oh, Lord, I didn't mean—"

My heart went out to him. Dear Colin. Open and honest and kind. Everything his cousin Lorne wasn't.

"I know what you meant, and you're quite right," I told him. "I'm not strapped for money, as you well know, and I'd like to buy Flora what she really wants. What is it, and where will I find it?"

"You can't miss it. It's a gold watch set with diamonds, and it's sitting smack in the middle of the display case in John Sinclair's front window. John's shop is in George Street, that's parallel with the Esplanade." Colin laughed. "I wish I had a shilling for every time Flora's dragged me to that display window to have a look at the watch. She fairly covets the thing. You'd really make her happy, Glenna."

As Colin waved us off in the gig, I knew from the furtive glances Donnie kept darting at me that he sensed the strained atmosphere that had developed between Lorne and me. Donnie had seen us start out on our leisurely rides far too often not to realize something was wrong. Of course, his training and his intuitive good manners prevented him from saying anything.

I had the young groom drop me off on the Esplanade in Oban, arranging a rendezvous for several hours later. I didn't go directly to Dr. MacColl's office. Already I was wondering if I'd made the wrong decision in deciding to visit him. I spent some time strolling along the quay, trying for a glimpse of one of the spotted harbor seals, watching the Glasgow steamer edging into the North Pier, before I left the waterfront to window-shop in the little stores selling Scottish handicrafts and woolens.

I found John Sinclair's jewelry shop without difficulty. Its owner, a cheerful rotund little man, was overjoyed to sell me the watch prominently displayed in the front window. "I ha' had this piece for some time, Miss," he confided. "I ordered it all the way frae Edinburgh for a gentleman over in Appin, ane o' the Stewart family, and then his wife died, and Mr. Stewart ha' no use for it. Quite understandable, I'm sure, but still . . . I'm thinking ye'll enjoy wearing the watch. A beautiful piece."

"I won't be wearing it, Mr. Sinclair. It's a gift for a friend." Personally I considered the gold pendant watch, loaded with diamonds and fastened with a clasp in the shape of a bow, as garish as it was expensive, but I took a perverse pleasure in writing the jeweler a draft on my Boston bank. I was looking forward to seeing Lorne's face, if I lived long enough, that is, when he watched Flora unwrapping a gift he couldn't afford to give her.

As I was saying good-bye to Mr. Sinclair at the door of his shop, a voice behind me exclaimed in surprise, "Miss MacDougall?"

I turned, gazing politely at the man who had spoken to me, not immediately recognizing the impassive, rather joyless face of Flora's father. "Yes? Oh, it's you, Mr. Cameron. How are you?"

"Verra fine, thank ye. Ye've come tae Oban alone, Miss MacDougall?"

"Yes, I've just bought Flora's birthday gift, as a matter

of fact."

"Ach, that was kind o' ye." Mr. Cameron paused. "Now that ye're here, would ye care tae visit my store? 'Tis juist over the way in Stafford Street, near the pier."

"Why, yes, thank you," I said, unable to think of a good excuse to refuse the invitation. Also, I reminded myself, I could put off for a little longer my visit to Dr. MacColl.

Dutifully I inspected the contents of Mr. Cameron's ship chandler's store, which to my ignorant eyes seemed to contain every imaginable kind of ship's stores: ropes and canvas and caulking and carpenter's tools, winches and capstans and compasses. Glancing at the one clerk on the premises, I remarked, "I imagine you're a bit short-handed with Colin on holiday."

"Indeed. I miss Colin. He's a guid lad, hardworking, reliable. Ah . . . Miss MacDougall, would ye have a cup o' tea wi' us? Mrs. Cameron would be delighted tae see ye."

His dry voice held an odd note of embarrassment. Suddenly I wondered if something besides an urge to show me hospitality had prompted him to invite me to the shop. Again, I couldn't think of a polite way to decline.

Mrs. Cameron, appearing somewhat flustered, welcomed me into her drawing room, which was painfully neat, smelling of wax and pine oil. The furnishings looked brand-new, glistening with varnish, and probably came from the biggest furniture factory in the Midlands.

"You must be looking forward to Flora's wedding, Mrs. Cameron," I remarked, as she busied herself making the tea.

"Oh, aye. It will be a fine thing when the lass ha' her own home. That's the way it should be."

Poor Flora, I thought. Colin was right. Mrs. Cameron obviously saw her stepdaughter's marriage, not as a source of joy and fulfillment to Flora, but as a means of being permanently rid of her.

"It be a wonderful thing for the Laird and his mither,

having a kinswoman visit a' the way frae America," Mr. Cameron observed, sipping his tea. "Doubtless ye ha' lang talks wi' the Maister?"

"Yes, sometimes," I replied cautiously. I didn't think Flora's father was a man for making small talk. What was he up to?

"I spoke tae the Laird about Flora's settlements, her marriage contract, ye ken, when I attended the ball at Dungariff. He didna seem disposed tae talk o' it then. Weel, he had guests, forbye." Mr. Cameron continued with an air of casualness, "I wouldna like tae think the Maister ha' problems."

So that was it. Mr. Cameron had heard a rumor about Lorne's money difficulties and he was trying to pick my brains.

"Oh, I don't think you have to worry about my cousin," I said, rising. "Mr. MacDougall seems perfectly cheerful to me. Thank you for the tea, Mrs. Cameron. I'll see you at Flora's birthday dance."

Back on the street outside the ship chandler's shop, I couldn't invent another reason for delaying my visit to Dr. MacColl. A passing urchin gave me directions for finding the doctor's surgery.

There was no one in the small waiting room when I entered. I recalled that Dr. MacColl had said he'd opened his offices very recently. It would probably take a young doctor some time to build up his practice. I didn't have to wait long. Five minutes later he opened the door of his inner office to usher out a patient. When he spotted me in the waiting room he seemed pleased to see me, but not particularly surprised. It was almost as if he'd been expecting my arrival.

"Miss MacDougall! This is a pleasure. Please, come in and sit down." Eying me with concern from across his untidy desk, he said earnestly, "I can see you aren't feeling well. I'm sorry you felt you had to come all this distance to see me. If you'd sent me a message, I would have been happy to go out to Dungariff."

"Oh, but I'm not ill, Doctor," I replied hastily. "It's . . . I haven't been sleeping well lately because I've been . . . well, a little worried about some rather odd things that have been happening to me, and I recalled our talk about your studies in Paris, and so I thought—" I floundered to a stop, wishing I'd put more thought into what I wanted to say. I was suddenly sure I couldn't bring myself to tell Dr. MacColl everything.

He leaned back in his chair, watching me steadily. "You mentioned my studies in Paris. I take it, then, that you're not referring to . . . to problems of a physical nature?"

"I . . . no." Doggedly I plunged into a description of my continuing sense of familiarity with the Argyll landscape. "And on a number of occasions I've seen . . . I've thought I've seen . . ."

"Persons from another time, another place?" Dr. MacColl said calmly. "Bonnie Prince Charlie, for example?"

"Yes. How did you know about my foolish fancies?" I asked in astonishment.

"When I talked to you, after you fainted at the ball, I suspected you had experienced an incident of what is known as déjà vu. Now, some older physicians might dismiss this phenomenon as being outside the practice of medicine, but . . ." He shook his head. "Actually, I'm not at all sure we're talking about a medical matter, but I'm glad you came to me about it, Miss MacDougall. I can certainly assure you that you haven't been experiencing mere foolish fancies."

"Oh. What are they, then?"

"Well, I'd say that these happenings definitely fall within the field of psychic research."

I must have sounded as taken aback as I felt. "Psychic research? Do you mean the supernatural?"

"Indeed not, Miss MacDougall. We're living in a scientific age." The doctor sounded pained. Then his thin intent young face relaxed, and his voice took on a tinge of enthusiasm. "The word psychic simply means that events or happenings are of an inexplicable nature, beyond orthodox scientific explanation. Such happenings occur all the time, and it was to study them that the Society for Psychical Research was formed in London in 1882. I myself joined the Society in my undergraduate days." Warming to his subject, he went on, "As a matter of fact, it's really a little odd that you should be speaking to me about this subject, because only yesterday I received the latest journal of the Society, in which there was a long article about the déjà vu phenomenon."

He gazed at me with a look of such concentrated interest that momentarily I felt as if I were a laboratory specimen being examined under a microscope. "Tell me, Miss MacDougall, are these incidents of déjà vu all of recent occurrence?"

"Yes. I find it so puzzling that nothing like this ever happened to me before I came to Scotland. You've heard, I suppose, that I'm visiting Argyll because my uncle's will required me to live here for a year."

Doctor MacColl nodded. "Well, I think there's a very down-to-earth explanation for your episodes of déjà vu. I believe your father and your aunt, Mrs. Murray, both came from this area, did they not? Undoubtedly they talked to you about the places where they grew up, and when you arrived here, you simply recognized landmarks from their descriptions." He smiled at me. "There, you see, it's not such a great puzzle after all."

"You're mistaken, Doctor," I said sharply. "My father and Aunt Aillie never spoke to me about Argyll. They'd been so unhappy here that they deliberately buried all their memories of their past life when they went to America."

Dr. MacColl looked skeptical. "It doesn't take very much to trigger this sense of déjà vu. Perhaps it was only a few remarks you overheard, or you may have read about Scotland in a schoolbook."

"You're saying, then, that my experiences definitely aren't due to any psychic cause?"

"Please don't misunderstand me, I don't discount the psychic element out of hand. As a scientist, however, I must always look first for a natural explanation. But no, certainly I don't deny the possibility that you may be one of a small minority of people who has the faculty of extrasensory perception. Let us say, for the moment, that you may have been in touch with the phenomenon of retrocognition, which I understand is fairly common. Recently, for example, I studied a well-researched story about two respectable English ladies, who, while on a tour of Versailles, suddenly found themselves as guests at a garden party hosted by Queen Marie Antoinette. They didn't find the situation alarming or threatening in any way."

Dr. MacColl paused, looking at me closely. "That's why you came to see me, isn't it, Miss MacDougall? You *do* feel frightened, threatened. Is there something you haven't told me?"

I admitted reluctantly, "I've been having some very disturbing nightmares."

As I described my dreams, Dr. MacColl's interest seemed to deepen. When I finished, he said, "You remember our talk about Dr. Freud, the Viennese neurologist who's been studying the problems of the mind, the study they're now beginning to call psychiatry? Well, Dr. Freud has a theory that dreams are often a clue to a patient's underlying problems. He thinks that beneath the manifest content of the dream—what the dreamer actually remembers when he awakes—there is a latent content, which usually embodies a wish, often a repressed wish." Dr. MacColl smiled ruefully. "But don't let me get carried away with my enthusiasm for Dr. Freud's ideas. You tell me that your dream recurs in the identical form in which you first experienced it. That's most rare, to have an identical dream recur more than twice, at most."

"Does Dr. Freud believe that dreams foretell future events?" I asked, my throat tightening.

"No, not at all. Now, there are those in psychic research who claim that dreams are often premonitory, but Dr. Freud doesn't agree with them."

I said slowly, "So then, a more likely explanation for my nightmares is that I'm mentally disturbed, is that what you're saying?"

The doctor stared at me, aghast. "My dear Miss MacDougall, I never said that, I never meant to imply it. However, and please remember that I'm not a specialist, I would venture to suggest that, behind these frightening dreams of yours, something is very definitely troubling you."

I opened my mouth and closed it again. We were coming very close to my most deeply seated fears. But that part of my mind that was still functioning normally told me that the doctor could hardly help me if he didn't know what those fears were. Slowly, hesitantly, I told him everything, or almost everything. I described how, on two occasions, reality had seemed to merge with nightmare. Once, on the ramparts, the night I arrived at Dungariff. Again, on the night of the ball, when I'd seen Lorne change into a completely different person out of the past. And then, swallowing hard, I told him how uncannily Lorne and I resembled Angus and Catriona, and how my life since my arrival in Argyll seemed to parallel the story of my tragic ancestress. One thing I didn't say. I didn't accuse Lorne of trying to kill me.

As I finished my account, Dr. MacColl's look of eager interest had changed to one of incredulity. "You can't be suggesting . . . surely you can't believe . . . that you've been reincarnated as Catriona MacDougall?''

"You don't believe that's possible?"

"I do not," the doctor snapped. "Reincarnation is out of the question. No medical doctor, no scientist, could entertain the notion for a moment."

"I see," I said between stiff lips. "Then I go back to my only alternative. I'm going mad."

He reacted immediately, as if he'd been stung by some noxious insect. "No, no, no, that's sheer nonsense. Let me say categorically, you are not mad."

"Well, what then? You can't convince me that what's been happening to me is quite normal, ordinary, run-of-the-mill."

"Admittedly, there are those who would interpret your experiences entirely in psychic terms."

"You mean, some people would consider me crazy."

"Please, Miss MacDougall." Dr. MacColl leaned back in his chair, his hands folded together, obviously picking his words with great care. "In my opinion, you're being troubled by memories from your childhood that are now surfacing. According to Dr. Freud, so many things are buried in our memories. Now, you say that Argyll was never mentioned in your home in America, that you have no memory of ever hearing about Scotland until you learned about your uncle's will. I say you might easily have overheard a conversation between your elders when you were a very small child, perhaps they thought you were safely tucked into your bed! Or you may have read a short description of Scotland in your school geography book. You aren't going to insist, I hope, that school-children remember everything!"

He chuckled at his own pleasantry and relaxed, as if he believed he'd covered all aspects of my case satisfactorily. He went on, "As for your nightmares, and your feelings of anxiety occasioned by what you conceive to be parallels between your life and that of the other unhappy lady—

Catriona, was that her name?—well, you seem to me to be an extremely sensitive and imaginative person, and you've recently made a drastic change in your way of living. Under the circumstances, it's quite natural that you should react strongly to the atmosphere and to the family traditions you've encountered here. Take the ball at Dungariff: you may simply have been nervous at the thought of being on display before so many strangers. For I assure you, Miss MacDougall, you've been the object of much curiosity in these parts from the moment you arrived here!"

Slumping back in my chair, I said dully, "What you're saying is that I've simply been the victim of an overly vivid imagination."

"Come now, don't put words in my mouth," the doctor objected. "Believe me, I'm not trying to make light of your experiences. However, I do think you should try to be more relaxed, try to keep your mind away from these nightmares and other anxieties. Do that, and take the light sedative I'm going to give you to help you sleep, and I feel sure that soon, you'll see an improvement in your state of mind."

On the drive back to Dungariff, I sat huddled beside Donnie in the gig, lost in a silent, bleak despair. It had been a mistake to go to Dr. MacColl. Oh, he'd assured me I wasn't losing my mind, but I wondered if his opinion would have been the same if I'd told him I thought Lorne was trying to kill me. Did I have any certainty that the doctor had told me what he really believed? Perhaps he was trying to keep the seriousness of my mental condition from me, hoping his reassurances would have a calming effect. At the very least, he obviously considered me a flighty girl obsessed with trivial fears.

I knew his sedatives wouldn't help me. Perhaps nothing could help me. If I wasn't losing my mind, there was only one alternative. I was being stalked by a merciless man who meant to kill me.

Chapter 12

I saw Dr. MacColl on a Thursday. As I lived through the next few days, I had no inkling that my ordeal was coming to a climax. All I knew was that the coils of terror and menace seemed to be closing more inexorably around me, with no end in sight.

I spent Thursday night in my tower room, reading and rereading Reverend Archibald's account of Angus and Catriona until I knew those crabbed, scandalized sentences by heart. By morning I'd come to a decision. I had to leave Dungariff as soon as possible. It might prove useless. If I were really losing my mind, or if indeed I were undergoing a kind of reincarnation, then moving to another place would be no solution. Away from the castle, however, even living in some other locality in Argyll, as I was bound to do according to the terms of Uncle Niall's will, I would at least be out of Lorne's physical reach. It was all I could do to help myself.

The next morning I didn't go down to breakfast, hoping to avoid seeing Lorne. My delaying tactic didn't work. Shortly after nine o'clock, coming down the turret stairs, I ran into him in the circular area at the foot of the staircase.

"Oh, there you are, Glenna," he exclaimed. "I was coming up to tell you about this. Go ahead, read it. It came a few minutes ago."

My fingers brushed Lorne's as I accepted the letter he was holding out to me. Why, I thought despairingly, did I still feel that frisson of excitement when he touched me, now that I knew who he really was and what he was capable of?

The letter was headed by the MacDougall crest. "My dear Ellen," it read. "Alastair and I would be delighted to see you and your family at Dunollie House this afternoon to take tea with us. We are especially looking forward to renewing our acquaintance with Mrs. Murray and her niece, and, of course, to seeing Miss Cameron again. Affectionately your friend, Margaret MacDougall."

"Mother and I thought you'd be pleased by the invitation. It was obvious to us that the Chief and his wife were very taken with you." Lorne added with a wry smile, "Flora's excited about her first visit to Dunollie House. She's having a dreadful time trying to decide what to wear."

"I'm sure she'll look lovely whatever she wears." I handed the note back to Lorne, saying, "Thank you for showing me this," and made a move to edge past him.

Lorne put his hand on my arm. "Glenna, wait a moment. I'd like to talk to you about yesterday—"

I shook off his hand as if it were a burning coal. The words poured out of me before I could stop them, "Don't touch me."

His eyes widened in shock. "Glenna, what is this? What's happened between us? Why are you so angry with me?"

I took a deep breath. I couldn't give myself away like this. "I'm not angry. I'm in a hurry this morning, that's all."

"I see." It was clear he didn't. "Well, I'll only keep you a minute."

"I can't talk now, Lorne," I interrupted him. "I told you

I'm in a hurry. I have to talk to Aunt Aillie."

"But . . . can't it wait a moment?"

"No." I pressed past him, practically forcing him against one wall of the narrow space. "Please excuse me, Lorne. We'll talk later."

No, we won't, I resolved, as I walked away from him down the corridor. I felt even more strongly that I'd made the right decision to leave the castle. Lorne knew that something had happened to mar our relationship, and he was bent on restoring our old footing. To lull me into a sense of false security, I presumed, making it easier for him to make his next move against me. It would be difficult to keep avoiding him as long as I remained at Dungariff. Not that my physical danger existed only in Lorne's presence. He'd proved very ingenious about arranging accidents that took place when he was far from the scene.

I found Aunt Aillie in Ellen's sitting room, embroidering still another antimacassar. She looked up with a smile. "So you decided to get up at last, sleepyhead. Pick up that embroidery hoop and get to work."

As I began pushing my needle through the fabric, I tried to think of the best way to broach the subject of leaving Dungariff. I'd rushed downstairs intending to confront Aunt Aillie with my decision to leave, but within moments of sitting down with her, I realized I'd have to tread very cautiously. I couldn't tell her my real reason for wanting to go away. She'd been concerned about my mental health for weeks now. If I told her Lorne was trying to kill me, she wouldn't believe me. Her worst fears would be confirmed. She'd have me heading straight for Bedlam. Even if, by some miracle, I managed to convince her of my physical danger, what excuse could we give for leaving the castle so abruptly? An excuse that wouldn't hurt Ellen's feelings, that wouldn't arouse endless speculation on the part of Colin and Flora? I'd grown very fond of Ellen, and I was prepared to go to great lengths to prevent her from finding out what kind of man her only son had turned out to be.

"Glenna!"

I jumped at my aunt's exasperated tone.

"Sakes alive, Glenna, I've spoken to you three times without getting an answer. You were off wool-gathering somewhere."

"Sorry, Aunt Aillie. What were you saying?"

"Nothing important, I guess. I was saying that it was flattering to be invited to Dunollie. Ellen says the Chief and his wife don't socialize much except at large formal gatherings. Lord, my poor mother must be turning over in her grave at the thought of her daughter and her granddaughter taking tea with the Chief of the Mac-Dougalls!"

"Yes, it was nice of Mrs. MacDougall to invite us." I couldn't summon the enthusiasm Aunt Aillie seemed to expect. At the beginning of our stay at Dungariff, I would have been wildly excited at the thought of visiting Dunollie House, but now all I could think of was that I would be forced into Lorne's company for most of the afternoon. Granted, there was safety in numbers. I wouldn't have to be alone with him.

"That was quite a present you bought for Flora," Aunt Aillie observed. "A little ostentatious for my taste, though. Expensive, too, I'll be bound."

"According to Colin it was what Flora wanted. As for the expense, I'm rich now, remember? I don't have to count the cost."

Aunt Aillie looked up from her embroidery to peer at me thoughtfully. I'd forgotten how sharp she was. She'd caught the note of cynicism in my voice. But she said merely, "I'm all for keeping our Flora happy. Matter of fact, I contributed to the cause this morning. I sent a note to Mr. and Mrs. Cameron asking them to join us for the luncheon party I'm giving in Flora's honor tomorrow."

"They won't come, you know. It would please Flora immensely if they did come, but Mr. Cameron would never leave his store in the charge of a single clerk on a busy Saturday."

"We'll see. I must say, Glenna, I've been pleasantly surprised at how smoothly this last week has gone, with Flora here permanently. Not a tantrum, not a trace of jealousy. Maybe she's convinced finally that you're not trying to steal her fiance."

"I should hope so. Nothing could be farther from the truth," I blurted. I went on, searching for words, "Aunt Aillie, I need to talk to you about something important."

"Here, you two, get yourselves into these things quickly. We have work to do," came Ellen's laughing voice from the doorway.

Aunt Aillie and I stared at the voluminous aprons and the rather ancient straw hats and rough gloves Ellen was holding out to us.

"I'm playing Simon what's his name. You know, the nasty slave driver in your American story," she explained. "I've decided it's time to tidy the family cemetery." She raised an eyebrow at my questioning expression. "You look dubious, Glenna. Surely you don't neglect your family plots in America."

"Very few people in America have private family plots. We certainly didn't," Aunt Aillie said tartly. "What did you have in mind, Ellen?"

"Nothing earthshaking. Just what I do every spring. Pull up the weeds, remove the dead leaves, trim back the shrubbery. It should have been done weeks ago, but I've been a little distracted by very welcome guests from America! I could ask the gardener to do it, I suppose, but he has enough on his hands at this time of year with his other duties, and besides," Ellen smiled self-consciously, "I like to think that all those long-gone MacDougalls appreciate having their last resting places taken care of by their family."

"I'm sure they do, Cousin Ellen," I said, jumping up from my chair. "I'd love to help."

"Good. Flora and Colin are waiting for us in the courtyard with the rakes and trowels."

So was Lorne, to his mother's surprise. "I thought you were going to see Jock MacCabe about the Fort William field trials," she said.

"I'll see Jock tomorrow. I decided I should help out with tidying the family plot. All those years I was at sea, you did it alone, Mother."

Ellen looked pleased at this evidence of filial concern. However, I soon began to suspect that Lorne had another reason for wanting to come with us. As we filed out of the courtyard and turned into the narrow path leading off the main approach to the castle, he fell into step beside me, chatting pleasantly, as if he didn't have a care in the world, but I knew it would be only a matter of time before he tried to maneuver me away for a more private talk.

The MacDougall family cemetery was situated on a low bluff overlooking the sea. It was surrounded by a stone wall, flanked by a line of wind-torn fir trees on the seaward side. In the middle of the enclosed area was an ancient stone chapel, roofless and windowless and doorless. Only the sturdy old walls were still standing.

"The chapel dates from the fourteenth century," Lorne told me as we approached it. "It was in use as a place of worship until the Covenant wars in the seventeenth century, when a lucky shot from a Campbell artillery piece destroyed it. About a hundred years ago the family began to inter the Lairds and their ladies in the ground inside the chapel."

Entering the chapel through the ruined archway, we found Ellen already on her knees before one of the graves, attacking the creeping weeds growing in the crevices beside the slab. A vase held the spray of flowers she'd brought with her. "My father," Lorne murmured. I moved closer to study the simple inscription: "Lachlan Boyd MacDougall, Laird of Dungariff, 1839-1896."

"Mother, we'll leave the chapel to you," Lorne said. He handed me a rake. "Come with me, Glenna. We'll get to work on the graves outside."

"Oh, I think I'll stay here with Cousin Ellen," I replied pleasantly. "You don't need me out there. You have Colin and Flora and Aunt Aillie."

He looked at me with a faintly baffled expression, as if he weren't quite sure my refusal was deliberate. He shrugged. "Whatever you like, of course. Mother and I certainly have no intention of turning you into a hired hand!"

Ellen gazed after him as he went through the archway. "He doesn't like to come into the chapel," she said sadly. "It's as if his father's spirit were hovering about the place, and he's afraid to be near Lachlan's grave for fear they'd start quarreling again. I'm surprised he came with us today."

We worked, Ellen and I in the chapel, the others in the cemetery outside, for most of the morning. Afterwards, as we stood, grimy and tired, surveying with satisfaction the mound of branches and weeds and dry leaves we'd heaped up beside the gate, Flora exclaimed, "Look over there. Isn't that another grave outside the wall?"

Lorne and his mother exchanged embarrassed glances. At last Ellen said, "Angus MacDougall is buried there. Your direct ancestor, Glenna."

"But why wasn't he buried in here, with the other members of the family?" I inquired, puzzled. "Was it because he was hanged as a traitor and it was felt he'd disgraced the clan? And where's his wife, Catriona?"

Ellen answered my second question first. "Catriona was a MacLean. She's buried on Mull. As for Angus—" She spread her hands helplessly. "I've gathered you don't know a great deal about the history of your branch of the family, Glenna. Angus wasn't only a traitor. He . . . he did some terrible things."

"Oh, what difference does it make, Glenna?" Aunt Aillie interrupted. "You don't want to know about those old scandals. Whatever the reason Angus wasn't buried in the family plot, it's nothing to do with Lorne and Ellen. Let's get back to the castle. I'm famished."

"In a minute. Cousin Ellen, if you don't mind I'd like to take a look at the grave."

I walked out of the gate and across the rough turf, my steps gradually slowing as I began to feel a sickening reluctance to approach the low mound with its simple headstone. I stood looking down at the grave, my inexplicable sense of dread growing. The mound appeared very peaceful, very ordinary. The grass around it was neatly cropped—sheep had been grazing in the vicinity lately—and the mound was covered thickly with heather.

I didn't realize Ellen was standing beside me until I heard her voice saying urgently, "Lorne, come here. Look at Angus's grave."

When Lorne came up to us with his long, ground-covering stride, he took a quick, incredulous look at the mound and muttered, "My God. I can't believe it."

"What is it?" I asked, looking from one bemused, vaguely perturbed face to the other. "Is something wrong?"

"No. No. Not really. It's—" Ellen spread her hands. "You've visited the battlefield of Culloden, Glenna. Were you told the story that heather has never grown over the clansmen's grave? Well, the heather has never grown over Angus's grave, either, not for a hundred and fifty years. Not until now."

I stared down at the scalelike, overlapping leaves of the ordinary-looking little plant, and my flesh began to crawl. Perhaps the heather was growing now over the grave because the spirit of Angus MacDougall no longer had any involvement with the moldering bones that rested here. The heather was growing again because Angus's spirit had moved on to a living man's strong and vital body. The body of the man standing beside me.

Choking back the sour taste of fear, I tried to dismiss the evil fancy. "There must be some simple explanation for this little mystery," I said weakly. "Maybe it has something to do with the weather. All of you keep telling me we're having unusually fair weather this year."

"Of course. Why didn't we think of that, Lorne?" Ellen took up my silly suggestion with an air of relief.

Lorne shot me a keen glance. Did he realize how shaken I felt? But all he said was, "It's only a legend, Mother. The explanation may well be that there's something about the soil at Culloden that inhibits the growth of heather."

"But that wouldn't explain why Angus's grave—" Ellen took hold of herself, saying briskly, "Well, enough of that. Now, then, we've done a good morning's work and we should be getting home. We've barely time enough to have lunch and dress for tea at Dunollie House."

During lunch I managed to act normally enough, but later, while I was dressing for our engagement with the Chief, I renewed my determination to speak to Aunt Aillie at my earliest opportunity about leaving Dungariff. Here at the castle, I was not only facing a physical danger from Lorne but I ran the risk of encountering, everywhere I turned, something that would trigger another of those malignant dark thoughts that led to madness. Today it had been Angus's grave and the heather that shouldn't have been growing on it.

More to keep my thoughts at bay than from any real interest in my appearance, I dressed carefully for our visit to Dunollie. I wore Aunt Aillie's pearls with a pale pink silk dress made with long tight sleeves and the new sun-ray, accordion-pleated skirt, and I topped my ensemble with a large straw hat trimmed with lace aigrettes and flowers. Flora, it turned out, went to even greater lengths. She must have changed her clothes half a dozen times before Ellen dragged her away from her mirror, still protesting that she wasn't ready.

"Flora, I don't know what you're concerned about, you look beautiful," Colin reassured her as he handed her into the landau.

Flora looked down at her lacy blouse worn with a tiny bolero and deeply flared skirt. "What do you think, Glenna? Do I look all right?" she asked anxiously.

"Colin's quite right. You look lovely," I said truthfully. Beneath the jaunty little toque trimmed with feathers, her normally pallid face had a blush and a glow that animated her features into real beauty.

"I hope so," she murmured. "This visit is so important, my first time at Dunollie House. After Lorne and I are married, I expect we'll be entertaining the Chief often."

We drove to Oban and along the curve of the bay sweeping north of the town. Beneath the ruins of Dunollie Castle, surmounting the prow of a small headland, was the modern residence of the Chief of Clan MacDougall.

The Chief and his wife received us with such cordiality into their comfortable but hardly imposing mansion that Aunt Aillie appeared visibly impressed. I suspected she was thinking of the old sad days when she and my father and Uncle Niall were the family poor relations. Margaret MacDougall put Flora at her ease almost immediately by complimenting her on her costume. We were soon seated in the drawing room, consuming a lavish tea.

"Your house is so beautiful, Mrs. MacDougall," Flora observed, sipping her second cup of tea. "Sometimes, when I think of living at Dungariff, I almost have the feeling that I'll be keeping house in a museum!" She flashed Ellen an arch smile. "But there, Lorne and Mother MacDougall *like* living in a museum, so there's nothing more to be said about it."

Glancing at Lorne and Ellen, who kept their faces carefully wooden, Margaret MacDougall diplomatically changed the subject. "If you'd like to see the rest of the house a little later, Miss Cameron, I'd be delighted to give you a tour. But first, Alastair wants to redeem his promise to show Miss MacDougall the family treasure." She added, her eyes twinkling, "Alastair and I like to think we ourselves are the reason why people like to visit us at Dunollie, but in our secret hearts we know we take second place to the Brooch of Lorn."

We all trooped into the library, where the Chief stood aside to allow me an unimpeded view of the object in the glass case. It was a large brooch of heavy gold, intricately chased and set with precious stones, not outstandingly beautiful as a piece of jewelry, perhaps, but giving off, to my vivid imagination, at least, an almost palpable aura of power and violence.

"Lorne told me the Brooch once belonged to King Robert Bruce," I remarked, looking up from the case. "How did it come into MacDougall hands?"

The Chief smiled broadly. "The MacDougall of Bruce's time—Lame John, he was called—caught up with the King in a skirmish in 1306. The Bruce managed to escape, but not before one of Lame John's followers snatched away the brooch that pinned the King's plaid to his shoulder. Our clan treasured the brooch for over three hundred years, until it was stolen by the Campbells when they captured Gylen Castle in 1647. It was restored to us in 1826. It turned up in a sale room, believe it or not."

"It wouldn't be a bad idea if the Campbells restored a few more of the MacDougall possessions," Colin remarked with a laugh. "Think what a wealthy clan we'd be today, if we still owned all of Lorn."

"To do that we'd have had to win all our battles instead of losing most of them," Lorne retorted. He spoke jokingly, but I caught the undercurrent of bitter anger I'd heard so often in his voice recently.

Although he hadn't tried to speak to me during the drive to Dunollie or while we were taking tea in the drawing room, I'd been very much aware of his straight, intent gaze. I shivered. He was biding his time until he could get me alone.

"Oh, I think you're a little hard on us, Lorne," the Chief smiled.

His wife spoke up briskly. "Well, now, if you've all seen enough of our precious heirloom, I'm going to show Miss Cameron the rest of the house."

"And I'm taking Miss MacDougall to see the ruins of Dunollie Castle," the Chief replied promptly. "Anyone else who cares to come along is welcome."

"Not me, thanks," Colin grinned. "Lorne and I explored those ruins years ago. I broke my ankle, matter of fact, climbing the walls of the keep."

"Thank you, Mr. MacDougall," Aunt Aillie said. "If you don't mind, I'd rather see your house."

In the end, the Chief and I and Lorne were the only ones to climb to the ruins looming above the house. We prowled around the enormous old keep, which the Chief explained dated from at least the twelfth century. "Though we have some evidence that it was built over an earlier fortification sacked by the Irish in the seventh century." As I stood talking to the Chief outside the entrance to the keep, Lorne wandered away a short distance to poke about in the ivy-covered fragments of several much smaller outbuildings.

Alastair MacDougall paused, watching Lorne. "Do you know, much as I love this estate, I often think that Lorne should have been the MacDougall of MacDougall," he said musingly. "The clan heritage means far more to him than to most of us. When he was a lad, he seemed to have the uncanny ability to attune himself with the past. He

215

used to come here often—as you probably know, Dunollie Castle has always been the principal seat of the clan—to play at reliving the days of glory when our ancestor Dugald was recognized as King of Lorn." The Chief's face grew troubled. "I've heard rumors . . . I hope they aren't true . . . I think Lorne would sicken and die if he lost Dungariff."

So he might, I thought. But before he reached that point, Lorne would fight savagely to keep Dungariff, using any means, fair or foul. Including murder.

The Chief cleared his throat, probably realizing he had said too much. "Lorne," he called. "I think Miss MacDougall might like to see the remains of the old moat across the isthmus."

Lorne rejoined us, saying, "That's a good idea, sir. Glenna, I think you'll find it interesting, even though the outworks and drawbridge have disappeared. You'll have a much better idea of how these fortifications were defended."

We started the descent, with the Chief saying jocularly, "You've a strong young arm, Lorne. You make sure Miss MacDougall doesn't slip."

Lorne put a supporting hand on my arm, and at the touch of his strong slender fingers a skittering of fiery arrows shot through my bloodstream, succeeded a fraction of a second later by the chill of revulsion. I pulled away from him. "I can manage, Lorne, thank you. I'm quite surefooted." I couldn't resist adding, "Remember that day at Dunard Point, when I fell into the rock slide? I didn't need your help to extricate myself."

He looked at me sharply. Had he caught the hidden barb in what I'd said? I would have to watch myself. I couldn't let him know I was on my guard.

As we approached the end of the descent, one of the Dunollie servants came running up to us. "Maister," he called to the Chief, "could I ha' a word wi' ye?"

After a brief conversation with the servant, the Chief turned back to us. "I must ask you to excuse me. A crisis in the stables. My favorite mare is foaling, and I fear she's having a difficult time. Lorne, do take Miss MacDougall down to the moat. You don't need me to find it."

I thought I detected a flicker of satisfaction in Lorne's face as he replied, "Of course, sir. I hope your mare will be all right. It's Chloe, isn't it? A beautiful animal. Come on, Glenna. The moat's not far from here."

"I believe I'll wait to see the moat another day, Lorne. I'm a little tired. Mr. MacDougall, I'll walk back as far as the house with you."

I didn't even glance at Lorne to check his reaction as I fell into step with the Chief. I was sure he must feel thwarted. Not only had I wriggled out of the private talk he'd been angling for since yesterday. I'd certainly prevented him from staging an attempt to get rid of me down on the shore. He knew I couldn't swim. For his fertile mind it would have been a simple matter to arrange an accidental drowning.

On the return drive to Dungariff, Flora was so talkative that no one, not even Aunt Aillie, noticed I wasn't saying much. Apparently Flora had been thrilled to the tips of her toes by her reception at Dunollie. "The Chief's wife gave me a list of the best shops in Edinburgh," she said excitedly. "And she especially recommended her favorite modiste, and said she'd write to the woman about my requirements before I go to Edinburgh to buy my trousseau. And guess what, Mother MacDougall? I invited the Chief and his wife to my birthday ball and they accepted!"

"Oh . . . how kind of them. It's such short notice . . ." Ellen hesitated. "You did tell Mrs. MacDougall, didn't you, Flora, that your birthday dance will be a very small affair? Otherwise, they might wonder why we hadn't invited them in the first place."

"Oh, that's all right. The Chief and his wife aren't the least bit snobbish," Flora said blithely.

Colin edged his horse closer to the landau. "I'll wager you don't remember what date it is, Aunt Ellen."

"The date? Why, it's the twenty-third! Oh, Lord. Colin, I *had* forgotten."

"I didn't remember it, either, not until the Chief mentioned the preparations for the estate bonfire as we were leaving."

"What's so significant about the twenty-third?" inquired Aunt Aillie. "And what's this about bonfires? Good heavens! It's the Eve of Saint John. Midsummer's Eve. I hadn't thought of it in years. We didn't make anything of it in New England, Glenna, but here, when I was a girl, Midsummer's Eve was the most exciting night of the year."

"It still is to many of us, the children especially, and the young people," Ellen said indulgently.

"What happens, precisely?" I asked her.

"Oh, the main thing is the village bonfire. The children play games around it, and I'm afraid there's often a little too much liquid refreshment. Pastor Munro doesn't really approve of the festivities. He says the Eve of Saint John is a corruption of ancient pagan ceremonies organized around the summer solstice. He makes no effort to abolish the celebration, though. It's been going on for too long, many centuries, I'm sure. At any rate, the villagers expect the Laird to appear at some time during the evening. Lorne and I will do our duty, but there's no reason for the rest of you to go."

"No, you don't, Aunt Ellen," Colin exclaimed. "You're not depriving me of one of life's great pleasures. Lorne and I used to look forward to the village bonfire all year. Glenna, Aunt Aillie, I'm sure you wouldn't want to miss it." He leaned over in his saddle to pat Flora's shoulder. "I'm counting on you, too."

Flora's eyes sparkled. "Lorne," she called. "Colin's just reminded us of the Midsummer's Eve bonfire. I'd love to go. I've never been at the castle on the Eve of Saint John."

Lorne had been riding ahead of the landau, apparently lost in his own brooding thoughts. He looked back when Flora called him, his expression faintly bemused. After a moment he said, "Fine, if you'd like it, Flora."

"Aunt Aillie, Glenna? We haven't heard from you yet," Colin said with a cheerful grin.

"Well . . ." Aunt Aillie hesitated, looking slightly self-conscious. "I guess I wouldn't mind attending the celebration for a bit."

I smiled. "Make that two of us, Colin."

"That's settled, then," Ellen said. "We'll all go. If it's agreeable to the rest of you, we won't start until it's full dark. Yesterday was the longest day of the year, remember."

Our plans to take part in the Midsummer's Eve celebration seemed to increase Flora's high spirits. I suppose it was natural for her to feel exhilarated, a little giddy. This afternoon she'd made a social call that was obviously very important to her, and tomorrow she would be the center of attention for the entire day, beginning with Aunt Aillie's luncheon in her honor on the island of Seil and ending with her birthday dance in the evening. If Colin was right, and she'd felt overlooked in her father's home since his remarriage, this weekend should make it up to her with a vengeance.

Watching her at dinner, however, laughing, voluble, teasing and playful to Lorne, I did wonder if her behavior wasn't too frenetic. She was so unlike her usual colorless self. She appeared overly stimulated, caught up in a mood of euphoria. If the pendulum should swing too far the other way . . .

After we finished eating, Flora vetoed the concept of sitting quietly in the drawing room over our coffee until it was time to go to the village. "Let's do something interesting," she exclaimed. "We could dance, or . . . no, I have it. We'll play a game of charades. We haven't done that in ages."

Without pausing to inquire if her suggestion was agreeable to the rest of us, she proceeded to organize the game. "Mother MacDougall, you're a shark for word games, so I think we'll draw lots for team members," she decided. "That would be more fair. Here—" She darted over to the secretary in the corner, tore a page of note paper in small pieces, scribbled briefly on a number of them, and folded each one over. She came back with the bits of paper on a small tray, extending it to each of us in turn. "Those of you who pick the three numbered slips will form one team."

I don't think she was best pleased at the result of her little lottery—Colin and Lorne and I ended up with the numbered slips—but her gaiety seemed unaffected. "All right, Lorne, we'll let you go first," she giggled. "Take your team over there by the fireplace and decide what words you'll act out. I think it would be fun to do titles of famous poems, don't you?"

After a lukewarm start—Lorne seemed disinclined to participate and I couldn't summon up much enthusiasm, either—the game of charades turned out to be surprisingly enjoyable.

For our team's first turn, I stood facing Lorne and Colin, gazing soulfully into their eyes while they pantomined drinking from a glass. At the end Colin pressed his fingers to his lips and then into his imaginary glass before gravely handing the pretense glass to me.

"A kiss? Wine?" Ellen repeated doubtfully. "I can't think of any poems with those things in the title."

"How about that Persian fellow? Omar something . . . the one who wrote about a loaf of bread, a jug of wine . . . no, that's not it. Do it over again," ordered Aunt

Aillie, whose face, I noted with amusement, was beginning to glow with interest.

"I know," Flora said suddenly, after we did a repeat performance. "I taught that poem to the children last term: 'Drink to me only with thine eyes, And I will pledge with mine; Or leave a kiss but in the cup, And I'll not look for wine.' *To Celia*. Ben Jonson."

"That was right clever," Aunt Aillie said admiringly.

"Clever it might have been, but it wasn't fair," Ellen retorted. "You're supposed to act out the *title* of the poem, not the first few lines. You can't break the rules like that."

Colin chuckled. "Flora was right, Aunt Ellen. You're a real Tartar at charades. We promise not to do it again."

In their first effort, Flora's team succeeded in mystifying Colin and Lorne and me for a short while, until I detected a gleam of mischief in Aunt Aillie's eyes.

"We're on the wrong track," I murmured to Colin. "We've been thinking English poetry. I have an idea. Let's ask them to do it over."

The skit began with Flora and Ellen having a mute conversation. Then Flora walked over to Aunt Aillie and plumped down on her knees in front of her. Aillie shook her head sadly and Flora, returning to Ellen, spread her hands in a gesture of frustration.

"Flora, you make a wonderful John Alden," I observed.

She collapsed in helpless laughter. "Mrs. Murray said you'd never guess *The Courtship of Miles Standish*," she gasped. "She said you'd be expecting Shakespeare, or Tennyson. Someone British."

As a matter of fact, the game did end with Tennyson. Flora stood watching in mock adoration as Ellen paraded gravely in front of her, completely ignoring her. Then Flora lay down on the carpet, her eyes closed, her hands folded together prayerfully on her breast, while Aunt Aillie sat beside her making rowing motions.

"They're on a boat," I said tentatively. "Is Flora sup-

221

posed to be dead or is she asleep?"

I got up from my chair, pacing up and down in an effort to get my creative juices flowing. That was how I happened to see Jane Henderson enter the drawing room and leave it precipitously a moment later.

"Excuse me. I'll be right back," I murmured. I walked into the passage, finding Jane leaning against the wall. Her face was pasty white and she was barely conscious, trying feebly to stay upright. I put my arm around her, saying softly, "Let me help you to your bedchamber, Jane. You're ill."

The sound of my voice seemed to galvanize the housekeeper. She struggled to release herself. "Thank ye, Miss Glenna. Ye needna concern yersel'. I'm not sick. 'Twas the lassie, Miss Flora. I saw her flat on the floor wi' her eyes closed and not moving so much as a finger, and it gave me a turn."

I studied her bony face. Her color was better but she still looked shaken. "You saw a fetch," I said slowly.

She stared past me, avoiding my eyes.

"Jane, I'm positive you had an episode of the second sight. Why won't you tell me about it?" I caught my breath. "Was it something about *me?* Did you see danger ahead for me?"

Straightening her gaunt frame, Jane wearily brushed a damp strand of hair away from her forehead. "Nay, Miss Glenna. If I saw anything, it had naught tae do wi' ye," she said heavily. Turning to go, she added, "Would ye juist tell the mistress that Donnie has brought the carriage around? 'Tis time tae gae tae the village."

I don't believe you, Jane, I thought, as I watched her go down the passage. Of all the people in the castle, you'd be most sensitive to the miasma of doubt and fear and uncertainty that was engulfing me. You saw another fetch, and you lied when you said it had nothing to do with me.

I walked slowly back into the drawing room, feeling

drained and blank and unable to respond to the burst of hilarity that met my ears.

Pulling a laughing Flora to her feet, Colin turned his head at my entrance, crowing, "Lorne solved the riddle without your help, Glenna. Flora's team was acting out *Lancelot and Elaine*. Remember how they put poor dead Elaine on a barge with a lily in her hand and rowed her down the river to King Arthur's palace? If only they'd cheated a bit and put a flower of some kind in Flora's hand, I'd have guessed the answer sooner."

"There you go, making excuses, Colin," Flora teased. "Lorne knew we were acting out Sir Lancelot and his love because he's a true knight at heart himself." She darted off across the room to a chest that held a large bowl of Ellen's yellow hybrid tea roses. Pulling out one of the blossoms, she walked back to Lorne, exclaiming in a theatrically exaggerated voice, "Sir Lorne, I choose you as my gentle parfait knight. Receive you the guerdon of my favor." She drew the rose through his buttonhole with a triumphant flourish.

I was watching Lorne's face as Flora went through her performance. If he was embarrassed, he didn't show it, although I saw Ellen bite her lip and Aunt Aillie looked as if she'd swallowed something unpleasant. Lorne put his arm around Flora's shoulders, saying quietly, "Thank you. It's an apt favor. Your name means flower."

Ellen glanced at the clock on the mantel. "It's time to go."

"I forgot to tell you, Cousin Ellen," I said quickly. "Jane was here a moment ago to tell you the landau is waiting."

The long northern twilight was merging into a velvety dusk as we drove toward the village of Finlay. We could see a glow in the sky even before we reached the outskirts. Leaving the carriage on the narrow village street, we walked down to the shore, guided by the flames of an enormous bonfire. Some of the adult villagers came up to greet Lorne and his mother respectfully, while their children, who should long since have been in bed, chased each other around the fire, screeching boisterously. Many of the young people were dancing a reel to the music of a pair of energetic fiddlers.

Colin disappeared briefly when we first arrived. He emerged from the shadows of the dunes a little later, wiping his mouth with a handkerchief. "Had to sample that liquid refreshment Aunt Ellen was telling you about. The lads have a handy keg back there, far enough from the fire to be out of the way of disapproving teetotalers," he said jauntily. He grabbed my hand. "They're striking up a strathspey, Glenna. Let's show the villagers how well an American can dance."

Within minutes I discovered that the spirit of revelry on the shore was contagious. My cares and doubts floated away for a while at least as Colin and I raced through the strathspey and several reels. "I've got to catch my breath, Colin," I gasped after the third reel. We stood on the sidelines in the semidarkness watching the other dancers, who showed no sign of weariness although they had probably been dancing steadily since the beginning of the evening.

"Enjoying yourself, Glenna?" Colin asked after a moment.

"Oh, yes. I'm glad you urged me and Aunt Aillie to come." I must remember this, I thought. I won't ever dance again on the soft yielding sand of a Highland beach in the flickering gleam of a leaping bonfire.

"We could come every year if you'd agree to marry me." Colin put his hands on my shoulders, looking down at me with a wistful smile. I could smell a faint malty whiff of whisky on his breath. "Have you thought about it, Glenna? My holiday will soon be over. Won't you send me back to Oban as an engaged man?" He bent his head, brushing his lips against mine in a soft kiss that deepened and clung until, instinctively, my mouth responded to his warm, urgent pressure.

"Glenna, say yes. Say it now."

"I can't." I pushed him away gently. "Colin, I don't love you, not—not that way, not the way you want."

He was silent for a moment. Then he said roughly, "You've loved someone *that* way. Perhaps you still do. Who is it, Glenna? Is there a man waiting faithfully for you back in Massachusetts?" He took my hands, drawing me close to him. "Forget about him, love. Your life is in Scotland now, with me."

A dry cough sounded close to us as a tall gaunt form emerged from the gloom. Colin and I moved hastily away from each other.

"A guid evening tae ye, Miss MacDougall, Colin."

"Pastor Munro," I said in some confusion. "I didn't expect to see you here. Cousin Ellen told me you didn't approve of the celebration."

"I ha' no quarrel wi' the bonfire itsel', ye ken, e'en though the custom comes tae us frae pagan times. In the olden days the fires were simply beacons tae announce the change of seasons tae farmers and sailors." The pastor sighed. "'Tis what goes along wi' the bonfire I canna stomach. The strong drink, the lewdness. Look at that, noo, will ye," he added with a glare of disapproval as a young man lurched out of the set of dancers, dragging his partner behind him. He collapsed on the sand near us, shaking his head helplessly when his partner tried to pull him to his feet.

"Tae full o' whisky tae walk," Pastor Munro snorted.

"Colin, isn't that Donnie?" I exclaimed.

"Lord, so it is. One of our grooms," Colin explained in an aside to the pastor.

"Aye, and the lassie is young Sheila Gordon," Mr. Munro said grimly. "Ane o' my flock. I'll juist take the lass tae her mither, tae keep her out o' harms way. Colin, ye'll oblige me by removing yer groom tae some place whaur he can sleep off the drink."

After the pastor had left to escort his obviously unwilling charge to her mother's care, and Colin had gone off with a sodden and stumbling Donnie, I stood by myself for a moment, peering into the gloom for a familiar face. Lorne suddenly materialized by my side. His face was indistinct in the flickering half-light from the fire, but the sentimental guerdon Flora had bestowed on him, her yellow rose, was clearly visible in his buttonhole.

I edged away from him, feeling cornered, though I wasn't really afraid he would try to harm me in this crowded gathering. It wasn't the right occasion, either, for that confidential talk he'd been pressing for all day, but I didn't want him near me. "Where is everybody?" I asked casually, glancing behind him.

"Some ladies from the church festival committee seized on Mother and Flora and your aunt. They'll be along soon." He said with a hint of laughter, "I saw you talking to Pastor Munro. Did he tell you how much he dislikes the goings-on of the Eve of Saint John? Mother and I could hardly drag ourselves away from him earlier tonight. He says the same thing every year, of course."

'The pastor was concerned about the drinking, I think. He said something about lewdness, too." I stepped back to avoid being overrun by a shrieking girl fleeing from a drunken young man. She seemed to be enjoying the pursuit. Certainly she wasn't trying very hard to escape.

Gazing after the pair as they disappeared into the darker stretches of the shore, Lorne observed dryly, "That, I fancy is what the pastor most objects to. It won't surprise anyone if there's an illegitimate birth in the village nine months from now. "Sorry," he added perfunctorily. "I shouldn't have said that."

"I have heard of such things, you know. I lived for years

226

in a small town," I replied drily. "Your mother says Mr. Munro would really like to abolish the celebration."

Lorne nodded. "He knows better than to try, though. He's convinced there's some kind of powerful malign influence at work in the village tonight, a carryover from the perverse heathen fertility rites practiced here centuries ago. I think he more than half believes what the villagers believe, that this is the one night of the year when supernatural beings wander about freely."

Lorne's voice lowered, grew slower, took on a brooding, measured cadence. I listened, mesmerized, as the words seemed to flow out of some dark trancelike state. "I can feel it too," he muttered. "There's something still here, some vestige of the life force the ancient ones invoked on the night of the summer solstice, a call to love, to savor the beauties of the flesh . . ." His voice died away, and he reached for me with an odd, groping gesture, as if he didn't fully realize what he was doing. Helpless to prevent myself, bound by the same sensual spell that held him in thrall, I swayed toward him . . .

"There you are, Lorne, I've been looking all over for you."

At the sound of Flora's voice, Lorne stepped abruptly away from me, drawing a ragged breath, like a swimmer surfacing from a deep dive.

"Glenna and I have been right here," he said, sounding dazed. He cleared his throat. "Are all of you ready to go?"

"Mother MacDougall certainly is. She says she's had enough of the Finlay bonfire to last her until next year!" Flora lifted her head, listening to the fiddlers. "They're playing a waltz, Lorne. Can't we stay a few minutes more? You haven't danced with me tonight."

I watched them go off to the dancing area, grateful that Flora had come along when she did. A few seconds more, and she might have had ample reason to be jealous. I clenched my hands into fists, willing myself into an artificial calm that lasted until we drove into the courtyard of Dungariff. Hastily refusing Ellen's offer of bedtime chocolate, I escaped to my tower room. There I rushed to the wardrobe, driven by an impulse I couldn't deny, dragging the family history from the upper shelf of the wardrobe with shaking fingers.

I sat down with the book, opening it to the section dealing with Angus and Catriona. I didn't have to read the passage. I knew it by heart. I read it anyway. "The Laird viewed his lady wife with the blackest of hate, he wished her dead so he could continue to indulge in the vice of fornication with his unworthy mistress, but still he could not overcome his lust for his wife's body . . ."

The Reverend Archibald's bald, repressed words faded away and I could see Angus striding into the Laird's bedchamber, his lean dark face twisted with hate. I wasn't experiencing a hallucination. I was fully conscious. I was here in the tower room, now, in this moment of time, but I was also present in the Laird's bedchamber . . .

. . . "I told you to move your miserable belongings out of this room," Angus snarled.

Catriona, dressed in a long silken robe of deep crimson, sat on the bed, brushing the waving masses of her dark hair. "I'm your wife," she snapped with a baleful flash of her blue eyes. "The Mistress of Dungariff sleeps in the Laird's Bedchamber."

"I married you. I don't have to sleep with you." Crossing the room, Angus seized Catriona's arm, dragging her off the bed. He grabbed her shoulders, his fingers grinding into her flesh. "Get out," he rasped between clenched teeth. "I won't allow you to soil my bed. I'd rather sleep with a snake."

She put up her hands to break his hold, wrenching herself free. "Sleep on the floor then, or go off to your whore's bed. I'm staying here."

His features contorted with ungovernable rage at the

scathing reference to his mistress, Angus grabbed for Catriona again, and as she attempted to twist away from him, the gossamer silken robe ripped and fell from her shoulders. He stopped short, staring at her naked white body as the robe slithered into a crimson pool at her feet. His eyes widening, he put out his hands, gliding his fingers lingeringly, caressingly over her arms and shoulders. "You have skin like velvet," he murmured huskily, his hands moving to her breasts.

As if released suddenly from a spell, Catriona jerked away. "Angus, please, I don't want—"

He reached for her again, ignoring her struggling, burying his face in her throat, lifting his head to trail a line of fiery kisses across her cheek. "You're a witch, Catriona, I can't resist you," he muttered, grinding his mouth against hers in a ruthless kiss. She ceased to struggle. With a low moan she strained against him in a bruising embrace that ended only when he snatched her up to carry her to the enormous Tudor bed with its paneled wooden canopy . . .

I stood up, the family history falling to the floor beside my chair as I covered my eyes with my hands in a vain, foolish attempt to block out the scene I'd just witnessed—no, *imagined*—in the Laird's bedchamber. The scene hadn't been real. What *was* real was the flaming passion felt by Angus and Catriona, an irresistible sensual attraction binding them together despite their mutual hatred. The same overwhelming physical urge Lorne and I felt for each other, even while he was trying to kill me, and I was fully aware of what he was doing. If Flora hadn't interrupted us, a few hours ago on the beach at Finlay, she would have found us in each other's arms.

The tower room was very still. It was always quiet, situated in the highest part of the castle, removed from the rest of the family living quarters. The soft knock echoed like a whiplash in the silent room. I sank to the floor, unable to control my trembling limbs, seized by a numbing terror as I stared at the massive old door leading to the ramparts. For weeks now, ever since I came to Dungariff, I'd tried to dismiss my illogical fears that danger waited for me outside that door. Now the danger was here.

The knock sounded again, a little louder. A moment later I heard Lorne's low, urgent voice. "Glenna, I'd like to talk to you."

Of course. It felt inevitable. Lorne—and no one else in the castle—had access to the ramparts from the Laird's Bedchamber.

"Glenna, I hope I haven't awakened you, but I must talk to you. Please open the door." A short pause. Then, "I promise I won't take more than a few minutes of your time. Please, Glenna."

Slowly, using the arm of the chair for support, I pulled myself erect and stumbled over to the door, leaning my weight against it because my legs still felt hollow. I tried to speak. "Lorne—" It was only a whisper of sound, but he heard it.

"Glenna, you're there, aren't you, on the other side of the door? Won't you let me in?"

I swallowed against the obstruction in my throat. "Lorne, it's late. I'm tired. I'll see you tomorrow."

"I don't want to wait until tomorrow. I . . . I wasn't myself tonight at the shore. I don't remember exactly what I said to you. I'm afraid I—"

"You needn't worry about what you said. It's all right." How could I make him go?

"Glenna, I've been trying to talk to you alone for two days. I know I've offended you in some way, but how can I apologize to you, how can I make it up to you, if I don't know what it is I've done? Please, unbolt this door."

I rested my cheek on the heavy old bolt, unutterably glad it was there. For the moment, it was my salvation. "I can't talk to you now, Lorne. I'm too tired. I have a headache.

Go away so I can sleep."

The seconds dragged by, and the silence was almost palpable, but I knew he was still there. Then I heard the slight scraping sound of his shoe against the pavement. He was gone.

I moved back into the room with dragging steps, like an aged and infirm crone. I went through the motions of preparing for bed, taking off my clothes, putting on my nightdress. I was tired to death, but the frantic thoughts swarming through my brain wouldn't let me rest. I didn't want to think any more. The box of sedatives Dr. MacColl had given me when I visited his surgery in Oban were still on the table next to my bed. I hadn't taken any of them. One of the pills . . . better, two . . . might give me temporary oblivion.

I slept, but I must have begun to dream almost immediately. Even as I closed my eyes, I seemed to feel the first drops of rain on my face and the buffeting of the wind . . .

. . . The dim figure came racing at me down the line of the ramparts, and now at last I could make out the chiseled features beneath the broad Highland bonnet. It was Lorne. In a moment I felt the cruel fingers tightening around my windpipe and I was gasping desperately for breath, clawing at those murderous hands . . .

Then I was awake, still struggling to breathe, tearing frantically at the object that was smothering me.

"Glenna?" It was Aunt Aillie's voice.

Instantly the pressure on my face relaxed. I pushed away the smothering pillow, sensing rather than seeing or hearing the departure of the person who had been standing over my bed. The door leading to the turret stairs creaked open, and as I sat up, I could see Aunt Aillie standing in the doorway, holding a lamp.

"Did I wake you? I'm sorry." Aunt Aillie put down her lamp and walked over to the bed. "I suppose you'd like to murder me for coming up here at this hour," she observed defensively. "It was the oddest thing, though. I woke up out of a sound sleep with the strongest feeling there was something wrong with you. I couldn't shake the feeling, so up I came."

She shivered at a sudden blast of cold air. "Good heavens, child, do you want to catch pneumonia?" she exclaimed. She walked over to the rampart door, closed it and slammed home the bolt. "You always were too much of a fresh-air fiend," she observed affectionately when she returned. "Well, I guess I should be going."

"Goodnight, Aunt Aillie. I'm glad you came up. I . . . I was having a nightmare."

"Oh." She nodded understandingly. "That's all right, then. Good night, Glenna."

I waited until after she left to pick up the yellow rose from the floor beside my bed. Flora's token of favor to her gentle knight. The rose Lorne had been wearing in his buttonhole this evening. The sure proof he'd tried to kill me again.

Chapter 13

Nobody commented on my appearance next morning at
the breakfast table, though I'd taken another of Dr.
MacColl's pills after Aunt Aillie's visit to the tower room,
and I felt sluggish and unrested after my drugged sleep.
My nerves were as taut as piano wires, but that seemingly
went unnoticed, too.

I'd come down this morning with only one thought in
my mind, to convince Aunt Aillie that we ought to leave
Dungariff immediately. Last night's experience had left
me feeling more uncertain than ever about my mental
stability, but I had no doubt at all that Lorne was trying to
kill me. The innocent yellow rose beside my bed had been
the conclusive proof of that. To persuade Aunt Aillie to
leave without revealing my real reasons for wanting to do
so, however, wouldn't be easy. For that I needed a quiet
corner and an uninterrupted block of time with her.

However, quiet and privacy were in short supply on this
June Saturday. For one thing, my own problems had
caused me to forget the birthday luncheon Aunt Aillie was
giving for Flora on the island of Seil. And tonight there
would be the excitement and commotion of the birthday
ball. Then, to everybody's surprise, Mr. and Mrs. Cameron
arrived from Oban shortly after breakfast.

"Aunt Aillie told me she'd invited Flora's parents, but I never dreamed they'd come," I murmured to Colin.

He rolled his eyes. "I would've bet against it. I've never known Mr. Cameron to be absent from the store for a full day *and* an evening, unless he was on his death bed. On the other hand, he doesn't have a daughter marrying the Laird of Dungariff every day of the week, either."

When I went up to greet the Camerons, they were chatting with Ellen. "I was juist telling Mrs. MacDougall that I had the honor tae show ye my store on Thursday last," Mr. Cameron observed.

"You never mentioned visiting the Camerons, Glenna," Ellen said, raising a puzzled eyebrow.

"Didn't I? It must have slipped my mind. It was very kind of Mr. Cameron. His store is a fascinating place," I said quickly. I wondered why Flora's father had brought up the subject of my visit. Perhaps he was testing the waters, trying to discover if I'd suspected he was picking my brains about Lorne's financial condition. Looking at his pinched, sour face, I reflected that he and his future son-in-law richly deserved each other.

We started for Seil in two carriages shortly after eleven. I felt a pang when I considered how pleasurably I would have anticipated the excursion in the early days of my stay at Dungariff. Today it would be a strain to show any interest or enthusiasm when I had only one overriding topic on my mind. And it would be difficult to stay out of Lorne's company completely without arousing the curiosity of the others in the party. I hadn't spoken to him this morning. I'd kept my eyes averted from him at breakfast, and I'd made it a point never to be alone when he was in the vicinity. He appeared out of nowhere to hand me into the landau, holding my hand a split second longer than necessary, riveting me with a straight intense gaze that said more clearly than words that I couldn't evade him forever.

In other circumstances I would have reveled in the

scenic drive through the village of Kilninver and over the mountains to Clachan Sound, a narrow channel of the sea, only a few yards wide, that separated the island of Seil from the mainland. The sound was spanned by an ancient, humpbacked, single-arched stone bridge. Colin, who was sitting next to me in the forward-facing seat of the landau, remarked with a grin, "Take a good look at that bridge, Glenna. It's the only bridge across the Atlantic Ocean!"

Today the waters of the sound were calm and windless, and the old bridge's reflection in the water created a miraculously perfect circle. "It's Glenna weather again," Ellen said merrily. "Often it's too windy and rainy to see that lovely circle in the water."

On the island a short distance from the little bridge, there was an old ferry inn, the *Tigh-An-Truish*—Colin told me impishly that the name meant House of the Trousers—where we stopped for lunch. We sat at a long common table in the low-ceilinged dining room. Aunt Aillie, with a slight air of self-importance that I found amusing, arranged the seating.

"We aren't going to be too formal," she announced, "especially since we have a shortage of men! Mr. Cameron, in honor of Flora's birthday, will you take the host's chair opposite me? Flora, you're on my right, of course, and Mrs. Cameron, please sit on my left." She put me between Lorne and Flora, but I pretended to misunderstand her, slipping into Ellen's place next to Colin on the other side of the table. As I sat down, I could feel Lorne's eyes boring into me. The others hadn't noticed my maneuver. He hadn't missed it.

Safely away, at least for the time being, from Lorne's proximity, I began to relax. The food was excellent and Colin's cheerful nonsense as distracting as ever. "Does the inn's name really mean House of the Trousers?" I asked him. "Or was that another of your terrible jokes?"

"Trust you to want to know that," he laughed. "Let's

see. I think the name has something to do with the banning of the plaid after Culloden. Is that right, Dungariff?"

Lorne looked up from his cold salmon. He hadn't been taking much part in the conversation, but now his eyes kindled with interest. "Most things in Scotland were affected by Culloden," he observed. "As I'm sure you already know, Glenna, both the wearing of the kilt and the carrying of weapons were forbidden to the clans after Bonnie Prince Charlie was defeated in the '45. However, at the beginning of the next century the English government needed soldiers in the fight against Napoleon, and they were finding it difficult to recruit in the Highlands until they decided to allow the clansmen to wear the kilt and to carry weapons while they were on active service. Enough was enough, though. When the Highlanders came home on leave, they had to change out of the kilt and into hodden trousers for the duration of their visit. This inn was one of the change houses."

Thoroughly charmed by the story, I watched Lorne's aloof features come alive with enthusiasm, and I found myself wondering how this serious caring man could be guilty of the crimes of which I suspected him. In the next moment I answered my own question. That very caring, that abiding love and concern for every aspect of his Highland heritage, was the motivating force impelling Lorne to murder.

Aunt Aillie had decided that we would present Flora with her gifts at the luncheon rather than at the supper that would precede her birthday dance. Flushed and happy, she blew out the candles on the cake that was ceremoniously put before her at the end of the meal, and sat waiting with ill-concealed impatience in front of a small mound of packages while the cake was being served.

When it was time for her to open her gifts, she tore into the packages with an avidity that left me faintly disturbed.

She seemed overly excited again, at the apogee of one of her pendulum mood swings.

Entranced with a fan of painted gauze with tortoise shell handles, she reached for the card that accompanied it. "Oh, Mrs. Murray, I didn't expect . . . It's too much, this lovely thing and the luncheon, too."

She loved all her gifts—the chrysophase brooch of apple green chalcedony from her father and stepmother, a large bottle of eau de cologne from Colin, a turquoise ring from Ellen—but she went into near-ecstasy when she opened the box containing my watch.

"I can't believe it," she breathed in delight, holding the watch out in front of her, swinging it gently to and fro so that the diamonds sparkled in the sunlight pouring in from the old mullioned windows. "How did you know, Lorne? Oh, I suppose Colin told you I've been coveting this watch for ages. Never, never did I expect to own it." She blew him an impulsive kiss. "Thank you, darling. Thank you for the most wonderful gift I've ever received."

Lorne took the watch from her hand, examining it closely. "It's beautiful, Flora. There's only one problem," he added, handing the piece back to her. "You're thanking the wrong person. I didn't give this to you."

Flora's eyes widened. She rummaged through the mass of discarded wrappings until she found my card. "Glenna, this is your gift? How thoughtful of you. Colin must have put you up to it." She was trying hard to be gracious, but she appeared chagrined. She reached for the last of her gifts, a bulky package about a foot high and slightly greater in width. "This must be from you, Lorne, it's the only one left." She unwrapped the parcel, revealing a small water color painting of an old castle perched on a high crag above the sea.

"Why, it's Dungariff," Aunt Aillie exclaimed.

Lorne nodded. "Yes, it's by Andrew Burns, the young artist who settled in Oban last year."

"Lorne commissioned the painting months ago as a surprise fer your birthday. He thought it would mean more to you than a bracelet or a necklace," Ellen told Flora, who was staring at the picture with a curiously blank expression.

"Oh, of course. It's very nice, Lorne. We'll hang it in our new sitting room, shall we?"

The contrast between Flora's flat, perfunctory response to Lorne's gift and her ecstatic reception of the watch was so marked that the others at the table plunged into conversation to hide their embarrassment.

"It's not really fair of Lorne to give you this painting, Flora," Colin joked, "when in a few short months he'll be giving you the castle itself!"

And Aunt Aillie said briskly, "I don't want to hurry you, but if we're to see the quarries, we'd best be going."

Flora herself seemed unaware of her gaucherie, and Lorne's face betrayed not a trace of the disappointment he must be feeling. I almost felt sorry for him.

We collected our belongings and piled back into the carriages for a short drive to Balvicar Bay to visit Seil's famous slate quarries. At first glance the unsightly slag heaps and the mounds of debris that detracted from the lovely island scenery were a disappointment. Soon, however, I was fascinated, like the others in the party, to watch the activity going on below us in the great pit, over two hundred feet deep, which itself was the result of past blasting on the site. Another round of blasting had just been completed. The workmen were busily levering out the great jagged masses of rocks with crowbars and were placing them on wagons to be carried away to the slate huts, where the rocks would be split and dressed into slate. I became so absorbed in what I was seeing that I didn't realize Lorne had come to stand beside me until he spoke.

"There's something right over there that you'd be interested in, Glenna," he said in a low voice. Placing his hand under my arm, he propelled me unobstrusively but inexorably away from the rest of the group. He took me by such surprise that I still hadn't opened my mouth to protest by the time we stopped beside a large boulder, some yards from the great pit.

Lorne motioned to the faint tracings on the boulder. "Those are the cup and ring markings I was telling you about," he remarked. "Definitely pre-Christian, but of course I'm no archeologist, so I can't say exactly how old the tracings are."

I glanced briefly at the markings, making no attempt to study them. "Very interesting. Thank you for pointing them out." I turned to leave but Lorne put out his hand to grasp my wrist. The same hand that only last night had been holding a smothering pillow to my face. I jerked away from him, suppressing a shudder of revulsion.

"Please don't go, Glenna. You said last night that we could talk today."

"Well, yes, I did say that," I replied, smiling woodenly, "but this isn't really a good time or place, is it? We should be getting back to the others."

Blocking my way, he said quietly, "This is as good a time and place as any. You're very elusive these days. Glenna, why are you so angry with me?"

"I'm not. Why would I be angry with you?"

He put his hand under my chin, forcing me to look up at him. His dark eyes bored into mine and his chin was set grimly as he said, "Don't play games with me, please." He paused, picking his words carefully. "I thought we'd become good friends these past weeks. I thought you enjoyed our walks and talks as much as I did. You seemed to love Dungariff, you were as much a member of our family as if you'd been born here. During the past few days, though, I've felt a wall going up between us. You avoid me, you go out of your way to make sure we're never alone together. Why, Glenna? What have I done? What haven't I done?"

"You haven't done anything. You haven't *not* done anything," I burst out, twisting my head to free my chin from his grip. "Lorne, this is ridiculous. You're imagining thoughts and feelings that I don't have. We've become friends, as you said. Nothing's wrong. Is that good enough? Can we go back to the others now?" I made a move to step past him. He seized my arm in a grip that hurt.

"I don't believe you," he said harshly. "There was something between us, Glenna. It was more than friendship. It was a—a bonding. Sometimes I had the feeling that we could see into each other's hearts. That's all gone now. I want to know why."

My heart felt sore. He sounded so sincere, so hurt, so deeply perplexed. What an actor he was, what an actor he'd always been. "I'm sorry, Lorne, you're forcing me to say something I'd rather not," I said between stiff lips. "The truth is, I like you and your mother, and I've enjoyed my visit to Dungariff, but I'm getting a little restless. Even a bit bored. I think it's time for me to move on."

Instantly he released my arm, stepping aside to let me pass. "Thank you. All I wanted was a straight answer."

I turned away, telling myself I was mistaken, that I hadn't glimpsed the flicker of black despair in Lorne's eyes. Or if I had, it was counterfeit, like everything about him. He caught up with me a moment later. Not speaking, we walked back to the pit to join the others. I was relieved when nobody commented on our absence. Lorne and I must appear quite normal, I thought, with no outward sign of the emotional tension that crackled between us.

I said cheerfully, "Lorne found an example of those cup and ring markings he's been telling me about. Before I came to Scotland, I never realized people have lived here since the days of the cave men."

Lorne smiled. "If Glenna stays in Argyll long enough,

240

we'll make an amateur archeologist out of her."

Colin slapped him on the shoulder. "You've missed your calling, Lorne," he said jovially. "You should have been a teacher. I tell you what, if you and Flora want to go off together after you're married to open a school or some such thing, I'd be very happy to take over as Laird of Dungariff."

"What an idiot you are, Colin," Flora exclaimed. I was used to the teasing bantering they often indulged in. This wasn't one of those times. Flora sounded out of sorts.

We left the slate quarries and the island of Seil shortly afterwards. When we arrived back at Dungariff, I sat for a long time by my tower window looking out toward Mull, wishing I didn't have to dress for dinner, wishing this awful interminable day was over. Perhaps one good thing had come out of it: perhaps Lorne had realized the futility of trying to mend his fences with me by means of a cozy little talk. His next step would undoubtedly be direct action, an attempt ot arrange another accident, but now his time was limited. Tomorrow, after the elder Camerons returned to Oban, I'd find the opportunity to talk privately with Aunt Aillie. In days—hours—I could be leaving Dungariff.

I finally summoned the energy to begin dressing for dinner. I was arranging my hair when Flora walked into the room after a perfunctory knock, saying brusquely, "I want to talk to you, Glenna."

I stifled a sigh. Flora's face was strained and pale and she sounded hostile. I didn't think I could cope with any more oversize emotions today. "Of course," I said quietly. "Sit down, won't you?" I returned to the dressing table. "That's a beautiful dress," I said, looking into the mirror at the reflection of her apricot-colored gown of Persian silk. "Is that the gown your aunt sent you from Edinburgh?"

"Yes." For a moment Flora brightened as she looked at

herself in the full-length cheval glass. "It didn't come in time for the annual ball, so I decided to wear it tonight instead." Her voice took on an edge. "I thought of wearing my new diamond watch with it."

"Oh? Why didn't you?"

"Because I don't think I ought to keep it. Here, Glenna, I'm giving it back to you."

I swung around to face her, ignoring the hand she was holding out to me. "I don't understand, Flora. I thought you liked the watch. Colin told me how much you admired it."

"Gifts should come from friends. Today I finally realized you aren't my friend."

"Flora, what on earth—?"

"No, let me finish. For weeks now I've been making excuses for your behavior. I tried to tell myself that you were simply spoiled and selfish and unthinking. You couldn't possibly be trying to steal Lorne away from me. It was only natural you should be in Lorne's company a great deal. You were a guest, an honored guest, and I was away most of the time at my school in Oban. It wasn't important that you were spending far more time with him than I was, his own fiancée. When school was out and I came here to prepare for my wedding, I assumed you'd back off, give Lorne and me some privacy. Instead of that, you've been bolder than ever, forcing yourself on him at every opportunity. You even saw to it that he gave you the place of honor at the ball! This afternoon, though, you went too far. In front of everybody—your aunt, Colin, my parents—you dragged Lorne away for a private little talk. How did you think I felt, watching you standing so close to him, hanging on his arm, whispering in his ear as if you had intimate secrets you couldn't share with anyone else?"

Flora paused for breath, and I could only stare at her, torn by an almost hysterical desire to laugh. What a supreme irony, that she should accuse me of pursuing

Lorne, when in point of fact I'd been doing my best to elude him before he succeeded in killing me. I forestalled her next outburst, saying, "You're quite wrong, Flora. There's nothing the least romantic in my relationship with Lorne. He's simply been acting the kind host to Aunt Aillie and me as visitors from America and distant members of the family. We've appreciated his hospitality and Ellen's very much, and we're fond of them both. That's all there is to it."

"How can you expect me to believe that? I've seen you together. There's something—"

I cut in sharply. "Flora. Listen to me. I don't want Lorne. Even if you weren't engaged to him, I wouldn't want him. He doesn't want me, either. Why can't you understand that?"

The vehemence of my words seemed to reach her. She was still angry, still tormented, but now there was an element of uncertainty in her face. "It's you who doesn't understand," she muttered, looking away from me. "Even if it's true that you're not interested in Lorne, you should stay away from him. He has very . . . strong physical appetites. You—both of you—could easily get carried away. It wouldn't mean anything to Lorne, of course. To him it would be a purely physical thing, a part of his . . . his animal nature." She ended in a difficult whisper, "Men do these things, you know . . ."

"Flora, don't say any more, please. There's no danger I'll get carried away, believe me."

"You might not be able to help yourself," Flora said in a shaking voice. Her face flooded with color. "I never thought that I . . . I never dreamed I'd let him touch me that way . . . Please, Glenna, I beg of you, stay away from Lorne. You already have so much. You're beautiful and wealthy and free to go wherever you like. Colin's falling head over heels in love with you, if you must have a man to care for you. Don't take Lorne, too. He's all I have, I love him so much." She broke into a torrent of hysterical weeping that racked her fragile body.

I watched her, appalled at this naked, indecent exposure of another human being's soul. She was far more unstable than I'd guessed. I'd never liked her, and she was even more distasteful to me now in her stew of wrong-headed jealousy, but it was impossible not to feel pity for her. I put my arm around her, guiding her to a chair, wiping her eyes. Over and over again I assured her that her fears were groundless, that she and Lorne would soon be happily married. I felt like a hypocrite. How could any woman, even the woman he loved, be happily married to Lorne, once she knew what he was really like?

Gradually Flora grew calmer. She rose, mopping at her eyes with the handkerchief I'd given her, and walked to the door. As she left she said tightly, "I'd like to believe you, Glenna. Unfortunately, I can't. If I lose Lorne, it will be your doing."

I sat down at my dressing table to finish arranging my hair, trying not to think about the implications of what Flora had said to me. It was useless. My thoughts kept returning to the subject, like a dog with a bone. I wondered if she realized how much she'd revealed. It seemed unmistakable that this prim, strictly reared, rather phlegmatic girl had succumbed with Lorne to what Pastor Munro would direfully term carnal pleasures, and that she had strong feelings of guilt about it.

A hot anger began to flood through me. Could Lorne have forced himself on Flora? Oh, she adored him, and perhaps she wouldn't have been entirely unwilling, but if a rape had occurred, it would certainly help to explain her deep-seated insecurities. No wonder she was so convinced I had designs on Lorne. She seemed to believe that no woman who caught Lorne's fancy could possibly resist his sexual advances. I slammed down my hairbrush at the thought, picked up my shawl, and started down the turret stairs. It was really too early to go down to dinner, but if I stayed up here, I'd only go on stewing about Flora.

At the door of the drawing room I ran into Flora's parents.

"Ach, Miss MacDougall, ye're an early one like oursel'," Mr. Cameron said with his tight, difficult smile. "We're the first down, I believe." He flashed his wife a meaningful glance. "Ah . . . Mrs. Cameron and I thought we might juist go for a walk afore dinner. The Laird's mither ha' a braw rose garden, sae I hear. Wouldna ye care tae come wi' us?" He took my arm as he spoke, making refusal impossible. I thought the idea of a pre-dinner stroll was as unexpected to Mrs. Cameron as it was to me. What did Flora's father want of me this time?

It was still light enough to see Ellen's roses, and the Camerons praised them dutifully. Then, clearing his throat, Mr. Cameron said, "We're verra happy tae see the bonnie blossoms, Miss MacDougall. However, I maun confess I ha' anither reason for bringing ye here."

I nodded. "I was aware of that, Mr. Cameron. I must tell you, though, that I can't discuss the Laird's affairs. If there's anything else you want to talk to me about . . ."

He eyed me with a flash of understanding. "Ach, noo, I was telling my wife ye were a clever young lady. Little gets past ye, I expect." His expression sharpened. "I dinna wish tae speak of the Laird, but of yersel'."

"Me!"

"Aye. Tell me noo, Miss MacDougall, is it true wha' my Flora told us, not half an hour gone in our bedchamber? Are ye after the Laird tae break off his betrothal tae Flora sae ye can ha' him fer yersel'?" Mr. Cameron spoke as matter-of-factly as if he were asking his supplier the price of rope.

When I recovered from my brief stupefaction I spluttered, "No, it's *not* true. I haven't the faintest desire to marry Lorne MacDougall. Your daughter is welcome to him."

"But is it no' a fact that ye were in his pocket each and every day for weeks on end, while poor Flora was teaching the bairns in Oban?" Mrs. Cameron asked. "Didna ye prevail on him tae open the Dungariff ball wi' ye?"

"And this day on Seil, my wife and I saw ye oursel', a-cuddling wi' the Maister i' the gorse," Mr. Cameron chimed in.

If I hadn't been so angry, I would have laughed. So much for my idea that nobody had been paying any attention when Lorne dragged me away from the others during our visit to the slate pit. We couldn't have been under closer surveillance if each person in the party had had eyes in the back of his head.

"Mr. and Mrs. Cameron, I see no point in continuing this discussion," I said coldly. "You and Flora will believe what you want to believe, no matter what I say. I suggest we return to the drawing room now. The Chief and the other guests will be arriving soon."

I turned to go, striding swiftly under the vault of the gatehouse, not waiting or caring to see if the Camerons were following me. Lorne, dressed for the evening in his kilt and velvet jacket, came out of the side entrance to the hall house as I crossed the courtyard. Hurrying up to me, he said, "Glenna, your aunt was wondering where you were." He looked at me closely. "You're upset. What's wrong?"

Evading the hand he put out to me, I snapped, "Ask your—" I was about to say "your future father-in-law," but I stopped myself in time. I didn't want to talk to Lorne about Flora's accusations. I wanted to keep my relationship with him on a strictly impersonal level until I could make my escape from Dungariff.

"Nothing's wrong," I said hastily, stepping past him into the house. I left him standing outside the door, his forehead creased in a slight frown as he watched the

Camerons emerging from the gatehouse.

When I reached the drawing room, my entrance didn't attract much attention since the Chief and his wife had just arrived. However, Colin sought me out, saying with a troubled frown, "I'm worried about Flora. When I finished dressing a bit ago, I noticed a light under her door so I knocked. She told me to go away. She said she wasn't coming down because she had a headache. Glenna, she can't not attend her own birthday ball! I tried to tell her that, but nothing I said had the slightest effect. I don't know what to do. Should I tell Aunt Ellen about it? Or her stepmother? Or—Glenna, why don't you go up and have a word with her?"

I had to suppress a nervous giggle at the sheer irony of the situation. Here I was being besieged on all sides about the affairs of Lorne and Flora, when all I wanted to do was to see the last of both of them. I shook my head. "I'm the last person Flora would listen to, Colin. Talk to Lorne."

Catching sight of his cousin, who had just entered the room, followed by the Camerons, Colin said with an air of relief, "Why didn't I think of that? He'll make her see reason, if anyone can." He moved off to intercept Lorne as the Chief came up to me.

"Good evening, Miss Glenna. I've brought you something." He handed me a little book, a pamphlet, really, with a cover of stiff cardboard.

I opened the booklet to the title page. *A Little History of Dunollie,* by Alastair MacDougall," I read. I leafed through the closely printed pages. "You wrote this, Mr. MacDougall?"

"I fear I did." The Chief's smile was faintly sheepish. "I thought I'd given away all my copies, but yesterday, after you left the castle, I rummaged about in my desk and found this one. Mind, I'm not much of a writer, but you seemed so interested in Dunollie, and you *are* a Mac-Dougall, so I thought . . ."

"You thought right." I smiled at him. "I'm immensely pleased and flattered to have this. Thank you so much." If only things had been different, I thought, I might be making plans to stay in Argyll forever. I'd have the chance to deepen my acquaintance with this kind and friendly man. I might even begin to feel like a true member of his clan.

Out of the corner of my eye, I saw Lorne and Flora enter the drawing room. He looked grim. She looked like a wraith. They walked around the room, greeting the guests who'd been invited for dinner. When they came up to the Chief and me, Flora looked through me, as if I were invisible. She extended a limp hand to the Chief. "Thank you for coming to my birthday ball, Mr. MacDougall." Her voice sounded lifeless. Spotting her parents, seated by themselves in a corner, she murmured a brief excuse and walked over to sit beside them.

"Miss Cameron doesn't look well, Lorne," the Chief said in concern.

"She has a slight headache," Lorne said quickly. "This has been a long and exciting day for her." He reached for the pamphlet I was holding, in a transparent move to change the subject. "Why, it's your history of Dunollie, sir," he exclaimed in a tone of forced enthusiasm. "I haven't seen a copy in years. I didn't know there were any left. You'll enjoy reading it, Glenna. I wish some member of our family had written the story of Dungariff."

Dinner was a subdued affair. Ellen and Aunt Aillie and the Chief kept up a cheerful flow of conversation in an attempt to cover up Flora's depressed mood, but they weren't very successful. She sat with her eyes cast down, pretending to eat.

The atmosphere became a little lighter when the dancing began in the Great Hall. Lorne led Flora out for the first dance. He talked to her steadily while they waltzed and by the time the number ended she seemed far more relaxed. She smiled at the Chief when he asked her for the next dance.

"All's well that ends well. Whatever ailed Flora, she's coming out of it. Lorne can work magic with her," Colin observed as he took my arm to lead me onto the dance floor. He watched Flora floating by with the Chief. "Look at her, Glenna. She's so lovely when she's happy."

I glanced up at him quickly. I'd often suspected that Colin had more than a lingering fondness for Flora.

For the rest of the evening, I didn't lack partners. I even managed to forget my problems temporarily and enjoy myself. Toward the end of the ball, however, Lorne asked me to dance, and I couldn't refuse him without making my estrangement from him clear to everyone.

We danced in silence at first. I held myself stiffly against his arm, trying to avoid the slightest pressure of his body against mine. He said abruptly. "You're not wearing the MacDougall crest that Mother and I gave you."

Involuntarily I glanced down at the small silver brooch that fastened my tartan sash to my shoulder. "No. The clasp on the crest was a little loose. I'll have to get it repaired before I can wear it again," I lied. At the risk of hurting Ellen's feelings, I hadn't been able to bring myself to wear the MacDougall crest. Only a few weeks ago I'd been so delighted to receive the brooch. I'd thought of it as a token of Lorne's affection and regard. Now it was only a pretty piece of jewelry, a reminder of my gullibility.

The music seemed to go on forever. I prayed for it to end. When it did, I found that Lorne had maneuvered us to a spot not far from the inner door of the Great Hall. "We've got to talk," he muttered, pulling me through the door into the drawing room and then out into the passage to his study. Pushing me inside the room and closing the door, he stood with his back to the door, looking down at me in a hard-breathing silence.

"We've talked enough," I said with stiff lips. "Lorne, I

want to go back to the Great Hall."

"Glenna, hear me out. I spoke to Andrew Cameron a few minutes ago in this room. Do you know what he wants me to do? He wants me to throw you out of Dungariff before you succeed in tricking me into breaking my engagement to Flora so that you can marry me instead."

I swallowed hard. "Why would Mr. Cameron say such a thing?"

He stared at me, his dark face strained and angry. "Don't play the innocent. You know perfectly well why. He told me about Flora's visit to your room this afternoon. I knew something had happened when she didn't want to come down for dinner, but she wouldn't tell me what it was. Glenna, I want to know what Flora said to you."

I stared back at him. Clearly, he wouldn't allow me to leave until I answered him. "Flora was upset, jealous," I began reluctantly. "She misinterpreted that . . . that talk you and I had on the island today. She had the absurd idea I was trying to come between you. I assured her I regarded you simply as a cousin and a friend. I hoped that would end the matter. Apparently it didn't."

"Is this the first time she's made such an accusation?"

"Yes," I replied truthfully.

"But you knew, didn't you, that she was jealous of you?" Lorne burst out. "Oh, she tried to hide it, but we all knew it. She's a very insecure person." He put his hands on my shoulders. "Glenna, is this the real reason why you've been avoiding me? Because you didn't want to give Flora any grounds for jealousy?"

His face was so close that I could feel his breath on my cheek, and his hands on my bare shoulders felt like burning brands. I tried to choke it back, but my treacherous mind admitted the memory of my daydream about Angus and Catriona. I closed my eyes, seeing Angus's ruthless hands tearing Catriona's robe from her body. I could hear his smothered moan when he couldn't resist the lure of her gleaming white flesh. Then memory and reality merged, and I was crushed against Lorne's lean body, held so closely I could feel the quickening urge of his arousal. He claimed my mouth in a savage suffocating kiss that drained my breath as it caused my heart to beat so tumultuously that I felt a physical pain. I don't know how long we stood locked together in that molten embrace that was fusing our bodies into one identity. I wasn't aware the door had opened. Eventually a screaming voice penetrated the dark, warmly pulsating pool of passion in which I was drowning. I pushed frantically against Lorne's chest to free myself. Panting and disheveled, we both turned to face Flora.

She was out of control. She wasn't screaming any longer, but a stream of vicious words poured out of her, accusing me of unspeakable acts I'd never heard of, calling me names I didn't recognize. Whore was the least offensive term she used. I did know what that meant.

White to the lips, Lorne tried to quiet her. He put his arm around her, shaking her gently, speaking to her in a low, soothing voice. Gradually the terrible flow of invective died away. Flora collapsed against Lorne, the manic expression fading into a lost, little-girl look. He lowered her into a chair and sank down beside it, cradling her tenderly in his arms. Without looking up, he said, "Please go, Glenna. I'll take care of her."

Stumbling into the passage outside the study, I collided with Colin. I relaxed gratefully into the comfort of his embrace. I felt soiled, sickened, by Flora's tirade. "It was awful, Colin," I murmured into his shoulder. "Did you hear it?"

"Yes. Some of it." Colin's voice was husky. "Glenna, don't think too badly of her. She didn't really mean what she was saying. It's just that she's so jealous of you . . ."

"I know." Slowly I pulled away from him. "How did you happen—?"

"I've been worried about Flora all evening," he said simply. "She wasn't herself. I saw you and Lorne leave the Great Hall. A minute or two later Flora apparently became aware that both of you were gone, and she left, too." He shrugged. "I thought it might be better if I followed her. It didn't do much good, did it?"

"You helped me, Colin." I squeezed his arm. "I suppose we should get back to the Great Hall before somebody realizes four of us are missing. Five of us," I added, looking down the passage without too much surprise to see Aunt Aillie advancing toward us.

"There you are," she said briskly. She glanced through the open door of the study and turned her eyes away from Lorne and Flora without comment. "Your hair's a mess, Glenna. You can't go back to the ballroom looking like that. Come along with me to Ellen's sitting room."

Aunt Aillie didn't say anything until her skillful fingers had smoothed out the heavy masses of my hair and replaced the pins securely. "Flora's in another of her tantrums, I see," she said at last. "The moment I saw her jump up and skedaddle out of the ballroom I knew something was wrong. Of course she's been nervous as a cat all evening. Sometimes I think she's not quite normal."

There was an unspoken question in her voice. I stirred uncomfortably, and then, suddenly, I realized I could turn the dreadful encounter with Flora into something positive. I could use it to make my exit from Dungariff without revealing my deepest fears and suspicions.

"You may be right about Flora, Aunt Aillie," I said slowly. "Perhaps she isn't quite normal. Today she came to the tower room and accused me of trying to steal Lorne away from her. And tonight she thought we were having some kind of romantic tryst. She made a dreadful scene."

"Well, I never," my aunt gasped. "I've always suspected she was jealous of you, but this is beyond anything."

I nodded. "Yes, it is. I can't go on like this, Aunt Aillie. I can't go on living in the same house with a girl who watches me constantly for the slightest sign that I'm trying to steal her fiancé. I want to leave Dungariff. Tomorrow, if possible."

"Leave Dungariff? But what about the terms of your Uncle Niall's will?"

"You know as well as I do that Uncle Niall didn't specify I should live at Dungariff," I replied impatiently "I can live anywhere within the boundaries of Argyll until my year is up. We could travel in the county. Didn't you always want to see Inverary? We could even rent a house in Oban." We won't, though, I promised myself. Oban isn't far enough away from Lorne.

"I don't know, Glenna. What would Lorne and Ellen think? They've been expecting us to stay the summer. They'd be so hurt, so offended, if we left for no good reason. Because, of course, we couldn't very well tell them we're being forced out of the castle by Flora's jealousy."

It would have been amusing if the situation hadn't been so desperate. After fighting so fiercely against coming to Dungariff, Aunt Aillie had clearly become so attached to her life at the castle that the thought of leaving was very unsettling to her.

"Lorne's all too aware of Flora's jealousy," I said shortly. "Ellen knows, too. If you were to go to her privately and explain our feelings, I'm sure she'd understand why we want to leave. There wouldn't be any hard feelings, and I have an idea she'd help us to go as easily and inconspicuously as possible. That's what we want, isn't it? We wouldn't want to cause Lorne and his mother any embarrassment."

"Oh, no." Aunt Aillie looked blank. "It's so drastic, though, so sudden . . ."

"We only came to Dungariff for a visit," I reminded her. "In any case, we could hardly have stayed on after Lorne and Flora were married."

"That's true." Aunt Aillie sighed. "I know you're right. We can't stay on here under the circumstances." She added, brightening, "It isn't as if we're leaving forever. We can always come back to see Ellen and Lorne and Colin."

I didn't have the heart to tell her that after my obligatory year was up, we'd probably never see Argyll again. "So you'll speak to Cousin Ellen? How about tomorrow after the service at the kirk?"

"So soon?"

"The sooner the better. That way, we could actually leave on Monday, or Tuesday at the latest."

"Oh, we couldn't do that, Glenna. Have you forgotten about the excursion to Dunadd on Wednesday? Lorne's gone to an enormous amount of trouble to arrange the trip. And it was mostly for your benefit, you know, because you're so interested in the local history. He's asked his archeologist friend to be our guide to the site, he's even made reservations on the steamer. We'd be dealing him a slap in the face if we decided not to go at the last minute."

"All right. We'll leave on Thursday."

A few days more at Dungariff couldn't make that much difference. Could it?

Chapter 14

On Wednesday morning, the day of our long-planned excursion to the ancient fortress of Dunadd, the weather was dreary and gray. As I stood waiting in the courtyard with Colin, I could feel the beginning of a fine cold drizzle. I pulled the collar of my coat more closely around my throat and put up my umbrella.

"It looks as though you've lost your magic influence over the weather, Glenna," Colin said jokingly. "What we're getting today is much more like normal weather in the Western Highlands. Lorne and I will need our oilskins for the ride into Oban."

Colin's good humor sounded a little forced today. Just then Donnie drove the landau into the courtyard, and Colin, taking out his watch, muttered impatiently, "What's keeping them? If we don't leave on time, we'll miss our sailing. You don't suppose Flora's changed her mind about going?"

I shrugged. "She didn't come down for breakfast this morning. Perhaps she's feeling ill again."

The past three days had dragged by interminably. Everyone in the household seemed on edge, as if I'd communicated my mounting tension to those around me. Aunt Aillie had spoken to Ellen and we'd be leaving

Dungariff tomorrow, but I hadn't been able to stifle a lurking fear that *something* would prevent our departure.

Lorne had covered Flora's abrupt departure from the ballroom on the night of her birthday ball by announcing that she'd taken suddenly ill. One of her sick headaches, he'd said tersely. Until yesterday, when she appeared at the dinner table, Flora had remained secluded in her bedroom. She still had a headache, Ellen had reported; sometimes Flora's headaches lasted for days. By an unspoken decision, nobody mentioned the scene in Lorne's study. At dinner last night, however, though she looked wan and languid, Flora had made an attempt to act normally. She even mustered a little enthusiasm for the excursion to Dunadd. She didn't address a single word directly to me, though. I might have been an invisible guest at the table.

Lorne, too, had been practically invisible since the birthday ball. He'd left on his estate rounds every morning before the rest of us were up, returning for dinner as we were sitting down to table, and then he'd spent his evenings in his office. Doing his accounts, Ellen said.

I was grateful for his absences. I couldn't stand the thought of being with him, of looking him in the face. I was too bitterly ashamed of myself for the way my treacherous senses had responded once again to the urgent pull of his sexuality. How could any sane woman be attracted to a man she feared and despised, a man who was trying to kill her? There was a ready answer to that, of course, but I wouldn't let myself consider it. After I made good my escape from this place, after I was safely out of Lorne's reach, I'd worry about my sanity.

Colin was impatiently consulting his watch yet another time when Flora emerged from the hall house with Lorne, Ellen, and Aunt Aillie. "Sorry to keep you waiting," she said pleasantly when she came up to me and Colin. "I couldn't get my hair to stay up. It always frizzes so when it's damp." She appeared to be speaking to both of us, but her glance slid off me as if I were an inanimate object.

As she and I settled ourselves in the landau opposite Ellen and Aunt Aillie, I stole a covert look at Flora's face. She still looked ill. Her skin had a pasty pallor and there were dark circles under her eyes. She began to talk quite naturally, however. The casual observer wouldn't have suspected anything was wrong. But I knew. She never met my eyes.

The rain began in earnest as we left the castle. During the drive to Oban, Lorne and Colin huddled miserably in their saddles beneath their enveloping oilskins. With the curtains down the interior of the landau grew uncomfortably sticky. We were all glad to reach the North Pier and board the inter-island steamer bound for the south. As we trooped into the crowded saloon, the boat began edging out of the harbor.

Shortly after we entered the Firth of Lorn, the driving rain slackened enough to allow us to go on deck. Ellen and Aunt Aillie settled into deck chairs, their legs warmly wrapped in lap robes. Arm in arm, Lorne and Flora began strolling along the deck. I stood at the railing, watching the wildly lovely Argyll scenery slip past me and contrasting my desolate mood today with the anticipation I'd felt a few short weeks ago, when Aunt Aillie and I had sailed along the shores of Loch Linne, making for Oban and our visit to Dungariff.

Colin came to stand beside me at the railing. "We may have fair weather yet for Dunadd," he commented. "I can't say I relish the thought of climbing that hill in a sea of mud. It's almost two hundred feet high, you know." He looked down at me, his face unwontedly serious. "Aunt Ellen told me about your plans, Glenna. You're still set on going?"

"Yes, Aunt Aillie and I will leave Dungariff tomorrow. Meggie is packing for us while we're off on this excursion."

Colin flashed a wry smile. "I never dreamed you'd leave Dungariff so soon, even before my holiday was over. Glenna, my heart will ache when you go away, but I think you're doing the right thing."

"Yes, we've imposed on Ellen's and Lorne's hospitality long enough. They're too polite to say so, but I'm sure they never expected us to stay so many weeks when they invited us to Dungariff."

"Glenna, don't put words in my mouth," Colin said roughly. "You and your aunt would stay forever, if Aunt Ellen had her way. She didn't tell me your real reason for leaving Dungariff. She didn't have to tell me. She said you and Aunt Aillie wanted to travel a bit. I didn't believe that for a minute. You're going away because of Flora." He glanced aft down the deck, where Lorne and Flora stood close together at the railing, immersed in their conversation. "I hope you won't think I'm being ungracious," Colin added, "but Lorne and Flora never seemed to have any difficulties until you came to Dungariff."

"Yes, I'm sure they can work things out once I'm gone," I murmured, keeping my eyes fixed on the increasingly wild shoreline, pierced by innumerable lochs, with gaunt hills descending steeply to the water. Everyone had accepted the fiction that I was leaving Dungariff to avoid provoking Flora to further jealousy. I didn't like telling lies, but Colin and Ellen and Aunt Aillie would be brokenhearted if they knew the evil truth behind my decision to leave.

After a moment Colin grasped my hand and squeezed it. "It's all right. You don't need to talk. You've given Flora her happiness. You're also taking away mine."

"Oh, Colin . . ."

He shook his head. "Aunt Ellen said your aunt spoke of coming back for a visit, or even of renting a house in Oban. Maybe Aunt Ellen believes that, but I don't. You're not ever coming back to Dungariff, are you?" He forced a

258

smile. "Wherever you go, though, remember my offer is still open. Any time you want to change your name from MacDougall to MacDougall, I'm your man!"

"You're a darling, Colin."

"I wish I were yours," he replied ruefully. "I'm sorry, I didn't mean to get this serious. Look, would you like a cup of tea? It won't take me a moment to fetch it."

After Colin left, I continued to stand at the railing, although it had started to rain again. I didn't feel like talking to anyone. All I really wanted was to get through this last day before I left Dungariff.

"I hope nobody offers to give you a penny for your thoughts. They'd be expensive at half the price."

Caught completely off guard by her harsh voice, I whirled to stare at Flora, who, the last time I'd sighted her, had been standing at the stern of the vessel talking to Lorne. Her eyes were glittering with rage and hate, but she didn't seem completely out of control as she had the other night.

"I'm warning you, Miss Glenna MacDougall. You'd better not start celebrating your victory too soon. You've won the first battle. The war isn't over yet."

"Flora, what on earth—?"

"Oh, don't play innocent with me," she sneered. "You know exactly what I'm talking about. You'll do anything to get what you want, won't you? Lying, cheating, stealing! It's all the same to you. You don't care if you ruin someone else's happiness. All you care about is getting your own way. Well, it won't work this time. If it's the last thing I do, you won't get away with it."

She swung away, passing Colin as he came out of the saloon with my tea. He cast a quick look around the windswept deck, deserted now by even the most diehard passengers. Thrusting the tea at me, he said, "Go on in, Glenna. Flora seems upset. I think I'd better stay out here and talk to her."

A tight knot beginning to form in my stomach, I walked back to the saloon. What had happened to set Flora off this time? I hadn't seen her talking to anyone except Lorne since the ship sailed.

As always, Colin was good for Flora. When they returned to the saloon shortly afterwards, she seemed quite calm, although I suspected it was a very brittle composure.

Several hours later we disembarked at Crinan, a bustling port whose small harbor was crowded with yachts and fishing boats. Waiting for us as we trooped down the gangplank was a tall gangling sandy-haired man with pleasant features and bright inquisitive blue eyes.

"Oh, you MacDougalls," he called exuberantly. "It's wonderful to see you again."

"Aillie, Glenna, Flora, this is Duncan Forbes," Ellen said with a fond smile. "He and Lorne were at school together. Even then Duncan was interested in digging up things. He was ecstatic when he came for a visit to Dungariff and discovered that prehistoric cave at Dunard Point."

"That's when I really made up my mind to be an archeologist," Duncan grinned. "I owe it all to you MacDougalls. Over here, please. I've hired a landau and a pony trap. They ought to hold all of us." As we walked over to the vehicles, he glanced up at the sky, observing, "It's cleared in the past hour. I can actually see the sun. We'll have a nice day to see Dunadd."

I made it a point to get into the pony trap with Duncan and Colin, leaving Lorne to ride with his mother, Flora, and Aunt Aillie in the landau.

As we drove away from the docks, I remarked, "I believe Lorne said you teach at the University of Glasgow, Mr. Forbes."

"Duncan, please. Yes, I teach at the university, but I can hardly wait each summer to get back here to do field work.

This is probably the most intensively concentrated area of archeological significance in all of Scotland. Hill forts, cairns, circles, standing stones, we have them all." He added smilingly. "When Lorne wrote to arrange this excursion, he told me you were an enthusiastic amateur archeologist, Miss MacDougall."

I smiled back. "It's Glenna. Amateur was exactly the right word to describe me. I'm certainly no archeologist. I *am* enthusiastic, especially when I find some connection with my own family almost everywhere I go in this beautiful country."

"Then you'll be very interested in seeing Dunadd. As you perhaps know, your ancestor, Fergus, of the Irish royal house, came to Argyll in the fifth century. He built a fort, or *dun*, and made it the capital of his new kingdom of Dalriada. He and his followers were the first Scots, of course."

After a pleasant drive of five or six miles along the Crinan Canal, with the low wooded hills of the Knapdale Forest stretching along the south bank, we turned north into flat farming country, a large area of land known, as Duncan informed me, as the *Moine Mhor*, or Great Moss.

"There," Duncan said suddenly. My eyes followed his pointing finger to see a great rock, clothed in grass, rising abruptly from the plain. We drove uncomfortably along a painfully rutted cart road into the yard of a small farm. Here we got out of the carriages to walk along a rough path to the rocky entrance of a deep gully that led into a large natural enclosure, carpeted with lush grass and populated by grazing sheep. From the enclosure, which Duncan explained had formed the lowest defensive works of the fort, we laboriously negotiated a winding, even more difficult path that followed the natural contours of the rock to the very top of the hill, the site of the original citadel.

Aunt Aillie and Ellen, who had been muttering rebelliously to each other during the climb, now collapsed on the grass. "We must have been out of our minds, Ellen," Aunt Aillie declared roundly, "to agree to come along on this excursion. Why didn't somebody tell us you needed to be part goat to climb up this mountain?"

"Now, now, Mrs. Murray, don't exaggerate. Mountain is a pretty strong word," Duncan grinned. "Seriously, though, it was a strenuous climb. You ladies rest for a bit while I show Glenna the treasures of the site."

Taking my arm, Duncan brought me to a tiny terrace near the very top of the hill, where he reverently pointed to some rocks in which I could discern the imprint of a human foot, a faintly carved outline of what seemed to be a boar, and a shallow basin scooped out of the stone.

"These are all sacred relics," Duncan observed, "in some way connected with the inaugural ceremonies of Celtic kingship. The foot imprint is believed to be of Fergus, and all subsequent kings of Dalriada placed a foot in it as part of the ceremony. Probably the basin was used for the ceremonial washing of the foot before it was placed in the imprint." He sighed. "These things really ought to be under glass, roofed over in some way. They're much too exposed to the elements, or even to vandals."

I gazed down at the artifacts, feeling the wave of compulsive awe that always came over me when I encountered a place or an object that linked me to the misty, far-off Celtic past.

"Speaking of vandals," Duncan exclaimed suddenly. "Look at that, will you?" He darted off to investigate a heap of broken glass.

"Picknickers. Or drunkards. Duncan doesn't like people who come up here and strew whisky bottles around," said a quiet voice beside me.

I turned my head with a start of surprise. Absorbed in Duncan's comments, I hadn't realized Lorne had followed us.

"I'm glad you had the opportunity to see Dunadd before you left Dungariff," he went on. "You seemed so interested in the site when I first mentioned it to you. I hope you haven't been disappointed."

"Oh, no. It's fascinating." It was eerie, the two of us engaging in this polite, formal conversation atop one of Argyll's famous landmarks, after everything that had happened between us.

We hadn't been in such close quarters since the birthday ball. As I looked directly at him, I felt a shock. His face was haggard and worn, as if he hadn't slept for nights on end.

"Mother says you plan to leave Dungariff tomorrow," Lorne said heavily. "She's terribly unhappy about your decision. She's grown so fond of you and your aunt. I think she feels guilty, too."

"Guilty? That's ridiculous," I exclaimed involuntarily.

"She's sure she could have done something to keep Flora's jealousy in check. I didn't tell her you'd decided to leave Dungariff even before Flora's outburst at the birthday ball. She'd be even more hurt if she knew you hated her son so much that you couldn't bear to live in the same house with him."

If I hadn't known him so well, I might have thought the bitter unhappiness in his voice was genuine. "Lorne, what's the point—?"

"Glenna, please listen. We may never have another chance to talk. Is there anything I can say that will persuade you to stay, at least for awhile? For my mother's sake? I promise I won't come near you. Flora won't bother you either. There's Colin, too. You know he's in love with you."

"No. No. Don't say any more." My heart ached with an almost physical pain. I'd reached the limit of my endurance to this constant emotional assault. As Duncan Forbes came up, I turned away from Lorne in relief.

"I'll have a word with the local historical society about

263

this," Duncan grumbled. "Five whisky bottles and a pile of chicken bones. We can't have rubbish littering our national monuments. Well, now, where was I, Glenna? Did I tell you about the Stone of Destiny?"

"No, but I'm sure you will."

Duncan looked pained. "Did you hear that, Lorne? The young lady is beginning to know me too well. It's the schoolteacher in me. The Stone of Destiny, Glenna, was the Coronation Stone of the High Kings of Ireland. Fergus brought it with him when he arrived in Scotland. It was kept at Dunadd for centuries. Eventually the Stone was taken to Scone, where it was used for the coronations of the later Scottish kings. Do you know where it is now?"

"Yes," I laughed. "The English stole it and took it to Westminster Abbey, where it's been used ever since for the coronations of *their* kings."

"Tell her, Lorne."

The strained look left Lorne's face. His eyes crinkled with merriment as he said, "The chroniclers said the Stone was a highly carved, saddle-shaped piece of marble or possibly of meteorite. Something very different from that crude lump of sandstone the English are so proud of." For a moment he could have been the man I first knew, drawn out of his natural reserve by a desire to show me the places he so deeply loved.

"Lorne and I are true-blue Scottish patriots," Duncan told me as he took my arm to help me down the slope. "Back at school, if we'd ever found a stray Stewart heir or two to champion, we'd have started our own version of the '45."

On a lower level of turf below the coronation relics, Aunt Aillie and Ellen had spread out a blanket and were in the process of setting out a lavish picnic lunch, including a spirit lamp for making tea. As I helped them remove the food and plates and cutlery from the heavy hamper that Colin and Lorne had carried up together from the farmyard, I looked down the twisting path we had taken and exclaimed, "Are those really our carriages down there? They're like a child's playthings. It's hard to believe we actually climbed that far."

"Well, *I* believe it, every foot of it," Aunt Aillie said feelingly. "From the way my back and legs feel, I suspect I'll be permanently crippled." She lowered her voice. "Is that wretched girl going to throw another of her tantrums?"

I flicked a glance at Flora, who was standing some distance away, apparently lost in a brooding personal fog, taking no interest in what the rest of us were doing. She was looking out over the view from the opposite side of the hill. She was so self-absorbed that I doubted she was really seeing the magnificent vistas of the islands of Jura and the Inner Hebrides.

"I hope she holds together through today anyway," Aunt Aillie muttered. "We won't have to worry about her after tomorrow. You were right, Glenna. We couldn't have stayed on at the castle."

In other circumstances I would have enjoyed this picnic lunch in the midst of some of the wildest, most beautiful scenery in all of Europe. The food was delicious and the West Highland weather had redeemed itself. The rain had completely stopped, the sun shone sporadically, and there was a cool, steady breeze, redolent of grass and wild herbs and the distant beguiling tang of the sea.

The problem was with the human element of the picnic. If Duncan Forbes hadn't been there, the meal would have been a disaster. Ellen and Aunt Aillie and I made an effort to keep the conversation going, grasping at topics like the weather and the smoothness of our steamer voyage, but our hearts weren't in it. Lorne and Flora scarcely opened their mouths to speak. Neither of them ate more than a mouthful. Even Colin was unnaturally silent. That left Duncan, who kept his air balls of persiflage dancing aloft until lunch was over.

"I often think back to those summer visits at Dunga-riff," he told Ellen at one point. "My mother used to swear there was something in the Argyll air that destroyed fabrics. I'd come home from the castle with holes in all my clothes."

Ellen laughed. "After your first visit I wrote telling her that I'd tried my best to keep you from climbing every rock in sight. She wrote back that I wasn't to blame myself. She said your clothes had been in tatters from the moment you learned to walk."

"Mothers," Duncan said sadly. "You'd think they'd keep our secrets." He turned to Flora, sitting next to him on the ground. "The wedding will be in September, is that right?" he asked with a friendly smile. "I suppose you and your mother and Mrs. MacDougall are knee-deep in preparations. I remember when my sister got married, there was no living in the house with her and my mother."

Shrewd as he was, I thought, Duncan couldn't help sensing the oppressive atmosphere that hung over us. His well-meant effort to draw Flora out wasn't very successful. She was slow in answering him, and her reply, when it came sounded wooden, as if she were reciting by rote. "The wedding. Yes, it will be in September. I hope you'll come, Mr. Forbes."

Lorne stirred, setting down his untasted cup of tea. Rising abruptly, he said, "I think I'll climb up to the top of the citadel. Who knows, there might be a minor artifact or two up there that's gone unnoticed."

Gazing after him, Duncan shook his head, smiling. "Lorne the eternal optimist! The archeologists, amateur and otherwise, have gone over this site inch by inch."

"I can't think what ails Lorne today," Ellen said suddenly. The words seemed to force themselves out of her mouth. She bit her lip.

"He hasn't seemed quite himself," Duncan remarked,

with a faint air of relief that the subject had been broached. "I did wonder . . ."

"You know him so well, Duncan." Ellen looked at me. "You were talking to Lorne, Glenna. Did he say anything to you about . . . about what might be bothering him?"

"No. He was telling me about the relics." Another lie. I was being entangled in a web of guilt. "You know, better than any of us, Cousin Ellen, that Lorne's not very talkative about his affairs."

Ellen said, half to herself, "That may have been true once. You can't say he hasn't been talkative to *you*, Glenna."

Flora had been sitting with her head down, staring at her fingers as they methodically tore a piece of bread into minute shreds. Now she rose slowly, her face like a mask, and without saying a word she began walking up the slope toward Lorne, who stood on a shallow outcrop of rock on the edge of the opposite, more precipitous side of the summit, looking out to the distant view of the islands.

"Something's the matter with her," Aunt Aillie exclaimed. "She looks as if she's sleepwalking. Perhaps we should go after her, Ellen."

"I wouldn't worry about Miss Cameron, Mrs. Murray," Duncan said reassuringly. "Lorne's up there. He'll see to her."

Colin broke out of his silence. "If you'll excuse me, I think I'll stretch my legs, too." He got to his feet, walking purposefully up the hill. Flora had already joined Lorne on the rocky outcrop.

I gazed after Colin, the vague unease I'd been feeling all day beginning to intensify. My eyes shifted beyond him to Lorne and Flora, outlined on their rocky perch against the vault of the sky. I couldn't hear them, of course, but it was obvious from the tension in their figures and Flora's wild gestures, that they were arguing bitterly. Colin had almost reached them when a scream of terror ripped through the

267

air. Immobilized in frozen fear for a moment, Aunt Aillie and Ellen and Duncan and I rose as one and raced toward the top of the hill.

I reached the rocky outcrop first. Colin, gripped with hysteria, made an ineffectual attempt to bar my way. "Oh, Glenna, she's gone, she's gone. Don't look," he babbled, but I pushed past him to find an ashen-faced Lorne staring transfixed at Flora's crumpled body on the rocky slope below. For the first time since I had known him, he was totally unnerved. He muttered the same few words over and over. "She lost her balance. I tried to catch her arm as she fell, but I missed."

Duncan Forbes broke the spell of horror that enveloped the rest of us. He glared at Colin and Lorne, shouting, "Good God, what's the matter with you two? We've got to get down there to help that poor girl." He started down the precipitous slope, catching at every available handhold to break his sliding fall. Within seconds Lorne's eyes cleared and he plunged after Duncan. Colin, gulping down his horror, followed.

Aunt Aillie's fingers dug convulsively into my arm as we watched the three men scramble down to Flora's still body. "She broke her fall," Aunt Aillie murmured. "She didn't fall all the way. She'll be all right, Glenna, you'll see."

I knew she was wrong. I'd known, from the first moment I glimpsed that pathetic broken figure, that Flora was dead. She'd tried desperately to prevent herself from plummeting to the bottom of the cliff by clutching at a projecting branch of a scrub pine, and she'd succeeded. But she couldn't avoid the sharp rock that cracked her skull and broke her neck.

Chapter 15

The grass in the old cemetery was soggy with moisture, and the air was dank and clammy from the driving rain that had beaten against the walls of the church during Flora's funeral. The large crowd of mourners—relatives, friends, pupils, and former pupils of the dead girl—formed patiently into a long line, waiting to say their last good-byes by tossing the ceremonial handful of earth over Flora's coffin. Hugging my arms against my chest in an attempt to ward off the penetrating chill, I stood to the rear of the line, numbly waiting my turn, feeling unutterably weary and drained. I clung to the comforting thought that soon the sad and lengthy ceremonial of Flora's last rites would finally come to an end and Aunt Aillie and I could leave Dungariff as we had planned.

Despite myself, my mind kept returning to that ghastly afternoon at the citadel of Dunadd. I couldn't erase from my thoughts Flora's scream of mortal anguish as she fell to her death. Duncan Forbes's presence had been a near miracle. For the first time since I'd known him, Lorne's iron self-control had broken, and Colin was in a pitiable state of shock, Duncan had taken charge, carrying Flora's body up the cliff and wrapping it tenderly in a carriage robe for the drive back to the port of Crinan. It was

Duncan, too, who had made the return steamer trip to Oban a little less grim than it might have been. He'd made quiet arrangements for a modest wooden coffin and kept vigil over Flora during the voyage, leaving her survivors to huddle together in dazed grief.

As I moved slowly behind the line of mourners, I was grateful that for a few moments, at least, I had become separated from the rest of the family, without the necessity to murmur perfunctory small talk. Ellen and Aunt Aillie were up ahead of me a short distance, and over a sea of intervening heads I caught sight of Lorne standing by himself beside the wall of the cemetery. Even from a distance I could see that his features were still set in the mold of rigid, masklike endurance that had settled on his face during the return trip from Dunadd. If I'd ever had any doubts about the depth of Lorne's feeling for Flora, they were resolved now. The man had obviously come to the brink of despair.

A tall figure loomed beside me. As I looked up at Colin, I felt a shock. I hadn't seen him for several days. He'd remained in Oban after we came back from Dunadd, working in the ship chandler's store to relieve Mr. Cameron of responsibility while the family made their preparations to bury Flora. Surprisingly, he hadn't sat with Lorne and Ellen and Aunt Aillie and me at the funeral. Perhaps he hadn't attended the services, I thought now, looking at his haggard face. In him, even more than in Lorne, the vital spark seemed to have been extinquished. Once more I wondered if he had continued to love Flora even after she became engaged to Lorne, though he'd seemed to convince everyone, including himself, that his affections had never been seriously involved.

"This is indecent," he mumbled. His eyes looked glazed, unfocused. I wasn't sure he was aware he was talking to me. "All these people crowding around her grave to throw earth on her body, pretending to mourn

270

her. They never cared about her when she was living. I think I'm going to be sick—"

"Colin, come with me," I said urgently. I took his arm, pulling him away from the line of mourners to a secluded spot near the gates of the cemetery. "Put your head down, Colin. Breathe deeply. Try to get hold of yourself, for Flora's sake. It'll soon be over."

As he gulped in great breaths of air, his color improved and his eyes seemed to clear. Obviously, however, he was still under enormous stress. He exclaimed savagely, as though the words were being forced out of some seething pit deep inside him, "It'll never be over, Glenna, not until my cousin Lorne pays for what he's done. He killed her, you know."

I stared blankly at him for a moment. Then I put my hand on his arm, keeping my voice low and soothing. "You know you don't mean that, Colin. It was an accident. Flora lost her balance and Lorne couldn't catch her in time."

Colin shook his head. "No," he said heavily. "I meant what I said. He killed her. He deliberately pushed her off the cliff."

"Colin, listen to me—"

"No, you listen. You weren't there. I was. As soon as I started toward them, I saw they were quarreling. Halfway up the slope, I could hear Lorne shouting, 'I can't go on with it. It's finished, but by God you're going to tell me where he is.' I don't know what he meant by that. Then Flora screamed something like, 'All right I'll tell you, but you've got to give me another chance, because I'll never let you leave me.' At that second I suppose Lorne realized Flora would never give him up, no matter what he said. He'd have to get rid of her. So he pushed her. My God, I'll never forget the sound of her screaming as she fell, never until the day I die."

"Colin, I know Flora's death has been a terrible blow

271

to you, but you've got to get a grip on yourself. Those few words you overheard don't prove Lorne killed her. Why would he do such a terrible thing? He loved Flora. They were going to be married."

Colin grabbed my hands, glaring down at me with a desperate urgency, as if it were essential that I accept the truth of what he was saying. "But that was just it, Glenna. Lorne wasn't going to marry Flora. She told me that he broke their engagement during the voyage to Dunadd. Don't you remember how they stood talking for the longest time at the stern of the boat? That was when he broke the news to her."

And it was right afterwards that Flora accosted me, I thought, accusing me of destroying her happiness. "I don't understand, Colin," I said stupidly. "Why would Lorne break his engagement?"

"He told Flora it wouldn't work out, that they'd be better off going their separate ways," Colin replied heavily. "Flora knew the real reason, of course. He wanted to get rid of her so he could go after you and your money."

"No . . . no." Wrenching my hands free, I stepped back, shaking my head against the sickening horror that was creeping over me. "It's not true. Lorne never wanted to marry me, it was always Flora."

"Then you were the last to know it, Glenna," Colin sneered. "Apparently it wouldn't greatly have surprised anybody in Oban if you and Lorne had announced that you were getting married. Even before I went on holiday, I'd heard rumors that Lorne was having financial difficulties. Mr. Cameron tried to pump me about it. Now it's all over town that the Master of Dungariff owes thousands to the bankers in Fort William and hasn't a prayer of meeting the loan when it comes due. And Mrs. Cameron's been spreading the gossip that Lorne's been neglecting her stepdaughter in favor of the wealthy heiress from America. Didn't you notice how people avoided you and Lorne and the family at the funeral? You were sitting by yourselves in the church, with acres of empty pews around you. Maybe folk aren't saying yet that Lorne murdered Flora to save his financial neck, but it won't be long, especially after I get through with him."

Taking me completely by surprise, he lurched away from me, heading purposefully toward Lorne. I stood petrified, staring after him, a hard knot wrapping itself around my heart. In my desolation I realized Lorne was capable of more evil even than I had imagined. Colin's terrible accusations were true. In his desperation Lorne had killed the woman he loved. He'd failed to eliminate me with his "accidents," and as soon as I left Dungariff, I'd be beyond his reach. The silica mining scheme had fallen through and the banks would certainly not extend him any more credit. His only chance of saving his beloved estate was to dump Flora and marry me for my fortune. It didn't matter that I'd told him I was bored with him and Dungariff; he was sure, from the fiery response he elicited every time he touched me, that I wouldn't resist him if he were free. But Flora had refused to be cast aside, and so he'd killed her.

Encased in a kind of icy numbness, I watched Colin accost Lorne where he stood alone on the opposite side of the cemetery, his hands stuffed in his pockets, his head bowed as he stared unseeingly at the ground. He looked up with a start as Colin came up to him, and I could make out the shock of surprise on his thin dark face when Colin began to speak.

The ice cracked around my emotions, and with a gasp I darted toward them, seized with a sudden instinctive conviction that I couldn't allow Colin to confront Lorne with his ghastly suspicions, not in this hallowed place, with poor pathetic Flora not yet resting in her grave, not in front of Lorne's mother and the Camerons.

I was too late. As I came up Lorne was exclaiming

incredulously, "My God, Colin, you can't—" He broke off as Colin lunged toward him. Sidestepping to his right to avoid Colin's flailing fists, Lorne pivoted his body adroitly to catch Colin from the rear, pinning his arms to his side.

"Let me go, damn you," Colin panted, struggling desperately to release himself. "I'm not finished with you."

With a lightning-swift movement, Lorne grabbed Colin's right wrist and twisted the arm behind his back, up toward his shoulder blades. "I want your word you'll stop this idiocy," Lorne said grimly, "or I'll break your arm. You know I can do it, Colin."

Impulsively I stepped in front of Colin, putting a hand on either side of his face so he was forced to look at me. "Colin, let be. You can't fight here. You owe something to Flora's memory."

He gave a great sigh and relaxed against Lorne's hold. "All right," he mumbled. "You've won, Lorne. This time."

Instantly releasing his grip on Colin, Lorne stepped back. He looked at me, his eyes cold and bleak, but before he could say anything, I turned away, taking Colin's arm. I spoke gently to him. "Let's join the line, Colin. Everyone will expect you to do this last thing for Flora."

"Yes," he muttered. "She'd want it. She always liked things done exactly right." As we walked slowly away, Lorne silently fell into step behind us. Several heads turned when we attached ourselves to the end of the line. I wondered if the incident between Lorne and Colin had been noticed. The three of us, Lorne and Colin and I, had been well to the rear of the line of mourners moving to the grave site, and the encounter had lasted for only a few brief seconds. For Ellen's sake and that of the Camerons, I hoped nobody had observed us.

My eyes filmed with tears and my hand trembled, as I

scattered the earth over Flora's coffin. I sensed rather than saw the shudder that shook Lorne's tall frame as he stood beside me, hesitating for an agonizingly long moment before he jerkily performed the same sad duty.

The experience was too much for Colin. He stumbled blindly away from the grave and I rushed after him, catching at his arm to prevent him from caroming into the mass of mourners who were preparing to leave the cemetery. Lorne followed us, saying in a low voice, "He doesn't know what he's doing. I'll get him away until he comes to himself."

"I can take care of him," I said tightly. "He doesn't want you. Please go away."

He recoiled, as if someone had hit him between the eyes, and Colin, drawing a deep, ragged breath, recovered himself enough to snap, "Glenna's right, Dungariff. Leave me alone. Get out of my sight." He turned his back on Lorne. "Glenna dear, thanks for your helping hand. I'll be all right now, but I've got to get out of here. I can't face going to the Camerons' house. I've always thought it was ghoulish, all that eating and drinking after a funeral. It's like eating a picnic meal over somebody's grave, and I've seen all I want to see of graves today."

He stalked away in the direction of the cemetery gates, and I didn't try to stop him. He was still in deep pain, but I thought he was rational again. Aunt Aillie and Ellen came up then, looking after Colin's retreating form with worried frowns.

"What's wrong with Colin?" Ellen asked Lorne. "He nearly fainted at the grave site. I never thought he'd be so affected by Flora's—" She bit her lip, her frown growing deeper. "Lorne, were you and Colin fighting? Somebody told me—"

"We had a little misunderstanding, Mother," Lorne said evenly. "Nothing to concern youself about. Colin's very upset. He and Flora were so close. They saw each other every day for several years. He didn't want to go to the Camerons' house."

I glanced at him sharply. Clearly he was implying that he and Colin had had a minor disagreement about the necessity of taking part in the post-funeral baked meats at the home of Flora's parents.

"Oh, was that it?" Ellen seemed relieved. "Well, I'd rather not go either, but we can't offend the Camerons."

Half an hour later, I slipped my plate with its barely touched food onto a serving table in the drawing room of the Cameron's big old house off Argyll Square.

"Glenna, you should eat something. You haven't had a morsel since breakfast," Aunt Aillie scolded.

I shook my head. "I don't want anything."

Despite her exhortations to me, Aunt Aillie herself had eaten very little. She and I and Ellen and Lorne were sitting together at the side of the room. The chairs to either side of us were unoccupied. People had been avoiding sitting near us since our arrival. It wasn't that we were completely ostracized. A number of persons had come up to talk to us, but they looked vaguely uncomfortable and didn't stay long. Mr. Cameron, circulating through the rooms to greet his guests and thank them for coming, had acknowledged our presence with the briefest of cold nods. No one unfamiliar with the situation would have dreamed we were two families who had nearly been united by marriage.

"Must we stay much longer, Cousin Ellen?" I murmured.

"There doesn't seem much point to it, does there?" she replied under her breath. "Lorne, shall we go?"

The drive back to the castle in the landau was accomplished in almost total silence. Neither Ellen nor Aunt Aillie commented on our chilly reception, both at the church and at the Camerons' house, although it would have seemed the natural thing to do. Perhaps they both felt that by asking the questions they would be letting the demons out of the bottle. Lorne sat with his head turned away from us, lost behind the curtain of his black thoughts. I gazed doggedly at the passing landscape, which, as if complementing the dark mood of all of us, looked inhospitable and subdued under the intermittent buffeting of slashing gray rain squalls. Incongruously, I remembered Colin's frequent laughing references to the beautiful "Glenna weather" I had brought to Argyll.

Colin. What would he do now? He'd accused Lorne to his face of murdering Flora. Would he try to bring home the crime to Lorne legally? I didn't see how he could succeed in that. He couldn't prove that Lorne had killed Flora, any more than I could prove any of Lorne's frequent attempts on my life. In the end, Lorne's punishment would probably be a variant of the Scottish legal verdict, Not proven. He'd live out his life ensnarled in a miasma of suspicion that he was a murderer. Not guilty, not innocent, just not proven.

The landau rumbled under the arches of the gatehouse and rolled to a stop in the courtyard of Dungariff. Donnie rushed down from the driver's seat to help Ellen and Aunt Aillie out of the carriage. Ignoring Lorne's extended hand, I jumped to the ground and turned to follow his mother and my aunt as they hurried across the slippery cobblestones to the side door of the hall house.

Lorne blocked my way. "Glenna, we must talk."

"Later. Inside. It's starting to rain again."

"Then come over here." He forced me into the little medieval chapel in the wall opposite the stables. Out of the corner of my eye, I could see Donnie eyeing us curiously as he drove the carriage into the stables. It was damp and dark inside the tiny space, and the cold crept up my legs from the ancient stones. I retreated against the wall as Lorne advanced toward me, looming over me with a controlled menace that sent my heart hammering so hard it seemed inconceivable that he couldn't hear it. Donnie saw us come into the chapel, I thought. Lorne can't do anything to me here without getting caught.

Lorne's face was haggard as he asked, "Glenna, did Colin tell you I deliberately pushed Flora off that cliff?"

On this subject, at least, we were past pretense. "Yes, he did," I replied, my lips stiff.

"But you didn't believe it? You couldn't have believed it . . ." His voice trailed off as he stared at my telltale face. He pleaded with me, "Glenna, in God's name, tell me you don't think I'm a murderer."

The torment in his voice sounded so real. Even now he was trying to win me over. "How could you do it?" I demanded harshly. "How could you bring yourself to kill the woman you loved?"

Lorne's dark eyes flashed, and the words came pouring out as if a dam had burst deep inside him. "But that was the whole point, don't you see? I didn't love Flora. I've never loved her. That day on the boat, I finally told her I couldn't go on with the farce any longer. She wouldn't accept it. At Dunadd she kept after me to change my mind, using the same old arguments over and over again, and I was so tired of it . . . She grabbed my arm, trying to get close to me. God help me, I brushed her away and she lost her balance, but you've got to believe me, Glenna, I never pushed her."

"Believe you? Why should I? You've been lying to me since I first met you and you're lying now," I spat out. "Flora told me you'd made love to her. You asked her to marry you. Why did you do that if you didn't love her? You loved Dungariff more, that was all. When the banks wouldn't give you any more credit, when you tried to get rid of me so you could inherit my fortune and all your attempts failed, then you killed Flora."

He turned ashen. "Oh my God," he whispered. "That's why you turned against me. You thought I was trying to kill you." He swallowed hard. "Glenna, will you listen to me? I'd known Flora for years before I quarreled with my father and went to sea, though she was closer in age to Colin than she was to me, and I always thought she and Colin would marry some day. About two years ago I came home on leave. Mother gave a small party for me and Flora was among the guests. I drank far too much that night . . . the visit wasn't going well, I'd quarreled with my father again. I can't remember much that happened. Apparently I talked Flora into going down to the beach with me. We had a bottle of wine with us and before long we were making love. Afterwards she was so overwhelmed with guilt, she was so convinced she was going straight to hell, that I promised to marry her."

A muscle twitched in Lorne's cheek. "After I went back to sea, though," he went on after a pause, "I realized that Flora and I couldn't build a marriage on the basis of one sexual encounter, and I wrote to tell her so. I was sure she'd eventually get over her feelings of guilt. I didn't know she'd been in love with me for a long time . . . or thought she was. When my father died and I came home for good, I discovered that Flora hadn't told anyone that our engagement was broken. After she received my letter, she found out she was pregnant. She went away to have our child in secret. She wouldn't tell me where the baby was, she threatened to keep him away from me forever, unless I agreed to marry her. What else could I do? I didn't love her, but the arrangement seemed bearable until you came to Dungariff, Glenna. I fell madly, desperately in love with you."

I shrank back in instinctive horror. He'd say anything, do anything, to get out of the trap he was in. "That's another lie," I said, forcing the words out of a dry throat. "I don't want to hear any more." I tried to slip past him.

"No you don't," he said, his voice brittle. He put his hands against the wall on either side of me, leaning toward me so I couldn't move. "This time you'll hear me out. There's not much left to tell. Gradually I came to realize that I couldn't marry Flora under any circumstances. She thought she could make me change my mind by holding the baby over me. That's what we were arguing about in those last seconds on the cliff at Dunadd. At the very end she did tell me. There'd never been a baby. She'd lied about it to get me to marry her."

Some of the tension that was keeping him as tight as a watch spring relaxed a little as he finished speaking. He dropped his arms, encircling my waist. I felt a sudden heat all through my body and the familiar racing excitement began to quicken my heartbeat. He lowered his head, murmuring, "Glenna, my darling, tell me you believe me. Let me hold you, let me love you."

Oh, God, was it all going to begin again? Hadn't I learned my lesson? I couldn't let myself turn into another Catriona, forgetting everything—honor, decency, ordinary common sense—in the searing embrace of a man who wanted only to use me. "Love me?" I gasped. "I can't bear to have you touch me with your bloodstained hands. After today, thank God, you won't have the chance to paw at me ever again."

I gave him a violent shove, startling him so that he stumbled backwards. Running out the door of the chapel, I raced across the courtyard into the hall house. In the corridor I collided with Jane Henderson, knocking a stack of linen out of her arms.

"I'm sorry, Jane." I knelt to pick up the scattered towels. "I hope you won't have to wash these again."

"Nay, Miss Glenna. It will be a' richt." The housekeeper looked at me keenly. "Are ye ill?"

"No. It's been a wearing day. I hate funerals," I said with a sudden ferocity.

"Oh, aye. Puir Miss Flora." Jane hesitated. "I was expecting Maister Colin tae come back wi' ye frae Oban.

The Mistress didna seem tae ken when the laddie might be arriving."

I thought it likely that Colin would never visit Dungariff again, but I couldn't tell Jane that. She'd find it out soon enough. "He became quite upset at the cemetery," I said cautiously. "He was very fond of Miss Cameron, you know. And then she died so tragically . . . I think Colin wanted to be by himself for a bit."

"I see." It was clear she didn't. "Weel, noo, Miss Glenna, ye dinna ha' tae hurry wi' changing yer dress for dinner. It willna be ready until eight. I didna ken juist when ye might be coming back frae the funeral."

One more dinner. One more night, I thought wearily, as I trudged up the turret stairs. When I opened the door, the first sight I saw was the row of valises and portmanteau neatly ranged beside the wardrobe. The little maid Meg had packed up my belongings while I was gone on the trip to Dunadd and I'd refused to allow her to unpack more than one small valise for my immediate needs. I was still determined to leave Dungariff the next day.

Removing my hat and taking off the dark coat I'd worn to the funeral, I walked over to the dressing table. Except for my jewelry box and the dress and shoes I'd be wearing for dinner tonight, very little remained to be packed. Tomorrow morning I'd put my comb and brush and mirror into my toilet case and I'd be ready to leave.

Extending my hand to close the jewelry box, I paused, picking up the silver MacDougall crest-brooch that Lorne and his mother had given to me. I turned it over in my hands, my eye lingering on the family motto: *Buaidh no bas*. To conquer or die. Yes, I thought, the motto summed up Lorne's whole character. To save his proud, ancient heritage, to remain as Master of Dungariff, he hadn't hesitated to sacrifice everyone and everything in his path. And how well the Gaelic word *dughall*—the origin of the family name—suited him. To me he'd always been that, the dark, unfathomable stranger. And never more so than today, when, with all the barriers down between us, with the horrifying details of what he had done in the open at last, he'd still apparently been convinced he could win me over by the naked power of his sexuality.

I replaced the brooch in the jewelry box and slammed down the lid. I couldn't bear to look at it, though I knew I'd have to take it with me. I certainly couldn't leave it here where Ellen would find it. My only consolation, in this stark and horrifying tragedy that was unfolding, was that Ellen might never learn about the crimes her son had committed.

A soft knock sounded and Aunt Aillie poked her head around the door. "Can I come in for a minute, Glenna?"

She walked in, her bemused expression at variance with her usual air of down-to-earth practicality. She went over to my dressing table, absently rearranging my toilet articles for a moment before she turned to say abruptly, "Do you know what ails Lorne? I was standing outside the sitting room talking to Ellen when he came storming into the passage from the courtyard, looking as though he'd seen the Angel of Death. For the first time since I've known him, he was almost rude to his mother. He wouldn't talk to her, wouldn't answer her questions . . . Glenna, you stayed behind in the courtyard to talk to him after we returned from Oban. Did he tell you anything?"

I shook my head. I had to keep the harrowing truth from Aunt Aillie, at least until we were out of this place. If possible, forever. Perhaps she could go back to Massachusetts with only beautiful memories of her time in Scotland. I said quietly, "I think you're forgetting something, Aunt Aillie. Lorne buried his fiancée today."

"That's another thing," she exclaimed. "What on earth was going on today at the funeral? I felt like a leper. Nobody sat near us in the church. Mr. Cameron looked ready to throw us out of his house. And I don't care how much he denied it, I think Lorne had a fight with Colin at the cemetery."

She looked at me expectantly, but I shook my head again. "People aren't themselves at a time like this. Flora died so young. Colin and Lorne simply can't accept her death."

"I suppose . . ." She sounded dissatisfied. After a moment, her eyes wandering to the row of packed luggage, she said, "Glenna, I've been wondering. Do you really think it's necessary for us to leave Dungariff tomorrow?"

I looked at her in surprise. "Yes, I do. Why should we change our plans?"

"Well . . . now that Flora's gone . . ." She put her hand to her mouth, flushing a beet red. "Glenna, you know I'm not glad the girl's dead, but she was the reason we were going away. Don't you think it would help Lorne and Ellen in their grief, if we were to stay on for a few days?"

"Aunt Aillie, I won't stay another day in the same house with Lorne." I don't know where the words came from. They simply exploded out of me.

Aunt Aillie's eyes widened. "What's Lorne done to make you talk that way, Glenna? No, don't put me off. I've felt all day that something's wrong."

I had to give her an answer. It would have to include at least a small shred of the truth or she wouldn't believe me. "Aunt Aillie, I'm afraid Lorne's begun to . . . to have strong feelings for me. I wouldn't feel comfortable staying here."

She gasped. "Glenna, are you saying Lorne mentioned love to you on the very day of Flora's funeral?" she asked bluntly. "Is that why he—both of you—are acting so strangely?"

"Yes. You understand, don't you, why I didn't tell you? You've always liked Lorne."

Aunt Aillie seemed dazed. "It crossed my mind once or twice . . . well, you remember, I hinted at it to you . . . that

Lorne regarded you as more than a distant cousin. And I never could understand what he saw in that poor pathetic girl. But this! It's monstrous that he should attempt to court you just hours after he buried his fiancée. What kind of a man would do a thing like that? You're right, of course. We can't stay here now." She paused, a worried frown forming between her eyes. "Glenna, you don't . . . care for him?"

"I never want to see him again, Aunt Aillie." That much, at least, was the truth.

She nodded. "I'll ask Ellen to have the landau ready first thing in the morning."

Dinner that evening was a ghastly parody of the meals I'd eaten these past weeks at the castle. Most of the food went back to the kitchens unconsumed. We sat in virtual silence as the courses came and went. Ellen and Aunt Aillie and I did make a few stilted remarks to each other, "We've enjoyed our visit here so much," and "It's been delightful having you." We sounded like strangers. Ellen's thoughts were obviously on Lorne, whose chair remained empty. When it became apparent, after the soup had been served and taken away, that Lorne wasn't coming to the table, Ellen murmured a brief apology. I could tell, from the many times I caught her hunted eyes resting on me, that she connected her son's absence and his earlier aberrant behavior with me.

It was an enormous relief to rise from the table. Aunt Aillie and I refused coffee in the drawing room; it was later than usual, we wanted to make an early start in the morning, the coffee might keep us awake. Ellen didn't press it on us.

When I returned to the tower room, I stood for a long time before my windows, gazing out over the sound toward the hazy outline of Mull in the last dying glow of the sunset, memorizing the view I'd come to love so much in all weathers and at all times of the day. The rising moon was attempting to show itself from behind a scattering of rain clouds before I turned away from the windows.

I moved restlessly around the room, checking the wardrobe and the heavy old chest of drawers for any of my possessions Meg might have left behind. She'd been very thorough. Tomorrow after I left there'd be no trace of the weeks I'd spent in this room. I paused before the wardrobe, looking at the thick leather volume on the top shelf. Meg knew the family history belonged at Dungariff. I had no desire to open the book again. The sooner I could forget about Angus and Catriona, and the eerie foreshadowing of their lives with mine and Lorne's, the better.

I jumped when the knock sounded at the door. "Yes?" I called apprehensively. Surely Lorne wouldn't try to see me again.

"It's Jane, Miss Glenna. I've brought you some chocolate."

"I don't . . . Come in, Jane." Perhaps I wouldn't get the chance to say good-bye to her tomorrow.

"Ye didna ha' coffee the nicht," she explained, setting her tray on a small table. She gazed curiously at my luggage. "The Mistress told me ye were leaving on the morrow. Will ye be coming back?"

"No, I don't think so, Jane."

"Ye'll be gaeing tae America?"

"Not immediately. Mrs. Murray and I will be staying in Argyll for the next few months, perhaps for a time in Oban."

"Ach, ye ken we'll be sorry tae lose ye."

"I'll miss you too, Jane. I'll miss Argyll."

"But why leave, then? Maister Colin would make ye sae happy here if ye'd gie him the chance."

"I'm sorry," I said gently, touched as always by her fierce attachment to her nursling. "I don't think Colin and I were meant for each other."

"Ah, weel, 'tis no' my place tae say. The laddie will no

doubt be telling ye himsel'." She nodded at my surprised look. "He came a wee bit ago. He want tae talk wi' ye."

My heart sank. Undoubtedly Colin wanted to see me to rehash his recriminations against Lorne. "It's so late, Jane."

She said apologetically, "I dinna like tae insist, but Maister Colin is bent on seeing ye. He told me tae tell ye,"—she screwed her eyes together in an effort to remember exactly—"he says he needs yer help tae make sure he doesna get awa' wi' it. The laddie said ye'll understand wha' he means."

I felt a shiver of apprehension. How could I help Colin make sure Lorne didn't get away with it? Surely Colin must have realized, as I had, that Lorne had covered his tracks too well. An official police investigation, if that was what Colin had in mind, would come to nothing. Or had he decided to take Lorne's punishment into his own hands? I couldn't let Colin do that. I couldn't let him become a murderer, too.

"Very well," I told Jane. "I'll see him. Ask him to come up."

"Nay, Miss Glenna. Maister Colin wants ye tae meet him on the parapet walk outside the tower room. In aboot an hour, after the family ha' gone tae bed."

"But why, Jane?" I frowned, feeling a rush of aversion at the thought of venturing out on the battlements. "Why doesn't he come up here?"

Her long face clouded over. "He said he wanted tae be verra sure ye wouldna be overheard. Miss Glenna, I fear for the lad. He's no' himsel'. Would ye believe it, he came out here in secret. He wouldna let me tell a soul save ye that he was here."

Increasingly disturbed myself, I eyed Jane's worried frown and took a sudden decision. "All right, then. Tell Colin I'll meet him at—" I glanced at the clock on the mantel "—at midnight."

The next forty-five minutes seemed like forty-five hours.

The minute hands on the clock didn't appear to move. I kept glancing at the door leading to the parapet. I felt more strongly than ever a chilling sense that evil lay in wait for me out there. Once I thought I heard in the distance the quavering echoes of Catriona's lost, anguished cry. At one minute to midnight, I slipped into the heavy hooded cloak that I'd retrieved from the packed portmanteau. Walking over to the heavy old door, I drew a deep, difficult breath and slowly drew the massive bolt. If I hadn't known that Colin would soon be with me, I couldn't have forced myself to step across the threshold.

The parapet walk was cold and dark. The pallid moon emerged only fitfully from a bank of black and scudding rain clouds, and a chill wind pulled at the hood of my cloak in erratic gusts. I shivered, drawing the heavy cloak more securely around me. As the seconds slipped leadeningly by, my skin began to prickle with a rising sense of apprehension and my breath came faster, as if I'd been running. Where was Colin?

Then a sudden fierce blast of wind whipped the hood from my head, causing my hair to stream out wildly behind me, and I heard a voice calling my name. Turning to look down the long line of the battlements, I saw Lorne running toward me. I knew with the sick certainty of inevitability that nightmare and reality had finally fused into one. The man who had menaced me for so long in my dreams at last had me at his mercy. He was racing to throw me over the parapet to the jagged rocks below, just as, so many years before, Angus MacDougall had returned from Culloden to kill Catriona.

My throat opened in a scream of despairing terror. Whirling around to try for the safety of my tower room, I ran straight into Jane Henderson's strong arms. "Oh, Jane, Jane, thank God you came," I was sobbing in relief, when the words choked in my throat. A pair of sinewy hands wrenched me away from Jane's hold. I flailed out with my legs, I clawed at the iron-hard arms that would soon force me to the embrasures from which, for so many centuries, the defenders of Dungariff had rained down their arrows and boiling oil and quicklime upon their enemies.

Jane must have leaped at Lorne. Suddenly I was thrown against the cold slippery stones of the parapet walk, striking my head so hard that I lost consciousness for a few fleeting seconds. A shrill, keening sound, carrying with it overtones of such terror that my heart constricted, brought me to my senses. I staggered to my feet to find Lorne grappling with Jane, trying grimly to subdue her. She was resisting him with such superhuman fury that the combat seemed very nearly equal, even though Lorne was so much bigger and stronger than she was. As she fought, she spewed out a stream of Gaelic, not a word of which I could understand, but there was no mistaking the venomous anger she was conveying.

I stood paralyzed, watching helplessly as Jane writhed and twisted desperately in her titanic struggle to break Lorne's merciless grip. Suddenly the fog of frozen terror that had enveloped me miraculously lifted in the face of my realization that Lorne was bound to win in the end. By myself, I couldn't help Jane. There was no way I could drag Lorne away from her. There was nothing out here I could use as a weapon. I had to go for help, rouse the household, before Lorne killed both of us.

For a second more I was mired in indecision as I glanced from the open door of the tower room to the stream of light coming from the Laird's Bedchamber farther along the parapet walk. The tower room was closer, but to reach help from there I would have to go down the winding turret stairs, through the first floor rooms and up the stairs again to the family quarters on the second floor. Gathering up my skirts I raced along the battlements and into the Laird's Bedchamber, which looked incongruously neat and serene, with a banked fire casting a soft glow on the ancient furnishings.

I tore open the inner door of the room and plunged down the stairs to the second floor, screaming at the top of my lungs as I neared the landing, screaming even harder as I ran down the dark corridor to Ellen's room. Before I could lift my hand to pound on her door she'd opened it, standing before me in her nightdress, shocked and frightened.

"Glenna," she gasped. "I thought I heard someone screaming!"

"Cousin Ellen, call the servants and then come up to the parapet walk immediately," I broke in frantically. "Jane needs our help."

Without stopping to answer her bewildered questions, I moved on to Aunt Aillie's room. She was already at her door, stuffing her arms into her dressing gown. "What's this about Jane?" she demanded, staring at my cloak. "Now, don't tell me you've been wandering about—"

I seized her arm, dragging her with me along the corridor, cutting off her angry protests. "Aunt Aillie, we've got to hurry," I panted. "We've got to save Jane. It may be too late already."

She closed her mouth, drawing her full skirts up around her knees so she could follow on my heels as I pelted back up the stairs to the Laird's Bedchamber, where I slowed my furious pace momentarily to pick up a stout walking cane from a chair where Lorne had tossed it. I hadn't noticed it on my previous mad dash through the room. Armed now with a weapon, I tore out the door onto the parapet walk, praying I'd brought help in time.

"Oh, God," I screamed in horror. His back to us, Lorne was kneeling beside Jane's prone, unmoving body. I was too late.

He jerked his head around at my scream and scrambled to his feet. "Good for you, Glenna," he exclaimed breathlessly as Aunt Aillie and I ran up. "You've told my mother? Jane's in a bad way."

I stared at him uncomprehendingly. Aunt Aillie answered for me. "Yes, Ellen will be here soon. She's rousing the servants." She slipped to her knees beside Jane, who, to my unutterable relief, began to moan. Perhaps I'd been in time after all. Lorne would hardly try to harm either Jane or me with Aunt Aillie here. Behind me I caught the scuffle of running footsteps and the sound of excited voices. Ellen and a handful of servants burst onto the parapet walk.

"Lorne, in Heaven's name, what's been happening here?" Ellen demanded, her voice unsteady.

"I really don't know, Mother," Lorne replied heavily. "When I came out here I found Jane trying to throw Glenna off the parapet. I think her mind must have snapped."

After a petrified moment of shock, I opened my mouth and screamed, "Liar!" Startled faces turned to stare at me. Before I could scream anything else, Aunt Aillie rose, putting her arm around me and murmuring, "I know you don't want to accept it, Glenna, dear, but you must. Lorne is right. Poor Jane has gone mad."

I looked down at Jane, who appeared to be partially conscious. She was tossing her head restlessly from side to side and her lips were moving, muttering phrases in Gaelic, but her eyes, when they met mine, were completely blank. She *was* mad. Lorne's brutality had driven her mad. She couldn't act as my witness if I accused him of attempted murder, and without her corroboration nobody would believe me. He'd slipped out of the noose again.

Chapter 16

Aunt Aillie and I sat in Ellen's sitting room, waiting for her to return with news of Jane. Lorne had carried the housekeeper to her bedroom and Ellen had remained to see that Jane was comfortable.

"Glenna, what were the three of you—you and Jane and Lorne—doing out on the ramparts at this time of night?" Aunt Aillie asked curiously.

I couldn't say Lorne had tried to murder me. I had no proof, and Aunt Aillie would only start worrying about my sanity again. I muttered, "Jane brought me a message that Colin wanted to talk to me. Then . . . I'm not sure what happened after that . . ."

"Colin wanted to see you at such a late hour? Whatever for?"

"I don't know, but needless to say he wasn't there . . ." The room was quite warm. Meg had rekindled the fire, but I felt a clammy chill creeping through my body.

"Glenna, you don't look well."

I shook my head. "I'm all right." I wasn't, although, except for a stabbing headache, there was nothing physically wrong with me. I was beginning to hear voices in my head, growing loud, and then dying again. Familiar voices from the past. I thought I recognized Mama's voice, and Papa's, but I couldn't distinguish a word they said. And images, some of them terrifying, were flashing in and out of my mind. It was as if I had a vast echo chamber in my head.

Ellen came into the room, followed by Lorne.

"How is she?" Aunt Aillie asked.

"She's much worse," Ellen replied, tight-lipped. "She's raving now, talking gibberish. She's trying to get out of bed, and she's so strong that three of the maids can hardly hold her down. Lorne, we can't wait for morning, we'll have to call a doctor. Oh, how I wish old Dr. Easton hadn't retired and moved to Glasgow. Jane was so used to him."

"How about Dr. MacColl?" Lorne suggested.

"Yes, I suppose so . . . he's so young, though." Ellen sounded doubtful.

"Yes, call Dr. MacColl," I cried out suddenly. For a fraction of a second, I'd seen my father lying on the floor, drenched in blood.

"Glenna, what is it?" Aunt Aillie shrilled.

I sank back in my chair, trembling with reaction. The image had gone. I was sure it would come back.

"She fell on the ramparts tonight," Lorne said. "Glenna, could you have hit your head when you fell?"

Aunt Aillie took charge, parting the thick masses of my hair and running her fingers gently over my head. "There's a huge bump behind your right ear, Glenna," she reported. "I'm putting you to bed. Dr. MacColl will have a look at you after he's seen Jane."

In the tower room, Aunt Aillie helped me undress and pulled the coverlets up over me as I lay in bed. I closed my eyes, not because I felt drowsy, but because I hoped to avoid any more of my aunt's questions. The images were coming faster now, fragmented, revolving in my mind like a kaleidoscope, and the voices were still echoing meaninglessly in my ears.

Oban is almost ten miles from Dungariff, and it seemed

an eternity before Dr. MacColl strode into my bedroom. Aunt Aillie, sitting beside my bed, had fallen into a light doze.

"Well, now, what have we here?" Dr. MacColl said, putting down his bag. "Mrs. MacDougall tells me you may have hurt your head in a fall. Let me have a look at you."

As he leaned over me, his skillful fingers probing the bump on my head, Aunt Aillie asked, "How is Jane Henderson, Doctor?"

He shook his head. "A very sad case. I've given her an injection, and she's quiet now, but I don't have much hope for her."

"Oh, my. You don't think she'll recover?"

"I should say it's extremely doubtful." Having finished his examination of my head, Dr. MacColl popped a thermometer in my mouth. Pulling up a chair, he consulted his watch while he took my pulse. Several minutes later he said, "You've nothing to worry about, Miss MacDougall. You don't have a skull fracture, nor a fever. I'll give you something for that headache, and I think you should stay in bed for the rest of the day."

As he rose to go, I said quickly, "Doctor, could I see you alone?"

"Why . . . yes. Mrs. Murray, would you mind . . . ?"

Aunt Aillie would clearly have preferred to stay. She left the room dragging her feet, tossing a curious glance at me over her shoulder.

Dr. MacColl leaned back in his chair, his arms crossed over his chest. He studied me gravely. "How can I help you, Miss MacDougall?"

"I'm not sure you can," I said slowly. "I had to talk to someone, though . . . You see, I've begun to remember the most terrible things that happened to me when I was a little girl. You understand, I don't see anything clearly, just partial glimpses, flashes really, each more frightening than the last."

"Ah." The eyes behind the thick glasses became intent. "Perhaps you'd like to talk about it."

"Well, first I think I should tell you that I literally lost a whole summer out of my life when I was ten years old. I woke up one morning and looked out the window to find that the leaves were beginning to turn. My last memory, looking out that same window, was the sight of my mother's peonies in full bloom. My aunt told me I'd been ill for months, in a coma, and that both my parents were dead. Now, though, I'm beginning to remember what happened during those lost months . . ." I paused, clenching my hands tightly together, as my whole body started to tremble.

Dr. MacColl leaned over to place his hand over mine. His long, serious face didn't look at all surprised. "Try to be calm," he said. "Now, then, you say these fleeting memories are frightening?"

"Oh, yes," I shuddered. "I see my father struggling, attempting to choke a man I somehow recognize as my Uncle Niall. I see my father raising a pistol to his head. And I see myself running in terror out of the house and then falling headlong down a flight of stairs. I don't know if these things are connected. I don't even know if they happened at all."

Dr. MacColl's hands clasped mine more closely. "When you came to see me in my office, you described to me your recurrent nightmares, your disturbing feeling you'd lived in Argyll in another time. If you'll recall, I said you might be experiencing symptoms of déjà vu, or even of precognition, and indeed you may have been. However, I was convinced from my reading of Dr. Freud that you had such a painful experience at some point in your life that you'd felt compelled to bury it below your conscious memory, into what Dr. Freud calls your unconscious mind."

I became very still. "Are you telling me that what I suspected is true, that I'm losing my sanity, like poor Jane?"

"Not at all. Your problem isn't insanity. I believe it to be amnesia."

"Amnesia? But isn't that a total loss of memory? I've heard of people who found themselves in a strange place with no memory of who they were or where they came from. With me, it's only a few months of one summer I can't remember."

"Yes, the most common form of amnesia, what Dr. Freud calls dissociative syndrome, results in a total loss of memory that's usually of short duration, although it can last for years until some stressful situation restores the memory spontaneously. However, as in your case, amnesia can also be circumscribed—covering one interval of time—with the patient having full memory of events before and after that interval. What I think happened to you is this: you had an experience so frightening to you that you ran away from it. During your flight you fell and struck your head so hard you suffered a concussion. The head injury induced a lengthy coma, and when you finally recovered consciousness, you'd suppressed all memory of the event that had caused you to flee."

I fixed my eyes on Dr. MacColl with a painful intensity. "Is this all I will ever remember, these fleeting impressions that come and go in my mind?"

"Oh, I think your memory has been returning for some time," said the doctor calmly. "That's why you've been having nightmares and these incidents of déjà vu. They're certainly connected with that childhood trauma. Yes, Miss MacDougall, I feel sure you'll completely regain your memory. I think it might happen faster if you talk with some member of your family who's familiar with your past life. Your aunt, for example. Isn't it likely she knows something of what happened to you that summer?"

I sat bolt upright. Of course, I thought. Aunt Aillie knows *all* about it. She's been keeping something from me for years. It explains her silence about our family background, and why she was so reluctant to have me go to Scotland. It explains her apprehension when I began remembering places I'd never seen before.

"Yes, I'm sure Aunt Aillie does know what happened," I told the doctor. "I don't think she'll be willing to talk about it, though."

Rising, Dr. MacColl took several turns around the room. When he turned to face me, he spoke with a curious mixture of reluctance and anticipation. "It's possible I could help you by placing you under hypnosis. Mind, I'm not a qualified practitioner, but I did participate in a number of experiments in hypnosis while I was at university. You might not respond to hypnosis, of course, but if you did, I believe your full memory might return immediately."

My uncertainty must have shown in my face. Did I really want to probe into these disturbing memories that had begun to surface? Perhaps I'd uncover even more frightening things, things it might be better not to know. On the other hand, could I live the rest of my life knowing that a large part of my past was missing?

"I want you to put me under hypnosis, Doctor," I said suddenly. "Do you need to make any special preparations? Could you start now?"

Dr. MacColl was taken aback. "But Miss MacDougall, it's already very late, and I've no idea how long the hypnosis session would last. You're tired, too, and you've had a head injury." An uneasy note crept into his voice. "Your family might think it odd for us to be closeted together for a long period at this time of night. Or morning, I should say."

Despite my agitation, I had to suppress a smile. Here was the prudish, Calvinist side of Dr. MacColl's grave

Scottish nature surfacing rather unexpectedly. "We could ask my aunt to be here during the session," I said calmly.

"I wouldn't like to risk violating the privacy of the doctor-patient relationship," he replied doubtfully. "However, if you insist on having the treatment immediately . . ." He crossed the room and opened the door. Aunt Aillie was waiting patiently and uncomfortably on the cramped landing at the head of the stairs.

"Mrs. Murray, I'd like you to be present when I perform a certain medical procedure on your niece." At Aunt Aillie's startled glance, the doctor continued, "Miss MacDougall has just realized she's suffering from partial amnesia. She has no memory of the summer of her tenth year. Tonight she began to remember snatches of what took place that summer. We both feel it would be better for her peace of mind if she could remember everything. To that end, I propose to place her in an hypnotic trance."

Turning very pale, Aunt Aillie groped for a chair. "I forbid it! It could only cause more trouble, more suffering. Dr. MacColl, you must not do this thing!"

"Aunt Aillie, I've already remembered some terrible things. Papa fighting with a man I'm positive is Uncle Niall. Papa with a pistol to his head. I *must* know the rest. If you don't want the doctor to hypnotize me, you must tell me yourself what happened."

Trembling so violently she could hardly speak, my aunt managed to say, "No, I can't tell you. I wasn't even there. Glenna, you're right, something dreadful did happen that summer, but you mustn't try to remember it. You've been happy all these years, not knowing it, why dredge it all up now?"

"I must, Aunt Aillie. Please begin, Doctor."

Although he looked uncomfortable at my aunt's distress, Dr. MacColl drew up a chair next to my bed, saying, "Lean back against the pillows, now. Try to relax as much as possible. Concentrate all your attention on this watch I'm holding in front of you." In a low, soothing voice, he suggested I was feeling very sleepy. He asked me to count backward from one hundred. I have no memory of counting back past eighty-five . . .

. . . I looked at my ten-year-old self complacently in the mirror above the mahogany table in the foyer. I was wearing a crisp new gingham dress under a starched white pinafore. My brand-new high-button shoes were polished to a dazzling gloss, and my long thick braids were tied with bright red satin ribbons. In my childish conceit, I thought I'd probably outshine every other girl on the opening day of fifth grade classes at the Acton Grammar School.

"Well, Glenna," came my mother's amused voice from behind me, "don't you think you've admired yourself quite enough? It's time to start for school."

I turned to find my mother and my Uncle Niall standing in the door of the parlor. They were both tall, slender and handsome, with hair as raven black and glossy as my own. "I represent the dark Celtic side of our ancestry," Uncle Niall had once told me laughingly. "Your father and your Aunt Allison must have inherited their red hair from one of those Viking marauders who tried to breach the walls of Dungariff during the Middle Ages."

"Mama, do I have to go to school today? Uncle Niall will only be here for another week. Couldn't I start classes after he leaves? I'm sure Miss Brewster wouldn't mind a bit if I missed the first few days of school. Nothing much happens then, anyway."

"No," my mother replied firmly. "I won't have you skipping school. And it isn't as though your uncle had only been paying us a brief visit. He's been here most of the summer."

"But Mama, I don't feel very well. My stomach hurts. I think I've got a fever."

Placing a hand on my forehead, Mama said crisply, "Nonsense. You don't have a fever, and your upset stomach probably came straight out of your imagination."

Uncle Niall chuckled. "Well, Mary, I guess children don't change very much. I remember trying to convince my own mother that I was too sick to go to school. Look, Glenna. You trot along now like a good girl, and when you come home from school, I'll walk you downtown for an ice cream soda. How about that?"

Even at the age of ten, I could accept the inevitable. I picked up my lunch bucket, slowly descended the high front steps of our house and began even more slowly the long walk along the tree-shaded streets of Acton to the primary school in the center of the town.

Miss Brewster greeted me warmly when I entered the classroom. The pretty and sprightly fifth grade teacher was very popular, and I'd been looking forward all summer to being in her class in the fall. However, as the morning dragged on, I found I couldn't concentrate on what Miss Brewster was saying. When, at lunch time, I pushed away the contents of my lunch bucket without swallowing a bite, my new young teacher took me aside.

"Glenna, aren't you feeling well? You're a little flushed. And you didn't answer even one question in class this morning."

"I've got a headache, Miss Brewster. My stomach hurts, too," I admitted, wondering apprehensively if the Lord was punishing me for fibbing about my symptoms to Mama earlier that morning, when I'd been feeling perfectly well.

"I'm sorry to hear that," Miss Brewster said, putting a comforting arm around my shoulder. "You don't have a sore throat, I suppose?" she asked offhandedly.

"Not really a sore throat. It feels a little prickly."

"Well, Glenna, I want you to go to the back of the room

to an empty desk and put your head down on your arms and try to rest a bit. I'm going to send a message to your father at the hardware store. I think he ought to take you home and put you to bed."

Papa's small store was only a block away from the grammar school, and he arrived a few minutes after Miss Brewster dispatched one of my classmates to fetch him. However, even in that short time, I was feeling much worse. Papa insisted on carrying me out to the store delivery wagon we'd never been able to afford our own carriage. As he was settling me on the floor of the wagon bed, I could hear snatches of his low-voiced conversation with Miss Brewster. After we were in motion, I propped myself up on an elbow and asked anxiously, "Papa, does Miss Brewster think I have typhoid fever?"

"Oh, I shouldn't think so, Glenna."

"I heard her mention the word typhoid," I insisted stubbornly.

"Well, you see, her cousin died last year in a typhoid outbreak in her hometown, so naturally she was a bit alarmed to find you had some of the symptoms. I don't want you to worry, though. There hasn't been a case of typhoid in these parts for years. You've probably got a touch of the summer flu."

Papa sounded so confident that I was reassured. I settled down in the back of the wagon, beginning to feel drowsy. I was glad enough to allow him to carry me into the house. When we entered the foyer he called out "Mary" a number of times. After a moment he said vexedly, "There! I'd clean forgotten that Mary and your Uncle Niall were going to hire a buggy at the livery stable today to go out to the Morris farm to buy some goose down. Well, Effie can take care of you until your mother comes home."

When I reminded him it was our hired girl's half-day off, he said, frowning, "I can't stay, Glenna. I have a salesman from Boston coming to see me this afternoon."

"I'll be all right by myself for a while. Mama will be home soon."

"Well, if you're sure . . ." He still sounded worried, but he began to carry me up the stairs. "I'll come home myself as soon as I finish with the salesman—" He broke off as we reached the upstairs landing, glancing in perplexity at the closed door of the bedroom he shared with Mama. This door was always left open in the daytime, and now, as we stood there, we could hear a kind of strangled moan coming from behind it. Allowing me to slide gently to the floor, Papa strode to the door and wrenched it open.

The blinds at the window of the bedroom were drawn, but enough of the bright September sunlight filtered in so that I could see quite clearly the two naked, sinuously entwined bodies on the bed. The sound of the opening door and my strangled cry of "Mama! Uncle Niall!" brought them leaping to their feet.

His eyes blazing, Papa launched himself across the room at Uncle Niall, grasping him by the throat with both hands and shaking him like a terrier after its prey. Mama, a sheet swathed awkwardly around her naked body, tried frantically to drag Papa's hands from my uncle's throat, but Papa seemed oblivious of her presence. His entire being seemed concentrated in a fury of revenge.

As I stood by the door in a sort of frozen immobility, watching the terrible tableau, Papa's arms gradually grew still, and he opened his hands to drop Uncle Niall in a limp heap on the floor.

"Oh, Ian, Ian, you've killed your brother," Mama whispered.

"Yes. He deserved it," Papa said in a lifeless monotone that was even more chilling than his previous outburst of rage. As Mama and I watched him with uncomprehending eyes, he walked over to the wardrobe, reached under the clothing on the top shelf and pulled out a pistol. Without a moment's hesitation, Papa put the gun to his head and pulled the trigger.

I found my voice at last, releasing a shrill, keening scream of such intensity that the blood vessels in my head seemed about to burst. Then I bolted from the bedroom, down the stairs, and out the front door of the house. I missed the top step of the high flight of stairs leading down from the porch and tumbled headlong toward the neat brick paving stones at the foot of the steps . . .

. . . "Miss MacDougall, open your eyes."

I turned my head to find Aunt Aillie standing beside the bed, her face crumpled in grief. Wordlessly, my eyes welling with tears, I lifted my arms and Aunt Aillie folded me close to her. Drawing away at last, I muttered dazedly, "But Uncle Niall *didn't* die."

Aunt Aillie clasped my hands tightly. "No, he didn't die. He was only unconscious. But your father thought he'd killed his brother, and so . . ."

I went on speaking, almost as though I hadn't heard my aunt's reply, my voice sounding curiously trancelike. "I remember Uncle Niall now. I can see him clearly. He looked a little like Papa, except for his dark hair. We spent so much time together that summer, tramping through the woods and fields, picking wild berries, looking for Indian arrowheads, reading books together. But mostly we talked. Or, rather, *he* talked. He told me so much about Scotland and Argyll and our family traditions. He loved Argyll so much, he was so proud that our family had once owned a great castle there. And he told me the story of Angus and Catriona, and how Angus had pushed her to her death from the ramparts of Dungariff in a jealous rage—"

Stopping short as I realized what I was saying, I stared at Dr. MacColl, who had been sitting quietly listening to me and Aunt Aillie. My eyes were wide with questioning.

"Yes," he nodded. "When your uncle committed that terrible act of betrayal, you buried all memory of him and the tales he'd told you in your unconscious mind. Then, when you learned you'd inherited Niall's fortune, your memories of him were stirred, and they began to surface in your dreams. However, Dr. Freud says that the mind acts as a sort of censor even in sleep. What he calls the manifest content of the dream—what the dreamer remembers—is often different from the latent content, the true meaning of the dream. Your sense of pain and betrayal was so deep that, instead of allowing you to dream of Niall himself, your mental censor permitted another frightening scene to surface, one connected to Niall but not involving him directly: the story of Angus and Catriona, of which he'd so often spoken."

I remained silent for a moment, feeling a tremendous sense of relief. Those disquieting moments of déjà vu, those recurring nightmares that had so often left me quivering with dread, were neither symptoms of insanity nor bouts with the supernatural. They could be explained by rather simple medical terms. Then, as my mind reverted to that terrible scene I'd blotted from my memory for so many years, I burst out, "But why, Aunt Aillie? Mama and Papa loved each other. We were so happy together before Uncle Niall came to visit us that summer."

Aunt Aillie shrank back against her chair. "Don't think about it any more, Glenna. Try to put it out of your mind."

Dr. MacColl gave Aunt Aillie a long thoughtful look. "Mrs. Murray, you're keeping something back, are you not?"

"Of course not," she flared. "I've already told you, I wasn't in Acton when those awful things happened."

"Perhaps you discovered something later? And if so, wouldn't it be better to tell Miss MacDougall? As her doctor, I think she needs to know everything that happened to her in her childhood, to be assured that there's nothing else hidden in her past, so she *can* put these sad memories behind her."

My aunt didn't speak for a long time. She sat with her face turned away, her hands clenched tightly together in her lap. At last she said, her voice slow and dragging, "I suppose I must take your word for it, Doctor, that this is the right thing to do." She fixed her eyes on me. "I arrived in Acton the day after your father died, Glenna—I'd been notified by the police—to find Ian a suicide, your mother in a state of shock and you in a coma from a blow on the head. Niall was gone. The authorities assumed, as I did, at first, that he was a callous man who'd refused to stay and face the unpleasantness of his brother's suicide.

"I stayed on in Acton to nurse you and your mother, Glenna. Mary was shattered. She was experiencing a difficult early pregnancy and showed little desire to live. Gradually she told me the truth, not only about what happened on the day of Ian's suicide, but what led up to it." Aunt Aillie reached over to grasp my hand strongly. "My dear, she admitted to me that you were Niall's child, not Ian's."

I cried out in horror and disbelief, and Aunt Aillie, gazing accusingly at Dr. MacColl, exclaimed, "You told me to tell her the truth, Doctor."

"Indeed, Mrs. Murray. I still consider it good advice. Please go on."

Now that she had revealed her most closely guarded secret, Aunt Aillie seemed to find it easier to go on. "You'll recall, Glenna, that when your father and I left Scotland to join your Uncle Niall in America, we arrived in Boston to find that Niall had left the city. At loose ends, Ian and I stayed for a while in the boarding house where Niall had been living. Soon Ian fell in love with your mother, Mary Fraser, the daughter of the proprietor. What Ian didn't know was that Mary and Niall had been lovers, and that she was pregnant. She married Ian without telling him about the baby, who was born 'prematurely.' No one ever suspected the truth, because you were a very small baby.

"Ten years later, when Niall returned to America and visited his brother's family, Mary had no intention of telling him you were his child, and no intention, either, of resuming their affair. But Niall guessed the truth almost immediately, when he learned the date of your birth. For another thing, Glenna, you're the exact image of Niall, and always have been, since the day you were born. I noticed the resemblance the first time I ever saw you. I thought you looked exactly like my father. It escaped my mind completely that Niall looked like Father too."

Aunt Aillie sighed. Then, shaking her head, she continued. "Well, after Niall discovered he had a child, the old attraction between him and Mary apparently sprang to life, stronger than ever. Mary told me that she and Niall both fought against it, but 'this thing,' as she called it, was so compelling that neither of them could resist it."

My aunt paused, turning a dull red, and I knew how difficult it must be for her, with her rigid sense of morality, to talk about the sins of the flesh. She added suddenly, "Glenna dear, for what it's worth, I believe your mother and Niall truly loved each other. I also believe Mary loved your father, though in quite a different way, and she was so torn by guilt by what had happened, that she really didn't want to live any longer. She had a miscarriage a few weeks after Ian's funeral, simply hemorrhaging her life away."

Aunt Aillie answered my unspoken question. "I don't know whose child it was, Glenna. I've always supposed it was Niall's."

I stifled a little sound of protest. It was still another blow, although not the greatest I'd received this morning.

Continuing to prod Aunt Aillie, Dr. MacColl said, "Please go on. Ian and Mary are both dead, and Niall has disappeared. The child Glenna is ill, still in a coma . . ."

My aunt nodded. "We thought you might never come

305

out of the coma, Glenna, that you'd die without recovering consciousness. God help me, I almost hoped that would happen. If you recovered, you'd have to cope with the tragedy of your father's death all over again. But then, finally, you did come out of the coma, and it was like a miracle! The entire summer had been wiped from your mind. You had no memory of Niall's visit to Acton, and, since you'd never previously heard of this long-lost uncle, it was as if he'd never existed for you. I told you that both your parents had died of typhoid, and that you'd been a victim of the disease yourself. Then, before anyone in Acton could tell you how Ian and Mary died, I whisked you off to Atwater to live with Malcolm and me. I hoped you'd never remember what had happened. As the years went by and your memory never returned, I began to feel a little easier."

"So that was why you never talked about Scotland or the family connection with Dungariff and Argyll, and why you never told me I had an Uncle Niall."

"Yes, that was why. I tried never to mention anything that might trigger your memory of him. When the news came that you'd inherited his fortune, I was so afraid you might begin to remember everything. I tried to talk you out of going to Scotland, where you'd be exposed, virtually every moment, to places and people that could remind you of Niall. In the end, though, I had to give way. It was only right that Niall should leave his fortune to his daughter, and in order to receive the money you had to go to Argyll. I had a few really bad moments at first when you seemed to be recalling details about the area that you could only have learned from Niall, but it did seem to be working out." Aunt Aillie's voice turned wistful. "I should have followed my instincts, Glenna. If you'd never come here, you might never have had to relive all this tragedy."

Suddenly feeling very tired, I leaned back against my

pillows. "Don't be sorry, Aunt Aillie. It was hard for you to tell me, and even harder to hear, but I'm glad I know the truth at last. It's given me . . . it's given me a sort of peace."

Dr. MacColl stirred, pointing toward the windows, where the morning sun was already streaming into the room. "Yes, Miss MacDougall, I think our hypnosis session has been a success. However, it's been a very long night and you must be exhausted. I want you to sleep now. Drink this, and I'll come back to see you later in the day."

But after Aunt Aillie had kissed me and had left the room with the doctor, sleep wouldn't come easily, even with the mild sedative Dr. MacColl had given me. My mind was still too occupied with my aunt's revelations. The memories of that summer in Acton were flooding back now, and the anger and bitterness I'd initially felt for Mama and Uncle Niall were beginning to ease. It was true, what I'd told Aunt Aillie; I was feeling a sense of peace. I knew with a sudden certainty that Mama had genuinely loved Papa. She simply hadn't been able to resist the raging passion she felt for Niall. I could even forgive my uncle. In a sense, he'd been a victim as well as a victimizer, and in his own way he'd done his best to make up for the tragedy he'd caused. He left me his fortune, he sent me to Scotland in the hope, I was now convinced, that I'd marry Lorne and become the Mistress of Dungariff.

My limbs became rigid. In the sorrow and excitement of learning the truth about that sad summer of my tenth year, I'd forgotten what had taken place on the parapet walk the night before. Lorne had tried to kill me again, and poor Jane Henderson, in a vain attempt to prevent my death, had fallen into the abyss of the very insanity I'd been dreading for myself for so long. Was Uncle Niall, I wondered, stirring restlessly in his grave? Wherever he was, did he realize that in sending me to Argyll under the terms of his will, he'd been signing my death warrant?

Chapter 17

When Aunt Aillie came to the tower room later that day—it was well past noon—I was already dressed.

"Glenna, for Heaven's sake, what are you doing out of bed?" she expostulated, setting down the tea tray she'd brought with her.

"I'm perfectly well," I said firmly. It was true in a sense. I'd awakened still tired and somewhat groggy from the effects of Dr. MacColl's sedative, but also, for the first time in many weeks, I was free of the suffocating fear that I was losing my mind. Once I put as much distance as possible between me and Lorne MacDougall, I could start taking charge of my life again.

"Are you all packed up?" I asked, continuing with my task of putting the contents of my dressing table into my toilet case. "I'd like to leave for Oban as soon as we can."

Aunt Aillie said blankly, "Surely we can't carry out our original plans to leave today after what happened last night? I think you should rest a little more. Say what you like about feeling well, it must have been a terrible shock to you, learning about—about your father. And there's Ellen, too. She's in a dreadful state about Jane Henderson."

"Aunt Aillie, I won't stay at Dungariff one minute

longer than I have to. I feel trapped here, I—" I broke off, swallowing hard, as Ellen came into the room. Her face was pale and her eyes were red-rimmed. It was obvious she'd heard what I said.

"Cousin Ellen, I'm sorry."

"It's all right, dear. I was hoping you and Aillie could stay with me for a day or two, but after the dreadful things that have been happening, I don't blame you for wanting to get away." She tried to smile. "You're looking so much better this morning. Thank God for one bit of light in the midst of all this darkness."

As Aunt Aillie flashed me a beseeching look, I felt a wave of compunction. I'd been concentrating so much on myself and my own problems that I'd failed to take into account how deeply Ellen would be affected by Jane Henderson's shocking descent into madness, coming so soon after Flora's violent death. Ellen needed friends with her now. My determination to leave must seem unfeeling to her. And yet I couldn't stay, not even for the few days she was asking for. She didn't know—and I didn't want her to know—that if I stayed, I'd be in mortal danger from her son.

"How is Jane this morning?" I asked gently. "Is she any better?"

Reaching for her handkerchief, Ellen dabbed at her eyes. "She's lying in her bed like a stone. Her eyes are open, but they look dead. She doesn't respond when I speak to her, in fact she seems unaware that anyone's in the room with her."

"Perhaps Colin could reach her," I ventured.

Ellen nodded. "Yes, I thought of that. He's the person Jane loves most in the world. If anyone could get through to her, he could. In any case he had to be notified about her breakdown. I sent Donnie to Oban early this morning to fetch him, but Donnie couldn't find him. Colin wasn't in his rooms or at the ship chandler's store or anywhere you'd expect him to be. I'm worried about him, too, Glenna. He was so upset yesterday at the funeral." She blew her nose and gave her eyes a last resolute wipe. "That's enough worrying about what can't be helped. If you two are really leaving right away, you'll want some kind of meal before you go. How about an old-fashioned high tea? I'll ask Cook to make a cottage pie. You've always liked that, Aillie."

The little maid, Meg, burst into the room, her eyes wide as saucers. "Mistress, I didna ken wha' tae do! The Laird and Maister Colin are fighting sae fiercely."

Ellen rushed for the stairs with Aunt Aillie at her heels. After a moment's hesitation I raced after them. I dreaded the thought of meeting Lorne face to face. I'd hoped to leave the castle without seeing him again. But I had to do anything I could to break up this altercation with Colin. In his present desperate frame of mind, Colin didn't really know what he was doing. I didn't want him spewing out his accusations against Lorne in front of Ellen, accusations that couldn't be proved and would only uselessly spoil and embitter Ellen's life. I didn't want Colin injured at Lorne's hands, either.

When Ellen and Aunt Aillie and I made the turn from the lower turret landing into the first-floor passage, we found Lorne leaning against a wall, wiping a streak of blood from the corner of his mouth as he watched Colin struggle to his feet.

"Lorne, Colin," Ellen cried despairingly, "what's gotten into you? Why are you quarreling at a time like this?"

"It's over now, Mother. I'm sorry I had to hit you, Colin."

Bracing his hand against the wall as he got up, Colin shot Lorne a glance of chilling contempt. Making an obviously enormous effort to control himself, he said quietly, his eyes deep-set and haunted in his pale face,

"Aunt Ellen, this is between Lorne and me. I never meant to hurt you, please believe me. I came out to see Jane, only that. After I've visited her, I'll leave."

"Colin, if you'd talk to me . . . if both of you would only tell me what's wrong—"

"I can't, Aunt Ellen. I'm sorry." He touched her shoulder in a brief, tender gesture of affection. Then, as if noticing my presence for the first time, he held out his hand, saying, "Glenna, come with me. I don't know if I can bear seeing Jane alone. They're saying she's gone stark raving mad."

"Of course, Colin," I replied without an instant's thought. I had to do this one last thing for him. Perhaps I owed it to Jane, too. If she hadn't tried so desperately to save me from Lorne's last murderous attempt, she might not be in the state she was in.

Hand in hand, Colin and I went off down the passage. The housekeeper's bed-sitting room was behind the kitchens. As we stood before the closed door, Colin lifted his hand, waiting for a long difficult moment before he knocked softly. "I'm afraid, Glenna," he uttered. "She's all I have left in the world now."

The housemaid who was sitting with Jane opened the door and stepped aside for us to enter. Colin and I stood silently beside the bed. The woman lying there was a shell of Jane Henderson. Though her eyes were open, she was like a stone, as Ellen had said, rigid, unmoving, insensible to her surroundings. Colin began to speak softly to her. "Jane, darling, I'm here. Please come back from wherever you are. Let me help you." Jane didn't respond by the quiver of an eyelash to the murmured endearments. After a while, Colin slipped to his knees beside the bed, burying his face in the coverlets, his hunched shoulders betraying the despair he was feeling. My eyes filling with tears, I slipped out of the room, leaving him to his private grief.

I gasped as steely fingers grasped my arms. I stared up

into Lorne's face. It looked strained and worn and years older than his age. Shaking off his hands, I stepped back. "You shouldn't be here," I told him savagely. "Haven't you done enough harm?"

A muscle twitched in his cheek. He made an involuntary move toward me and checked himself. "Colin still thinks I killed Flora," he said tightly. "I'm trying to understand. I see now he never got over loving Flora, and he's lashing out at someone to blame. But you, Glenna, you've had time to reconsider since yesterday, surely you don't think—"

"Don't you ever give up, Lorne?" I lashed out. "Yes, I think you killed Flora. I *know* you tried to kill me last night. You'd have succeeded too, if that poor creature in there hadn't stopped you at the price of her sanity."

"God . . ." He was white to the lips. "What are you planning to do, then? Are you going to report me to the authorities, try to get me hanged?"

"I would if I could, but I can't prove anything against you," I said harshly. "My only witness is in there," I motioned to the closed door of Jane's room, "and she can't speak. I'm leaving Dungariff today, Lorne, and I hope I never see you again. I haven't told your mother anything, by the way, and I don't intend to. I'm leaving her happy in her ignorance. She's one person you won't try to harm."

"Good-bye, Glenna." He went away then, without another word.

I sank back against the wall of the corridor, trembling with a delayed reaction to this latest bitter encounter with Lorne. I couldn't forget the expression in his eyes. He looked mortally wounded.

Gradually I became aware of voices coming from Jane's bedroom. Straightening up, I pushed open the door. Jane was no longer lying in frozen immobility. She was threshing about with her arms and legs, mouthing broken phrases in Gaelic and English. Colin and the housemaid were using all their strength to hold her down.

"Jane, dearest, I'm here. Nothing can hurt you now," Colin kept saying over and over. He must have reached her at some level of her consciousness. Slowly she became calmer. Her speech was still wildly incoherent, but I could begin to make out snatches of what she was saying. She was talking about Colin, though she seemed not to comprehend he was actually in the room with her. At one point she glanced around her with a triumphant smile— looking at an imaginary Colin, I presumed, not at the real man kneeling beside her—and exclaimed, "Ach, my bonnie laddie, ye're the Maister noo."

I don't know how long Colin and I remained in that room listening to Jane's ravings. It seemed to go on for an eternity. When at last the broken old voice died away, I sank, unnerved, into a chair, covering my face with my hands. "Oh, Colin, Colin, we've been such fools."

"Yes, and worse," came Colin's dragging reply after a long silence. "Now we'll have to repair the damage, Glenna."

With one last glance at Jane, who had lapsed back into her stonelike trance, Colin and I left the room. We passed through the kitchens and walked along the passage to the sitting room, where Ellen and Aunt Aillie sat before untouched cups of tea.

"Aunt Ellen, where's Lorne?" Colin demanded. "It's all right, we're not going to fight," he added reassuringly.

"He went off on that new horse he bought, the one that's not completely broken yet," Ellen replied, apprehension shadowing her eyes. "He didn't say where he was going."

"I know where he went." I spoke with absolute conviction. "Colin, I'm going after him. No, I don't want you to go with me. You stay and talk to Cousin Ellen and Aunt Aillie."

I swept out of the sitting room, paying no attention to objections from either Colin or Aunt Aillie. Running up the turret stairs, I tore into my carefully packed portmanteau and dragged out my riding habit. Ten minutes later I was in the stables telling Donnie to saddle Jeannie.

"Ye havna been riding verra much o' late, Miss," said the groom. "Jeannie ha' missed ye."

"I've missed her too, Donnie."

"Ye'll no' be riding alone? The Maister willna like it—"

"The Master won't mind at all." As Donnie helped me into the saddle I asked, "Did he say where he was going?"

"Nay, Miss."

I headed Jeannie at a gentle canter around the head of the loch and into Glen Fingorm. As I rode along the banks of the little river, I thought back to the day Lorne and I had ridden into the lonely reaches of the glen. I could hear his voice saying, "I love to come here. I can leave all my problems behind me for a while. When I quarreled with my father I'd come to this place to nurse my wounds and I'd find a kind of peace here . . ."

Long before I reached the end of the glen, at the spot where the River Fingorm burst out of its rocky ravine into a line of foaming cascades, I could see a grazing horse and near it Lorne's tall figure, standing beside the trout stream. He was so deep in his thoughts that he wasn't aware of my presence until Jeannie and I were almost upon him. As I reined in, he lifted his head to stare at me, making no move to approach me.

"Lorne, please help me down."

He walked slowly over to me, stopping beside Jeannie but not raising his hands to help me dismount. "Are you sure you want me to touch you?" he asked coolly. "Aren't you afraid I'll reach for your throat to strangle you? We're alone here, you know. There's no Jane to rescue you, or anyone else."

I gazed down into his dark eyes, the torment in their depths belying his tone of stark bravado. "No, I'm not afraid of you, Lorne," I said softly. "Not any more. Help me down."

His expression changed, the grim hardness dissolving into a look of confusion. He lifted his arms to me, and as I slid to the ground I leaned against his taut body for a fraction of a second longer than necessary. Instantly I felt a rush of the devouring physical hunger I'd resisted for so long. He felt it, too, and stepped back from me abruptly.

"So why aren't you afraid of me any more, Glenna?"

"Because now I know you didn't kill Flora, and you never lifted a finger against me. Poor Flora's death was just what you said it was, an accident. *My* accidents—most of them, anyway—*were* deliberate attempts to kill me, but you had nothing to do with them."

A flash of overwhelming relief crossed Lorne's face and he stood taller, as if a mountainous weight had lifted from his shoulders. Almost immediately, however, he said sharply, "You're mistaken, Glenna. Nobody at Dungariff would want to harm you."

"One person would. Jane Henderson." I took his arm. "Let's sit down over there on those rocks at the edge of the stream. I have so much to tell you."

His dazed expression gradually fading away, Lorne listened with frowning intensity as I told him what Colin and I had learned from Jane's last crazed outburst.

"Jane didn't actually tell us any of this, Lorne. She was babbling, speaking in disconnected snatches. One second she'd be talking about Colin's babyhood. In the next breath she'd be bringing me tea in the tower room. Colin and I had to put the bits and pieces together.

"You and Cousin Ellen always thought Jane was devoted to the family, though Colin was her undoubted favorite. As Colin grew up, though, Jane began to feel he wasn't being treated fairly. Over the years, she built up a fantasy in her mind in which you and your parents had deprived Colin of his rights to Dungariff. She thought it was monstrous that you should be the next Laird of

315

Dungariff, while Colin could only look forward to working for a salary in Mr. Cameron's store. Then, when Colin fell in love with Flora, only to have her choose you, Jane thought of that as deliberate betrayal."

Lorne made a sudden sharp movement, instantly controlled.

I went on, "If I hadn't come to Dungariff, perhaps nothing would have happened. Jane suddenly saw a chance for Colin to triumph over you, Lorne: if he married the immensely wealthy American heiress, he'd be the most important citizen in Oban, more important than the Master of Dungariff. For a little while Jane thought her plan was succeeding. It was obvious I liked Colin very much.

"Then her scheme started to unravel, as she began to suspect that you and I, Lorne, were falling in love. Do you remember the day of the boating accident? I know now, by the way, that my near drowning was simply another accident. You were trying to save me, not push me into the water. But Jane found out from Colin that night about Flora's fit of jealousy on the island before the boat capsized, and that set her alarm bells ringing. And earlier that day she'd had an incident of second sight."

"But surely that didn't have anything to do with—"

"Yes, it did," I interrupted. "That, and the boating accident itself, are what really set Jane off. After I almost drowned that day, I suspected Jane had foreseen my danger in her episode of second sight. It wasn't my death she saw, however. It was Flora's."

Lorne stared at me in horror.

I nodded. "Jane had a sudden glimpse of Flora falling to her death from a great height. She didn't know when it would happen, of course. Perhaps not for many years. Before it came to pass, Colin might have persuaded me to marry him. But, as a precaution, she gave me a love potion that night, hoping it would make me fall in love with

Colin. All it did was make me horribly ill. Later I was convinced you'd poisoned me. Remember, you insisted I have some whisky for my chills?"

"Good God, Glenna—"

I had to smile at his exclamation of outraged anger. "Lorne, that's behind us now."

He drew a deep breath. "I hope so. You'd better tell me the rest. You started having a string of accidents, and Jane Henderson was behind them all?"

"Yes. At first she was only trying to scare me. She wanted me to fear and distrust you, so I'd turn to Colin. So she cut the cinch on my saddle, she put a dreadful doll in my room and told me somebody was attempting to bewitch me, she brought me the MacDougall family history to read in the hope that I'd begin to believe you and I had become reincarnated as Angus and Catriona, and that you were trying to kill me for my fortune."

"Reincarnation?" Lorne said blankly. "You couldn't have believed in something so ridiculous."

"Not if I was in my right mind, no. But you see, Lorne, at that point, I thought I might be going mad." Drawing a deep breath, I told him about my hypnosis session with Dr. MacColl.

"Glenna, no wonder you were troubled, with all those terrible memories trying to surface," he said, reaching out to clasp my hand with a ready sympathy. "Does it hurt much, knowing Niall is your real father?"

"No, not really. It brought me to Dungariff."

He gave me a quick, uncertain look, drawing his hand away. "Go on about Jane. You say she was only trying to frighten you at first."

"So I'd turn to Colin, yes. The turning point came when I refused Colin's proposal of marriage. Jane was getting desperate. She stepped up the attacks on me. She rolled a boulder down on top of me from the castle walls, she stretched a rope across the turret steps to trip me, she tried to smother me on Midsummer's Eve, leaving the yellow rose that Flora'd put in your lapel to convince me you'd done it."

"Damnation!" Lorne leaped to his feet, lifting his clenched hands into the air. "No wonder you thought I was a murderer. If I had that woman's throat between my two hands—" He walked about for a few moments, trying to control his anger, before sitting down again on the boulder. Frowning, he said, "Any one of those last incidents could have been fatal, I suppose, but if Jane were really trying to kill you, she wasn't being very skillful. Why would she want you dead, anyway? If you died childless, your fortune would go to me."

"Not to you, Lorne," I said quietly. "To the Laird of Dungariff, whoever he might be. Uncle Niall's will was quite explicit. It showed Jane how she could take advantage of Flora's death, which at first she must have thought was the end of all her hopes for Colin. With Flora out of the way, Jane was certain you and I would marry some day, leaving Colin with neither wife nor money. So she tried one last desperate scheme. She told me Colin wanted to meet with me on the parapet walk late last night, after everyone was in bed. I found it easy to believe her. Colin had quarreled with you at the funeral, and he wouldn't want to risk running into you. And she gave you a message that I wanted to see you."

"I couldn't wait to keep the rendezvous," Lorne muttered. "I thought . . . I *hoped* that you'd realized I wasn't guilty of all the crimes you'd accused me of. Then I stepped out on the parapet walk and saw Jane about to attack you. I think I must have frozen in place for a fraction of a second, I was so dumfounded, before I came to my senses and raced to drag her away from you."

I shuddered. "She was planning to push me off the parapet to my death and blame you for it. She had a story all made up to tell the authorities. She was going to tell them she'd become suspicious about my accidents, especially after Flora's death, so when you gave her a message for me to meet you on the ramparts, she followed me and saw you hurl my body onto the rocks below. You'd have hanged, Lorne, and Colin would have inherited your title *and* my money."

We sat in silence for a few minutes. Lorne was obviously having difficulty digesting all the gruesome facts I'd thrown at him. I was weary and drained. I'd been fighting so hard for such a long time for my sanity, for my very life . . . and now it was over.

Finally I rose, shaking out the divided skirt of my riding habit. "I think we should go, Lorne. Your mother and Aunt Aillie will be worried."

He stod up, reaching out a long arm to catch me as I turned. "Are you still planning to leave Dungariff today, Glenna?"

"Do you want me to stay?"

"Do you have to ask that?"

"I'm not sure. I've called you a liar, I've mistrusted and misjudged you. I've accused you of heinous crimes. Why would you want my friendship after all that?"

"I don't want your friendship," he said roughly. "I want your love. I want all of you. Almost from the moment we first met, you've been a raging fire in my veins. For Flora's sake, I tried to choke off the way I felt about you, but it was never any good." He pulled me against him, wrapping his arms around me so tightly I could feel the lithe strength of his body through the enveloping skirts of my habit. "Oh, Glenna, Glenna, this is where you belong," he murmured, crushing my mouth in a hungry urgency that brought the salt taste of blood to my bruised lips. I wound my arms around his neck, straining even closer to him, letting myself surrender at last to the tide of passion I'd tried to resist for weeks.

It was Lorne who pulled away first, his eyes still

319

burning with the fierce heat of desire, his breathing labored and erratic. "You couldn't kiss me that way if you didn't love me, Glenna. I want to hear you say it."

I put up my hands to cradle his dark intense face. "I adore you, Lorne," I whispered. "I'd rather die than leave you."

He snatched me back into his arms to kiss me again, and after a long deliciously mindless interval, I pulled away to say mischievously, "It just occurred to me that Uncle Niall got his own way, after all. Now Dungariff will be back in our branch of the family."

Lorne looked down at me with his rare radiant smile. "Remember what I told you the day you came to the castle? So you've arrived at last, Miss MacDougall. Welcome to Dungariff. Welcome home."